To Peter Allum

with my best *u*

Andrew

01/07/02

Caesar's Passage

Caesar's Passage

Andrew Smyth

 **Calypso Press**

Published by Calypso Press
15, Camden Square
London NW1 9UY

Copyright © 2002 Andrew Smyth

Published in Britain in 2002

A CIP catalogue record for this book is available from the
British Library

ISBN 0-9542270-0-X

Printed and bound by T.J. International Ltd, Padstow, Cornwall

Cover design by Katy Hepburn

"It has been well said that an author who expects
results from a first novel is in a position similar to
that of a man who drops a rose petal down the
Grand Canyon of Arizona and listens for the
echo."

'Cocktail Time' P.G. Wodehouse

Prologue – 2000

The narrow passage is completely hidden from the sea. It leads to Šipanska Luka – literally Port Šipan – the principal village of Šipan, a small island off the Dalmatian coast in the Adriatic Sea. It's one of the prettiest islands in the entire Mediterranean, but unless you know it's there, you'll miss it.

The passage leads past a pinnacle of rock, almost awash just beneath the water's surface, and then turns back on itself towards a deeply indented bay with the village at its head. The island is green and soft, quite unlike the harsh mountains whose shadowy outlines are just visible on the mainland beyond, where the heat of summer and the bleak winds of winter have flayed the landscape into barren, brown fields.

As the passage opened into the bay, we passed a small, Venetian-styled palace on the waterfront. Its shutters were hanging open, swinging on broken hinges. Above the vaulted entrance, a terrace ran along the width of the building, but it was now crumbling and stained with years of rust washed from flaking balustrades. A couple of ornamental urns lay cracked and overgrown at each end. A date, carved high above the principal, double-fronted window, was just legible through the overgrown moss. It read '1909'.

A man took our lines as we moored alongside the quay. There was hardly anyone else about. Three old men were sitting without speaking on a bench underneath a sparse clump of trees. Next to us, at the foot of the paved breakwater, part of an imposing old villa had been converted into a small café, while the rest of the building was open and abandoned. Towards the centre of the town, at its heart, a large open area had once been an ornamental park, but was now also neglected and forlorn. The shrubberies were overgrown, the flowerbeds long since covered by weeds, while the paths were rutted and unkempt. An old fountain was dusty and dry and its inscription was weathered and illegible.

A large, three-storey building of uncertain age and style occupied the head of the bay, and had been converted quite recently into a hotel. In front of it, several old wooden boats were moored stern-to against the long quay which ran around the entire length of the town's waterfront. It must once have been a quarter of a mile of stonework, but now it was cracked and worn, its joints forced open by the roots of wild plants which penetrated deep inside it. Beyond the quay, all around – even high above the town – the hillsides had once been terraced, and although a few sparse olive leaves were still visible amid the overgrown pines, the stone retaining walls had given way, washed into gullies by the winter rains.

We walked towards the small park. Surrounding it, the stuccoed façades of the once-elegant villas were peeling, while the roof of a small chapel had partially collapsed and lay rotting where it fell. Past the trees on the far side, we could see a row of massive columns, and as we walked through we came across a dilapidated mansion, built in the style of the Deep South of colonial America, with an imposing Georgian portico. Building materials were piled up inside the porch which ran behind the columns, but the decaying steel beams supporting the narrow veranda at first-floor level indicated that the attempted restoration was already too late.

As we looked at the building, the man who had helped us to moor came out of it. We studied him with interest. It was almost impossible to guess his age – sixties or seventies certainly, but that was as far as we could tell. 'What an extraordinary mansion,' we said as he approached. 'Who owns it?'

'Me,' he replied almost casually. 'My brother, and my sister of course – she lives here as well.' We looked at him in surprise, but he didn't seem to notice. 'I live in Canada now, but it's still in the family. My name's Stepan, by the way, Stepan Beran. My grandfather built most of these houses.' He looked up at the peeling masonry and shrugged. 'They're too far gone now. We're just going to have to watch them fall down.'

I looked at him enquiringly. 'But what happened?' I asked.

1862

Chapter One

'She's coming, she's coming.' Milo ran quickly down the steep steps of the narrow alleyway leading towards the bay. He was a short but sturdy boy, just approaching his thirteenth year, with fair hair bleached almost white by the sun. 'Niko, Niko!' he shouted. 'She's coming. She's nearly at Caesar's Passage!'

He leapt off the bottom of the steps, skidding on the dusty surface as he ran through the open square towards the peninsula which protected the bay from the open Adriatic Sea. The waterfront was still busy, even though the catch had long since been landed and taken across to the mainland. Along the entire length of the quay, dozens of brightly painted boats of various sizes lay with their bows towards the wall, moored tightly together in rows, in places three deep. The few fishermen still on board were cleaning up before hauling their gear ashore. Nets were piled everywhere, some still pink from a recent dye-wash, others faded to a muddy brown. Dotted along the waterfront were men sitting on short, round stools, checking the nets for damage caused by the previous night's catch, passing the small squares of netting rapidly from hand to hand with practised skill.

Niko was standing opposite his father, Mato Boskovich. Between them they held the ends of one of the nets tightly, gathering it together carefully to stow on the boat. Niko glanced at Milo as he ran past the quay up the bank, allowing the tension to loosen. Mato sighed and took the net from the boy's hands. 'All right, off you go, lad.' He shook his head. 'I'll get Vigo to help me with this later.'

Niko took off his cap and clenched it tightly in his fist as he rushed to join Milo in a frantic dash around the quay. He caught up with him as they jumped across the dried-up gully at the head of the bay, and ran off towards a small beach. They climbed a low ridge and looked out across the Adriatic. The calm sea was a deep blue, and a lazy swell rose and fell, foaming gently as it washed over the rocky shore. A boat, ageing and battered, sailed slowly past, its faded lateen sail barely filled in the light north-westerly wind. The boatman, whose long grey smock, stained with tar and grease, was as neglected as his boat, looked ahead impassively. The dark blue cap lodged precariously on his head might once have been smart, but now its white lining was sticking out in tufts through its many tears. In front of him, on the thwart, sat a smartly dressed woman whose careful clothes contrasted sharply with the boatman's. Her oatmeal-coloured jacket was buttoned to the neck, and she had collected her long skirt together carefully to avoid staining from the dirty rags lying in the sole. The boat approached the narrow channel at the head of the peninsula, navigating inshore of a sharp rock which jutted out menacingly through the water's surface.

'Fräulein Wolff, Fräulein Wolff!' the two boys shrieked in a ragged chorus. The woman turned on her seat and looked back towards their shouts, squinting against the sun with her hand over her eyes. Recognising them, she waved back briefly as the boat disappeared behind the headland. The two panting boys stayed for a few moments to catch their breath, before turning and rushing back to the quay.

The boatman furled his sails and pulled alongside the steps with a final sweep of the long oars, which he shipped as they bumped unsteadily against the stone wall. Milo jumped in, took Elsa Wolff's case and handed it up to Niko, who carried it off. Tethering the boat alongside, the boatman spat on his hands, as if to clean them before offering to help his passenger ashore; she hesitated briefly before accepting with a light laugh. Milo clambered out and ran along the quay after her. 'I've done it, Miss. I've worked it out.'

Elsa turned and looked back towards him. 'You have?' she asked. She paused for a moment. 'And what was it?'

Milo stopped in front of her. 'You've forgotten, haven't you? You told us last time a trick with numbers. But I've worked it out – you put a number in and then took it out again. It didn't make any difference what the number was.'

Elsa suddenly remembered what he was talking about. It was a puzzle she gave all her children, never expecting any of them to understand it. She only told them in an attempt to get them interested in numbers. She looked at Milo and hesitated. 'That's right,' she said, looking at him in surprise. 'How long did it take you?'

'That night,' said Milo. 'I kept thinking about it, so I took a piece of paper and wrote it all down. It was simple when I knew. It wasn't magic at all.'

Elsa smiled uncertainly. 'I didn't say it was. I said it was a riddle.' She turned and walked on, thinking quickly. No one had ever tried to solve it before. Not for the first time, she found

Milo's approach disconcerting. She changed the subject. 'Apart from working out the numbers,' she asked, 'what else have you been doing since my last visit?' A young girl was cleaning the large windows of the villa at the end of the quay. Elsa turned past her towards the park in the middle of the village. 'How's Peter been?' Peter was Milo's pet mouse and during her last visit he had insisted that it had caught a cold. 'But he's sneezing,' he had protested in the face of her doubts.

'Oh, he's better now, Miss. I fed him lemon juice on a plate with some honey mixed with it.'

Elsa still couldn't be sure whether he had been serious or just trying to tease her, but she had decided to play along with it, uneasily aware of the tenuousness of her authority. She suspected that if she challenged him he would probably simply come up with something else and surprise her again. They walked along the quay, past the park towards a small gully which led up the hill towards the centre of the island. Niko caught up with them, and handed her a bundle of assorted papers. 'I've collected everything for you to mark, and your case is in the schoolroom. Are you going to the Bossanos?' he asked.

'Thank you, Niko. Yes, I'm spending the night at the estate, so I'll see you both in the morning. Can you tell all the others?' As Niko ran back towards the village, Elsa walked on with Milo.

'Will we ever see your brother at school again?' she asked.

'I shouldn't think so, Miss,' replied Milo. 'Jurica's hardly ever at home now he's found a part-time job off the island. Mam told him he should keep up with his lessons, but he's not like me, he just wants to get out and earn some money. He thinks because he's five years older than me, he's too old to go to school.'

'Well, he's lucky to find any work, the way things are in Dalmatia. Where's he working?'

'On the mainland, Miss. In the docks at Gruz,' Milo replied. 'Not that they're paying him anything. They say they're allowing him to learn the business and he should count himself lucky. Though Mam says it's a funny sort of luck to work for nothing.'

Elsa laughed. 'You can see her point, can't you? I'm really looking forward to meeting your mother, she sounds like a very sensible woman. Anyway, I need to talk to both your parents soon about your future.'

They passed over the ridge behind the village, into the small valley which ran through the middle of the island. A vineyard ran up the slope towards a large rambling villa. From the house, a gravel path snaked down through the vineyard towards a pair of wrought iron gates. Down the path they could see a figure walking rapidly towards them. 'If you want to talk to my Dad, there he is now,' Milo said proudly, and called out. Andro Beran looked up from the ground, as though disturbed in his thoughts, and Elsa studied him as he approached. He was tall, with strong, broad shoulders. Long black hair spilled from under his cap and curled over the back of his collar. He was panting slightly and his clothes were a little dishevelled, as though he had been running. Milo looked up at his father's weather-beaten face, flushed even darker with anger.

'That woman!' Andro spat the words out, almost unaware of his audience. 'Just who does she think she is? Hasn't that family done enough to us already?'

Milo was bewildered by his father's strange mood and embarrassed that he was ignoring the teacher. He looked at Elsa apologetically and tugged at his father's sleeve. 'Dad, Dad, you haven't said hello to Fräulein Wolff. She says she wants to talk to you.'

Andro recovered himself with an effort and gave the teacher a weak smile. 'I'm sorry, Miss. It's a bad time. Mrs Bossano is a friend of yours, I know, but to the rest of us...' He let his words trail away and clenched his jaw, as the anger flushed over him again. 'I'm sorry, I've got to go,' he said abruptly. 'Afternoon, Fräulein.' He touched his cap briefly and strode off down the hill, without even a glance at Milo.

'Dad, Dad. What's the matter?' shouted Milo, as he watched his father disappear behind the trees.

Elsa saw the confusion on the boy's face. 'I'll take the bag now,' she said briskly, and Milo didn't seem to notice as Elsa grasped the case from his hands.

She pulled the gate closed and Milo finally turned back to her. 'I'm sorry, Miss, I don't understand what's gone wrong. I'll see you in the morning.' Elsa smiled and nodded. For a few moments she watched him run down the path, wondering what could have happened. She knew Rusa Bossano could be rude to her staff, but this seemed to be something more than that. Shaking her head, she turned along the driveway towards the imposing villa at its end. As she approached, she noticed one of the huge, oak double front doors was half open, and in the darkness of the hallway beyond there were signs of movement. Elsa tugged cautiously at the creaking bell pull and stepped back in alarm as the door was suddenly flung open. Rusa Bossano stood in the doorway, her normally pale face flushed and her eyes damp.

She recognised Elsa with difficulty and stepped backwards. Attempting to recover herself, she pushed at the strands of hair which had become loose. 'I'm sorry, Elsa,' she stammered.

'I didn't, that is, I wasn't…I mean…' The effort to control herself was too much and she cried out impulsively. 'Did you see him?' She pointed along the driveway. 'Did you see him leave? How could he? Thinks he's God's gift, but I'll not let him get away with it.'

Elsa looked at her in alarm. 'What's happened?' she asked. 'Are you hurt?'

Rusa looked at Elsa strangely. 'Hurt?' she repeated. 'No, he didn't hurt me. It'll take more than a man like that to hurt me.' The thought seemed to comfort her and she slowly regained her poise. 'I'm sorry. I'm sorry. Just leave your bag there. I'll get someone to take it to your room. Now come along with me.'

Rusa led her to the top of the steps and ushered her into a long, high-ceilinged room which seemed to take up the complete width of the house. Large windows opened onto a balcony which looked over the vineyard and along the valley. Rusa inspected the room and scowled. She was still shaking, barely keeping control. She sniffed loudly. 'On top of everything I've just been through, I have to cope with lazy servants. They haven't even laid out tea yet. I'll go and see what's happening.'

As Rusa left, Elsa went out onto the terrace and looked across the valley. Even at the end of the long summer, it was green and verdant. The forests of dark oak and Mediterranean pine encircled fields of regularly spaced, bushy green olives. Why did Rusa never seem to appreciate the beauty of the place? Elsa Wolff had been teaching here for less than two years, but the island had captivated her the moment her foot stepped on Šipan's quayside. The sheltered turquoise water, mottled by the shadows of the sea urchins, rocks and plants on the seabed, made her feel that time had no place here. It was an island insulated from the present, and the dim outlines of the distant mountains of the mainland were just a hazy reminder of another world.

Hearing sounds behind her she went back into the drawing room. A maid was laying out cups from a large tray, setting them down noisily on the table. 'How many times have I told you to do that quietly?' Rusa's piercing voice came from the doorway, and Elsa saw the maid jump and almost drop a plate. Rusa walked into the room. She had changed her dress and rearranged her hair, and appeared to have regained her composure. Her usual confidence had returned and she seemed to have forgotten her earlier outburst. 'What did I tell you about the staff?' she continued, as though they were alone together. 'Either they're doing nothing, or they're doing everything wrong. It's a miracle any of my chinaware has survived such handling.'

The maid's eyes started to water, and Elsa realised she must change the subject if the girl wasn't to burst into tears. 'How is Mr Bossano?' she asked desperately.

'Frano? Same as ever. Still spending hours in that study of his. What he does in there I can't imagine.' Rusa waved away the maid. When the door closed behind her she leant forward. 'It's going to change, though. I've never understood why he ever agreed to put up with Andro Beran managing the estates, but after what happened today it's going to end. It's about time Frano took an interest himself.'

'But what did happen today? What did he do?' Despite her wish not to get involved, Elsa couldn't restrain her curiosity.

Rusa looked at her for a moment before replying. 'It wasn't so much what he did,' she answered hesitantly before shaking her head. 'But I don't want to talk about it. He's not going to be around any longer. Let's talk about something else. I want to hear everything that's been happening on the mainland. You know how dull it is here.' She reached out for the teapot. 'I really can't understand why you left Austria when you must have had such a fine life in Vienna. Palaces and grand balls, all that music – how could you leave the centre of the Empire for this outpost?'

'Palaces and grand balls indeed! My brother and I were brought up in an orphanage, as you well know. The nuns didn't hold many balls and the convent certainly wasn't a palace. Dalmatia might be an outpost, but it's still part of the Austrian Empire and we owe our duty to all of it, not just to favoured parts. Besides, I like the people who live here.'

'The people!' Rusa snorted. 'The people here are lazy and worthless, they have no concept of manners and they certainly don't recognise breeding.'

Elsa sighed inwardly. Following her fortunate marriage to Frano Bossano, Rusa had adopted what she considered to be the manners of the aristocracy, trying to conceal her own modest origins under a veil of her imagination that represented her family as forming part of society's elite. Her haughty manner was wearing and Elsa hesitated before replying, well aware of Rusa's views on what she dismissively called 'the people', even though she wasn't too far removed from them herself.

She knew it was pointless to argue, but Elsa couldn't help herself. 'But don't you see that's why I'm here? The people need education. More and more families are sending their children to my brother's school in Slano, and if they have proper schoolrooms on the mainland, then surely it's only a matter of time before they can build them on the islands? Perhaps your husband could become a Patron of a village school here in Šipan, as well as at Slano. You could get a permanent teacher, and I wouldn't have to visit every few weeks to teach the few children who can be spared from the land.' As she said it, Elsa immediately realised how unlikely it was.

Rusa smiled at her condescendingly. 'The islanders would never appreciate it, my dear. They've never shown us any gratitude for what we've done for them in the past. I simply don't know why you bother.'

Elsa wondered at how often Rusa Bossano managed to turn the conversation around to the 'ungrateful' islanders, and couldn't quite understand what they had to be grateful for. 'But I love coming to these islands,' she said attempting to deflect Rusa's bitterness. 'Especially Šipan. You know it's my favourite, and the children here are the best. Take young Milo Beran: he's such a joy to teach, as sharp as a needle.' Absently, she temporarily forgot Elsa's problems with Milo's father. 'If only I could get him to join the school on the mainland he could go a long way – he's already almost fluent in German.'

'Beran? What do you want to talk about them for? The whole family act above their station. Andro's wife Olga is just as bad – you should see the way she looks at you.' Rusa started to become agitated again. 'On the mainland they wouldn't be allowed to get away with it. Just because it's an island, they think that position isn't important and forget their true place.' She paused to collect herself. 'Anyway, I can't see what you can teach these children that'll do them any good. What do they want to learn German for? The only thing they need to learn is how to work properly and show some respect to their betters.'

Elsa laughed. 'We don't teach German to them all. We're supposed to, but it's so remote down here in the south – the inspectors never get beyond Peljesac. We're only too grateful if the families want their children to learn anything at all; we only attempt German with the bright ones, and even then it's usually only quite basic.'

'How you can spend so much time with those children I can't imagine,' Rusa said briskly. 'Why don't you just stay here in the villa for a few weeks instead, and forget about them? It's always lovely to see you and we'd have so much to talk about. These children will never understand what real values are.' Rusa sniffed. 'It seems that the further away from Vienna one goes, the lower standards one finds.' Rusa always talked as though she were a regular visitor to the Viennese Court, although in fact she had never been north of Zadar. 'These days people don't seem to show respect to their betters, and they certainly don't seem to understand that standards can be maintained only if you work at it.' Rusa stood up and walked out through the open windows and looked along the valley. 'You know the Bossanos came from Italy?' she said over her shoulder. She made it sound like an illness and sniffed with disapproval. 'When Frano was small, they even had to speak Italian.'

Elsa followed her onto the terrace. Rusa gazed out, lost in her memories. 'You know, I had such plans when we got married. It's almost twelve years ago and I was so excited about it all. Coming here to Šipan I thought I could finally make my mark on society. Everyone knew Frano's reputation, but all my friends still envied me.' Rusa noticed the expression on Elsa's face. 'No, really. You wouldn't think it now, but he used to be so good looking. He had a sort of willowy charm, and all the girls fancied him; but he was so unreliable and headstrong that he was almost out of control. His father gave him lots of money and he was difficult to resist – several scandals were brushed under the carpet. Old Mr Bossano tried to pretend nothing was wrong, but the stories grew worse and worse until even he had finally had enough. He cut Frano's allowance and kept him here on the island.' Rusa laughed bitterly. 'His father thought Frano couldn't get into much trouble here. But he still tried it on with the local girls. I saw it as my chance, because I could see what no one else could. He was headstrong and careless, but at heart I knew he was weak. I could give him a direction in life – at least I thought I could. I thought I could control him and get him to settle down and understand his duties. I planned to turn this place into an estate to rival those in the mainland, so we'd be accepted by the best families in Dubrovnik.' Rusa stopped and looked out across the fields for several minutes.

'He tried at first,' Rusa continued. 'But old Mr Bossano had already taken on Andro Beran to manage the estate. I never understood why. It meant that Frano didn't need to do any-thing. And after his father died, he just sort of lost interest. Beran always acted as though he was special, but there were many better-qualified people on the mainland who at least had some level of breeding. As Frano's done less and less, we've become dependent on an uneducated estate manager. It's humiliating. He's such a rough man. He…' Rusa stopped, aware that her voice was starting to rise. 'Well anyway, he's going to suffer for it,' she added finally.

Elsa was uncomfortable at witnessing the force of Rusa's anger, but found it difficult to counter such bitterness. 'I'm sure Mr. Bossano has good reasons for employing him.'

'Well, whatever they are, after today I've had enough of Andro Beran. I don't care what Frano says. It's time he started to take an interest and did the job himself.'

Elsa brushed down her dress nervously. She didn't think she wanted to hear any more of Rusa's complaints. 'I'm sorry,' she said. 'If you will excuse me, I've got to check the lessons for tomorrow and mark the papers.'

Rusa pulled herself together quickly and turned away from the terrace. 'Yes of course, my dear. Make yourself at home as always. You know what it's like on this island and how much Frano and I enjoy visitors from the mainland. At supper you can tell us all the news and I can find out everything I'm missing.'

Elsa could hear their raised voices from the landing. She came down the stairs quietly, unsure whether she should make her presence known. 'I've always wondered why you've kept him on,' Rusa spoke with familiar petulance. 'You could have found a better-qualified manager on the mainland, someone who'd been brought up on estates and understood some culture. Someone we could even have to dinner occasionally. After your father died there was finally nothing to stop you. Instead we've had to put up with an uncouth islander all these years.'

'He's not uncouth,' Frano Bossano answered truculently. 'And he's proved to be good at the job: why shouldn't I have kept him on? You think everyone has to have a good family. I'm not employing the family, I'm employing the man.'

'So his family has nothing to do with it?' Rusa's voice was ominously low. 'Not his wife even? She's still a fine-looking woman; she must have been quite a temptation for any man.'

'What's that supposed to mean?'

'You know perfectly well what I mean,' replied Rusa tersely. 'The way you used to carry on before I came here. There wasn't a woman on the island who felt safe when you were around. You just did what you pleased.'

'Let's not go into all that again.' Frano sounded less sure of himself.

'I don't know what you would have done if I hadn't taken you in hand. You know none of the girls here could risk standing up to you.' Rusa thought for several moments before adding: 'Anyway, what did he mean when he said to me "after all we've done to his family"? What have we done to his family?'

Elsa heard the floorboards creak as Frano walked across the room. His voice came through the doors more faintly. 'I don't know what he's talking about. Anyway, if you dislike him so much, why don't you keep away from him?'

'I do, but he always tries to search me out,' Rusa retorted angrily. 'I've always told you that I don't like him around me. I've always said he makes me uncomfortable, but you've never taken any notice. Well, after today I've had enough of him.'

'Today? What are you talking about? What did he do?'

'He…' Rusa stopped suddenly. Elsa thought she could almost hear her think. 'He's always had that look about him. I always knew he was dangerous.' Rusa said it defiantly, as though she had made a decision. 'And today it finally happened – just as I feared.'

'What happened?' Frano repeated impatiently.

'He tried to kiss me.'

'Kiss you?' Frano was incredulous. 'What d'you mean, he kissed you? I mean… Why? Where were you?'

'I warned you about this. I've never liked his manner. Arrogant. Too sure of himself. Thought he could do as he liked. Well, not with me. He may be a big man, but by the time I'd finished telling him my mind he was only a couple of inches high.'

Elsa thought back to her brief meeting with Andro. She realised she couldn't bear to listen any further. Impulsively she pushed open the door and walked through as calmly as she could, trying to appear as though she had heard nothing. Frano turned from his wife and looked at Elsa blankly, but she held her fixed smile and approached him. If he had once been good looking, Elsa could find little sign of it now. His once-trim moustache was straggling and unkempt, while his belly hung heavily over his belt band. His clothes were sagging and crumpled, the lapels scarred with burn marks from his cigars. Elsa held out her hand. 'Mr. Bossano, once again I'm in your debt for letting me stay.'

Frano was unsettled by the interruption. It took him several moments to recognise his guest. 'Fräulein Wolff, you know you are always welcome.' He recovered himself slightly and kissed her lightly on both cheeks. 'But you must excuse me. Rusa has been telling me some terrible news about my estate manager.' He turned to Rusa. 'Does Fräulein Wolff know about this?'

Rusa looked at Elsa nervously. 'No, no,' she said quickly. 'I didn't want to upset her and it might make her feel vulnerable.'

'Vulnerable?' Elsa remembered that she wasn't supposed to have heard their conversation. 'Why, what's happened?'

'He's…' Frano searched for the right way of saying it. 'He made a pass at her,' he said eventually.

Elsa looked at Rusa. 'Indeed,' she said coolly. 'Are you sure it wasn't a misunderstanding?'

Rusa tossed her head. 'I know what happened,' she said and faced Frano. 'He's got to go. I can't have him on the estate any more.'

'I suppose you're right,' he said glumly. 'Perhaps he has gone too far.'

'Perhaps?' said Rusa. 'There's no perhaps about it. You must tell him immediately.'

Elsa watched the indecision on Frano's face. He wasn't accustomed to making his own decisions; life was a lot easier if he simply fell in with his wife's wishes. 'All right, then,' he said finally. 'I'll just have to take my chances. Andro's taken his position for granted for too long now. I don't care what he says about me.'

'What do you mean, you don't care what he says?' Rusa asked sharply. 'What can he possibly say about you?'

'He can say...' Frano hesitated. 'Well, for example, he could say that I'm a bad employer,' he ended weakly. 'He could say...'

'He can say what he likes,' Rusa interrupted. 'He's got to go.'

Frano walked slowly towards the window and looked out at the darkening fields. He realised he had no choice. 'He's coming here tomorrow at midday. I'll tell him then.'

Elsa Wolff cried out without thinking. 'But what about Milo? What's going to happen to the boy?' She saw Frano looking at her strangely. 'I'm sorry,' she said recovering herself. 'I know it's not my business. But if he could just spend another year at school, he could achieve so much. If you dismiss his father, I don't see how Milo can stay on.'

'The boy,' repeated Frano. 'Yes, I suppose there's always the boy. But if my wife has made up her mind, I don't see what I can do.'

'Why should you worry about the boy?' asked Rusa. 'Andro should have thought of that before.'

'Before what?' thought Elsa, but she said nothing. How could she face Milo the next morning knowing what was about to happen to his father?

Chapter Two

Even though the summer was fading, the morning was already hot as Elsa entered the small building that passed as the island's school, the room kept cool by the thick stone walls. Taking off her hat and hanging it on a peg under the shelf next to the doorway, she took the case from where Niko had left it and sat behind the desk, patting the stray wisps of her brown hair into place. Pulling out her books and papers, she stared at them vacantly for a moment. Her watery brown eyes were the colour of her hair. She sighed as she thought of Milo. She couldn't see how he would be able to attend lessons for much longer, yet she had never come across a child with so much potential. She questioned again whether it was all worth it. Perhaps Rusa Bossano was right; why give these children education when they had no opportunity to use it? She looked up as the first of her class came in and took his place behind his tiny desk. She returned his greeting, but her doubts remained. These children were willing enough – but what was the point, when their futures remained on an island with only a choice between fishing or working the land?

But as the lesson progressed, she forgot her reservations; the children's unaffected interest exhilarated her, as it always did, and she wondered why she had questioned the work she was doing. Afterwards, as she walked back towards the square, she took her small basket of bread and cheese and sat down alone in the harsh sunlight. She looked across the bay and imagined what she could achieve if she could come more often. Who knows what she could discover in some of the children? If only young Milo could study full time…

'Fräulein Wolff?'

Elsa took several moments before she responded to her name, and then looked up blankly. The woman looking down at her was no longer young, her long dark hair was streaked with grey and the smooth skin of her face had fine lines gathering around the eyes. In spite of this it was clear that she had once been a beauty, and it was the eyes themselves that no amount of time could dull. They were a deep chestnut, with a warmth and confidence and humour that Elsa found almost mesmerising. She stirred herself. 'I'm sorry, I was miles away, Mrs…er, Mrs…'

'Olga Beran,' the woman said and held out her hand. 'I'm Milo's mother.'

Elsa's heart fell. Of all the islanders, this was the woman she most wanted to meet – but why now? After the previous evening at the Bossanos, she had found it difficult enough to face Milo in the morning class, but to meet his mother like this was more than she thought she could take. She forced a smile. 'Mrs Beran, I've been looking forward to meeting you all year, but I'm afraid –'

Olga interrupted her. 'We should be ashamed of ourselves leaving you here on your own.' She looked down at Lisa's basket and tut-tutted loudly. 'Now that's not going to see you through the day. You must come up and eat with us.'

Elsa felt near to panic. 'That's very kind of you but – but…' She stood up and looked around desperately for an escape. 'But I've really got to get back to the schoolroom and mark the children's work. I'm sure you understand. Please – another time. I'd like to visit you, but another time.'

Olga smiled and put her hand softly on Elsa's arm. 'Please don't be embarrassed, Fräulein Wolff. Just treat us as you find us. For our part we won't be giving you any special treatment and you'll only eat what we eat. There isn't anything else. Besides, what would the children say if they heard you wouldn't join us?'

Elsa saw she had little choice but to give in gracefully. She would have to steel herself to forget what she had heard the previous night and try to leave as soon as possible. 'Thank you,' she said. 'Perhaps just briefly. But after that I've got to get back.'

Elsa followed Olga up the steep alleyway. At the top of the village she passed through a doorway leading onto a narrow terrace. Underneath the vine that shaded the terrace during the hot summer, a simple meal was laid out on a large wooden table. She walked across the terrace and gasped at the extraordinary view spread out before her. The air had an eerie clarity, which allowed her to see from the harbour beneath, across to the mountains above the Peljesac peninsula on the mainland. To the west, beyond the village and the bay, the sparkling Adriatic was now clear to the horizon. 'You must never tire of looking at all this,' she said.

Olga Beran looked out across the sea. 'No, never,' she said after a few moments. 'And it's always changing. Today it's so clear – in the summer you can hardly see the mainland for the haze, but it's starting to get cooler now. Different times of day, different seasons, different weather: it's never the same.'

Elsa sat down at the end of the table and looked out across the islands. 'How can anyone bear to leave a place like this?'

'The people who leave don't normally have a choice,' Olga said. 'Fortunately, with Andro's job, we've been able to keep our children with us.'

Elsa suddenly felt cold, utterly powerless in the face of an overwhelming destiny. 'If only...' She looked back along the valley towards the Bossanos' estate. 'If only people could see how lucky they are, and what they could make of this place.'

'You're talking like someone from the mainland. There aren't many opportunities on an island. The only job Jurica could find was at Dubrovnik.' Olga laughed. 'They're not paying him yet, so they shouldn't complain when they find things take twice as long whenever he's around. I always do,' she added good-naturedly. She paused for a moment and then continued more seriously. 'But it's Milo I worry about. The school came here a bit late for Jurica and he wasn't interested in his lessons anyway, but Milo...' She hesitated. 'I know he's my youngest, but it's more than that.' Olga looked across the terrace towards the mountains and spoke as though to herself. 'He's not like his brothers. They're both impulsive, but he's quieter and not as outgoing. They'll rush at things, but he takes his time thinking about it before he acts. But if there's something he wants, he'll always find a way to get it.'

The sound of running footsteps made Elsa look up. Milo ran in from the alleyway, panting heavily. He stopped in surprise as he saw Elsa. 'Fräulein Wolff?'

Olga cuffed Milo playfully. 'Your teacher is joining us, so you can show some manners for a change.' She looked towards the tall young man who had followed Milo through the gateway. 'You can start by introducing Vigo.'

Milo's brother approached Elsa with an easy confidence and held out his hand. Elsa shook it and looked over to Olga. 'There's not much doubt who he is – he's much more like his father than Milo.'

'His father?' Olga looked at her curiously. 'You mean Andro?' She frowned and sat down at the table, reaching out absently for some bread. 'I didn't know you'd met him already. He didn't tell me.'

Elsa reddened, unsure of herself. 'I only saw Mr Beran briefly. He was -' she glanced towards Milo who was washing his hands in the stone sink. 'He was obviously very preoccupied, so we didn't talk for long.' Her misery deepened. She had obviously said something wrong and, knowing what Frano had decided, she felt like a spy in the enemy camp. She looked in desperation at the food laid out on the table. The sooner she could finish it, the sooner she could leave. 'This looks good,' she said. 'And to think I almost turned it down.'

'Please help yourself,' Olga said and turned to the boys. 'I found her sitting alone by the quay. She comes all the way here to teach our children, but it seems that we're so ungrateful that no one takes the trouble to look after her.'

The mention of 'ungrateful islanders' made Elsa wince inwardly. 'No, that's not true,' she protested. 'This has always been my favourite island, and I don't find the people at all ungrateful.' She put some food on her plate and attempted to change the subject. She turned to Vigo, who had sat down beside her. 'Milo tells me you're going to be a fisherman.'

'That's right, Miss. It's not regular yet, but I help out if a skipper is short of a crew, so I can learn all the tricks. I'm going out all this week with Mato Boskovich – that's Niko's dad. But soon I'll be on my own. I've been building my own boat and it's nearly finished.'

'It's a beautiful boat, Miss,' Milo interrupted. 'You should see it. Vigo's so clever with his hands. He's only got the seat left to fit.' Elsa saw the look of admiration on Milo's face as he looked up at his big brother.

'I'll be ready soon,' said Vigo. 'I'm not in a hurry and the older fishermen still have a lot to teach me. But when I get established, then perhaps I can get a second boat, or even a third.'

'He knows all the places, Miss,' Milo said proudly. 'He's shown me all the bays and coves right around the island. There's nothing Vigo doesn't know about Šipan.'

Vigo laughed. 'I don't know about that.' He reached out and tousled Milo's hair. 'Perhaps you can come and join me as crew. What d'you think?'

'Don't say that!' Olga's shrill cry echoed around the bay.

Elsa looked up in alarm, stunned at her vehemence. For several moments no one said anything

'I'm sorry, Vigo.' Olga collected herself finally, but her face was still white with fear. 'It's just that after, after…' She turned back to Elsa. 'I worry about them so much. It's so dangerous out there and I want something better for Milo.'

'We'll be all right, Mam.' Vigo looked at her anxiously. 'Milo will be fine, and I'll make a good living with the boat. I promise. In a few years I'll be able to provide for all of us, even when Dad's finished working. Though I can't imagine how he will put up with the Bossanos for so long.'

'Don't talk about them like that,' Olga said sharply. 'You're embarrassing Fräulein Wolff. You know she's a good friend of theirs.'

Elsa cut in quickly. 'Not a good friend,' she said. 'They're kind enough to have me to stay when I'm visiting the island. I really don't know them that well.'

'You know, you shouldn't think too badly of Frano Bossano,' Olga said. 'It's his wife. She set out to change him from the very first day of their marriage. He wasn't always as he is now. I know he acted like a spoilt child, but he could also be quite kind, even generous. Even after his father died, Frano's always been good to Andro.'

Elsa thought back to the conversation she had overheard the previous night. If Frano Bossano did carry out his threat she had no idea how the family would manage, and they would always associate her with the Bossanos' betrayal. She finished her plate and stood up quickly. 'I really must get back. I told you I couldn't stay long – I've still got some lessons to prepare. Perhaps you and Milo's father could come down to the schoolroom sometime to talk about his future.'

Vigo looked questioningly at his mother, who nodded back at him. He stood up and, taking Elsa's hat off the peg, he handed it to her. 'We're all very grateful to you, Fräulein. For what you're doing for Milo. I wish you'd been here when I was a lad.' He grabbed Milo and held him tightly across his chest. 'Though how you manage to put up with this little monster I have no idea. Milo's mouse is cleverer than he is.'

To Elsa's dismay, Olga took off her apron and followed her to the doorway. 'Let's leave these two arguing, Fräulein Wolff. I'll come down with you and you can tell me about Milo's progress.'

Elsa said nothing as they walked together down the alleyway. 'I'm sorry about just now.' Olga said finally. 'But I get so frightened. After their father...' She stopped suddenly, and turned to Elsa. 'You really didn't know that Andro isn't Vigo's natural father?'

Elsa looked back at her in consternation and shook her head.

'Andro's my second husband.' Olga said. 'I thought you knew that. I thought everyone knew it – people used to talk about it often enough behind my back. But if you're teaching Milo, then you ought to know. My first husband was called Pasko Rosich. But he died at sea before...' She hesitated. 'Before Milo was born.

'He'd only signed on for a short passage, but it was nearly a year before we found out what had happened.' She shook her

16

head sadly. 'His ship hit a reef during a gale – the light on the headland was out. The wreckers on shore waited for the storm to end before rowing out to steal whatever they could find. By that time most of the crew had drowned and my Pasko was one of them. But they didn't care. It seemed the wreckers put out the light deliberately and it didn't worry them that they'd taken a father from his sons.

'It wasn't easy after that, not with the two boys. My family's not from this island and I was on my own. It was very difficult.' She paused, groping for the right words. 'But whatever people say, I did what I had to do,' she continued, almost defiantly. 'There was no one else to support me. But Andro was so good to me. He'd been Pasko's friend, and I think he'd always had a thing about me. He wanted to get married, and it seemed best for us all. And then, afterwards, when Milo was born, Andro was always so good to him – he's been a good father to all of them. He's never tried to take Pasko's place, but they all accepted him. The older boys still remember Pasko, but Milo…' Olga looked unseeingly across to the boats bobbing against the harbour wall. 'I promised myself that after Pasko, none of my boys would go to sea. But what can I do? At least I'm grateful that Andro's got a job on the land.'

Elsa clenched her fists tightly. 'There must be a way,' she said. 'We've got to find something else.'

'That's the strange thing,' Olga said. 'Vigo loves the sea and he wouldn't hear of doing anything else. If that's what he wants, then I can't stop him, but Milo's different. If he has to join him, then I know I'll have failed. Milo deserves more.'

Elsa felt on firmer ground. 'He's done so well this year,' she said more confidently. 'I can hardly believe the progress he's made. It would be such a waste if he couldn't continue his studies. Just a year longer and he would certainly get a certificate on the mainland.'

'A year!' Olga looked doubtful. 'I'll have to see what Andro says about that. He's getting reasonably well paid by the Bossanos, but it's not easy for him. You know what Mrs Bossano is like; she seems to have taken control of her husband. He wasn't always like that.'

'Perhaps,' said Elsa, unconvinced. She looked along the quay suddenly. 'Isn't that your husband now?' Andro was striding towards them, and Elsa could see his face was even darker than on the previous day.

Olga looked up. 'Yes. That's my Andro. You must come and meet him properly.'

'No!' Elsa cried desperately. 'No, I'm sorry. Later, perhaps. I've got to get back to the schoolroom. I'm sorry, but I've already spent too long away as it is. Thank you for your hospitality, Mrs Beran.' She turned and walked rapidly away.

Olga watched her in surprise and called after her. 'Olga, please call me Olga. After all you're a friend of the family now.'

Elsa felt the words like a bullet in the back. The family's livelihood had been taken away from them, and she hadn't had the courage to warn them, or even help them. But what could she have done? Frano Bossano had once told her, in an unguarded moment, that he didn't know how he could manage the estate without Andro. Perhaps he had reconsidered. Perhaps he had finally found some independence and had decided to keep Andro after all. But seeing Andro Beran's glowering face, she knew this was a false hope. It would be a tragedy if Milo was forced to leave school to work on the fields or, even worse, to be sent to sea. But what could she do? She couldn't change the way the island's life had always been.

She had to think about the other children as well. It was Frano Bossano who helped support her brother's school on the mainland, allowing her the time to visit the islands. Although none of the others approached Milo's ability, they all worked under great difficulties to prepare their scraps of writing. In some cases it was almost a miracle that they produced anything at all, and she was determined not to let any of them down. But her thoughts kept returning to Milo. After what she had heard, she could only guess at his future.

At the end of the afternoon Elsa normally stayed on to talk to the children, but this time she left the schoolroom hurriedly as soon as lessons had finished. Milo called after her, 'See you in the morning then, Miss,' but she hurried back towards the Bossano estate without answering. Milo shrugged and wandered down towards the quayside with Niko. Dusk was starting to fall and the evening stars were already visible in the transparent sky.

'Vigo! Vigo! What are you doing?' Milo looked in surprise at his brother, who was heaving his unfinished boat towards the water.

Vigo looked up. 'Haven't you heard?' He gave a sour laugh as he answered his own question. 'No, I don't suppose you have.'

Milo was mystified. 'Heard what? What's happened?'

'It's Dad.' Vigo put the bows of the boat down on the flagstones. 'Lord High-and-Mighty has finally done it. That bitch Rusa Bossano put him up to it. He knows he can't manage on his own.'

'Manage what? I don't understand.'

'Dad's been dismissed. Mr. Bossano called him in at lunchtime and told him to go. Just like that.'

'But he can't.' Milo clutched at his brother's arm. 'He can't, not after so long. Why? He must have told him why?'

'Dad said there was a reason, but he wouldn't tell us. He said that Rusa had become almost impossible and there was nothing he could do. He said he'd been thinking of leaving anyway.'

'And go where?' Milo cried. 'There isn't anything else. You know that – not on Šipan. What are we going to do?'

'I know what I'm going to do.' Vigo bent over the boat again and started pulling.

Milo looked at Vigo in confusion. 'You're not going out?' Vigo didn't answer. 'But the boat's not ready.'

'It'll do,' said Vigo. 'I have to do something to help. I've been working on this boat long enough – it's time to make it pay.'

'But you can't go out on your own,' Milo pleaded. 'You haven't finished it yet.' He turned. 'Niko, tell him. You know your father would stop him. The older men aren't going out.'

Niko looked away in confusion. 'I – I'm sorry, Milo,' he stammered. 'I – I – don't know what to say. I think Vigo should wait, but my father would know what to do.'

Vigo couldn't ignore his brother's distress. He put down the boat and walked over to Milo and put his hands on his brother's shoulders, shaking him gently. 'Come along now, I'll be all right. I owe it to Dad.' He paused and looked down at Milo affectionately, his voice tinged with pride. 'And to you. I'll always be just a fisherman – but you? You've got a better future. What's a big brother for if he can't help you achieve it? Anyway, didn't you say I knew the island like the back of my hand? Nothing's going to happen to me.'

'But what about the weather?' asked Milo. 'If the sky's so clear, it could mean a storm's coming – even a *Bora*.'

Vigo looked up at the brilliant sky and a moment's fear pulled at his stomach. He shrugged it off quickly. 'No, it'll be all right. It's clear because it's autumn, that's all.' Vigo put his arm around Milo reassuringly and walked him towards the boat. 'You and Niko can give me a hand launching her, but after that you'd better go up and comfort your mother.'

'Does Mam know what you're doing?' asked Milo, suddenly realising that Vigo probably hadn't told anyone.

'She'll find out in the morning,' Vigo grunted with the effort of pushing the boat over the stone edge into the water. 'I have a feeling that it's going to be my lucky night. I've got this hunch about a place. I'll show them that we don't need the Bossanos.' The boat slid into the water and settled alongside the quay. Vigo looked at it with satisfaction. 'Isn't she a beauty? Now you get back and see your mother. She'll be waiting for you.'

Milo left Niko and ran back up the hill. He slowed as he approached his house and walked quietly through the gateway onto the terrace. His father and mother sat at the table talking quietly. His father looked up as Milo sat down beside him. 'Dad?' Milo said softly. 'Are you all right?'

Andro turned away slowly and looked across the bay for several moments before nodding almost imperceptibly. 'We'll manage, son; we always have. We're not going to let Rusa Bossano steal our happiness. 'We'll sort it out. Don't you worry.'

Beneath them, down in the sheltered harbour, Vigo felt the chill of autumn as he pushed the boat out and sculled expertly into the darkness – there wasn't enough wind for the sails and he couldn't row until the seat was fixed. The new moon was not due for a couple of days but, as the daylight faded, the stars pierced the darkness so brightly that even the tiny waves shimmered with the reflections from the sparkling night sky. On the horizon the powerful acetylene lamps of the sardine boats flashed as they rocked up and down on the swell. Vigo knew exactly where he was going to try. He had spent all his life swimming in the bays and his navigation around the islands was almost instinctive. As he pulled further from shore, the other fishing boats from the town went off to the west and soon became invisible in the dark. Rounding the point to the north of the island, he turned and headed past the tiny island of Mishnak towards the rocky point. He took a deep breath of the still air and the pit of his stomach fluttered gently. The boat might not be completely ready, but this was his first night as a professional fisherman. He looked at the black night around him and smiled at it.

Far from Dalmatia, nearly a thousand miles inland, the air pressure had been building up throughout the afternoon. As the pressure grew, it pushed a gentle north-easterly wind towards the valleys of the western Balkans. Between the valleys and the southern Adriatic, the moving air was blocked by the high, steep-sided mountains that fringed the coast. In the cold night, the mountains were covered with their first frosts of autumn and the cold air hung around them, heavy and still. The pressure rose and the force of the wind grew, pushing the air higher into the foothills of the forbidding mountains. The rising air cooled and as it did so, it became heavier and pushed back against the air from the valley. Away to the north, a field of low pressure moved towards the high pressure, strengthening the wind which funnelled between them. The pressure grew, pushing the wind higher up the mountains as the air became increasingly colder and heavier. Some of it condensed, forming layers of cloud that swirled around the peaks, but the mountains still resisted the wind, like a breakwater against a wave. Along the narrow coast and far out to sea, the air was still and quiet.

As the pressure gradient steepened in the north, the wind grew stronger, increasing the pressure on the cooling air. With a renewed effort, the immense force of the wind from the valleys finally pushed the dense air up, and then over even the highest ridges of the mountain range, and all resistance disappeared instantly. With nothing to stop it, the heavy, freezing air literally fell down the steep sides of the mountains to the sea at their feet. Millions – billions – of tons of air were released and cascaded down onto the Adriatic coast a mile below and as they did so, the dense clouds expanded like a small explosion and sent a fierce pressure wave swirling across the water. The north-easterly wind, finally freed from any constraint, blasted the formidable *Bora* across the open sea.

The wind hit the sea like an avalanche, smothering everything in an invisible blanket of violent air. Within minutes the flat water was whipped into furious turmoil. A wind of this force, out in a great ocean, has thousands of miles to build the seas into huge, spread-out waves, but so close to the coast there was no space for waves to form. Instead water was flung upon water and wave upon wave, with no recognisable troughs between them. The sea churned and raged, and the spray was atomised into fierce jets of spindrift. In less than half an hour, the calm, warm waters of a peaceful Adriatic autumn had turned into a merciless and unstoppable threshing machine.

With no pattern to the tumultuous water, there were no waves for a small boat to ride over. Even when a pattern tried to emerge, it was crushed by a vicious cross-sea. Vigo struggled with the oars, but with no thwart to sit on he was forced to kneel with his legs biting into each side of the keelson. Each time he managed to heave the bows into the wind, a wave hit the boat from the side, forcing him to drop an oar and lose his balance. But, unable to steady the boat into the sea, his task was hopeless. He shouted into the searing wind in pain and frustration. If he had been further out to sea, there would have been space for him to pay out a line; he could have trailed a drogue to keep his bows into the wind, but close inshore there was nothing he could do. The boat slewed sideways against the storm, tripling the force against the hull. A steep, cruel wave bore down on him and as the little boat rose up its side, the crest flipped it into the air where it was hit by an intense gust of wind and flung backwards towards the rocks beyond. The boat was dragged across the foaming water, scooping up the boiling sea and, in an instant, it was swamped amidst the debris of its equipment. Piles of nets unravelled under the force of the spray and the floats were blown apart by each breaking wave. Vigo was thrown clear and kicked out in a frantic lunge for the surface. As his head broke through the surface, he gulped a lungful of air. A wave washed up behind him, briefly raising him into the force of the wind. The spray lashed against his face as he looked around for his boat. It wasn't meant to be like this, he thought grimly, not tonight, not when he had so much to look forward to. To one side he glimpsed briefly the orange shadow of a fishing float and he turned towards it, sucking down a breath before the undertow of a breaking wave pulled him under. Again he struck out wildly, knowing he had to get back to the boat, but the waves smashed against his face, leaving him disorientated, while the darkness of the night covered everything. He had spent his childhood playing in these waters and, through his confusion, he resolved that he would not let the waves take him. This was his island: he was in home waters. Instantly the thought of Milo's pride flashed across his fading consciousness – he couldn't let his brother down. With a final effort he pushed himself upwards and as he swung his arm forward, his fingertips brushed against the nets swirling around the boat. Exhilarated with the relief of imminent safety, he kicked forward through the netting as another waved crashed over him. He lunged towards the boat and the palm of his hand hit something solid. He reached out to grab the top of the waterlogged hull.

Chapter Three

Milo lay awake as the shrieking wind battered the island. He strained to hear the sounds of Vigo's return, but as each gust hit the old house, all he could hear were the roof tiles clanking just above him and the creaking windows rattling in their frames. Just before the morning's light, he bundled up his clothes and crept downstairs. Through the doorway, on the terrace, Olga and Andro were silhouetted faintly against the sky. They were sitting together silently, staring across the dark bay. Milo crept up to them uncertainly. 'Is he back yet?' he asked softly. Olga shook her head slowly. There was something unfamiliar in her manner, a frailty he hadn't seen before – she was normally so confident about everything, so much in control. 'It'll be all right, Mam,' he said, sliding his hand into hers. 'Vigo knows the coast, he'll be safe. He'll be back soon.'

His mother stirred and shook almost imperceptibly as though forcing herself out of a private dream. 'But he's not as experienced as the others,' she said. 'He should have asked me. I would never have let him go out alone.'

Andro stood up abruptly and stared across the bay. He could hear the dull rumble of the wind as it buffeted the island. Out at sea, dawn was slowly lightening the sky and streaking the white-crested waves with undulating layers of light. He looked back at Olga, knowing what must be going through her mind, feeling powerless to offer any comfort. 'He didn't have to go,' he said fiercely. 'Not tonight.'

Milo looked up at him, taken aback by the anger and frustration in his voice. He couldn't mistake the fear on his face. For the first time Milo realised that Vigo might never come back. He knew it was because of him.

The suddenness and ferocity of the storm had taken the small community by surprise. Vigo was the least experienced of the fishermen – most of the older men had stayed in port, fearing in the clarity of the day an imminent *Bora*. Most of those who had gone out had put out to the west, in the lee of the island, where they could make for shelter in St George to the south. Others had given themselves enough sea room to hoist a patch of sail and make for shelter elsewhere. Out at sea, the wind was more constant and the waves more regular, allowing the boats to ride out the storm until it faded – such a fierce wind cannot sustain its fury for long. By the middle of the next morning its energy was largely spent, and during the afternoon most of the straggling fishermen had found their way back to port. But by early evening, there wasn't an islander unaware that Vigo had still not returned.

Olga Beran felt an increasing desolation. Memories of her first husband kept returning to her and, sitting beside Andro on the wall beside the quayside, she felt powerless and desperately afraid. She felt herself sinking into a black certainty that the sea had claimed another of her family.

Mato Boskovich approached them from along the quay, his manner diffident. Milo and his parents looked at him expectantly. 'Have you heard anything?' Andro asked.

'No, nothing,' Mato replied. 'Jurica's back from the mainland. He's gone with Fräulein Wolff to organise the children to bring messages from St George. They're both over there now.'

'This is all my fault. If it hadn't been for me he would never have gone out.' Olga and Andro froze at Milo's anguished cry. They looked at him in despair.

'I'm sure Vigo's all right,' Mato said quickly. He put his arm around Milo and squeezed him encouragingly. 'There are so many inlets around the island – he could have sheltered in any of them. He might even have gone off to one of the other islands. If his mast is broken then it would take him a good while to get back.'

Olga shook her head. 'He can't have got to another island, Mato, there wasn't time. The other boats went to the west, and none of them saw him. If he went east, where could he have found shelter? We should have heard from St George by now.' She started to pace up and down, glancing up at the hillside every time she turned. 'Why doesn't someone tell us what's happened?' she kept asking herself. But the path above them remained empty.

Andro watched her helplessly until he could stand it no longer. He walked a little way up the path. In the distance he could see some figures approaching and he turned and called down the hill, 'I think it's Fräulein Wolff.'

'Is Vigo with her?' Olga cried, but before he could answer Jurica ran past, slipping on the stony path, and with a cry he flung himself into her arms.

Andro Beran looked at the boy in alarm. 'What is it, what have you heard?'

Jurica could barely talk. He pulled himself away. 'Vigo's not coming back,' he howled. 'He's, he's…' Unable to get the words out, he looked backwards up the path.

Andro and Olga followed his look towards the hillside. Fräulein Wolff appeared through the trees and stumbled down the path. Olga watched her in terror as she approached, afraid of what she might read in her face.

Andro stepped forward. 'What's happened? Where's Vigo?' he asked desperately. Elsa looked from Jurica across to Andro. She seemed dazed and her voice trembled as she tried to speak.

Milo tugged at her dress. 'Have you heard anything, Miss?' Elsa looked down at him and saw the fear in his eyes. Tears started to course down her face. She brushed them away clumsily. 'I'm afraid they've found him,' her voice caught in her throat.

'Afraid? What's happened?'

Jurica faced his stepfather and cried out. 'They've found his boat off Point Tiha – it had capsized. The fishing nets were washed overboard and they were floating everywhere, all tangled, and…' he stopped to gather breath. 'They found him in the nets; his feet were caught.' Olga reached out and held him. He couldn't understand why it had happened. 'They said there was no way he could free himself. He was trapped.'

Elsa looked on helplessly. She couldn't control her grief any longer. She broke down and wept. 'I'm sorry, I'm so sorry.'

Andro held out his arms and gathered his wife and sons into them. 'Not Vigo, not our Vigo,' he cried. 'Why? He was just starting. He was so young, why him?'

Mato looked on, stunned. 'Point Tiha – why did he go there?' He looked at Elsa as if in entreaty. 'I should have been with him, I could have helped. If only I'd been here I would never have let him go.'

Olga pulled herself away, fighting back the hysterical misery which she feared would overwhelm her. 'Oh my God! First you take my husband, then my boy. Why have you taken my Vigo?' she moaned and then suddenly stepped backwards, clenching her jaw in an effort to find strength. Taking her husband's hands, she cried. 'Whatever happens now, we must stay together.'

Milo pulled himself away from his father. 'I tried to stop him.' His anguished voice quivered as he fought to keep control. 'He only went out because of me. What have I done?' Milo broke down and fell to his knees, wailing helplessly. 'What have I done?'

The loss had been so sudden, the grieving family's transformation so cruel, that in the sombre days that followed, the community tried to provide what little help they could. Vigo could so easily have been their own son, husband or brother. Over the generations, few families had remained untouched by the cruelty of the sea, and they had come to live under its threat with resigned fatalism. Storms, like hunger, were accepted as one of the perils of their precarious existence; life throughout Dalmatia was harsh and few people had any reserves to fall back on. Their poverty allowed little time for mourning. It was just a few days after Vigo's funeral that Andro Beran felt compelled to raise with Olga the family's uncertain future. 'Without Vigo it's going to be difficult to manage,' he started uncertainly. 'We can't expect the neighbours to support us forever. I can help with some boatbuilding for the moment. That will give us a little time, but we must think about the future.'

'But Milo; we must keep a place for Milo,' replied Olga woodenly. 'Whatever happens we can't let him go.'

'We must try, but there's no work on the island to support him.' He took her hands in his. 'You know that. There's no boat seeking a crew and he's still too young.'

'Not on a boat,' interrupted Olga. 'He's not going on the boats.'

Andro looked at her sadly. He sensed how hard she was fighting against her desolation and how much she wanted to regain control of her life. But although it was left unsaid, they both knew that without permanent work, without Vigo's contribution to the family, there wasn't enough money to keep Milo on the island.

'We'll find something,' insisted Olga and she turned abruptly and looked inland across the valley. 'Frano Bossano – he'll have to help now. He must have some work on his estate.'

Andro shook his head. 'Even if he had any work, after what's happened there's no chance that Rusa would do anything to help us.'

'But it's not for you,' Olga said vehemently. 'It's for Milo. I don't care about Rusa: it's Frano we must speak to. He might not listen to you, but he'll listen to me.'

Andro felt helpless, but anything was better than watching his wife tear herself apart. 'We can go and ask,' he said gently. 'I'll go and see him tomorrow.'

'No, not alone,' Olga said firmly. 'We'll all go. We'll take Milo with us.'

'He was doing it for me, Niko.' Milo flung the pebble high into the air above the sea in Caesar's Passage. A seagull dived across to investigate. Milo always came here when he wanted to think:

its romantic name stimulated his imagination. Everything that the outside world had to bring came through this narrow passage and beyond it lay things he could only guess at. Milo watched the gull fly off and turned to Niko. 'It's my fault he went out.'

Niko looked at his friend sadly. He didn't understand the events that had changed Milo's life so suddenly and completely, but knew he must support him. He couldn't bear to think of his best friend leaving the island; more than anything he wanted Milo to stay. 'Things will sort themselves out, you'll see,' he said helplessly. 'I know it must be difficult, but...' his words trailed off. Milo had always been the lucky one; but now? Now, he couldn't tell what might happen. 'It'll be all right, I promise.' He said it without conviction.

Milo looked at Niko and smiled weakly. 'I know you only want to help, but it won't be all right; how can it be after everything that's happened? It's all been so sudden. How can our lives have changed so fast?'

Milo was silent for several moments, lost in thought. 'You know, I thought everything was settled. Vigo's boat was nearly finished; Jurica was getting established on the mainland. But I've always been different from them. While Dad had a good job, I thought I could go on to the school on the mainland and make something of myself. My family has always expected more from me and I've always felt I owed them more. My brothers were never interested in lessons, but I was. I enjoyed the sense of discovery. The challenges which Fräulein Wolff gives me are...' Milo shook his head. 'I can't explain it. They seem to give me such...such power. When I solved one of her problems, I just felt so good. I felt I could go on and do anything.' He looked down at the water lapping around the rocks at his feet. 'But I always thought that whatever happened, this would always be my home. My family would always be here when I came back. At times, during the night, I've woken up in panic thinking I'm at school on the mainland and could never return. I've always been happy here, until, until...' Milo searched for the right words. 'Why must it all change? Everything I want is here, except the most important.' Milo caught Niko's bewildered look. 'Work,' he said. 'Islands aren't places for working; they're places to return to when work is finished.'

Niko leaned forward and looked earnestly at his friend. 'Your father will find something here. You know how much everyone respects him. In time you'll get established with something.'

'Not now!' The force of Milo's response made Niko recoil. 'Not now. Until this week I'd never even thought about my future. I just took it for granted that Fräulein Wolff could arrange everything.' Milo stopped and threw another pebble into the water. 'But that's the past and it's over. They were all trying to do their best for me. It ended up killing my brother.'

'That's stupid,' Niko surprised even himself when he said it. 'Vigo always wanted to be a fisherman, you know that. He talked about nothing else. It was his choice.'

'Was it?' said Milo sharply. 'It's all right for you: your father's a fisherman and he'll be able to teach you until you're ready to get your own boat. Vigo wasn't ready. His boat wasn't ready. He only went out because of me.'

'He would have gone anyway,' said Niko. 'There was nothing you could do. It really wasn't your fault. As the time passes, you'll get over it.'

'I don't want to get over it,' Milo said, still angry. 'Why should I? He was my brother, he was my friend. He taught me how to swim, and the best rocks to swim from – he taught me all his secret places. Nothing will be the same now.'

'Not the same perhaps,' Niko searched for what he was trying to say. 'But I'll always be here,' he said it diffidently. 'I'll be able to help you.'

Milo laughed bitterly, but seeing Niko's face he stopped. 'I know you will,' he said gently. 'But can't you understand? It's different for me. You're like…' Milo faltered. 'Look out there,' he pointed past the entrance to the passage, towards the open sea. 'That's where the rest of the world is. Šipan is such a tiny part of it. All those places Fräulein Wolff told us about.' Niko looked across the water in bewilderment and Milo knew that he didn't understand. 'You'll be happy staying here, Niko, but how can I? Whatever there is out there, I have to find out. With Vigo gone, I have no choice.'

'But what about your parents? You've always been such a happy family. You made me so welcome.' Niko turned away in embarrassment. 'I've always been so envious of you.'

Milo looked at him intently for a moment. 'You see? All that's in the past.' He looked back across the passage. 'Fräulein Wolff tried to tell me I could control my future, but she was wrong. I've got no more choice over what I do than anyone else.'

'Your mother will think of something,' said Niko desperately. 'Your mother always manages; she'll look after you.'

'They're going to see the Bossanos,' Milo laughed bitterly. 'But it won't do any good. Rusa will never agree to give me a job. You know what she thinks of our family. She won't do a thing to help us.'

'But after – I mean, after what's happened, perhaps Frano Bossano will want to help. With all that land, he must be able to find something for you to do.'

Milo shrugged. 'He can, but he won't,' he said shortly. 'Anyway, how could I remain on the same island as the Bossanos after what they've done to us? I can't just let them get away with it. I don't know how, but I'll get back at them somehow.'

Niko reached out and took Milo's hand. This was his best friend. How could he face things without him? 'Will you promise me something?' he said earnestly. He had never felt so serious in his life. 'If you don't find what you're looking for, will you come back?'

Milo smiled and squeezed Niko's hand. 'Don't worry. I'll find it. And then I'll come back. But not until then.' Milo paused. 'The Bossanos will still be here when I come back. I'll settle with them then.'

The following day, Andro and Olga Beran made their way slowly up the driveway towards the old villa where Andro had worked for so long. Milo walked several steps in front of them, as though to demonstrate his independence. The family was shown up to the first-floor drawing room, and Olga took Milo onto the terrace and showed him the vineyards in the fields below. As Andro stood by the window, Rusa Bossano came into the room. Frano followed behind her, pulling at his sleeves self-consciously as he sat down in a large armchair in the shade.

Even in middle age, Frano still resembled a spoilt child. He seemed to live with a permanent air of pained sufferance, as though people were not taking the trouble to understand him properly and were therefore unable to see his true qualities. He acted as though this was a handicap that he bore bravely, but as a result he could rarely summon up any interest in others. His mother died even as she brought him into the world, leaving him in the care of a doting father who had, until then, given up the idea of having a son and heir. His father found compensation for his wife's untimely death in indulging his unexpected son, and Frano soon learnt that if he wanted something, his father almost invariably gave it to him. As he grew, he found that there was almost nothing he could do to earn his father's disapproval – and he went further and further to seek it.

Rusa insinuated herself into his life expertly, recognising that her strength was a counterbalance to his weakness. Once she had decided upon it, their marriage was inevitable and Frano succumbed easily. It was as though he had finally found in Rusa the control that his father had never exerted and, perversely, Rusa's domineering ways provided exactly the restraint he had sought. He had little inclination to fight her anyway. His temper abated, but in Rusa the islanders found someone else to deal with. In addition to his estate, the Bossanos owned large plots of land around the island, which were occupied by his tenants, subject to his approval and to his wife's whim. Total dependence and absolute devotion were what she considered her due, and her capricious and random disapproval made her feared by all the islanders.

Frano gradually discovered that his life was less troubled if he relapsed into a sort of resentful acquiescence. He did exactly what his wife told him to do, while maintaining the air of acting only under sufferance. Once his wife's oppressive influence had replaced the freedom his father had given him, he discovered that little really interested him and there was nothing he wanted to fight her for. Except for Andro Beran.

Frano knew that in spite of Rusa's insistence, he couldn't look after the estate without Andro. He knew nothing about estate management and he cared even less. While Andro continued to do a good job, Rusa had no grounds on which to dispense with him. But this time it was different. Frano knew that she'd always acted strangely whenever Andro was around, and he couldn't quite understand why this time it should be so different. He knew that in some way he should feel affronted, but in fact he felt annoyed. Annoyed not at what Andro was supposed to have done, but angry that Rusa had finally been given her excuse to insist upon his dismissal. That morning over breakfast he had told Rusa that he had second thoughts, but it had been no good. Rusa's mind was made up and Frano was powerless to change it. Damn the man. How was he going to manage?

Frano looked across to his wife from his chair. She looked back at him sternly, and he just wanted to be somewhere else. He turned back to Andro; he had no choice but to go through with it. He cleared his throat nervously. 'I'm surprised that you can come back here after what you did to my wife.'

'Your wife, your wife?' Andro said coldly. 'And what exactly did I do to her?'

'I'm not prepared to discuss this with you.' Frano's old petulance returned. 'Will you please leave? I have nothing to say to you.'

'But you have something to say to *us*.' Olga came through the doorway, holding Milo's hand. 'You know what's happened to my family; how can you talk to my husband like that?'

Frano looked to Olga in astonishment. He clearly hadn't expected her to come, let alone thought that she might bring Milo. He was flustered and confused. 'Olga? I mean Mrs Beran.' He stood up to hide his embarrassment. 'I was so sorry to hear about Vigo,' he said awkwardly.

Olga looked at him intently for several moments. 'Every family on the island has tried to help us, except you. You know our situation. Why have you done nothing? How could you just ignore us?'

Frano looked down uneasily. 'Olga, I'm sorry…'

'How can you let her talk to you like that?' Rusa Bossano's voice cut through the room. She turned to Olga. 'Can't you show proper respect? You'll call him Mr Bossano while you're here.' Rusa knew what had happened to Vigo and guessed why they'd come. She could scarcely conceal her triumph, knowing how much this visit must have cost their pride. Finally, even the Berans were forced to recognise the power that she wielded for the Bossano family.

'But you naturally have my most sincere condolences.' As she spoke, there was a suggestion of a smile about her lips.

Frano Bossano realised that he had to finish this discussion just as soon as possible. His wife would allow no other course. He looked back to Andro with an expression of what he hoped was sympathy. 'Vigo was a fine boy,' he started. 'But…'

'He was indeed, sir,' Andro glanced across to Olga, as if seeking her support. 'But you will understand that it's Milo we've come to talk about. I'm no longer working here and now Vigo's… we just can't afford to stay together. We have to send Milo away.'

'Yes, it must be very difficult – but I can't see how I can help.' It was a statement, not a question.

'Well sir, if you could find young Milo a position… he's a very bright lad with a quick wit, and Fräulein Wolff says he's a fast learner.'

'You know we have no positions to fill,' Frano answered with a trace of irritation. 'Apart from the November harvest, winter will soon be here and we will all have to tighten our belts until the spring.'

Andro's eyes passed quickly over Frano Bossano's waistline. What does he know of tightening belts, he thought. Aloud he said, 'I thought, sir, that the shepherd might need some help. After all, he's not young any more and with the frosts coming, er…' his voice tailed off. The shepherd was unlikely to see through another winter. 'What I mean, sir, is that he could start to teach Milo about the flock before…well, before the winter, sir. You would find Milo very useful.'

Secretly, Frano Bossano agreed, but he looked tentatively across to his wife. He didn't need to ask her views. 'No, no, that's simply not possible; his grandson can always help out.' They both knew that the shepherd's grandson was far too unreliable to be left on his own.

Rusa Bossano interrupted. 'We can't be expected to help every family on the island which has difficulties. This is a working estate, not a charity.'

Andro felt as though he had been punched in the stomach. He could hardly catch his breath. Although he hadn't expected her help, he was shocked by her arrogant and unconcerned manner. Not daring to look at his wife, he managed a deep breath before trying again. 'You will understand, sir, that Mrs Beran has held our family together, and if Milo went away so soon after losing Vigo, then it would break her heart.'

But lift my wife's, thought Frano. 'No, I'm sorry,' he said. 'There is nothing we can do. You will have to find another way. After all,' he looked down at Milo and continued ponderously. 'The ships of the world are full of young men from the islands of Dalmatia, and we're proud of them and of our tradition. You will have a good future at sea. It will all come out for the best, I'm sure of it.' He walked towards the door to indicate that the interview was over.

'So you won't help us, Frano?' Olga said defiantly. 'Even though it's for Milo, you still won't help us?' Frano looked anxiously at his wife.

'You could find me a ship, sir.' Milo voice was steady and he looked at Frano with assurance. There was a shocked silence. Olga was too surprised to tell him to keep quiet. 'It wouldn't be difficult for you to find me a ship,' repeated Milo firmly.

Rusa recovered from her surprise. 'Don't speak until you're spoken to, boy,' she hissed at him and turned back to Olga. 'Haven't you brought up your boys to show us any respect?'

Olga looked at her steadily. 'I've brought my boys up to show respect when it's deserved.'

Rusa flushed with anger and looked at Milo with contempt. 'How d'you expect a boy like that to understand?'

Milo calmly ignored her. He knew what he wanted and that he wasn't going to get it from Rusa Bossano. He turned back to Frano. 'A ship, sir. After everything that's happened, that's the least you can do for us.'

Frano looked across to Olga. Olga shook her head helplessly. 'I didn't tell him to ask that. I don't want him to go to sea.'

Andro put his arm around his wife's shoulders. 'We have no choice, my love. If Mr. Bossano won't give Milo a job, then we've got no choice.'

'But he could find me a *good* ship,' said Milo.

Frano walked over and pulled on the bell pull. 'I'm sorry, there is nothing more I can do. Once again you have our condolences on Vigo's, er...' he let the words hung uneasily in the silence.

'You see, I told you,' Andro said sadly to his wife as they walked slowly away from the house. 'It's her: you can see it. It's Rusa Bossano; she has it in for us, and Frano simply can't stand up to her. It's her fault this has happened and she doesn't care.'

Olga was quiet for a moment, thinking. Suddenly she stopped and looked up at Andro. 'You know, I think that woman was *pleased*. Did you see her face? She was enjoying her power. I won't give her the satisfaction. If they don't want to help us and Milo has to be sent away, then I know he'll make good. You know what Fräulein Wolff says about him. When he comes back, then she'll see what my family is made of.'

As they returned to their house, Milo ran straight upstairs. Andro looked at Olga with alarm. 'Is he all right? Perhaps you'd better go up and talk to him.'

Olga shook her head and started to weep. There was nothing to say. They had no choice. She had lost her fight.

Upstairs Milo tore a page from his exercise book and took up his pencil. If Frano Bossano wouldn't find him a ship, then Fräulein Wolff could. As he composed his letter he realised that in the hopeless fight against his destiny, his brother had been killed.

In the weeks that followed, the decision was accepted as inevitable and the family attempted to adjust to its new circumstances. Dalmatia, this long, thin country, squeezed between the mountains and the coast, had an unbreakable and enduring bond with the oceans. Dalmatian forests had provided the timber, Dalmatian dockyards built the ships and Dalmatian families supplied the crews. When the olive harvest was over, Milo must submit to generations of tradition and go to sea.

Autumn came quickly; the olives ripened and were falling from the trees. The benign climate of the Adriatic islands allows olives, once established, to grow old at their leisure over hundreds of years. Each November, entire families set out from the mainland to harvest the crop, even from the remotest islands. On Šipan it was the only time during the year when there was work for everyone. Milo was sitting on a sheet gathering up the fallen olives when he heard his name being called. He looked up to see Fräulein Wolff approaching in the distance, from Šipanska Luka. Leaving his basket, he rushed to his feet and ran over to meet her. 'Fräulein Wolff, what are you doing here?'

'Well, that's a fine way to greet me.'

'I'm sorry, Miss. But surely you knew it was the harvest this week and we wouldn't have any time for lessons?'

'Of course I know,' replied Fräulein Wolff, 'but I haven't come here for the school. Since I got your letter, my brother and I have been asking around everywhere for a suitable captain, but most of the local ships are fully crewed. But there's a ship belonging to the cousin of one of the Patrons, which has come from up north. She's just put into Dubrovnik for a cargo and needs a boy. If the Captain likes the look of you, then he's prepared to take you along. But there's just one problem.'

'What's that, Miss?' asked Milo.

'Well, the ship is loading in Gruz and the captain wants to leave as soon as it's finished.'

'So when will that be?'

Fräulein Wolff looked at Milo anxiously. 'I'm afraid you've got to be there tomorrow. I know it gives your mother so little time, but Captain Maras is highly recommended and the opportunity might be too good to miss.'

'Perhaps it's as well if Mam doesn't have any notice,' Milo said. 'That way she won't have time to worry.'

Olga Beran took the news with resigned fatalism. That evening she prepared a special farewell meal, but without Vigo and Jurica it was an empty and sombre house. Andro tried to joke with Milo about the adventures ahead of him, but Olga could see how forced his efforts were. She knew that Andro remained bewildered that he had failed so dramatically to look after her sons. Later, Milo went upstairs and brought down a small, homemade cage that he carried out onto the terrace. He put it on the wall and pushed a finger between the bars. The little mouse sniffed the end of it inquisitively, his whiskers trembling. Milo tickled his ears. 'I'm going away tomorrow, Peter, and there won't be anyone to look after you.' He put his hand inside the cage, held the tiny animal gently and cradled it against his chest. He stroked its head softly. 'I'm going off to be a sailor, but one day I'll come back to Šipan again. I've got to send you out into the world, too. From now on, we've both got to look out for ourselves.' He kneeled down and put the mouse on the flagstone. The mouse stopped for a moment and then stood up on its hind legs sniffing. Milo watched as it ran towards the doorway. 'Good-bye, Peter. Good luck.'

The next morning, before the sun had risen and while only the faintly reddening sky lit Šipan's quay, the Beran family, having lost their father and their eldest son to the sea, prepared to say goodbye to their youngest. The ferryman's tattered blue hat hung at its precarious angle as though glued in place. He unfurled the dirty sails and let them flap in the light breeze. There was little that could be said, and the family was subdued as Andro grasped his son in an enveloping embrace. 'May God be with you, my son. God will always be with you. Be good and remember us always. We will be waiting for you.'

For Milo, the past few days had seemed exciting, but the reality now hit him that it would be months, perhaps years, before he would see them all again. His bravura left him and he crumpled in his father's arms. 'It'll be all right, Dad. I promise. I'll be back.' Andro lifted down Milo's bag containing his meagre belongings. He gave his son one last hug. 'I'm sorry,' he said slowly. 'I'm sorry I failed you.' With a last look towards Andro, Milo turned and followed Olga down into the boat. Milo would never forget the lines of anguish etched in his stepfather's worn face.

The ferryman pulled in the sheet, and the sails filled, pushing the long boat slowly out into the bay. Milo stood up at the stern looking backwards. 'I'll be back. Don't forget to leave food out for Peter.' He waved at them as they pulled away. 'We won't let the Bossanos win.' Olga's face was stony as she steeled herself to what had to be done. As the sky lightened, Milo stared at the passing shore, recognising and remembering the haunts of his childhood, where he had played and swum with Vigo. The boat slowed in the sheltered water as they passed through Caesar's Passage, but once through and out into the open sea, the wind was free and they sailed swiftly southward. Milo turned and looked ahead.

Chapter Four

The high walls of Dubrovnik encircle and protect the ancient city that for centuries ruled the tiny republic of Ragusa. Its fortifications, built on the steep slopes leading up to the mountain of Srd, dominate the bay to the south. From a distance its defences seem impregnable, but approaching past the island of Lokrum, a small quay at the foot of the sheer walls hides the narrow entrance to the compact harbour at the very centre of the city. Protected by tiers of defensive walls, breached by force just once during its centuries as an independent republic, the harbour allows access only for boats and is too small and too shallow to take ships. But behind the rocky peninsula on which the city is built, a narrow estuary winds several miles inland to meet the Riyeka River. At the mouth of the estuary, another deep inlet reaches back towards the rear of Dubrovnik's walls. Here, over the years, the port of Gruz became established and, as trading increased, it prospered in its protected bay.

The battered ferryboat sailed past Daksa Island at the mouth of the Riyeka Dubrovacka, threading its way through the dozens of ships lying at anchor in the sheltered water. A succession of lighters bustled back and forth to the busy quay at Gruz, loading and victualling, removing inbound cargoes, or transhipping for longer voyages. Gruz itself was a noisy mass of activity. At the head of the inlet, past the derricks on the quayside, a line of shipyards fringed the shore, the boats and ships on the slipways alive with carpenters and shipwrights. The ferryman sailed past the docks towards the slipways and turned in towards the public jetty. Pushing a way through the other boats moored by the steps, he made the boat fast and held it alongside to allow the passengers to step ashore. Olga stood up. 'We'll go and see Jurica first – he should be at the market,' she said, leading Milo out of the boat and through the heaps of ropes and ships' stores which were stacked in piles all around the dockside.

Gruz market had long ago become permanent. Situated just behind the docks, it was at the crossroads of all the commercial movements of southern Dalmatia. The overland route along the coast to the North was rugged and difficult; wagons were often shaken to destruction trying to pass along the neglected road.

No railway had been built or was even contemplated by the Austrian authorities, who were indifferent to the prosperity of an area so far removed from them. The fastest and most secure transport was by sea. The fresh-produce market served the entire region – the islands as well as the mainland. Jurica was employed here a couple of days each week, helping to load the ships' supplies. Through the crowds, Milo made out his brother pushing a cart towards the docks. He chased after him. 'Jurica, Jurica, wait. It's me.'

Jurica finally heard him and turned in surprise. 'What are you doing here?' He looked down at Milo's rolled-up bag. 'You haven't found a ship already?'

Olga caught up with them and embraced Jurica. 'That depends upon the Captain,' she said. 'Fräulein Wolff has given Milo an introduction to a Captain Maras, who might take him. The ship's called the Aurora. Can you find out where she is?'

'I don't need to. That's her over there,' replied Jurica. 'We were supposed to be loading her with fresh supplies this morning, but the agent cancelled it. They told us they'd got a cheaper price from the Kolarov brothers. It's not a ship that comes here often, otherwise they'd know better than to trust those two thieves.'

'Why?' asked Milo. 'I might be eating those supplies.'

'You've got to check everything they load. They put the good stuff on top, but underneath it's all rubbish – they hope that nobody notices until they're at sea and it's too late.'

'But surely the ships wouldn't use them again after that,' Milo said.

'The honest ones don't, but some still buy from the Kolarovs because they give the Captain a cut and provide him with separate supplies. That way he can say that he bought in good faith and it wasn't his fault that the supplier was crooked.' Jurica looked down at Milo. 'That's the sort of world you're going into. Take my advice, and don't trust anyone you don't know. And even then don't trust 'em.'

Olga frowned. She had steeled herself to bring Milo here and see that he got a good ship. She didn't want to be reminded of the harsh world beyond her protection. 'Where's the Aurora now?' she asked. 'If Captain Maras is to take Milo, he's got to make a good impression. He's got his best suit on and I've put his work clothes in a small parcel.'

'Dunnage, Mam: real sailors call it dunnage.' Milo said, showing off his little knowledge.

'Well, it's you who's going to be the real sailor, not me – and when you are, you can call it what you like,' retorted Olga.

'She came alongside a week ago,' said Jurica. 'She's taking on timber, so she couldn't be loaded at anchor. That's why the skipper wants to set sail quickly to avoid port dues. That's her over there.'

Milo turned and looked along the quay to where his brother was pointing, but there were too many ships moored and too many people working around them for him to make out the Aurora. 'I can't see her,' he said. 'Can you show us?'

Jurica led them along the dockside. 'Here she is,' he said. 'Funny little thing, ain't she? I hope the skipper likes the look of you.' He glanced anxiously back along the quay. 'I'd better get back to work. I'll see you later.'

Milo looked up at the short stubby masts and then along towards the prow. She seemed out of proportion, as though a piece had been cut out from her centre section and then the front and back joined together again without it. Her bows seemed too steep, and her stern too high. She might be a funny little thing, thought Milo, but if this is going to be my home, then I'll take to her whatever her faults.

Olga Beran called up to the man supervising the derrick on the foredeck. 'Excuse me, sir,' she called, 'I'm looking for Captain Maras.'

'And who is it who's wanting him?' the officer replied.

'Olga Beran,' she replied. 'I'm told he's looking for a lad to join the crew and my son has been recommended to him. And who are you, sir?'

The officer flushed. He didn't like such self-assurance in a woman. 'Ivan Dimitrov, Ma'am, first mate,' he said tersely. 'Captain Maras is busy. Would that be your lad?' She nodded and he turned to Milo. 'How old are you then, boy?'

'I'm shortly to be thirteen, sir.'

'Twelve years old, eh? But you're a little 'un. I can't see as how you can help pull in a sail.'

Olga Beran interrupted and asked impatiently. 'It's Captain Maras we need to speak to. When do you think he can see us?' Milo stiffened, seeing the mate's anger at being spoken to so directly by his mother.

'The Captain has one or two other duties, Ma'am,' the mate said sarcastically. 'But if you come aboard and wait outside his cabin, I suppose he'll see you when he's finished.' Olga didn't seem to notice his resentment. Instead she clambered up the narrow gangplank, while Ivan Dimitrov turned and walked off towards the bows of the ship. Olga stepped over the coiled ropes and sat on a sea chest outside the Captain's cabin.

Milo was too excited to sit still. He paced up and down on the deck, imagining what it must be like in a storm. He looked about him, wondering at all the ropes, astonished at the thickness of the warps, thicker than his wrist, which moored the ship to the quay. A log was being lifted from the quay and swung above one of the holds. A cloud of steam spurted from the valve of the engine as the operator pulled back on the lever. A voice called out for the mate; Milo looked over to see two men pulling a laden cart towards the ship and pointed them out to his mother. 'Those must be the Kolarovs,' he said. 'If Jurica is right about them, I hope the mate checks everything.'

But the mate was wise to the old tricks. As the brothers wedged the chocks under the wheels of the cart he went ashore and slashed open the top sack with his knife. Nodding approval, he put it to one side and delved down and pulled out another sack from near the bottom. Milo looked at the faces of the two brothers, who appeared unconcerned at this inspection. One of them even seemed to be smirking. The mate cut open the top of the sack and peered in, but seemed satisfied. 'It seems all right: you can load 'em,' he said, as he climbed back up the gangplank. But Milo watched the brothers carefully, and saw one of them turn away from the ship and nod to the man operating the steam derrick.

A sudden jerk of the loading rope was immediately followed by a splintering crash as the log fell heavily towards the hold, smashing against the hatches as it caught on the deck and slipped through its slings. The mate ran over to the hold and roared down. 'Clear out, it's loose.' Two men bolted up the companionway and onto the deck as the top of the log slid along the hatch and fell against the corner. All work stopped as the crash reverberated around the port. As the echoes died away, the mate shouted at them from the foredeck. 'Check that it's fast before we try and move it,' he bellowed.

They put their backs against the log and heaved together. 'That's not going nowhere without the derrick, sir,' one of them said.

The shock of the log's near miss seemed suddenly to strike the man, who sat down trembling on the hatch cover, his face white with shock.

The mate ignored his distress. 'Don't just sit there. One of you take that axe and go back down and fix the sling so's it don't slip.'

Milo looked back towards the Kolarovs. One of them was pulling a second cart from behind the machinery housing, while the other had kicked away the chocks and was pushing furiously at the first cart. By the time the mate had organised the log to be hauled up, the two Kolarovs had exchanged carts, and one of them was carrying the sacks on board. 'Where d'you want them, sir?' he asked.

'By the galley up forr'ard,' replied the mate, without looking back. He turned towards the crane operator. 'Damn fool! Why don't you watch what you're doing? We nearly copped it, you ignorant son of a whore.' Remembering Olga, he touched his cap again. 'Excuse me Ma'am, but a working ship's no place for women.' He looked down at Milo. 'Nor children, neither. I'll go an' see if the Captain can see you now.' He went down the companionway steps towards the cabin. After a few moments he put his head up. 'Follow me, Ma'am. You as well, boy.'

Milo's first sight of Captain Maras was a disappointment. Rather than the tall, imposing man he had expected, the Captain was short and slight, with a rather prim goatee beard. His tight-fitting naval jacket and peaked cap pulled low over his forehead made him appear even smaller in stature, and Milo was surprised that he had survived in such a tough business. But when the Captain spoke, his tone was confident, and he came straight to the point. 'Mrs Beran, your son has been recommended to me. I'm told his teacher thinks that he's a clever lad.' He turned to Milo. 'Well, I'm not interested in whether he's clever or not – I want to know whether he can work. Can you, lad?' He barked out the question, and Milo jumped slightly.

'Y-y-yes sir,' he stammered nervously.

The Captain inspected him for several moments. 'I'll tell you what,' he said finally, turning to Olga. 'You take him home, feed him every day for a year, and then you can bring him back and I'll see what I can do. This isn't a big ship and everyone needs to work and pull. The lad's so small the first storm'd blow him away.'

Olga looked down at her son standing next to her and imagined all that he'd have to go through. The Captain was right; he was too small for such a life. She started to turn back towards the doorway but she saw Milo clench his lips tightly together, fighting to hold back tears. This was what he wanted to do – what he had to do. She had no choice but to support him. She turned back to the Captain. 'He might be small, sir, but he's sturdy and strong for his age and he's got spirit. Give him a task and he'll stick to it. Will you not reconsider, Captain?'

'Indeed I will not, Ma'am. Apart from the mate and a boy, we take only six seamen. I need a lad who can lend a hand.'

'A ship needs more than muscle to get by. I've seen the biggest men lying useless with drink.' Olga glanced towards

Ivan Dimitrov. 'My boy is honest and reliable,' she continued. 'And what he's got, he'll give you all the time.'

'Well, Ma'am, if that's the case, all the more will I look forward to seeing him in a twelvemonth.'

Olga looked down again to Milo, not knowing what to say to him. She couldn't believe that even with Fräulein Wolff's introduction, they had wasted their journey. The Captain could have told her earlier that he wanted an older boy. But Milo's distress seemed to have vanished. He seemed to have controlled his tears and was staring steadily at the Captain.

The Captain looked back at him. 'Well, lad? What is it? You'll not change my mind, you know.'

'I think I should tell you what happened. What I saw.'

Captain Maras looked from Milo to Olga. 'What's the boy talking about?' His patience was being strained. He was accustomed to his decisions being accepted without question.

'Well, sir,' said Milo. 'It's just that when the log slipped just now, I think, sir, that they might have changed over the supplies.'

'Changed what?'

Milo looked across to the mate. 'Perhaps I shouldn't say this, sir. Not after Mr Dimitrov has checked everything. But the Kolarovs changed the cart for another one and unloaded that instead.'

'Did they, by God?' the Captain growled and turned to the mate. 'You'd better check this out, Mr Dimitrov. You can't have this young lad doing your job for you.'

The mate's face darkened with anger as he walked out, pulling his knife from its sheath. A short while later he came back, looking fiercely at Milo. He turned to the Captain. 'The boy's right, sir. They're not the goods I approved. Someone's switched them.' He looked back at Milo, as though the blame was his. 'I would have seen it before we left,' he added.

The Captain sat behind his table and looked at him thoughtfully for several moments. Then he looked across to Milo. 'Not been on a ship before, then?' he asked.

'No, sir. But I've been on lots of boats and I know how to tie knots and do some splicing, sir.'

'Well I suppose that's a start, but you've never been up the mast in a storm?' Olga shuddered and Captain Maras turned to her, 'Oh don't you worry, Mrs Beran; we'll take good care of him and bring him back in one piece.'

'So you'll take me, then?' Milo blurted out in excitement and relief.

'Aye, you've changed my mind after all. You're a bit small, but we'll knock you into shape.'

'May I ask where you're bound, sir?' Olga asked

'We're going right around to the English Channel, Ma'am, to London. Taking those northerners some decent Dalmatian timber for their ships. It's a new passage for us, but we're hoping it becomes regular.'

Olga looked at Milo with relief. The voyage couldn't take more than a couple of months. Turning to the Captain she asked, 'And when do you want him back on board, sir?'

'We'll be leaving this evening, so I expect you'll be wanting to use the next couple of hours to say your farewells to your mother. Report on board at eight bells.' Seeing Milo's anxious look he added, 'That's midday to you, son.'

Taking a sovereign from his pocket, he handed it to Milo, 'Looks like you've already earned your first pay. Well done, lad – if you can work as well as you think, then you've got a long way to go.'

They walked away from the docks and climbed up the hill towards the old town of Dubrovnik. Just opposite the city's central gateway they branched off and followed a narrow path through the trees, leading up towards the summit of Srd. After a few minutes' climb they were level with the city's battlements, and shortly afterwards the path levelled out into a grassy clearing. Olga always headed for this place when they visited the city together. As she spread out a cloth and pulled out some food from her bag, Milo walked over to a low wall and looked across to the layers of red roofs inside the massive defensive walls that protected them. Beyond the fortifications, to one side, the bay arched around into the distance. It was a clear, still autumn day and the coast was fringed with an aquamarine band, where the shallowing sea washed over the rocks along the shore. In the far distance a light cover of autumn snow had covered the mountain peaks. Milo looked back to his mother. 'London's not so far, Mam. I'll be back in no time.'

Olga said nothing for several moments, until she was satisfied that everything had been set out. 'I've cooked you a cheese tart,' she said. 'Sit down and have some. Over here, next to me.'

Milo walked back and sat down. He saw Olga's eyes were watering. He reached out and took her hand. 'It'll be all right. I promise.'

'I'm sorry, Milo,' she said. She wiped her eyes with her sleeve and then continued more cheerfully. 'Of course it will be all right. I don't want to spoil our last few hours together.'

'We'll have plenty more when I come back.' Milo reached out and took some of the flaky tart.

Olga pulled her bag towards her. 'This is for you.' She handed him a small box. Milo brushed his hands against his jacket before taking it and pulling out a chain. On the end of the chain was a small gold locket. He looked at it carefully. 'I wanted you to take something of mine,' Olga said, as she watched him open it. 'It's all I had.' She stared at the miniature portrait with a sad look. 'It's…it's your father.'

Milo examined the tiny painting. 'Is that really what he looked like?' he asked after a while.

'The likeness isn't important.' Olga took the locket abruptly and gazed at it for several moments. 'It's to keep you close to us. So wherever you are, you'll always remember Šipan.' She looked up suddenly as Jurica approached along the path.

He stopped and looked over her shoulder at the miniature. 'Who's that?' he asked. 'Have I seen it before?'

'It's, it's…I just wanted Milo to have something to take with him,' Olga replied in embarrassment. 'To remind him of how things used to be before…before everything…' Her voice trailed away.

Jurica took the locket and studied it. 'This must have cost something.'

Olga took the locket quickly and handed it back to Milo. 'You don't mind him having it?' she asked.

'Not as long as he brings it back.' Jurica sat down next to her.

Olga turned back to Milo. 'You will keep it safe?' Milo nodded. He folded the chain and put it carefully into the box.

'Milo?' Olga continued hesitantly. 'Whatever happens, you won't blame us for what happened?'

Milo stared at her blankly for several moments. 'How could I blame you?' he said finally. 'It's Frano Bossano's fault, not yours. If it hadn't been for him, none of this would have happened.'

'He wasn't always like that,' Olga said. 'It's Rusa. She changed him.'

'No, it's his fault. And I promise that one day he'll pay for it,' Milo insisted.

Olga forced a smile. 'Let's not waste our last couple of hours talking about them,' she said, but the strain in her face was still clear. 'I want you always to remember the good things.'

Milo stood on deck, next to the rail, watching the wake stretch behind them towards the horizon. The ship was gliding along steadily in a smooth sea and all the sails were set to a light south-easterly wind. Through his shirt he felt the locket hanging around his neck. He didn't quite understand.

When she had finally left him at the ship, she had turned and walked away steadily, not once looking back. What had she been trying to tell him?

He looked around at the equipment that he was slowly starting to recognise. He'd felt helpless as the ship had been warped out to sea and all sails set. But my mother was right, he thought. He wasn't as helpless as two of the crew who were carried on board dead drunk, not sobering up for nearly twenty hours. Not that the rest of the crew were much better; most of them had hardly managed to stand up as they set sail, although one of them, a gnarled old seaman named Marko, seemed to have taken pity on him and tried to show him what to do. There were so few able-bodied men that even the Captain, showing a surprising strength for his size, had joined the hands on the capstan. But in spite of the unfamiliarity of it all, Milo felt confident and optimistic. He had finally left the terrible misery of the last couple of months behind him. From now on, until he returned to his family in Šipan, he had only himself to look after.

He couldn't know that he would never see his mother again.

Chapter Five

Milo looked up as the Captain came out of his cabin and shouted across to the mate. 'Mr. Dimitrov, call all hands to get these sails taken in. The barometer's been falling fast these past few hours; I reckon a sirocco is on its way.'

'All hands! All hands!' bellowed the mate. He saw Milo. 'Boy! Stop daydreaming and lend a hand here. Now's your chance to show what you're made of. It ain't blowin' yet, so make your way along the bowsprit and help pay off the foresails.' Under his breath Milo heard him add, 'And with any luck ye'll fall off.' Milo went forward nervously and was joined by Marko, coming on deck from the fo'c'sle. 'Take the boy and gather in the fore staysail,' yelled the mate. He pushed one of the hands angrily. 'Get a move on there!' The man stumbled, still half asleep. Grumbling under his breath, he steadied himself against a rope and lurched slowly forward. At the bows, he swung himself over onto the bowsprit and pulled himself along over the sea rushing beneath.

Milo watched, terror-stricken. There was nothing to catch him if he fell. Marko saw his fear. 'Come on lad, lend a hand. Just keep holding tight on that rope and you'll be all right.' Milo was almost shaking with fright, but he was determined not to show it. He eased himself over onto the bowsprit and balanced unsteadily on the rope supported beneath it. 'That's right lad, hold tight. One hand for the owner and one for yourself. Ease off that rope there and we'll do the difficult bit.' Milo grabbed at the rope and let it slip through the soft skin of his fingers.

When Milo finally made it back to the deck, his hands were bleeding and his bare feet were raw. The sky had clouded over and the wind was increasing. The ship was starting to heave and roll in the rising sea and Milo suddenly felt his stomach convulse as a wave of nausea hit him. He staggered towards the rail, but the mate grabbed him. 'Oh no you don't, boy, we're not finished yet. Up you go and help them take in them topgallants.' In spite of the mate's rasping command, Milo hesitated and looked up. The top of the masts, which had seemed so stumpy in Gruz, now seemed to be lost in the clouds. 'Don't just stand there, boy – or perhaps you need some encouragement?' Milo flinched as the fraying rope end stung his back. 'I'll put that across yer again: now get up and start on them sails.'

Milo steeled himself. He grabbed hold of the netting and started to climb. As he rose higher, the swaying of the mast grew worse and at the first yards he stopped and hung on feebly, as he felt the seasickness turn him inside out. His head felt numb as he started blindly to work his way out on the spar. Marko came up fast behind him. 'No, son, you best keep on going, these are the topsails – them above you are the topgallants. To shorten the sails we starts at the top.' The other hand clambered up past him and Milo fought down his rising stomach and followed them both towards the topmost yards. Standing on the rope supported beneath it, they crabbed their way sideways out above the deck.

Marko patted his shoulder. 'OK then, boy, we've all got to start sometime. Now loosen off the halyard, that rope by your head, boy. Faster than that.' Another wave of nausea hit him and his face grew sticky with a clammy sweat. He clung to the crosstrees and tried to breathe deeply as the strengthening wind whipped his face. Fighting against the sickness, he found the rope-end cleated on a pin and untied it. 'Yeah, that's right, boy, keep it around the pin and pay it off gentle.' As the pressure came on the halyard it slipped through his hands, tearing more flesh off his palms. 'Keep the pressure on the pin, boy. That'll slow it down.' Milo pulled it against the pin and the rope held steady. 'That's good: now let it go slowly and we might make half a sailor of you yet.'

The ship plunged down into a deep trough and almost buried the tip of the bowsprit where he had been hanging just a few moments earlier. The mast dipped low to one side and then swung back steeply onto the other side as the ship climbed back up towards the crest of the next wave. Milo hugged the mast tightly as he was flung across like a stone in a sling. Marko looked at him anxiously. 'Are you all right, boy?' Milo was too ill to answer. He was weakening rapidly as the ship lurched and staggered through the building sea. But he could hold it down no longer, and his stomach contracted deeply as he retched over the sails below.

'You young bastard.' Milo looked down groggily and saw the stain had run down the sails over the mate's jacket. 'Look what you've done. Look at this mess. Get down here.' Milo was almost past caring, too relieved at being ordered off the mast. Slowly he made his way down, taking gulps at the wind to keep himself conscious. Marko looked down at him and shook his head.

As Milo lowered himself onto the deck, the mate grabbed him. 'D'you see this?' he shrieked, pointing to the stain across his shoulder. 'What kind of sailor d'you think you're going to be? I always said you shouldn't have been given a berth; now I'll give you what you deserve.' He lifted up the end of his rope and brought it down fiercely on Milo's back.

'Let that boy free!' The Captain stood at the companionway steps, and his sharp command cut through the wind.

The mate froze with his arm in the air. 'Aye-aye, sir,' he said finally, aware that the entire crew had heard the public reprimand. As he let go of Milo's collar he bent down and growled in a low voice. 'You little runt. Don't think I'll forget this, boy. You'll get the hiding you deserve when the Captain's not around to stop it.'

After the storm, the Aurora fell into its normal routine and, as they sailed westwards towards the Atlantic, Milo slowly gained his sea legs and started to learn and understand his new world. As they passed through the Straits of Gibraltar, the barren high mountains of Morocco reminded him of the Dalmatian mainland, and he was surprised at just how close the African shore was. He had never imagined that the two continents were separated by such a narrow stretch of sea. Milo felt a twinge of homesickness as they left his Mediterranean sea behind and turned north past Cape Trafalgar towards Cape St Vincent. The Captain retreated to his cabin, handing back the running of the ship to Ivan Dimitrov. But as they beat up the Iberian peninsula against the fluctuating Portuguese trade winds, the mate become increasingly brooding and preoccupied. Milo grew apprehensive. He slowly realised the mate was planning his revenge – the only question was when.

A ship's routine is governed by a sand-timer that takes exactly half an hour to run through. At the end of each half hour, the ship's bell is rung and the glass turned. After four hours – eight bells – the watches change and the process starts again. But the period between 4pm and 8pm is broken into two, staggering the port and starboard watches over successive days. These dogwatches are generally the only times, except during a storm, when all hands are about at the same time, and it became accepted as a time for relaxation and attending to personal matters – although there is little privacy on a ship. It was during such a dogwatch, when all the men were on deck mending their clothes or carving their keepsakes, that the Aurora passed Cape Finisterre and Ivan Dimitrov finally decided to act. He sent Milo down into the chain locker to check the flaking of the anchor chain and, making sure no one noticed him, he picked up a slender rope and followed him down through the fo'c'sle.

Down below, the mate grabbed Milo, pulled him down and thrust a balled cloth into his mouth. 'One peep out of you and I'll break your neck so you'll not be heard again.' Milo gagged on the cloth as the mate threw him onto the coiled chains. 'OK, you little bastard, you didn't think I'd forgotten, did you? The Captain might run this ship, but I'm first mate and no one's ever made me look a fool before you came on board. Now it's payback time.' Milo looked up at Ivan Dimitrov. The mate's face was scarred with a wild fury, he was almost out of control, unbalanced enough to kill. Milo dimly realised that if he offered resistance, it would only provoke greater violence. There was no one who could hear him anyway; he was beyond anyone's help. He had to submit and try to survive.

The mate grabbed Milo's arms, pulled them above his head and wrapped the heavy chain around his wrists. Tearing the shirt over his head, he stood back and brought the rope savagely across the uncovered back. Milo convulsed as the searing heat swamped his senses. Again the rope lashed down and his small body arched in pain. The darkness increased Milo's terror; all he could hear was the mate's grunting as each blow found its target. His muffled screams reverberated around the empty fo'c'sle, while the unrelenting rope continued to whip him almost into unconsciousness.

The mate finally stopped and pulled him to his feet with a strong hand around his throat. 'That was just a start,' he snarled as he untied the chains. 'Just a taster, so you'll know what'll happen next time. You so much as breathe a syllable of this to anyone, and you won't leave here alive. Understand?' He slapped Milo fiercely across the face. 'Do you understand?' Milo mumbled incoherently, insensible from the force of the beating. 'What was that, boy? Answer me. D'you understand what'll happen next time?'

Milo fell back, cutting himself on the rusting chains, 'Aye-aye, sir,' he said weakly and the mate turned and left him lying in the darkness. Milo tried to move, but an agonising pain paralysed him. He had never felt so helpless. Each movement of his arms tore at the welts on his back, and he could feel the wet blood oozing through his wounds and sticking to his skin. Groaning with pain, he pulled himself to his knees and struggled laboriously to his feet. As he stood, a wave of giddiness over-took him and he clung desperately to the locker, falling back against the door. The shock steadied him and he finally managed to stagger back to his cabin, where he fell onto his bunk.

Milo stayed below when his watch was called and the Captain sent Marko down to rouse him. 'I can't move, Marko; tell the Captain I'm ill again. Tell him anything – just leave me here.' Milo didn't doubt Ivan Dimitrov for an instant. If he said a word to anyone, he would be thrown overboard.

'What's the matter with you?' asked Marko. 'You've been crying, haven't you?'

'No. No. It's just this weather. It's making me ill. I'm not used to it.'

'Milo, come on. What's the matter?' Marko put his hand on Milo's back but jumped backwards as Milo cried out. 'What happened? Let me see your back.' Marko carefully pulled Milo's shirt up to his shoulders and gasped at the bleeding welts. 'Who's been laying into you? Milo, tell me what happened.'

'I can't. He said he'd kill me if I told anyone. Just leave me alone, I'll be all right. Tell the Captain I'll be up for the next watch.'

'Who said?' Marko thought for several moments. 'It's not the mate, is it?' He frowned. 'I've always thought he's unhinged, but it's been worse this trip. Son, if it's the mate, you've got to tell the Captain. We'll be none of us safe.'

Milo turned his head from his mattress. 'No. Not the Captain. But I'll not let him get away with it, Marko.'

'D'you want me to help?'

'No. No, you can't. It's not your fight. You've got to stay with the ship afterwards. I'll find a way on my own.'

'Just keep away from him. You're on the skipper's watch, so don't go near him. Next time he could kill you.'

Milo tried to prop himself up, but fell back with a cry. 'I'll think of something,' he said after the pain had subsided. 'If I'm going to survive at sea, I've got to fight back. If I do nothing, I'll be a victim for the rest of my life. I'm not going to let anyone beat me.'

Marko looked at him, slowly beginning to understand how determined the boy could be. 'All right then, lad,' he said finally. 'If that's what you want. I'll tell the Captain you've fallen and cut yourself. I'll bring you something to put on your back. When we get to London, then we'll see about Dimitrov.'

The Aurora sailed across the Bay of Biscay and Milo remained below. A continuous drizzle worked its way through the decks, and dripped on him incessantly as he lay recovering in his bunk. Once they had passed Ushant, a strong south-westerly wind helped them up-Channel and Milo eventually felt able to go on deck again, but his Mediterranean clothing was now sodden and offered little protection against the biting winter wind, which whipped his face raw. He had never felt so cold and had never been so miserable, nor felt so alone. He watched the dark waves rolling up behind and passing underneath them in the gloom. They slapped against the hull with a low hiss. In the sparkling waters of Sipan, he had never imagined that a sea could look as dull as lead.

As they rounded Dover towards the Thames estuary, Milo's spirits finally started to lift at the sight of a new land so near to, and by the time they entered its monochrome waters, Milo had almost recovered. He started to take an interest in the new sights around him, both annoying and pleasing Captain Maras with his questions. The Aurora ghosted up under her own sails as far as Greenwich, where the Captain pointed out the famous naval college and observatory. As they passed up-river, Milo looked on intrigued as a steam tug took their warps and pulled them towards the London Docks. Never had he seen so many ships; hundreds of masts surrounded him, grouped together in clumps – some apparently a considerable distance inland – lying immobile in the sprawling docks like the trunks of a petrified forest. Milo had always thought that Gruz was a busy port, but the huge docks in London were something he had never even imagined. Even along the banks of the river boats lay aground, high up on the muddy shore, waiting for the flood tide. Milo could scarcely believe that the tide could rise high enough to float them off.

The steam tug slowed as a boatman approached and hailed Captain Maras. 'Are you for the docks, sir, or for a mooring?'

'The docks,' bellowed the Captain in reply. 'But we need a mooring until we can get in.'

'Alongside the Newcastle over there.' The tug pulled them slowly alongside in the still-ebbing tide, and the hands made fast.

Milo looked around him with excitement. He could just make out the towering dome of St. Paul's Cathedral in the distance. The strange languages of the crews, the noise, the smoke; he found them all exhilarating. 'Captain, sir, is this the Thames river?'

Captain Maras smiled at him. 'Sailors usually just call it the London River, son. Even at low tide ships can go right up to London Bridge. What d'you think of it? Impressive, eh?' The Captain pointed ashore across to the row of steam derricks strung along the side of the lock. 'When the tide's risen enough, the lock gates can open and we'll go through into there. You can have a look round later, but it's a dangerous area, so you'd better stay with Marko.'

Milo watched as the tide rose and floated the boats off the mud. He'd never seen a lock before – with no tides in the Adriatic there wasn't any need for them. He was mystified by the process, and after trying to help the crew with the ropes they eventually sent him away as more of a nuisance than a help, and they locked the ship through into the dock and warped her alongside the derricks. Once again the Captain took charge of the manoeuvres, and a surly Ivan Dimitrov went forward to supervise the crew in the bows as the ship came alongside.

Captain Maras handed over to the mate, who kept the grumbling crew working for another two hours before allowing them to approach the Captain to draw an advance against their wages. Marko walked slowly over to Milo as he counted his money. 'How're you feeling now, lad?' he said looking up. 'Cap'n says I can take you ashore, but I'm to keep an eye on you an' protect you from the drunkenness and debauchery which surrounds this place.' He had a twinkle in his eye. 'Just as long as you don't do the same for me. Now you get cleaned up a bit and I'll take you to Ma Babich's.'

Milo joined Marko on the quay. 'Who's Ma Babich?' he asked as they walked out of the docks across the lock gate.

'Ain't you ever heard of Mother Babich? Why you're even more ignorant than I thought, boy.' Marko bent under a massive mooring cable and pointed along the grey river. 'See over there? That there's Limehouse Reach an' beyond that is Chinatown. That's where Ma Babich's place is. That's where all us sailors go in London.'

'Chinatown? Why is Chinatown in the middle of London Docks?'

'You'll see,' Marko said shortly. 'Now get a move on, I'm thirsty.'

Milo followed him along the dark streets, swaying with the unaccustomed feel of land underneath him. At one moment he nearly fell, and memories of his early nausea washed over him, but his curiosity soon overcame his unsteadiness as he looked around him at the dark, unfamiliar buildings. Is everything in London dark, he wondered? More low grey clouds covered everything and the air was thick with a dirty mist that hid the further reaches of the river. Queues of carts backed up at the dock gates and the sound of hooves clattering on the cobbles echoed and merged with the cries of the longshoremen unloading the ships. As they made their way further along the riverside, away from the docks, people of all nationalities crowded the streets, blocking the horses and carts which were trying to force a way through. Many of the men were staggering to stay on their

feet, some singing noisily. On several doorsteps unconscious sailors slept off their alcoholic stupor. The buildings
became taller and the streets narrower as they walked past
the storehouses lining the riverfront. Interspersed along the
uniform façades of the warehouses, Milo caught occasional
glimpses of the sky above the low roofs of the public
houses, creating gaps in the high buildings like missing teeth
in a fighter's mouth. Throngs of people milled around
outside each hostelry, shouting and arguing with a desperate
enthusiasm that only a few days' freedom ashore, with
money in their pockets, can give.

As they walked on, Milo noticed increasing numbers of
Chinamen bustling along the streets, stooped under laden
shoulder yokes. Shops, eating houses and godowns were
marked with faded signs in Chinese script, and through the
open doorways the interiors were concealed under swaying
clouds of smoke which merged with the greying haze of the
streets.

'See what I mean?' said Marko. 'This is the Chinese crossroads. They're always on the move. Coolies coming on the ships
from China and going out to the railways of America or the
guano islands of Peru. When they pass through here, for just a
short time they're at home. They live so closely together that
most of them still can't speak anything other than their own
languages. They hardly mix with anyone else. A coolie arrives
off a ship and stays in one of the houses until he finds another
berth. The old men keep opium dens in the back rooms upstairs; if you can pay them enough, it's the only time they'll
make you welcome.'

They were passing the door of another Chinese shop when
Marko grabbed Milo's shoulder and pushed him towards a
small alleyway leading away from the river. In the increasing
gloom it was almost dark in the shadow and it was difficult to
avoid the discarded rubbish, barrels and packing cases that
obstructed the alley. Eventually their path opened out into a
small courtyard, leading towards another street that ran behind
the docks. A small knot of men were lounging around the front
door of a large house. One of them turned towards them.
'Marko,' he cried. 'It is old Marko, isn't it? Lord! How long is it
since you were last here?'

'Well, if it isn't the Shark. Haven't they locked you up yet?'
Marko turned to Milo. 'You'd better watch out when he's
around; he'd steal the soles off your shoes if you weren't
standing on them.'

'Are you visiting Ma Babich's, then?'

'Of course,' said Marko. 'Come and buy me a drink and I'll listen to all your lies about what you've been doing.' He turned back to Milo as if suddenly remembering him. 'You wait outside, lad. I shouldn't be too long.'

Milo was quite happy to be left alone. He wanted to take in every detail of this strange place, and he paced around the small square investigating the buildings and examining the people. But as the time passed and Marko still didn't come out of the hostel, he became frustrated that he couldn't explore further. He sat down on the steps outside and started to imagine what the rest of London must be like. As his mind wandered, he thought of Ivan Dimitrov – could he really go back to the ship with the mate still there? What the mate had done once, he could do again – what was to stop him? Who could help him?

He got up and walked to an alleyway that ran down the side of Ma Babich's and disappeared into the gloom beyond. Silently he crept down it. Passing the dim light of a curtained window, he heard muffled voices from inside the Dalmatian hostel. He stopped and listened.

'You think we hurt him badly?' one voice asked.

'No way. We only gave him a black eye. He'll be fine after a few days. Just poorer.' There was an ugly laugh and the scraping of beer mugs on the table.

'How did you know he was carrying any money?'

'I can always tell who's been paid off after a long voyage,' the second voice said. Milo craned his head across the window ledge to get as close to the glass as possible. 'This one had the same look about him,' the voice continued. 'Like he was hungry to spend everything. Didn't I tell you that if you stick with me you'll do all right?'

Milo stood thinking carefully, as the men inside drank in silence. Making a sudden decision, he took a deep breath and rapped on the window. 'Christ, what's that?' the voice inside sounded frightened. 'There's someone out there.'

'I think I can help you,' Milo spoke quietly but distinctly. 'If you want to come outside, I've got some information for you.'

'Who are you?' the voice inside sounded wary.

'I'm only a ship's boy, but I heard you talking and you might be able to help me. If you want to come outside, I'll tell you about it.'

'Have you been listening to our conversation?' the voice growled. 'Why should we want to help you?'

'Because if you do, we could help each other. I'll explain outside.'

Milo could hear them talking furtively together. 'Wait out there,' one of the voices said finally, and there was a shuffling as the two men pulled out their chairs.

Milo waited until he could see the silhouettes of two men approaching from the end of the alley. His stomach lurched as he thought of what might happen if his plan went wrong. He decided to keep the initiative and before the men could challenge him, he ran up to them. 'I'm looking for someone to help me rob a sailor,' he said quickly. 'I'm not old enough to do it on my own and I heard you talking. You could be the men I need.' The men stopped in surprise, but Milo kept talking. 'Gold coins. The first mate on our ship in the docks. He keeps a pouch full of them. I don't know where he got them from, but I saw him counting them when I was doing an errand for the Captain. He doesn't trust the crew and takes the pouch with him whenever he leaves the ship.' As Milo had hoped, the men's expressions had changed at the mention of gold coins. 'If I point him out to you, d'you think you could take him on?' Milo looked at the men doubtfully. 'He's a big man,' he added.

The bigger of the two men rose to the challenge, just as Milo had hoped. 'Course we can. Ain't many who can beat me.' He laughed nastily. 'Not if I get 'em from behind, at any rate.'

Chapter Six

Milo was scrubbing the deck when Marko finally came up from below, holding his head and groaning loudly. 'I thought you might never regain consciousness,' Milo said cheerfully.

'It's a wonder that anyone survives the gut-rot they serve at Ma Babich's. Every time I go there I say it's the last.' Marko's voice was hoarse. 'Where did you get to, anyway?'

'I wasn't going to wait there all night, was I? I walked about a bit, made a few arrangements and came back.'

Marko groaned again. 'Did the Captain see you? He'll kill me if he finds out. Told me to look after you.'

'I don't think he'll care,' Milo said. 'Not when he finds out I've gone.'

'Gone?' Marko sobered up quickly. 'Where're you going?'

'That's what you've got to find out. I need your help, Marko. I told you I was going to get back at Dimitrov and it's all set up. But afterwards I won't be able to come back here. It'll be too dangerous. I want you to find me another ship.'

'Another ship? You've only just joined this one.' Marko looked at Milo suspiciously. 'What d'you mean, "afterwards"? What's all set up?'

'You mustn't get involved, Marko,' said Milo. 'But could you ask at the hostel, see if they know another ship looking for a boy?'

Marko coughed noisily. 'I s'pose I could.' He spat over the rail. 'But why should I, if you won't tell me what you're doing? Even after all the help I've given you, you still don't trust me.'

'I thought it would be better if you didn't know.' Milo looked around to see if anyone was close by. 'Last night, when we were at the hostel, I overheard these two sailors inside talking.'

'Well that's a surprise – most of 'em are senseless on the floor by suppertime.'

'No, wait – this isn't a joke,' said Milo. 'They were sober. They were talking about a sailor they'd robbed on his way back to his ship. So I tapped on the window and told them to come out.'

'Christ, Milo, they could be dangerous, you know. What d'you want to be messing with them for?'

'They did seem in a bit of a state when they came outside. But they calmed down quickly when I told them about an officer who always carried a bag of sovereigns with him. I said that if they'd help me get it off him, I'd give them a share.'

'What are you talking about?' Marko looked at Milo blankly. 'You don't know any officer who carries gold coins.'

'That's true: but they don't know that.'

Marko scratched his head. 'What're you up to? How can you get a couple of thieving sailors to …' He thought for several moments. 'You wouldn't be thinking of our first mate, by any chance?'

Milo looked at him steadily. 'Marko, you saw what he did to me. I told you I'd not let him get away with it.'

'So what are you going to do?'

'They'll be sitting at the same table tonight and I've arranged to knock on the window again when the officer arrives. They said they'd give me a share; but they agreed a bit too quickly and it seemed suspicious, so I settled for a smaller commission in advance, leaving them to deal with the mate themselves. I said it wouldn't be easy, though.'

'Why not?' asked Marko.

'Well, I sort of told them that even when drunk he's very strong and he'll fight hard. They got the impression that a block of wood might make it easier for them.'

'You're a nasty little lad, aren't you? You're not only getting two thugs to attack Dimitrov for you, but they're even going to pay you for doing it. What're they going to do when they find that Dimitrov doesn't have any money?'

'I don't know, but I won't be there to find out. That's why I want you to find me another ship. I've got to be at sea before they realise what's happened.'

Marko shook his head in confusion. 'You know, I just can't keep up. A few weeks ago you were completely helpless, and now you're getting involved in something like this. But I suppose Ma Babich can probably help. With all the deserters here in London, she's bound to know of someone who's looking for crew.' Marko thought for a moment then chuckled. 'It's a good plan, though. I just wonder – if you can do this sort of caper at your age, what're you going to get up to when you've grown up?'

'Oh, the plan's not perfect; there's a major flaw.'

'What's that, then?'

'I won't be around to see it,' said Milo.

The tug pulled the Hanover slowly downstream. Marko had persuaded Ma Babich to find him a berth, and she'd introduced him to Joachim Traub, the first mate of this immense clipper, bound for Australia. The first mate, a huge man with a chest as broad as an oak cask, had seemed surprisingly sympathetic when Milo had explained that he had to escape from Ivan Dimitrov. Getting him on board had been easy; a new Captain had taken over the ship in London and he wouldn't know that Milo hadn't been part of the crew before. As the river broadened, the buildings grew sparser and long, featureless banks spread ahead of them; but just as he thought they were about to cast off the tug, it turned, taking them sharply to the south towards a flat and deserted island surrounded by mud. Behind the island he could see a fortified hill, and as they approached he saw the large naval dockyards lining the banks of the dirty river. A low rope-walk stretched along almost the entire length of the quay and on the other side of the fortifications, well away from the dockyards, a long wooden pier led away from an enclosed part of the fort. The tug pulled them carefully alongside and Milo approached a sailor making fast one of the warps. 'What's happening? Why aren't we going out to sea? What is this place?'

The sailor shrugged. 'I don't know for sure, but this is the Chatham Navy Yard and the last time I was 'ere we took on a load of gunpowder.' As he coiled the rope, the heavy doors at the base of the pier opened and a row of carts emerged. 'Yeah, see there, the powder's all in sacks. It'll be hand-loaded to make sure it's safe.'

'Safe?' Milo cried, 'How can it be safe? We're not going around the world on a floating gunpowder store?'

'Oh, it'll be OK. We was told it's no more dangerous than salt – until you light it with a match, that is. But the first mate knows what he's doing – he'll make sure it's secure.'

Milo was sceptical, but was reassured as he watched the sacks stacked tightly into the front hold. I suppose they need gunpowder in Australia too, he thought, and someone's got to take it to them, but it's a pity it has to be us.

It took almost a day to load, until Joachim Traub finally checked the locking of the hatches. He looked up. 'Don't just stand there gawping, boy, lend a hand there! Get those ropes COILED!' The first mate's bellow startled him. Since he'd been on board the mate had hardly noticed him, and there'd been no sign of the Captain at all.

The two officers checked the forward holds again and gave orders for the tug to tow them out. Organising the few men who were on deck, they assigned one to the wheel and the others to set the lower sails and cast off the tow. With only a faint wind and the top sails furled, the ship had little more than steerage way as the pilot set a course through the mud banks of the estuary. 'Mr Recht, you can get the rest of the hands on deck now. I'll call the Captain and we'll allocate the watches.'

'Aye-aye, sir,' replied the second mate, and Milo had his first opportunity of seeing the other officer on board. Although he was quite small in comparison with Joachim Traub, he was stockily built and looked as though he was used to handling himself. His prominent forehead and bushy eyebrows gave him an imposing appearance, and his hoarse roar could almost be heard in his native Leipzig. There was no doubt about his authority, and normally he got even reluctant hands to follow his orders without resorting to his fists. Milo had been told that anybody who took him on usually came off worse, and from what he could see of the man he didn't doubt it.

Milo watched as a bedraggled group of men emerged from the fo'c'sle, some barely staying upright as they climbed unsteadily on deck, stepping over the men who still lay where they had fallen dead drunk the night before. His spirits fell. How can we ever make it with a crew like this? he thought, until he realised that it would be over three months until the men would have another opportunity to drink as they had the previous night. The second mate kicked at the prostrate figures; someone handed him a bucket and he threw the water in their faces. Spluttering and cursing, they slowly regained consciousness.

The chief mate returned from the cabin, but there was still no sign of the Captain. 'Now, men, most of us are new on this ship, so we're going to set new watches. Mr Recht and I will each choose our men, and when you're called you give your name to the steward there and your knife to the carpenter.' He looked towards the cluster of crewmen standing sullenly by the rail and pointed towards a man who was only slightly shorter than he was. 'You, what's your name and rating?'

'Calls me Bergen, zur,' the man answered with a thick accent. 'On account of no one can say my name.'

'Rated able, sir,' said Clarke, the steward, ticking his list.

'Right, Bergen, you're in my watch; give Chips your knife.' The Norwegian hesitated. 'The knife, man, give him your knife,' the mate ordered sharply.

Reluctantly, Bergen took his knife from its sheath and handed it to the carpenter, who quickly clamped into a vice and hammered off the point. Immediately the sailor started towards the wiry carpenter with a low growl. 'Stop that,' shouted the mate. 'If any of you are tempted to turn a knife on another then at least we can stop you stabbing them. I don't want to see a point on any blade on this ship. Right then, Mr Recht, you're next.'

One by one the two officers took turns in choosing the men for their watches, each man being signed on either as ordinary or able. The fact that the large Norwegian had allowed the point of his knife to be hammered off made the rest of the men accept it more easily, although some could still be heard grumbling softly. Two men remained, apart from the boys, and both had fallen back on deck and were out cold. Recht kicked one of them viciously and bent down to him. 'Name?' he shouted in his ear. The man lifted his head and looked at him groggily. 'I said, what's your name?' he shouted again – but the man continued to stare blankly.

'Can't, er, can't remb'r, sir. Forgot name, sir,' the man's thickly accented mumbling tailed off.

'Jones, sir,' called out the steward. 'Gave his name as Jones, sir, from Cardiff.'

'Hear that, man? Your name's Jones.'

The sailor stared at him for a moment puzzled. 'Aye-aye, sir, Yones, name's Yones. Yones from Cardiff, sir.'

The first mate laughed deeply. 'He sounds Swedish to me, and it's the first I've heard there's a Cardiff in Sweden, or a Yones for that matter. Whichever ship he's running away from, you'd think he'd choose a name he can remember. I'll take him in my watch, but I think we'll find it easier if we call him Johanssen. Even if it turns out to be his real name, they're not going to catch him in Australia.' He turned to Milo. 'You'd better join me, lad, on the starboard watch and young Arnie here'll go with Mr Recht's port watch.' Joachim looked back anxiously towards the poop. 'I'd best go find the Captain: he'll want a few words. You stay here, lads.' He walked off and went down into the cabin; Milo looked across towards and studied the other boy for the first time.

Arnie was obviously a couple of years older and a good head taller, but he was slighter and quite sallow, as though in weak health. Milo walked over to him and introduced himself. 'Are you German too?' he asked.

'From Bremen,' Arnie said. 'I suppose this is your first deep-sea passage?'

'Yes. And you?'

'Oh, I've got lots of experience. I started nearly two years ago, so I should've shipped as an apprentice, not just a boy. That way I wouldn't have been forced to share the fo'c'sle with the sailors.' He took a deep breath, as though unaccustomed to anyone showing an interest in him and he intended to get it all off his chest. 'I've been to New England and back several times,

and most of the crew leave me alone so I can study my navigation books. The last Captain recognised that I wasn't just an
ordinary sailor and was going to rate me as able, but now he's
left, I'm still paid as a boy, though I can do a man's work better
than most of these layabouts.' He gestured dismissively towards
the other sailors. 'I reckon I'll be an officer in a few years' time,
and I already know more than most. I don't suppose you've
learnt anything yet and I'll probably have to help you out the
whole time. If there's anything you want to know, just ask me.'
He ran out of breath and before he could start again, Milo
interrupted.

'Sounds like I'm lucky to have you on the same ship with
me,' said Milo, but Arnie didn't seem to notice the sarcasm.

'Yes, even though we're on different watches we'll still get
time to talk. Hold on.' He looked aft towards the cabin. 'Quiet,
I think the Captain's coming.'

The low talking of the men tailed off as the first mate came
up the stairs from the cabin. 'All right then, men, here's the – '
he paused and almost spat out the final word with disgust, ' –
Captain.' Behind him a short, fat man emerged slowly from the
companionway, holding tightly to the rail as he reached the
deck. He appeared to be swaying slightly even though no sea
was running. His face was pasty and large puffs of dark flesh
drooped below his watery eyes. His uniform was stained and
creased and he was breathing heavily merely from the exertion
of climbing the stairway. Some of the men started murmuring.
'Silence,' roared the second mate – and everyone stood and
waited to hear the Captain's first words as he cleared his throat
noisily.

The Captain reached the quarterdeck and looked around
slowly before speaking. 'I don't know you and you don't know
me – yet,' he snarled. 'But I couldn't care what you lot think of
me, because the only opinion which counts on this ship is mine.
D'you understand? You do what I say, follow the officers'
orders, then I'll form a good opinion and we'll all get on. But if
I get a bad opinion of a crew, even its officers, then there'll be
no peace till my opinion gets changed. An' it'll only change if
the crew changes, understand?' He paused again and waited as
though he'd forgotten what else he could say. Finally he turned
back towards the companionway. 'Carry on Mister, er,' he
hesitated, groping for the mate's name. 'Carry on Mister. I'll be
in my cabin.'

There was silence for a few moments as the entire crew tried
to assimilate the Captain's performance. Before anyone could
recover, Arnie turned to Milo. 'Seems like a sound man,' he

said. Everyone else ignored him. Was it possible? Was it really true? Were they adding a drunken Captain to all the other dangers they faced? Taking over the situation quickly, the first mate started to issue orders before anyone could argue. 'Let's get this ship under way. All hands get out the topsails and let's get this deck cleared UP!' Slowly the crew got to work, with varying degrees of efficiency. It was a long way to Australia.

The ship gradually established a new rhythm, as the hands learnt to work with one another and the officers established their discipline. The new Captain was rarely seen on deck, although he kept the steward busy, and most of the crew soon forgot he was even aboard and looked to the two officers to keep control of the ship. They both proved themselves competent and reliable, and since most of the hands were accustomed to discipline being enforced with the belaying pin and brass knuckles, even the most hardened of them began to develop respect for the first mate, whom they recognised was shouldering all the responsibility involuntarily. Drunken skippers were not unknown; most of the crew had experienced them before and knew that it was often when they tried to interfere that problems arose. They were all quite happy that he kept to his cabin, although they questioned where the steward's copious supplies of whisky came from.

As they approached the Tropics the weather became warmer, and Milo wondered whether he really could make it as a sailor if he had to deal with such cold seas again. He decided that he was a warm-country person. When he was able again to work on deck without a jacket or shirt, the dry wind healed the welts on his back and he started to adapt to his crew mates and the daily life aboard. Tough it might be, but if he stood his ground, the rest of the crew accepted him. Bergen, the big Norwegian, had almost adopted him and most of the crew came to learn that if they wanted to take advantage of Milo, then they would have to deal with Bergen, and so Milo managed to maintain a fairly peaceful life. He even found himself slowly warming to Arnie, whose posturing he came to realise was the result of loneliness more than anything else. The lad was simply unable to deal with the happy-go-lucky attitude of the rest of the sailors, and hadn't yet learnt that the prime requirements at sea were patience and equanimity. Milo saw that every situation Arnie faced he tried to control, and the result was increased frustration and incomprehension. Mr Traub, the first mate, held lessons most mornings for the two of them, and if the wind was light even let them take a turn at the helm. Although Milo was the faster learner and could work out the navigation problems easily and quickly, Arnie didn't seem to calculate the answers, but had an almost intuitive grasp of navigation and appeared to arrive at the correct answer without apparently even knowing why. If he just relied on his natural ability instead of trying so hard, he could make a first-rate seaman, but whenever the mate tried to say this, Arnie simply got more nervous and it only made things worse.

Milo was also learning from the crew. Johanssen, when he eventually sobered up, turned out to have been an officer himself, but every time he shipped as a mate, the first port he came to would be his undoing; he would get disrated and sent back before the mast. Sober, he was competent and thoughtful and although his knowledge of the great ports of the world was blurred, he knew the sea and seemed to have developed an almost uncanny understanding of its moods. When standing a trick at the wheel, even the first mate listened to him if he felt a change in the weather was on its way. Milo simply couldn't understand why he should waste his ability by drinking himself into insensibility at any opportunity. It seemed to him simple. If Johanssen could take on some of Arnie's anxieties, and if Arnie could absorb some of the Swede's fatalism, then the two might balance each other out and they could both become dependable officers.

But Milo appreciated the easy-going attitude of most of the rest of the sailors, unaware of how unusual it was to find a happy ship. There was just one he thoroughly mistrusted, a mean-looking Estonian from Tallinn called Olav, who was an accomplished shirker and always seemed to be placed well away from any work which needed doing. Milo was particularly irritated by the man's self-satisfied smirk and thought that if he were bigger, he would have tried to knock it off the man's face. But apart from Olav, Milo accepted his situation – it was a hard life and no one could survive who wasn't prepared to fit in with the harsh discipline. He recognised that sailors rarely received any justice and – at any rate while at sea – they simply had to deal with things as they came. Although true sailors rarely grumbled about the dangers, they all knew that against the power of the oceans they depended upon each other to survive. Most sailors were deeply superstitious and had developed complicated rules of fortune to explain the randomness of their lives. One of his watch, Claus, a greying, lugubrious Swede from Malmo, was constantly predicting disaster, convinced that the ship would founder with all hands before it reached Sydney. 'Dat Captain, what is he about, going to sea on Friday? Too much bad luck.' Even the company of a school of dolphins for the best part of a morning failed to cheer him up. 'Dey go away and den you'll see.' Early in the voyage, as they were crossing the Bay of Biscay and he was at the helm, he heard the second mate whistling softly under his breath. Leaving the wheel he ran to the fo'c'sle calling out to the first mate. 'Herr Traub, Herr Traub, vat is happening? Dere's goin' to be big storm if he don' stop de vistling.' The first mate laughed but, like all sailors, he secretly shared Claus' fear, suggesting to Mr Recht that he should know better and wait until they were caught in the doldrums before he attempted to whistle up a wind.

One of the crew members in the watch, an Irishman by the name of Tom O'Connor, was an accomplished musician. During the afternoon, in settled weather, the officers allowed him to play his fiddle on the foredeck, where the men joined in the dancing with considerably more enthusiasm than skill. He was also a good chanteyman, with a wide repertoire and a fine tenor voice. When hauling up the mainsail Milo was amazed at the power which the sea-shanty added not just to the pull of the sailors, but to their spirit and good heart. When a halyard had got caught, O'Connor had started a hauling chantey, which brought the Captain up from his cabin for the first time in several days. 'What's this damn noise?' he grunted at the first mate. 'Can't you keep any discipline on deck? Do I have to keep the men in line along with all my other responsibilities? Can't I rely on my officers for anything?' Joachim was genuinely speechless. Every other Captain he had served under had given an extra allowance to a good chanteyman; they were hard to find and worth a great deal to a hard-pressed crew.

'The men seem in good voice, Captain; it would be a pity to upset their rhythm. If they can get accustomed to pulling together, then we'll get the sail changes done that much faster. One day it might make the difference between the rocks and the open sea. I recommend you leave them at it, sir.'

The Captain looked at the men by the mast. 'I suppose if you say so, Mister, but it weren't done when I was on coasters.'

Suddenly Joachim realised the Captain's problem. 'Coasters, sir? Have you spent most of your time on coasters? Have you, er,' he tried to think of a way of putting it. 'Have you been to Sydney before, sir?'

'Same sea, isn't it, Mister? Still have to keep a keel under you.' He looked around once again and stumped off back to his cabin. 'Carry on.'

So that was why he kept to his cabin – he hadn't been master of a deep-water ship before. Joachim pondered on the problem and decided to keep it to himself. He had already passed his master's examinations and could do all that was required of a skipper. He just needed this one last voyage and the Captain's endorsement before he was eligible for his own command. He'd just humour the Captain and look after the ship himself.

The two boys were taking noon sights under the first mate's supervision. 'Now I want you to go away and calculate our position and let me know what's special about it,' said Joachim, but Arnie had already worked out what the mate was getting at.

'It's the line, sir. Isn't it? We're almost into the southern hemisphere and we'll be crossing the equator very shortly.' Arnie seemed excited at the idea. 'I've never crossed the line before.'

'Have you not?' the first mate seemed surprised. 'I know Milo hasn't, but I hadn't realised there were going to be two of you.'

'Going to be two of us who what?' asked Milo suspiciously.

The mate laughed. 'You'll see,' he said shortly. 'Now get below and let me know when we're going to reach it.' After the two lads had gone below he called over the second mate. 'Mr Recht, let the men know that we'll be crossing the line some-time tomorrow morning – they might want to make prepara-tions.' The second mate smiled and walked off forward and spoke quietly to the crew.

Milo had little idea what was going to happen. He was aware, the following day, that all hands seem to be occupied on deck, which was strange, and he had sensed a strange atmosphere during mealtime. People seemed to be whispering more than usual, but when he looked across at them, they stopped. He was talking to Johanssen when Olav suddenly grabbed him and held his arms behind him. Looking across he could see that Arnie had been grabbed by Tom O'Connor. Claus from Malmo looked down into the sea under the bowsprit. 'He's a-coming lads, get 'em ready.' A large man pulled himself on board next to him, wearing a large messy mop of seaweed on his head and waving a roughly made trident in his hand.

'My subjects are expected to kneel before their Monarch when they enter my kingdom.' Milo was pushed to his knees as the rest of the crew also knelt down on the deck. 'Is there anyone who is trespassing here without my permission?'

Olav enjoyed seeing the boys humiliated and tried to take a leading part in the ceremonies. He stood up and shouted out, 'Yes, your worship, these here are two lads who haven't crossed the line before and seek your authority. Here's one,' he pushed

Milo flat onto his face. 'And that, your honour, is the other one.' Milo looked up at Olav who was pointing towards Arnie. He was looking terrified and was struggling to get up.

'No, no, leave me alone, I say. Leave me alone: what's going on? What are you going to do?' Arnie's voice was breaking with terror and the crew seemed to be thoroughly enjoying it.

Milo looked towards Neptune who was advancing towards him and he recognised Bergen underneath the seaweed. 'Put on the blindfolds,' he commanded, as a piece of sailcloth was wrapped around Milo's head. 'If you are entering my kingdom, then you must prepare yourself to be received. You must both be shaved and bathed before I can accept you.' Rough hands grabbed Milo and his face was covered with a substance which felt like treacle but which, with resignation, he realised was tar. 'Now we will shave him.' A rough surface was dragged across his face, Milo was sure his skin would be stripped off, and he could tell that the crew was now crowding around to take their turn at scraping off the sticky tar. 'And now the bath!' cried Bergen and Milo was lifted into the air as hands grabbed his feet and swung him upside down. Sensing what was coming, he took a deep breath and held it as his head was forced downwards into a bath full of slimy solids floating in a oily liquid with a disgusting smell. Suddenly they let go of his legs and he was submerged in the mess while hands held him under. Trying not to panic, he waited until they released him and pulled him out and removed his blindfold. As he climbed out he recognised the smell. Pig-swill: all the slops the cook puts into a bowl to gave to the pigs. He gagged and pulled the mess from his face as Bergen came up to him. 'You are now a son of Neptune and may enter my Kingdom. Kneel and give me thanks.' Milo recognised that the best way to get this over with was to do exactly as he was told, and he knelt down as Bergen touched him on the head with his trident. 'And where is the other trespasser?' he asked, turning towards Arnie.

Milo got to his feet as someone handed him some oakum to clean his face. He didn't think Arnie was going to take this well and looked on as the excited crew surrounded the terrified boy. He probably thinks it is Neptune, thought Milo sadly as he looked on, willing the humiliation to be over quickly. Someone had stuffed some sailcloth into the boy's mouth, but he could still hear Arnie's muffled shrieks through the laughter of the crew. There was nothing he could do; even Joachim Traub was looking on and smiling broadly. If Arnie couldn't take this, then a ship was no place for him.

At last the crew allowed them to go below to clean up. The

cook brought a large bowl of hot water and grinned at them sympathetically. 'When I was a lad like you, they put you in a bowline, hung you from the lower yards and let you fall into the sea, and dragged you behind for several minutes before they pulled you in. I saw 'em do it three times to one poor lad who they thought weren't entering into the spirit. Several mother's children never returned after bein' initiated across the line. You'll be all right,' he said sympathetically, as he saw Arnie start to sob. 'Clean yourselves up with this an' I'll bring you some more hot water.'

Milo turned to Arnie and could see he was nearly in hysterics. 'It's all right, Arnie, they didn't really hurt you. I know it's humiliating, but that's the point of it. Listen to what the cook said: they used to drown boys in the past.'

Arnie sobbed as he pulled at the mess on his face. 'I wish they'd killed me. I never imagined it could be so awful. How could they do that to someone? Why me? I've never been so humiliated. Oh Milo, I just can't go on any more – most of the time they just ignore me. I can tell what they think; whenever I go up to anyone they move away or start talking to someone else. They just don't like me. They think I'm too good for them.'

'No, Arnie. It's you who thinks you're too good. If you didn't try so hard all the time … stop trying to impress everyone by making out you're someone you're not. Why can't you just try being yourself? Why feel humiliated by a ceremony that every sailor has been through? Why not just accept it? Look at me, I'm just as dirty as you are, my face is just as scratched. Why should you be any different?'

'But they like you, Milo – no one likes me.'

'People take others as they find them. They don't like me, they like what I do. I go out of my way to be nice to them. If you keep saying how clever you are, then it's hardly surprising that they don't want to know – even if you're only telling the truth. You are clever, Arnie. Look how quickly you worked out our position yesterday. A position within a mile of Mr Traub's. I can work it out too, but I don't feel it like you do. You're a natural – if only you had more confidence in yourself, you wouldn't have all these problems. Can you play cards?'

Arnie was taken aback at the question. 'I'm not going to gamble with sailors!'

'You see what I mean. You've never tried it and you're already thinking it's something it isn't. When you fetch the mate's tobacco for him, d'you keep any back?'

'Of course not: he might find out.'

'He probably wonders why you don't. I've got a hoard of the

stuff and when some of the crew let me, I join their game. They use the squares of tobacco instead of money. They don't mind if I bring some along – they think they're going to take it off me. Only trouble is,' Milo laughed, 'most of them are hopeless at cards.'

'So if you win, don't they want their stakes back?'

'Sure they do,' replied Milo. 'But they don't just grab them, they try and win them back. So I let them – why not? The important thing is that they see that I'm joining in. Sometimes I try to bluff them with a weak hand, hoping they'll call me. Next time I wait for a strong hand and pretend I'm bluffing again. That way they have to think about it. I don't let them take me for granted. Why don't you try it?'

'I wouldn't know what to do.'

'It's not difficult. I'll teach you. You'll probably skin 'em alive and they might not like it, but they'll start to respect you for it. Don't fight them all the time: try and join them. Why don't you treat Neptune's initiation as an opportunity? You could have a future as a sailor. I've watched you; it's not just navigation – I can see you going to the sails before the mate's even called out. If you want to stay at sea, you're going to have to bend with the breeze. Otherwise,' Milo shrugged. 'Otherwise it'll break you.'

Chapter Seven

Claus was grumbling again as Milo looked at the dorsal fin cutting through the water behind them. It had been following them for several hours. 'Said de ship is unlucky. Said ve'd never make Australia. First ve leaves on Friday, den ve have vistling mate and now ve're going to lose a man. Sharks are vaiting for someone to fall.'

Milo laughed at him as the first mate walked over and called across to Bergen. 'You can ask the cook for some pork fat and put a line over if you want. Claus, you help him.'

Claus cheered up immediately. 'Aye-aye, sir,' he said and walked forward to join Bergen and help him round up the hands. They bent a thick wire rod into a hook and attached it firmly to a length of chain the shark couldn't bite through. Baited with some pork fat, they trailed the line behind them and waited. Several pilot fish formed an advance guard for the big shark; they swam ahead and appeared to sniff the bait, while the shark held back. After a while the shark, too, moved ahead and nudged the fat repeatedly with its tapered snout, before eventually falling back again.

The men on deck watched with suppressed excitement. It was clear that the shark wanted the bait and it was only a question of time before it attacked. It did so with merciless speed. Twisting its body in the water, it opened its mouth and the rows of teeth flashed through the foam as it surged forward with a powerful thrust of its tail. The shark grabbed the bait sideways in its jaws and the chain rattled past its teeth and into its gut. The crew cheered as they saw that the hook had gone home and took in the tension of the rope through a block on the yard. Hauling in unison, they pulled the shark completely out of the water and made it fast with its tail just skimming along the surface. As the ship heeled, the thrashing body fell against the hull and with a mighty heave it flipped its tail with a force which would have stove in a lesser ship. 'Big bugger,' grunted Bergen approvingly, as he prepared a slip knot on the end of a line and slid it expertly over the chain and over the shark's jaws until it slipped down to the tail. 'Gotcha!' he shouted in triumph. 'Now heave away the line.' Even Arnie had joined the excited hands and was pulling as hard as the rest of them. Bergen strapped a knife to the end of a boathook, and as the shark was winched over the deck he slit its gullet and watched the contents of its stomach cascade onto the deck. Arnie turned a dull green colour and even Milo felt his own stomach turn as he recognised, amid the remains, the half-digested body of the ship's dog which had fallen overboard two days previously.

Bergen did his work expertly as he cut up the body and threw the flesh overboard. He carved off the fat, carried the huge jaws forward and lashed them down to dry in the hot sun. Bergen was an accomplished carver and the shark's jaws would provide him with material for this voyage and the next. Now that they were convinced the animal was finally dead, the crew lined up to run their hands along its razor-edged jaws. 'Vell at least zese aren't going to chew up no poor sailor-man,' said Claus, awed by the power of the tightly-packed rows of teeth.

'Now you've had your fun, let's get the deck cleaned up,' ordered the first mate. 'Arnie, get that shovel and dump this mess overboard.'

Arnie had recovered somewhat, but he was still shaking at the violence of what he had seen. However, he was determined to hide it as best he could, so he grabbed the shovel and approached the stinking mess. Shark was just about the only thing that sailors wouldn't eat, although they'd make a meal of almost anything else. The previous day they'd even stewed an albatross that had landed on board and couldn't fly off. The cook had refused to have anything to do with it, while Claus took to his bunk yelling out to anyone who would listen that 'ze ship vas doomed'.

Milo saw that Arnie's initiation had affected him deeply; he was more subdued and less inclined to rush in with his opinion, taking more time to listen to others. They both shared a cabin forward, next to the carpenter's, and spent many hours talking about their homes and families. Milo showed him his mother's locket, explaining how the Bossanos had forced him to leave the island. Arnie, who had grown up in the cold and damp of the north, found his description of Sipan almost magical. He was particularly affected when Milo told him about Vigo, and he kept asking Milo to tell him stories of the things they had done together. For him, tales about a green sunny island bathed in a warm sea conjured up images of the fantasy island he had always dreamed of. Nearly all Arnie's family were seafarers and he had been expected to go to sea from the day he was born.

Perhaps that's what made him such a natural sailor, thought Milo: it's in his blood. His brothers had gone to sea when he was very small and he could barely remember them, leaving his childhood a solitary one. Milo could see how, on previous ships, Arnie had either been bullied or ignored, strengthening his feeling of loneliness, and with no one to talk to he had tried to become the person he thought others wanted him to be. But as they talked more, Milo found Arnie starting to trust himself more. Fundamentally he remained insecure and lacking in confidence – but just give him time, Milo thought. If his obvious abilities were allowed to develop, he would win through – if he survived.

Arnie had even attempted to join the watch below during a card session. Olav had sneered at him. 'Decided to come down to our level, have you? Aren't you afraid you're going to catch our corrupted morals?'

Johanssen tried to intervene. 'Why don't you leave the boy alone? Let him join us if he wants to. Just as long as he can put up a stake, where's the harm?'

'I don't happen to like sitting opposite someone who's just a lad but still looks down his nose at me.'

'Let's face it,' said Johanssen. 'Most people look down their noses at you.'

Olav leapt to his feet. 'You don't dare say that to me outside: I'll lay you out.'

'No, you won't,' replied Johanssen calmly. 'No one's going anywhere. Now just sit down and play your cards.'

'Damn you and your cards, you drunken sot. You can only play when you're sober. Put you in front of a bottle of whisky and you're lost.'

'Maybe so, but since there's no whisky between here and Sydney, can we get on with the game?'

'That's what you think. Next time I play, I'll stake some real whisky, not this lousy chewing tobacco. I'll let you win and then watch you collapse. You make me sick trying to nursemaid this, this ... pasty-faced milk-sop.'

Arnie stood up angrily and lunged towards him. 'Sit down!' shouted Johanssen. 'Just ignore him, Arnie, it's not worth it. Whatever anyone says about you, at least you try – even if you try too hard. Olav just spends his time doing nothing. He lets the rest of us carry him and thinks no one notices when he slopes off every time there's any work to be done. We all know what sort of person he is; it's just that we don't see the point in telling him to his face.'

Olav was red with fury. 'You'll see what sort of person I am when you're grovelling on your knees. I'll remind you when you're begging me for a drink.' He slammed his cards on the table and, picking up his tobacco, stormed out.

'I wouldn't trust that man anywhere,' said Johanssen. 'At least everyone knows that I'm a drunk, but no one knows what he's capable of.' He turned to the boys. 'OK, Arnie, are you in?'

Later, in their cabin, Arnie told Milo what had happened. 'I wouldn't trust Olav either,' said Milo. 'Have you seen him with the steward? There's something going on between those two; they're always whispering together and if you walk past, they stop talking. My guess is that Olav wants to get his hands on the Captain's whisky, and he's trying to get the steward to tell him where it's hidden.'

As they voyaged southwards, Milo and Arnie continued their lessons with Joachim Traub, who pointed out the new constellations opening up ahead of them, as the Big Dipper give way to the Southern Cross. On deck, he named the seabirds which now escorted them. The petrels, the black spotted Cape pigeons which followed the ship, especially in stormy weather, and the tiny 'Mother Carey's Chickens' which, he told them, sailors called 'Little Peter' because they appear to walk on the water. A flock of these birds flew alongside, begging for crumbs which the sailors threw them. Milo attempted to catch one by putting a hook into the bread, but Claus stopped him with a blow that fetched him up in the scuppers. 'Vat you do, boy? They carry the spirits of departed sailors. Don't you know to kill 'em is bad luck?' As well as the petrels, exhausted boobies would frequently sleep on the yardarms and although it was simple to catch them, they were lousy and tasted so rank that they were left alone. Cape hens and the giant fulmar, a species of small albatross, often followed the ship, picking up any carrion they threw out. But it was the albatrosses themselves that fascinated Milo. He could watch them for hours as they sailed above the masthead, hardly moving their immense wings as they swooped down to take their prey while hardly breaking their glide. If they were ever to settle on the water, they could never get back into the air again.

It was after Arnie had left him to go on watch, just as he was turning in, that Milo heard a scratching from the other side of the bulkhead. He stiffened and listened intently. The wooden timbers creaked as the ship rolled in the sea and drummed against the deck, making the fo'c'sle alive with a cacophony of sounds, but Milo was sure this was something out of the ordinary. As he listened he heard it again: a metallic creaking, which rose slowly in pitch. Milo thought quickly of the layout of the ship and imagined the plan of the deck above him. His cabin was well forward, just aft of the heads, and to starboard there was the small skylight that provided ventilation for the hold – someone must have climbed into the narrow shaft which ran below. He pressed his ear against the timbers; there was now the unmistakable sound of bottles clanking. He rushed from his bed, ran on deck and looked forward, where he could just make out a figure, hidden from the officers by the ventilation hatch. The man appeared to stand up and another figure climbed up to him and crawled through the hatch, but it was too dark for Milo to make out who they were. Afraid he might be seen if he stayed on deck, he went back down into his bunk and waited, listening out for what they would do next. Soon, he heard the men creep quietly over his cabin and settle down behind the galley. There was a clink and a faint pop of a cork being pulled, the unmistakable sound of a whisky bottle. Milo was puzzled. Even if there was a consignment of whisky stored in the forward hold, how could they get through the sacks of gunpowder? He had seen the sacks being packed himself and there was no easy way through. Unless – and he didn't like to think about what might have gone on a few feet from his head – unless they had made a tunnel through the sacks. But for that they would have needed a light, and the officers were the only people with access to a Davy lamp. Milo thought hard. He had no qualms about informing on his shipmates if his own safety was involved, but until he could identify the culprits, he couldn't see how he could stop them. He decided to wait. Whoever it was, if they spent the night drinking, it should be pretty clear in the morning who they were. He pulled the covers over his face, turned over and went to sleep.

Milo went on watch as the dawn lit up the streaky sky. Unusually, the previous watch was still on deck; the abundance of seabirds had made them aware that the island of Tristan da Cunha would soon be close. Most of the crew were now lined along the rail, watching as they approached the high, steep-sided island. Sometimes, if they passed close enough and the weather was calm, boats would come out and sell them fresh fruit and vegetables. But with a light wind, the mate put Milo at the wheel, and with so many on deck he was too far aft to tell if anyone was missing below. He'd just have to wait and see.

After his watch he made his way into the fo'c'sle. Olav was sitting at the table with an open bottle of whisky in his hand. Milo thought he was looking too pleased with himself. 'Where's Johanssen?' he asked.

'What do I care?' sneered Olav. 'He's dead to the world an' no use on a ship.'

'What's the matter with him?' asked Milo.

'Drunk, he is. Dead drunk and snoring like a foghorn. I reckon it's the last we'll see of 'im till we dock.' Olav turned back to his bottle, but Milo grabbed his arm and shook it.

'You can't fill him with drink. If the mate finds him, he'll be locked up until we reach Sydney and then they'll fine him all his pay. Just like before, he'll slide right down to the bottom and have to start over again. You can't do that to him.'

'An' why not? It's his lookout. If 'e wants to pay me for the whisky, why shouldn't I sell it him?'

'Because it's not yours, that's why,' replied Milo quickly. 'Not only that, but you're going to blow the ship up searching around the front hold like that. There's gunpowder down there.'

''S perfectly safe, in't it?' Olav was getting rapidly very drunk and Milo was afraid of what he might do. He went over to Bergen's bunk and shook the big Norwegian's shoulder.

'Bergen, you've got to wake up. Olav's been selling whisky to Johanssen and he's passed out in his bunk. You've got to help.'

But Bergen had already heard. 'I ain't gotta do nothing. I've seen too many like him to feel sympathy. If he wants to drink himself senseless, then let him.'

'No, Bergen, it's not just him – it's us. I think I know where he's got the whisky from; it's the same place as the Captain's getting it.'

'So? It's nothing to me, either way he gets it. Just give me a quiet life. I'm keeping out of it.'

'No, you can't,' pleaded Milo. 'There's a consignment of spirits in the front hold. I saw the steward and Olav getting the bottles out.'

'Saw them, did you? When was this? It's none of our business anyway.'

'Well, I didn't see them exactly, but it must have been them and anyway it is our business. There's gunpowder in that hold.'

The Norwegian was not a quick thinker, and he lay in his bunk for several moments while he took in what Milo had told him. 'They're going through the powder?'

'How else can they get in there? You saw it being loaded. They've got to climb past the sacks to get at what's below. We've got to speak to the mate. Those two have got no idea what they're doing: they'll get us all blown up.'

Bergen continued to think silently. He looked towards Olav, but the Estonian was just staring at the bottle and was clearly in another world. Eventually he turned to Milo. 'If you tell the mate, then Johanssen will get put in irons anyway.'

73

Milo shook his head impatiently. 'Yes, but they'll let him out after a few days, and there'll be no more drink to tempt him. Now are you coming with me?'

Slowly the big sailor got to his feet. Every instinct told him that he shouldn't tell on his shipmates to an officer, but Milo's urgency made him realise they were all in danger, and so reluctantly he followed Milo aft to the cabin. At one point Bergen's nerve failed and he turned, but Milo ran in front of him and faced him. 'You've got to do this,' he said. 'For all our sakes.'

Milo followed Bergen aft. The Norwegian never felt comfortable in the officers' cabin and shuffled from one foot to the other, wringing his cap nervously between his hands as he haltingly and circuitously tried to tell the mate of their fears. Joachim listened impatiently before finally interrupting and asking Milo to interpret what Bergen was trying to say. Even before Milo had finished his explanation, Joachim jumped up and rushed forward, calling the second mate to bring the special Davy lamp to the front hold. The mate and Bergen were far too big to struggle through the ventilation shaft, and Bergen grabbed Claus and Tom O'Connor to help him lift the fore-hatch cover. Mr Recht climbed inside, but it was already clear to everyone what had happened. A trail of spent matches lined a worn burrow through the sacks. Joachim Traub raised his eyes to the heavens and his hand against his forehead. 'You sailors will be the death of me yet,' he groaned. 'Isn't there anything you won't do for a drink?' No one answered.

It took several days before Olav and Johanssen recovered. Joachim decided that it would achieve nothing to lock them up. The only thing that counted was to cut off their supplies, so he instructed the carpenter to secure the ventilation hatch and check that there was no other way in. He had no idea how the Captain was going to manage, but for the moment that was the least of his problems. The Hanover was racing towards the Roaring Forties, and Captain or no Captain, he had to muster a full crew for the hard work ahead.

Milo was relieved that the gunpowder had been made secure. It had worried him since they left Chatham, and seeing the ways of deep-sea sailors at close quarters had done nothing to improve his confidence. He was quite prepared to accept that if you dug deep enough, you'd find a heart of gold, but it was clear that most sailors left responsibility behind as soon as they set foot on deck. Perhaps life at sea was already so dangerous that it didn't make much difference even if the ship was full of dynamite – but Milo liked to calculate risks, and lessen them whenever possible. The increasing cold concentrated his mind on more immediate matters; he brought out his warm clothes again, but still couldn't keep warm. He couldn't understand why they had to go south of Australia rather than keep to the north, where it was warmer. The knowledge that they would find stronger winds and a shorter passage further south left him unmoved. He'd been happy in the steadier seas, and wasn't looking forward to a rough ride. But he plotted their course even more carefully than usual, and after each day's run he mentally ticked off the time left to Australia.

As they ventured further southwards, it became colder still, and the depressions ploughed through in a succession of unbroken gales which piled the seas up behind them. The huge waves towered over the masts, forcing the mate to put two men at the wheel, with a third backing them up by the rudder stock. As the seas built up, each massive wave lifted their stern into the wind as it rolled away underneath their keel. The winds reached hurricane force; both mates were on deck and only a scrap of sail was flying from the foremast. Eventually even the Captain came up, and it was clear from his pale face that he had never encountered such a sea before. He looked around as he hung on unsteadily to the leeward rail. 'Shouldn't we heave to until the wind abates?'

Joachim looked at him in astonishment. 'We'll never get her head around in this,' he shouted above the wind. 'We'll just have to hold on.'

'But in this sea and with this wind, we could broach,' shouted the Captain, his voice breaking with fear.

'We've got Bergen and Claus on the wheel, and they're holding her. We're doing all we can.' Another huge wave stormed up behind them, breaking over the ship's stern. The decks were swept as though by a tidal wave, and the men were washed against the downwind rail. The mate was clinging to the base of the mast as he heard a strangled voice yell out, 'Man overboard!' Wiping the sea from his eyes he looked back towards the helm, where the wheel was now swinging freely. There was no sign of Bergen or Claus. He grabbed at a rope and pulled himself towards the wheel. 'Get the helm!' he shouted with all his force as he worked his way towards it. The ship was rolling uncontrollably and as it pitched, he fell again onto the steep deck and dragged himself forward on his hands and knees. A second wave followed, whipping the ship's stern into the air and the unmanned wheel spun wildly. As the sea passed underneath, the ship ploughed down the front of the next wave and was turning towards the following sea. Joachim struggled aft and finally managed to grab the wheel. As he did so, he felt it stiffen in his hands and looked up to see that Bergen had struggled back and was heaving at the wheel's rim, forcing the ship away from the wind. The ship teetered on the edge of a wave as a furious gust laid its scuppers under water. Time seemed to stop. Everyone on board waited, sensitive to the precarious balance. If the crest of the next wave broke against them, they would be defenceless. The seas would rush in and flood them, taking them to the bottom in seconds. The crew were deaf to the angry noise of the storm. Even at its centre, as they hung in the air, in their minds it was silent.

Slowly, very slowly, the ship started to rise. The masts seemed to kiss the surface of the sea and swing back towards the sky. The two men wrestled with the wheel, praying it could take the strain. The bows were inched down-wind as they gradually regained control. 'Get a rope around this man,' yelled the mate, as hands came aft and strapped Bergen to the rails. 'Mr Recht, get me a damage report and find out what happened to Claus.' He stopped suddenly and looked around him. 'Where's the Captain?'

Recht bellowed back to him, 'I've got Claus here; he's got some broken ribs, but I think he'll be all right. I saw the Captain go below just before that last wave hit. But Johanssen is missing. I think he was washed overboard.'

The ship was a sombre place as they worked their way steadily through the storm. No one said much, but Johanssen's loss depressed them all deeply. When the storm finally started to abate, Milo watched sadly as a weak sun rose over the still-hostile sea. He'd liked poor Johanssen. Even though he had so little self-control, he had a kind of dignity. After all, it was his money that he'd spent on drinking himself into unconsciousness. It was his choice to go back to sea to win such hard-earned wages. Each time he got to a port, he was knocked back further than the sea had ever thrown him, yet knowing all the dangers, he had returned. What did it matter that he was so weak on shore? At sea he had been a hero. Where was the justice?

They reached the last of their stores just a few days out from Sydney, and Joachim looked at the pig sadly and decided that they had carried him far enough. Milo looked on without enthusiasm as they chased the condemned animal around the decks, providing just the lift in spirits that the first mate had hoped for. Even Arnie was crying out wildly as he dived headlong to grab its neck, missing by several lengths as it cantered down the companionway into the cabin. Milo couldn't help comparing its fate with Johanssen's. They had both been valued members of the crew. Everyone had scratched the porker affectionately behind the ear, to its obvious enjoyment, and whereas no one had gone quite that far with Johanssen, he too had been popular. While he lived. It didn't seem fair that neither of them would see the end of the voyage. For them both, Claus had been right. Their voyage had been doomed.

The cook served out generous portions of sizzling pork to the cheerful crew, who fought over the pieces of crackling like children. The mate looked on from the quarterdeck and called the steward over. 'Let them splice the mainbrace – issue a tot of rum all round.'

The blood drained from the steward's face, and he looked at the mate dumbly.

'What's the matter with you, man – can't you understand a simple order?'

'Aye-aye, sir. I mean, well, sir, it's like this sir,' his voice trailed off.

'What is it? Why're you just standing there?'

'Well, sir. You see. Well, er ...' The steward took a short breath, shut his eyes and clenched his hands in an effort to force out the words. 'The rum, sir. There isn't enough left, sir. You see, after the front hold was secured, I couldn't get at the whisky for the Captain, sir. And he hadn't got any left of his own supplies, so, well, er ...'

'So you provided him with the ship's rum?'

'Well, yes, sir,' answered the steward meekly. 'But it was the Captain's orders, sir. I wouldn't have done it on my own, sir,' he added quickly.

The mate turned towards him and the steward backed away against the rail. 'No, I guess you wouldn't. Your life wouldn't have been worth living if the crew found out that you'd stolen their rum rations. But I'm going to ensure that it's not worth living anyway.' He raised his hand, but then stopped. If the crew found out, he would run the risk of having a mutiny on board. They were nearly at Sydney and the weather was now set fair, so there was a good chance that no one would miss it. He brought his arm down. 'All right, then, but if you breathe a word of this to anyone, they'll pull you apart and feed you in pieces to the sharks. Get what's left of the rum, give it to Mr Recht and ask him to make it secure – and if I see you trying to get any for the Captain, then I'll hand you over to the men. Now get out of my sight.'

The mate was right. The weather remained fair as they left

Tasmania behind them and rounded up north, towards Sydney. As they approached Jervis Bay, the land finally came into view and for the next ten hours they worked their way slowly along the coast. Joachim had allowed Milo to take the helm in the steady breeze, and they arrived at Sydney Heads just as dusk was about to fall. Milo craned his head to get his first view of the famous harbour.

'You won't see anything from here,' said the first mate. 'You won't even see the entrance until we're close in; it's hidden by the cliffs. We'll have to heave to here till the morning and wait for a tug to pull us through.' He issued the orders to the crew, and the ship headed up into the wind.

'What's going on here?' At the sound of an unfamiliar voice, all hands stopped and looked aft, where the Captain had emerged from his Cabin and was making his way towards the first mate on the quarterdeck. 'Who gave orders to heave this ship to?'

The first mate straightened himself in anticipation of trouble. 'I did, sir. We've got to wait for a pilot and a tug to tow us in.'

'Tug? What d'yer mean, tug? What's wrong with the wind? Damned steamships, think we can't do without 'em. Now turn this ship about and we'll go in under sail.'

'Sir, you've not been here before – you don't know it. There may be a fair wind out here, but the entrance is narrow and the cliffs blanket the wind. We could drift onto the rocks in the darkness. Many a ship has done it before.'

'You think I'm waiting out here while some steamship decides to come and rob us with some outrageous charge for a tow? Now do as I say and turn the ship around.'

'No, sir. It's too dangerous.'

'Mutiny! That's what it is, sir! Mutiny! Put that man in custody,' he called out, to no one in particular. Milo, at the wheel, had heard every word, but was careful to look steadily ahead, remaining expressionless as though unaware of the argument. He knew the crew couldn't hear what was happening aft, though most guessed what the shouting was about.

Joachim Traub called out to the second mate, who ran back and up the steps to the deck. 'Mr Recht, will you take the Captain to his cabin and keep him there? I'm placing him under arrest for being drunk.'

'Drunk!' snorted the outraged Captain. 'How can I be drunk when you've taken away my spirits? I'll not be getting another drop till we get into Sydney, and the sooner we get in the better. Now turn this ship around!'

The second mate looked questioningly at Joachim. 'It's all

right, Mr Recht – it's best you don't become involved. I'll deal with this myself.' He moved in front of the Captain so the crew couldn't see what was happening and with a speed that made the second mate doubt his eyes, he swung a powerful blow at the Captain's head and caught the senseless body as it fell.

'Mr Recht, the Captain's taken poorly; get some help to carry him below.' He turned back towards the crew. 'What are you all staring at? Get back to work. Arnie, haul out the pilot flag and get the blue lamp ready. We're going to wait for the tug.' He turned back to the second mate. 'Whatever the consequences, Mr Recht, I'm not going through Sydney Heads at night under sail. I'd sooner be disrated.'

If the Water Police had seen what I saw, thought Milo, they'd not just disrate you – they'd throw you in jail. But then who's going to tell them?

Chapter Eight

The pilot left the ship at anchor opposite Port Dennison until a tug was available to tow them alongside Alger's Wharf. As soon as the Hanover was made fast, and before even the stevedores could come on board and start unloading, the Captain stormed ashore, hurling filthy oaths at Joachim Traub. It was a subdued crew who formed up in a line in front of the cabin for an advance to cover their time in port. Apart from Milo, none of them was quite sure what had happened off Sydney Heads, but most had been able to guess at a fairly accurate explanation of the nature of the illness which had affected the Captain so suddenly. Without exception – even the steward – they all sided with the first mate. Although unafraid to resort to violence when necessary, he had maintained order, as well as taking the place of the skipper, without bullying. And, moreover, they'd made good time for an old ship. Joachim Traub was an officer rare in the service. He was popular.

For his part, the mate was untroubled at the generous advances he gave the men. Since the old gold-rush days, when entire crews would leave the ship and make their way inland to stake a claim in the goldfields, the Australian police took a hard line on deserters. If necessary, they sent patrols deep into the outback to bring them back and Joachim could see little reason why any of his men should desert. The ship was sound and the crew, by most standards, was relatively competent and cheerful. In any event, whatever they got up to ashore, he was unlikely to remain as first mate and so it really didn't matter to him what they did. He had searched his conscience and was convinced that if he had the past twenty-four hours to live again, he would have done nothing different. He stayed on board and waited.

He didn't have to wait long. The Captain had lost not a moment in going directly to the Water Police to file his charges. Without returning to the ship, he had found lodgings ashore, and locked himself in his room, afraid of what his big first mate might do to him if he returned. Even before most of the crew had left the ship, the police patrol came on board and took away their first officer, the man who had guided them through the dangers of the past four months. They stood watching as he was taken to the station under guard, knowing that sailors' justice, however capricious, was always swift. Nor was his hearing delayed; it was just the following morning that Milo was called to the magistrates' court. 'Now listen,' the Captain said to him just outside the courtroom. 'You tell 'em what that big bastard did to me. You tell 'em that I'll not have anyone speak to me like that. Not on my own ship. You tell 'em.' The Captain stopped, suddenly remembering that he was only talking to the ship's boy. 'You know I've always looked after you, not like that mate.' He patted Milo on the shoulder. 'Mate, ah! He won't be one for much longer, not after I've finished with him.'

As Milo watched the magistrates file in, he reached into his shirt and started stroking his locket. The Captain started to present his case with relish. But once embarked on it, he became angry and incoherent and Milo started to relax. The magistrates listened to his tirade against his first officer with increasing impatience, until they finally interrupted, asking him to get on and present his evidence. The Captain stopped his accusations reluctantly, and called Milo as his only witness; it didn't occur to him that his evidence might not favour his skipper. Even Joachim was anxious about what Milo might say, and that he might be too frightened by the courtroom to lie.

'Tell the court what you saw, boy,' the Captain barked.

'Saw, sir?' Milo replied. 'When would that be, sir?'

'You know perfectly well what we're talking about, boy. Tell 'em what happened off Sydney Heads.'

'Well, sir, I'm not sure that I should.' Milo turned to the bench, looking worried. 'They always told me that when a sailor is aft on the quarterdeck, he never sees or hears anything.'

The chairman of the magistrates was a German. He leant forward, with a friendly smile on his face. 'You're obviously a good lad,' he said coaxingly. 'And you're right, you shouldn't normally let on you've heard any of the officers' talk. But this is different. The Captain is saying that the first mate knocked him out. You must tell us what you saw.'

Milo brightened. 'Thank you, sir. If you're sure it's all right.' The man nodded encouragingly and Milo continued. 'The Captain's right. It was just as we reached Sydney Heads. He rushed up from his cabin, and was obviously very upset about something. We were all really worried about him.'

The Captain nodded approvingly. 'Tell us what the mate did.'

'It was terrible, sir,' said Milo. The Captain looked towards the bench and nodded smugly.

'He looked a bit funny,' Milo continued, starting to enjoy himself. 'He was very pale, almost white, even though he seemed to be sweating a lot. He was mumbling something about pirates boarding the ship and stealing his supplies. He said he had to chase them and ran across to the rail; if Mr Traub hadn't stopped him, he would have jumped over, I'm sure of it. The next thing I saw was that he'd collapsed on the deck. Mr Traub was most concerned, and had him taken to his cabin immediately. I'd never seen the Captain that bad before, although he hadn't been too well ever since we left England.'

'There was nothing wrong with me!' The Captain's voice thundered across the courtroom. 'What d'you think you're talking about? The boy's lying, anyone can see that.'

The magistrate banged his gavel. 'You're not on your own quarterdeck now, Captain. I'll not have anyone bellowing like that in this courtroom. The boy's your witness and we want to hear him.' He turned to Milo. 'Just carry on, and tell us the truth.'

'Yes, sir, of course,' Milo frowned as if to remember what he had been saying. 'I never understood what was wrong with the Captain. When he was on deck, the illness made him a bit unsteady, so he spent most of his time below. But the first mate, he's a fine seaman, sir. I don't think we could have made it here without him. He was very worried about the Captain, and didn't want to sail through the Sydney Heads without him. Instead he told me to turn the ship into the wind and we waited for a tug.'

The Chairman frowned, and glanced across briefly at the Captain. Turning back to Milo, he said, 'Are you saying that the Captain was about to sail through the Heads?'

'Oh yes, sir. But after the Captain was taken ill, Mr Traub said that he'd only been through a few times, and he didn't feel confident enough to do it under sail. So we waited for a tug, sir. He said the Captain must know it very well to think of doing it alone.'

The magistrates turned to look at the Captain. 'The court is aware of just how many wrecks have been caused by skippers who thought they could do it alone.'

The Captain's face was by now a deep red. He stood up angrily. 'That's not the point. What about the assault? We're here to find the first mate guilty, and it's obvious that the boy didn't see what happened. I wasn't ill: the first mate hit me.' The Captain looked wildly around the court. 'Is anyone calling me a liar?'

After a few moments' silence, the Chairman finally stood up. 'I think we've heard everything, and we will now consider the matter.' He left through a side door, followed by his two colleagues. Milo looked across to Joachim and winked.

It didn't take long for the magistrates, all of them ex-sailors, to make up their minds. Whatever the true situation, a Captain's position had to be upheld, but that didn't mean they would break the career of an obviously promising officer. Joachim was sentenced to the minimum one month in prison and a report was sent to the Mercantile Marine Office. Milo watched sadly as he was taken away, but grinned when Joachim turned and winked back at him.

But although the mate might have got off lightly, Milo found his absence like being on a ship without bulwarks. Joachim had held everything together. Now they'd bring a new officer on board, and who knew what he would be like? He discussed it with Arnie, who had matured sufficiently to point out that, whatever happened, there was nothing they could do about it anyway. Milo shrugged, aware of the irony that Arnie was only telling him what he had been telling Arnie over the previous few months. A sailor couldn't change anything, except himself.

But after four months at sea, Milo was at least overjoyed to have the feel of solid ground under his feet again. It would take between one and two weeks to unload the ship and their time would be their own until the owner's agent received new instructions. After the depressing, dark and smoky streets of London, he found Sydney a delight. Full of wide streets, gardens and parklands, it felt open and welcoming. Certainly it had its share of hard men, but the harbour front was not dominated by crimpers and thieves, as he had been told. Most of the boarding houses were reasonably quiet and respectable, and there were fewer temptations to distract the sailors now that the gold rush was over.

They found Joachim after several days, at the Woolomoloo prison on the outskirts of the town, and persuaded the warders to let them see him for half an hour. He was cheerful and in good heart. He looked fit and healthy and seemed to be enjoying his brief stay. 'You know, I've heard some fascinating stories in here; you should come and join me. They're people from just about everywhere, and they've done just about everything, too. Some of them have committed crimes I didn't know were even possible.' He looked at the worried faces of the two boys. 'Come on, lads, cheer up. What choice did the magistrates have? If a ship's Captain ever has to answer to the crew, then it's all over. Everything would fall apart. The only security a Captain has against a mutinous crew is the certain knowledge that they'll stand no chance when they get ashore. There's no other way. But I got the minimum sentence, so it's clear what they thought of our Captain. Have you heard what's happened to him, by the way?' The boys shook their heads.

'Well, I'll tell you. This prison is full of old salts and it leaks more than a wooden schooner. The word is they've cabled the magistrate's report to London, and they're already looking for a new skipper. The agents found out how much whisky was missing, so they must've worked out what was going on. So don't you worry about me; there's plenty of ships here in need of a good first officer, and if I can't find a berth here, I'll take a steamer up to Newcastle and find one there. When the word spreads, no one's going to take the Captain on, even as mate. He'll probably end his days on the domain – that's where you'll find most old sailors who can't get a berth.'

Arnie and Milo walked slowly from the prison back towards their ship, deep in conversation. They were happy to find Joachim in such good spirits and for the moment they had forgotten their fear about who might succeed him. Suddenly a booming voice called out, 'Arnold! If it isn't me old shipmate Arnold.'

They stopped in surprise and looked around them. They were passing a large open area, with just a few scrubby trees and some tumbledown sheds. The smoke of dozens of small fires made the air acrid, but they could just see groups of men sitting around them. There must have been over a hundred of them, but they were all some distance away.

'Up here, my lads. I'm just above you. Won't you join me in my modest home?'

They looked up, into the branches of the tree that overhung the pathway. In a cleft, where several branches intersected, a small platform had been built, and leaning over it, grinning down at them, was a rotund figure with a grey bushy beard. Arnie stared up at him. The face looked vaguely familiar, but he couldn't place him, let alone remember the man's name. 'Why, ahoy there, shipmate,' he called out non-committally, searching his memory furiously for an identity.

The grinning figure climbed down laboriously from his perch and grabbed Arnie between outstretched arms. 'Don't you remember me, then? We shared watches together on the Allan Lines to Montreal.' He turned to Milo. 'He might have forgotten me, but who could forget him? Right snotty-nosed little know-it-all, weren't you?' He turned back to Arnie and shook him amiably. If he hadn't liked Arnie, he certainly gave no sign of showing it, and he laughed loudly. It was the laugh that did it.

'Dutch Joe!' said Arnie. 'We were on the Maria on my first trip out of Glasgow. I didn't recognise you at first; you didn't have the beard and you're, well, you're…'

'Fatter, boy. Just say it. I am fatter and what's more, I like being fatter.' He leaned forward conspiratorially, holding on tightly to Arnie, who turned his head away from the powerful fumes which the old sailor exhaled. 'Got myself a good little number here. Board an' lodging an' all expenses paid.'

Milo giggled in spite of himself, and Dutch Joe looked at him as if affronted. 'What you're laughing at, boy? You think ol' Arnie 'ere is too good for 'is ol' shipmates?' He let go of Arnie and advanced upon Milo.

'No, no, sir, it's not that.' Milo thought quickly as he backed away. 'He's told me all about you. It's Dutch Joe, isn't it?'

'Aye, that's right,' said the sailor, somewhat mollified. 'Sailed together on the Maria,' he repeated.

'So if you're getting your board and lodging paid, where are you staying?' asked Milo.

'Why, right here of course, in this tree. Number 11, Woolomoloo Avenue, The Domain, Sydney, New South Wales. Cosy, isn't it?' he said, pointing towards the platform.

'So this is the Domain?' asked Arnie.

'That's right, son. It's a sort of home for old sailors. Mind you, now autumn's coming on it's getting a bit chilly at night.'

Milo was fascinated. 'But what's this job you've got? Who's employing you?'

'The Professor,' said Joe proudly. 'That's who.' He leaned forward again and the boys took another step back. 'He's a remittance man.'

'Remittance man?' they said almost in unison.

'Aye, that's right. Sent here by his family,' he tapped the side of his nose knowingly. 'For 'is 'ealth, you un'erstand. Gets four pounds sent 'im each month, and my job – ' he paused proudly. 'My job is to see no evil sailor takes it off of 'im before it's spent. 'Cos he's a professor, you see. Always thinking. Got 'is 'ead full all the time, with thoughts, not like me. Each month, when 'e's got no money left, 'e gives us all a lecture and passes around his 'at at the end of it – that is if he can still remember. Told us all 'bout something called 'lectricity last month, not that I understood it all. Mind you,' he added after a moment, 'I don't think he did either.'

Milo suppressed another fit of giggles and clutched at Arnie's arm.

The sailor frowned and his smile turned to belligerence. 'Wot yer laughin' at, then? W'a's so funny? We's proud folk here. No one laughs at us on the Domain.'

Milo pulled at Arnie's sleeve. 'We've got to get back to the ship, we're late. Come on, Arnie.' He turned and ran down the street. Arnie clamped his hand over his face, trying to stop himself laughing, and ran off after him. They stopped out of sight behind a row of houses, both almost helpless with laughter. Sobbing with the effort, Arnie steadied himself against a wall. 'You know, it's not fair,' he said between breaths. 'We shouldn't be laughing at them. One day that could be you.'

Milo stopped suddenly, as though someone had slapped him on the face. He looked up at Arnie. 'Never,' he said. 'You'll never find me in a place like that.'

With the second mate in charge of the ship, Milo thought it prudent to make himself as agreeable as possible. With the Captain and Joachim gone and the crew spending most of their time in the alehouses, he judged – rightly – that Mr Recht was not enjoying his own company and was happy to have them join him for excursions inland. Now he didn't need to maintain the discipline of life at sea, they found him to be a cultured officer, and in spite of the differences in their ages, they were even asked to use his first name, Alex, while ashore. They were careful that Alex quickly became Mr Recht as soon as they were in earshot of the ship.

As they left the longshoremen to unload ship, their days together passed quickly, but it couldn't last. An idle ship made no money for its owners, and Alex Recht soon received new orders. Following a meeting with the agents, he returned with Mr Streicher, the new first mate. The crew inspected him warily as he came on board. A pale, lean man who looked more like a preacher than a sailor, he gave little away when he assembled the crew and told them curtly that loading was now finished. They would be sailing the next day up the coast to Newcastle, to take on coal for San Francisco. The new master, Captain Brockman, still hadn't appeared. He was being transferred from an Australian line and would be joining the ship in the morning.

Milo and Arnie realised that their brief holiday was over, and that once again they were hostages to an uncertain future. They made a final visit to Woolomoloo prison and managed to persuade the guards to let them visit Joachim one last time. As they said goodbye, even the stern first mate became quite emotional. 'We'll meet again, don't you worry. From the deck of a clipper the world might seem a big place, but to an old sailor it's like a village.' He hugged Milo. 'Thanks for your help, boy.'

'No,' replied Milo. 'It's you who's helped me. I won't forget it.'

~~~~~

The two boys looked around them gloomily. It was now nearly three weeks since the ship had dropped its anchor in

Newcastle Bay to wait for a vacant berth. No one had been allowed ashore and after the freedom of Sydney the inactivity was causing frayed tempers. Fights were starting to break out below decks, out of sight of the officers. Around them, several dozen other ships were anchored, all taking their turn to load. On shore, the line of ships loading alongside the wharves was partly covered in a mist of dark coal dust. Huge piles of coal lined the back of the wharf and a light breeze carried the fine dust across the harbour. Milo rubbed his eyes, but it only made the stinging worse. 'I see what they mean about taking coals to Newcastle,' he said. 'I always thought they meant England, but nowhere could have more coal than this place.'

The new Captain hadn't helped the atmosphere. He remained a remote figure with no time for the crew, but they reluctantly had to admit that he seemed to know his business and handled the ship expertly when he was finally given clearance to lay her alongside at King's Wharf. The coal was filled from chutes until the holds were overflowing and after washing down the decks, the steamer Challenger came alongside and towed them out to sea, casting them off in the light southerly. Milo watched as they sailed slowly out of sight of land towards America. Is the world really small enough to meet Joachim again, he wondered? It didn't seem so small.

A new, harsher rhythm became established, different from Joachim's routine. The new first mate was freer with his fists and with the end of the rope and, encouraged by the Captain, the Hanover was a more brutal place, with less time for reflection and socialising. The new mate seemed to disapprove of music and allowed Tom O'Connor his fiddle only on Sunday afternoons, and even then with obvious ill will. But Milo was now accustomed to life at sea and accepted things as they came, since there was no point in complaining. Instead he studied Captain Brockman. The skipper was much younger than the previous Captain, almost a different generation, and it was clear that his only interest was to achieve the fastest, or even a record, passage time. The man was quite good looking in his way, almost aristocratic. On land you would never have thought him to be a sailor; he didn't seem hard enough. But it was clear that this was deceptive, and he drove the ship and its men as hard as any skipper could. He was constantly reproving the first mate for missing any wind-shift, reminding him that records were made to be broken. It became clear from the start that there was no love lost between the two of them.

But no records were to be broken on this passage. Although the weather was fresh, after passing to the north of New Zealand the wind rarely reached gale force, and ahead of them lay the prospect of slow progress in the south-east trade winds. The crew didn't object to a slower passage; all of them preferred boredom to hurricanes. Their approach to the Date Line provided all the excitement they wanted, especially as the second mate estimated there was a good chance they would cross the following Tuesday. Several ounces of tobacco were bet on the chances of two days of plum duff, the crew's favourite. Claus, who had recovered from his broken ribs, if not from his innate pessimism, bet against, observing that 'Good things don't happen to me.'

As they neared the line and the prospect of hurricanes had almost passed, Mr Streicher ordered them to take in the best suit of heavy sails and bring up the old sails which wouldn't get damaged by the light winds of the Tropics. As they were hauling them up, the Captain came on deck and, in a bellow which would have brought the mermaids themselves aloft to investigate, he ordered them to pile everything back in the sail locker and shorten sails as fast as they could. Calling across to the first mate, he pointed to the black clouds ahead of them. 'Don't you keep a look-out on this ship, Mr Streicher? Can't you see that squall ahead? This is no time to change sails: get them all down before she hits.' The men sighed. In their experience, a first mate up-braided in front of all the hands invariably took it out on the crew later.

The men had still not completely found their sea legs and worked on the sails only slowly. Claus and Arnie were still on the yards when the wind hit with a sudden and ferocious blast that laid the ship on its ends. Arnie was growing fast and getting tougher by the day. He was hardly recognisable as the slender, almost frail boy Milo had first seen in London. He had taken to heart Milo's advice and was determined to show the new officers that he should now be treated as a man. The rest of the crew looked up at them anxiously. It was nothing that any of them hadn't experienced before, but it injected a new feeling of urgency which had been missing after the long stay ashore. It also provided a test for the new officers who supervised the frantic efforts of both watches, lashing down sails as they worked loose and tying down the ropes washed free by the waves sweeping across the decks. The squall lasted only a few hours, but although the wind dropped slightly, the sea remained confused, causing the ship to pitch and toss. Occasionally she seemed to stop dead as she buried the bowsprit deep into a trough. Captain Brockman didn't waste a minute before ordering the men back up aloft to set the sails.

At the first words of command, Arnie rushed impulsively up the ratlines to the main royal yard, unaware of the succession of waves building up behind them. Alex Recht shouted out a warning, but his voice was lost on the wind. The first wave rushed at the hull, lifting them high above the sea as it broke underneath them. The ship veered down the back of the wave and from his first steps, Arnie was fighting to keep his balance. The ship started to corkscrew as he climbed higher; each time he attempted to counteract the roll, he overcompensated and was flung against the rigging. The next wave hit and the mast swung over again, flinging Arnie along to the end of the yard where he grabbed at the toeline. A final cross-wave smashed against the hull and Arnie didn't have a chance. The juddering impact jerked the rope from his hands, and he fell into the sea below.

Alex Recht grabbed quickly at an orange life ring and flung it at Arnie as he swept past, yelling at the helmsman to put the ship into the wind. Captain Brockman had watched it all and shrugged. 'It's too late,' he said. 'The boy's had it.'

Milo had seen Arnie fall and rushed back screaming. 'Captain, sir. We've got to go after him, we can't leave him. Can't we lower the boat, sir?'

The first mate turned back to the Captain. 'There's no point, sir. The man who falls overboard is a dead man. We'll never get him back.'

'Can we try, sir? Please!' Milo's voice was breaking. Every moment they travelled further away from his friend. 'The wind's starting to drop, sir. We've got to try.'

Captain Brockman's face clouded. 'Got to?' he repeated angrily. 'You don't tell me what I've got to do on my own ship.'

'Captain, sir,' Recht interrupted, coughing respectfully. 'If some of the men want to try, there'd be no harm, would there? And Milo is right, the wind is dropping.'

The Captain looked around him at the sea. 'What do you think, Mr Streicher? I suppose there's just a chance they could make it. That is, if they want to try.'

'If they want to kill themselves, let them go ahead,' the first mate said without interest.

The second mate approached the Captain. 'It's possible, sir. I could lead a party,' he hesitated. 'Although I don't see the other men queuing up to save Arnie.'

'I'm not going to risk you,' snapped the Captain sharply. 'I don't mind losing some of the others, but I still need some people who know what they're doing.'

'Aye, aye, sir.' There was no future for a second mate who argued with his Captain.

Milo looked at Alex Recht in dismay. Without him, no one else was likely to lead a rescue party. In desperation he ran to the foredeck. 'Who'll help me?' he shouted frantically. 'He's a shipmate, we all have to rely on each other.' The men looked at their feet sullenly and no one moved. Milo laughed bitterly. 'If it was anyone else out there you wouldn't hesitate. Arnie has his faults, but he'd be the first to help save a shipmate, you all know that. No one can accuse him of not trying. You know he thinks of you all as his family – you can't just abandon him. If we don't get back to him now, it'll be too late – if it isn't already.' Milo looked at the waves surging around the ship. 'I couldn't live with myself knowing I'd done nothing to help a shipmate.'

Bergen stepped forward uncomfortably. 'He might be a difficult little bugger, but I admit his heart's in the right place.' Bergen looked questioningly at the Captain, but his expression was impassive, unconcerned whether they stayed or went. At the corner of his eye he saw Alex Recht nod slightly. Milo was right: how could he live with himself afterwards? 'I'll take a party.' He turned back to the rest of the crew. 'Who's coming with me?' He looked along the row of sailors. No one looked up.

'Come on, men,' exhorted Milo. 'It could be any one of us out there. He's a shipmate.'

The sailors looked at each other sheepishly. Hesitantly they shuffled aft and the Captain looked towards Bergen. 'I'm not going to stop you, but I'm not going to encourage you either. We've got a passage to make and if anything happens I won't be coming after you. I'll wear the ship around while you launch the boat, but I'll tell you now, you've only got the slightest chance of getting back.'

'Aye-aye, sir.' Bergen nodded glumly. 'Claus, launch the boat. Tom, you come with me.'

'And me, sir – what about me?' cried Milo.

'You're not strong enough to row, lad,' Alex Recht shook his head. 'You're safest here.'

'But sir, I grew up on boats. I can steer a boat better than anyone and I'm light enough not to be a burden.'

'We haven't got time to argue,' replied the second mate. Glancing at Milo, he saw the desperation in the boy's eyes and remembered how close he was to Arnie. 'All right, then, get in the boat as they lower it.'

Milo jumped in and held the long painter as the boat wallowed in the water. One by one the men climbed down the rope and settled themselves on the thwarts. Before they could shove off, another cross-wave smashed the small boat against the hull, stoving in several planks. Bergen saw the water rush in and pulled off his jacket and handed it Milo. 'Here boy, stuff that in the hole and hold it there, then try and bail us out.' He heaved against the ship and pushed them off. 'Now lads, ROW!'

Milo hadn't anticipated that so low in the water, they would see so little. Only when they rose to the top of a wave could they see anything, but if Arnie at that moment was in a trough, they would miss him. The coat had stemmed the water, which was now only trickling in and after he'd bailed most of the water overboard, they were starting to make good progress. Standing on the thwart, Milo held the tiller tightly and swept the sea ahead for any sign of Arnie. Turning back, he estimated how far they had gone from the ship. 'He should be around here somewhere. He can't have got much further away than this.' But there was no sign of him.

Claus stood and looked around. 'He must've been swept further away; we'd best get rowing again. Milo, steer directly downwind.' The men applied themselves to the oars but stopped after several minutes while Bergen looked around uncertainly. 'You two look through the starboard quarter and Claus an' me'll look to port. Milo, keep us on a steady bearing from the ship.' As the small boat rode the confused waves, the men stared out across the sea. Milo searched desperately ahead before turning back to check the ship, now quite some distance away, and adjust their course. As he turned back, he glimpsed a brief flash of orange in the sea behind them. As the boat rode up the wave, he saw it again.

'Over there, we've passed him.' He pushed the tiller hard over.

'All right, let's give it all we've got,' said Bergen. 'Milo, keep pointing at him.'

It was slow progress against the wind, but the glimpses of orange became more frequent as they pulled against the sea, until they were finally within hailing distance. As they reached him, it was clear that Arnie was hardly able to keep his head clear of the water. With each wave washing over him, he was growing weaker.

Claus grabbed a boathook and pulled him alongside. The men crowded to help and the boat tipped dangerously; a wave rushing over the gunwales dislodged the coat and the water sloshed around their ankles. Milo pulled the tiller hard, facing the boat into the sea as another cross-wave bore down on them. 'Sit down, men, or you'll have us in there with him,' he shouted, instinctively taking control. 'You two, stuff the coat back in between the planks and get this water out. Bergen, get a hand under Arnie's shoulder there and pull.' The two men lifted

Arnie easily over the side and he fell heavily onto the thwart next to Milo. 'Get him out of those clothes fast and rub him down hard. Put this coat on him afterwards. We'll steer with the oars.' Milo lashed the tiller and went forward to help Arnie. 'Now heave away. One, two – heave.' Without the tiller keeping them on track, it was difficult to pull a straight course and while Milo slowly rubbed Arnie's circulation back, the boat veered erratically back towards the ship. Arnie was as white as the foam which surrounded them. He grabbed his breath in gasps, but slowly, as Milo massaged his skin, his colour started to return. He's going to make it, thought Milo triumphantly, but his elation disappeared as quickly as it came. Milo looked across the foaming sea and understood how it must have been for Vigo.

His thoughts were cut short by a cry from Bergen. 'It's starting to get dark, lads, and we're hardly making progress.' Bergen stood up and peered ahead into the gloom and shook his head. 'There's the light – we've got to pull harder, now heave away.' For several minutes the men pulled silently, with just the creaking of the oars on their rowlocks and the slapping of Milo hands rubbing back warmth into Arnie's weakened body. 'We're only just holding our own, but we can't keep this up. We'll have to stop.'

'We can't just stop.' For the first time Tom O'Connor felt a tremor of fear. 'We'll get blown away and they'll lose us during the night. Even if they do find us, Arnie can't survive a night at sea.'

'We've got no choice. We're not making any progress. With any luck, Captain Brockman will run downwind of us during the night.'

'What, him?' snorted O'Connor. 'He made it clear he ain't going to help no one. Let's give it one last go,' he insisted.

'I suppose we've got nothing to lose,' said Claus morosely. 'All right lads, on the count of three.' Once again a strange silence fell on the boat as the men strained at the oars, and the evening gloom spread over the sea around them. Ahead of them, the riding lantern at the bows of the ship was swinging and its light grew steadily stronger against the darkening sky.

Milo watched it steadily. 'We're getting closer.'

'No, it's just getting darker, that's all.'

'No, no, we're getting closer. The wind's dropping, can't you feel it?'

The men had been rowing too hard to notice, but now that Milo had pointed it out, they could tell he was right. It had dropped. Even the sea seemed slightly quieter. 'Keep going lads,' Bergen shouted. 'We'll be back in time for supper yet.'

Milo tightened the coat around Arnie, and saw his colour was again starting to fade. He bent down and whispered in Arnie's ear. 'Hold on – you've got to hold on. We're nearly there.'

But Bergen had spoken too soon. The wind picked up again and the steady leak through the stove-in hull was making the boat heavier and slower. They were only just holding their own and he was aware that the men were flagging. 'It's no good, lads, we're going to have to skip supper. Will you settle for breakfast?'

'Look, look,' Milo shouted excitedly. 'There's something in the water just ahead. It's got a line on it.'

Bergen looked at it and shook his head. 'No, it's nothing. We're not going to make it back.'

Milo looked at the rope. A float was lashed to its end and he suddenly realised what it was. 'Mr Recht must've floated it down to us. The other end's on the ship. One last heave and we can grab it. Claus, get the boathook and pull it in when we're alongside. Once it's made fast they'll pull us in. Tom, give us a chantey.' Tired as he was, Tom O'Connor didn't hesitate. Starting on a low note, he launched into his shanty with gusto, and as everyone joined in they pulled with renewed effort. Echoes of the sound rebounded from the decks of the Hanover and with one last heave, Claus reached for the line, grabbed it and cleated it around the sampson post. Milo yelled out against the weakening wind. 'Mr Recht, we're secure on your line.'

They heard the second mate's faint voice from the deck. 'Just hold on, lads. We'll pull you alongside. Just keep the boat heading towards us.' Milo unlashed the tiller and looked down at Arnie. It was going to be close.

Chapter Nine

'What d'you think of that, then?' asked Alex Recht, as he leant over the rail and pointed out the city opposite. 'Thought you were never going to see 'Frisco, didn't you? Well there it is, over there, and a more evil place you can't imagine. Oakland here isn't much better. Just you wait and see what crimpers the devil sends on board. There's nothing we can do to stop 'em – you throw 'em off one side and they climb in the other. The 'Frisco boarding house runners make everyone else look like beginners. Whatever anyone offers you, just say no. Take my word for it – this is a dangerous place.'

'It can't be as bad as that,' Arnie said. 'I don't think I'll find anything as dangerous as what can happen out there.' Milo looked at his shipmate. Arnie was now almost fully recovered and his face was flushed with excitement at the scene in front of them.

The second mate laughed. 'Don't you believe it. The fore-deck will be full of crimps shortly.' He looked across at Milo. 'At least at sea you've got your shipmates to help. On land, most of them will be drunk by suppertime.'

'Here they come,' said Alex said. 'The Captain's putting you on night watch to keep you out of harm's way, so you'd best get your rations now.'

As Milo and Arnie went forward, a large, fat man puffed up the gangway alongside them. In spite of his size, he was care-fully and expensively dressed in a long frock coat, with a heavy gold watch chain disappearing into a breast pocket. He wore gold jewellery all about him and he clearly took great pleasure in showing it off. He waddled towards the foc's'le, and ap-proached one of the crew. 'Welcome to the Golden City,' he said, opening his arms as though to embrace the entire crew. 'And there's no finer city in all the world; the best girls, the best whisky and the best dance halls. You know, lads, here in 'Frisco,' he stopped and winked at Milo, 'even the ducks fly backwards so's their tails keep the sun from their eyes.'

Arnie laughed, and the man turned to him. 'Now then, son – are you a drinking man yet? There's no finer place to start than here. At my boarding house, we don't serve any knock-you-down hogwash which rots your guts and steals your sight. No sir, we have nothing but the finest Kentucky whisky, and for all you sailors,' – he looked up at the crew who were now crowding around – 'it's all free.'

The hands started talking to one another. 'Yes, indeed,' continued the fat man. 'When you stay in my boarding house, you won't need to put a hand in your pockets from the day you walk in until the day you walk out.'

'Get carried out, more like,' said Tom O'Connor, and the crew laughed. It was clear that the boarding house was starting to sound very attractive.

'That's right, lads.' The fat man knew he had their attention now. 'And when you leave, we kit you out in a fine suit. And did I tell you about the food? The best steaks, not the swill they serve you on these ships: everything we serve is fresh. Nine o'clock every night, we have dancing, with the prettiest partners you ever saw. Now what do you say to all that?'

'I say: "Lead me to it",' shouted one of the men, who was cheered by the others. It seemed from their flushed faces that someone had already managed to smuggle a bottle on board.

'I bet you do,' said the fat man. 'That's what any sane sailor would say. That's why the house is normally full – but today you're in luck, because it just so happens that we've got some rooms free. See, it's like this. After a man spends a few nights at ease, in good company, he gets to thinking that sailorising is a hard life. Why should he work so hard for so little, when all the thanks he gets is the mark of a rope on his back? So some of the sailors decided to sling their hook right here in 'Frisco, and I got a few of them jobs up-country. I know someone who was looking for bartenders, and with my recommendation they were made welcome.'

It was a master-stroke. Most of the men had asked little of life, but when they did, it was to get a job as a bartender. They simply couldn't imagine anything better. Only Bergen showed any objection. 'Don't listen to 'im, men. You know ye'll never see any of it. Ye'll all get shanghaied and wake up in just another fo'c'sle on just another ship.'

The second mate had walked up from the quarterdeck. 'Bergen's right, men. Don't you recognise the famous 'Shanghai Franklin'? Haven't you heard of the two-hundred-dollar watch he carries on the end of that chain there? Where d'you think he gets his money from? He makes it from taking advantage of poor sailors like you, that's how. Who d'you think gets your three months' advance?'

But it was clear that the men weren't listening to him, and he walked off in disgust. Milo and Arnie followed him. 'Is that true, sir, what you said? That he gets their advance?'

Recht snorted. 'Course it is – how d'you think a crimp lives? He gets all the sailors to leave their ships, promising to find 'em a better one, then the Captain has to go pay another crimp to get 'im a new crew. That's the way the system goes round. Why, Franklin once persuaded a sailor to leave his ship by giving 'im a bottle of whisky. The sailor started drinking it straight away – except that it was doctored. He passed out in the boat and Franklin rowed 'im straight over to another ship, telling them he was drunk. They took him on board and sailed away that night. Poor man, his feet never even touched dry land, but Franklin got all his three months' advance and the sailor not a penny.'

Milo was transfixed at the injustice of it. 'Why doesn't someone stop it?'

'And then where'd we get our crew from? Until they change the system we need the crimps as much as they need us, and who's goin' to change the system?'

~~~~~

Captain Brockman was a mean man. Although he'd drive his crew without mercy to save a day at sea, he couldn't understand that it was better to hire a tugboat than attempt to close the coast under sail and take a day longer in doing it. He saw a tow as the easy way out, the soft option. To his mind there was nothing that couldn't be achieved if he drove his crew hard enough, and in port he tried the same approach. But unlike the poor sailors out at sea, on land there was a choice, and it was obvious to everyone but him that pushing the stevedores was a waste of time. They knew no one else would unload his ship and were unimpressed by his threats to find longshoremen elsewhere. They held all the cards and everyone but the Captain knew it. It took two days before he finally agreed to their terms and took Arnie and Milo off the night watch, giving them a chance to visit the city. Arnie had been impatient to visit an uncle, an ex-sailor who'd set up home in San Francisco. He found Uncle Harold a sympathetic listener and after several visits, his uncle told him to bring Milo the next time, to enjoy what he called 'genuine American hospitality'. No one liked to point out to him that both he and his wife had been born and brought up in Hamburg and that he'd served most of his time on German ships.

Milo certainly wasn't about to quibble about the nationality of any hospitality on offer; it was a long time since he had eaten properly. Rarely had he seen a table like it, and he devoted himself to the food, paying little attention to the talk around the table. Uncle Harold had two young girls, one of them just a year older than Milo, but they spent much of the time giggling at the end of the table, and although he noticed Arnie blushing furiously once or twice, he ignored them and concentrated on his food. When he could eat no more, Uncle Harold turned to him. 'Young Arnie here tells me you're a good sailor. How're you enjoying the sea?'

'Well enough, sir. It can be a hard life, though.'

'It can indeed. You find some tough men out there.'

'Is that why you left then, sir?'

'Lord no, I don't mind it hard. No, I swallowed the anchor when I saw I had no future in it.'

'But weren't you an officer, sir? Couldn't you have got your master's ticket?'

'I could and I did, but I wasn't really cut out for it. I didn't like the way the men were treated, but no one seemed to care. I could never understand why they put up with it. Most of the time they were left with nothing.'

'They get their wages, sir, and their food and lodging.'

'Food? You must have a pretty good idea of what the food's like on most ships, and as for their wages, you know most of them never get to see it. When there's three months' advance available, there's bound to be greedy men sniffing around them. Especially in a place as corrupt as 'Frisco.'

'You mean the crimps, sir?'

'And the city. When I first left the sea, I set myself up in the police. You had to buy your beat, and still do. The more you pay, the better beat you get – the most expensive get a share of the backhanders from the dance halls and gambling houses. I could only afford three hundred dollars and that got me the waterfront, but I couldn't live on the pickings to be had there, so I had to give it up. But the crimps couldn't operate unless the officials supported them. It's not just the police; it goes right up to the Mayor. Everyone knows it, but no one'll do anything about it until they scrap the three months' advance, like the seamen's missions are asking for.'

'But the sailors don't have to go with the crimps.'

'That's what you think – if they don't go with the crimps, they'll like as not get shanghaied anyway, hit over the head when no one's looking and carried onto their next ship unconscious. The crimp tells the Captain he's drunk, but who can tell till it's too late? I've known crimpers who've carried dead men on board, swearing they'd be good seaman when they sobered up. But a sailor never seems to learn. He'll arrive at the wharves in Oakland with months of pay owing him. The Captain won't release him, but he deserts anyway, losing all the money he's earned. Then he gets his next advance taken off him by the crimps and has to work the next three months for nothing until he's paid it off, even though he never even counted it. Then it all starts again – and that's just the sober ones. Most of them are so drunk they don't remember a thing that happened to them on shore anyway – so perhaps it doesn't matter much what's done to them. I never worked out whether sailors become drunks, or drunks become sailors; not that it makes any difference.'

Arnie was taken aback. 'But Uncle Harold, it can't be as bad as that, can it? I mean there are a lot of good men at sea.'

'There're many more bad ones. Oh, sure, most of them have their hearts in the right place. Most of them'd do anything to help a shipmate, but that's the sea for you. It binds men together. Mind you,' – he appeared to muse on a private memory – 'it can do funny things to the girls. There's something that happens to a nice girl when at sea.' He pulled himself reluctantly from his private memories. 'The Pacific west coast is the worst. Especially Callao in Peru, on the West Coast of South America.'

Arnie looked at his uncle. 'The mate says that's where we're bound.'

~~~~~

None of the original crew returned to the ship for its passage south. Even Alex Recht was missing, and Milo could only assume that he, like so many others, had been shanghaied – to wake up on another ship going almost anywhere. Although it seemed difficult to make friends at sea, it was an easy matter to lose them on shore: but at least Arnie was still on board. Big Bergen, having looked after him for all those months, had gone, and his bunk was taken by a tall, rangy American who, when he eventually woke up, looked around him and asked what kind of bunkhouse he'd come to. For the first few hours he was convinced that he had the DTs; nothing else could explain why the floor kept rearing up and down. The cowboy had never seen the sea before and no idea how he had got there. Milo watched from behind the mast as the second mate attempted to relieve him of his six-shooter. The cowboy was too confused to understand and acted like a cornered animal, bellowing that it had kept him alive for the past ten years and no one was going to take it off him. At least, thought Milo, he wouldn't pine for the open spaces – he'd find plenty of them at sea.

It was a slow passage southwards under ballast, crabbing against the winds and the currents. Milo found the life unforgiving and the new crew harder than the men he had got to know on his way from London. The Captain's driving of the ship in all weathers led Mr Streicher, the new first mate, to even worse brutality, which seemed to be reflected in the sullenness of his shipmates. The sense of companionship and co-operation had evaporated. Food was inadequate, no proper rations were served, and Milo and Arnie found themselves constantly hungry. But although the men complained amongst themselves, none of them had the courage to lead a deputation aft to the Captain's cabin. Before, on their way to Australia, Milo had watched Joachim Traub build up a team who worked together and, within the limitations of the ship, take enjoyment wherever they found it. But not one of this crew was surprised by the harsh regime. This was how it was at sea – it was Joachim's benign approach which had been different. But he still couldn't understand why the new first mate led by fear, rather than by encouragement. Surely a ship would work better and faster if the men were healthy and in good spirits? But it was clear that such thoughts had never entered the mate's mind. He remained brutal and a sworn enemy of all the sailors before the mast, and never walked the deck without a belaying pin, brass knuckles, and a curse on his lips.

When they eventually rounded the rocky cliffs of San Lorenzo Island and drifted into Callao Bay, they dropped anchor under the fortress of Real Felipe. Throughout the bay there were ships of every type: sailing ships, men-of-war, store ships, coke hulks, lighters. Fringing the shoreline, the abandoned wrecks of rotting hulls lay unrecognisable. The port was alive with activity. As if infected by it, and even before the ship lay to its chain, the Captain ordered the companionway to be lowered for him to go ashore. Before it was properly in place, two men scrambled up onto the deck. One of them, a huge figure, made straight for the foc's'tle, while the other looked on from the rail.

'Jack Brett!' The man stopped as the mate called ominously from the quarterdeck. 'I see you have your partner Mr Olsen with you, Jack. I'd like to say that it's a pleasure to welcome you on board, but it isn't. There's no man leaving this ship till we've loaded at the Chinchas and I'll have no crimpers aboard to try and make it otherwise. If you're not off the ship in the next ten seconds, then I'll start some target practice with this six-shooter I picked up in 'Frisco.' The first mate approached the big man steadily. Olsen was well over six feet two and the mate's lean figure seemed to shrink as he approached, but his hand was steady on the gun and he showed no fear. They stared steadily at one another and the crew looked on, waiting to see who would back down first.

Jack Brett stood his ground. 'You wouldn't talk like that without that revolver,' he said. 'Put that away and let's see what kind of man you really are.' A shiver of excitement ran around the crew. Since Mr Streicher had boarded in Australia they had all wanted to see him beaten, and there was little doubt that Olsen would have killed him if he could.

'Since you're interested,' said the mate, 'I'll show you what kind of man I really am.' He raised the gun and squinted along its sights. With a dull thud, a puff of smoke flew out of the barrel and all hands looked towards Jack Brett, whose face blanched as the bullet hit his black felt stovepipe hat and shot it from his head into the sea behind him. Still he hesitated and the mate raised the gun again. 'Revolvers are a clever invention; there's still five more where that came from.' Jack Brett turned and jumped overboard, with Olsen close behind.

The Captain, apparently completely indifferent to the crimpers, was in no less of a hurry and had his gig lowered away without even a word to his first mate, calling Milo and Arnie to row him ashore. They nudged their way through the flotilla of boats plying busily between the ships and the shore. Along the mole, a row of boys and apprentices were guarding their skippers' gigs. One of them took their painter and made them fast while Captain Brockman stepped ashore. 'If anything's taken while I'm at the shipping office, then I'll hand you over to Mr Streicher,' he growled the words ominously. 'At least you won't be tempted by the liquor – the Callao *pisco's* too strong for either of you. Stay here: I'll be back later.' He stumped off through the crowds, who seemed to melt away in front of him.

The apprentice who had taken their lines came over. 'German ship?' he asked, and they nodded warily. 'First time in Callao?' They told him nervously that it was. They had never been so close to the Captain before and were still shaken by his threats.

'It doesn't get much worse than this,' said the lad, and they looked around gloomily. Beyond the shingle beach were row upon row of dilapidated houses. Crumbling masonry lay in piles, shaken off by previous earthquakes. Towers and spires of innumerable churches pierced the decrepit scene. The flimsy houses had once been painted, but the walls were now stained a dirty yellow, and were rotting in the damp. In places, the mud caked onto the bamboo laths had collapsed, leaving entire rooms open to the streets. The unpaved roads leading away from the docks teemed with people of all races, languages and colours, jostling and pushing, shouting, laughing and crying. Smoke from open fires swathed the sea front with pungent, acrid fumes. At the far end, just visible through the haze, work was under way on a new floating dock that jutted out into the bay. Nearer to, jars of *pisco* brandy were being guarded by armed men in dirty uniforms. Unrefined sugar cane was baled inside plantain leaves and clouds of flies covered them in a black, shifting blanket. Drunken cries were everywhere and dense crowds of people circled around numerous fights. A damp mist cast a grey pall over the port and the hills of Lima, a few miles beyond.

'So this is what hell looks like,' said Arnie.

'You've got it,' said the lad. 'And you'll be able to study it all day before your old man comes back.'

'How can they live with this disgusting smell?' asked Milo.

The lad laughed. 'You get used to it when you've been here long enough. This is my third trip; we were finally homeward bound when a shroud parted. Our Old Man reckons that someone cut it on purpose so he could jump ship when we came back, but he's not letting anyone ashore except me. He reckons that I'm too young to want a drink, though to tell the truth I'm too afraid of him to even think of it. I've seen how he deals with the sailors when we were loading at the Chinchas.' He paused. 'I suppose that's where you're going?'

'That's what the second mate told us,' said Arnie. 'Is it far?'

'No, but it's dead against the wind, so it'll take you a fair while. It's not bad when you get there. There's good fishing, and if you're waiting for the chute there's not much else to do.'

'You haven't met our first mate. He wouldn't let us waste time fishing. The only choice we have on our ship is working or a thrashing,' said Arnie. 'Anyway, what cargo can you get from an island?'

'Guano,' said the lad. 'You see the clouds of birds wheeling and diving before you even see the islands. There's so many fish in the sea the birds can eat all they want – and more. Doesn't matter how many birds there are, there's always enough fish for 'em. An' they leave their droppings all over. There's guano all along the coast south of here, but out in the Chinchas it's ninety feet deep in places. Just building up over hundreds of years with nothing to stop it. Fifteen years ago they took some to Europe and tried it out as a fertiliser, and it's been bedlam here ever since. They can't get enough of it.'

They relapsed into silence as they looked around the ships in the bay. 'Look at that Russian barque: ain't she an apple?' said the lad after a while. 'Only eight hundred tons, but she's logged over four hundred miles a day.' He stopped and they looked around some more. 'See that hulk over there being used as a store-ship? That's the Naiad – she was at the battle of Trafalgar.'

There must have been over eighty ships in the bay and the two boys studied them with interest. Finally Milo asked, 'What d'you think our Old Man's doing ashore? Why don't we go straight to the islands and load up?'

'Gone to find some native Cholos to trim the guano in the holds, I expect,' answered the lad. 'Most sailors can't take the ammonia fumes – they make your eyeballs bleed unless you're used to it.'

'It's still safer than gunpowder, though,' said Milo.

'Until you have a fire – then you should see it go up. I'll tell you there's more ways of dying at sea than you can think of. Why we do it?'

'Promotion,' said Arnie. 'I'm doing it for promotion, and the money.'

'There isn't enough money in the world to keep me at sea,' said Milo bitterly. 'Look at those poor beggars over there in that lighter. Where are they taking them?'

The lad looked across towards the small ship, low in the water, weighed down by what seemed like a solid block of men. 'Chinese coolies,' he said. 'Brought across to work the guano deposits. They're on contract, but when they're on board they're locked up below decks for the three-month passage, just like cattle. Dozens of 'em never make it across alive.' He shrugged. 'Those are the lucky ones. You should see it out there – I don't think any of 'em lives long enough to finish the contract. Poor bastards. No one sees it as slavery, but it's difficult to tell the difference. They might be Chinamen, but they're still human beings. You'd never guess that the owners and Captains are all God-fearing men, taking money for cargoes like that.'

As the lighter approached, the overpowering smell of the dirty, emaciated bodies hit them, and they watched the sullen and silent workers pass by. The pale figures, covered in grime and filth, were still, staring vacantly ahead without emotion and without hope.

'What a place,' said Milo finally.

They were loading at the Chinchas for nearly three months. For most of the ships, it was a diversion from the dangers of life at sea, but on the Hanover the officers kept the crew working, often on unnecessary tasks, and mutiny was never far below the surface. Milo watched moodily as crews from other ships organised boat races and fishing expeditions. He had never imagined there could be so many fish. They were packed so tightly that simply pulling a line through the shoal was enough to spear a mackerel on the hook. At night, the American ships were lit up with coloured lanterns and the Captains' wives kept up incessant socialising and even dancing. Such was the huge demand for guano that there were close on three hundred ships at anchor around the three islands, either waiting their turn to be loaded from the main big ship chute, or ferrying the sacks and loading from hired lighters. On shore, Milo had watched the Chinese labourers work on the sheer cliff faces of white guano, digging and bagging amid the dust and overpowering smell of the deposits. Each gang was worked by an overseer with a twenty-foot whip which was used skilfully and instinctively, without thought or mercy. Many of the coolies threw themselves into the sea rather than continue with the hopeless misery of their situation, preferring to take an early release from the slow and wretched death from which there was no other escape. Milo couldn't understand how such conditions could be tolerated so unquestioningly, when slavery in America was being fought at such cost. He was sickened by the pretensions of the Captains' wives, whose attempts to maintain their own elegant society afloat was sustained only by the inhuman conditions ashore.

Captain Brockman decided not to wait for the chute. Instead he got the first mate to organise loading from lighters. The work was backbreaking and desertion was impossible; there was nowhere to go to on the islands and no master would accept a man from another ship without the Captain's authority. To Milo it seemed that his future stretched away into darkness, offering no relief from the hopelessness of the seaman's life and the constant brutality that surrounded them.

'I can't take much more of this,' he said to Arnie, after supper one evening. 'There's no future in it. If we get this cargo back to Europe, there'll just be another one to pick up, and so it'll go on until I die. I want something more.'

'But if you stick with it, you could become an officer yourself, and then even a Captain. That's worth waiting for, isn't it?' Arnie looked earnestly at Milo. 'Can't you imagine it, being your own Captain? Able to do just as you please, making all the laws in your own kingdom? That's what I want one day.'

'Not for me,' said Milo. 'There's too much chance at sea — no wonder they're so superstitious. There's no pattern. It's too harsh, too aimless. How can you plan anything? You spend the whole time fighting whatever's thrown at you.'

'But there's money in it if you work your way up high enough. The ship's already covered its costs back to London and this guano will give the owners a clear profit of over five pounds per ton. The Captain's share of that is over a thousand pounds.'

'And what's our share — if we live long enough? Nothing! I want to work in a situation I can control.' Milo leant forward and lowered his voice. 'I'm not going to spend the rest of my life like this. When we get back to Callao, I've decided I'm going to stay there.'

'Jump ship? You must be crazy! You've seen the place — you wouldn't last five minutes.'

'I'll take my chances.' Milo hesitated. 'Arnie? Why don't you join me? There must be money to be made out there.'

'You were the one who told me to stick at it. I'm not going to give up now. We've both got to see this through — even if it does kill us.'

'No,' said Milo. 'Not me. I've had enough. When we get back to Callao the Captain will get us to row him to the quay. We'll be the only ones he can trust ashore, and that'll be our chance. There'll be no one to stop us.'

~~~~~

With the harrowing scenes of the guano fields still vivid in his memory, Milo found it an unlikely relief to be surrounded by the rancid stench of Callao bay. As he had anticipated, the Captain again chose the two boys to take him ashore to complete his paperwork with the Peruvian authorities. Waiting on the mole by the boat, they were free to go where they wanted, but Arnie remained adamant that he would stay with the ship. The most Milo could do was get him to walk into town to look around, convincing him that Captain Brockman wouldn't return until late in the afternoon. As they pushed through the crowds lining the streets, Milo was constantly heckled by the locals. 'It's the hair,' said Arnie looking around at the dark men surrounding them. 'No one else has fair hair. If you play your cards right, perhaps you can persuade them you're a God. That would stop you worrying about your future — you'd be immortal.'

Milo shuddered. 'Can you imagine it — an eternity in this place?' They walked past the peddlers lining the street. Card games and lottery sellers were side by side with *pisco* booths and trinket stalls. Boys pestered them continually, begging for food, offering worthless shells or the more enterprising offering lottery tickets. More boys lay in the doorways, immobilised by dreadful diseases, while in the windows above, handkerchiefs fluttered in outstretched arms as the women advertised their presence to the sailors.

Milo put out his arm out to stop Arnie. 'See that?' he pointed towards a stall on the corner. 'Let's just wait here a while.'

Arnie had no idea what Milo meant. 'What are we waiting for?' he asked.

'Look, they're playing Find the Lady. You've got to gamble on which thimble the pea's under.'

'No one's ever won on that,' said Arnie. They're always too fast.'

'You've just got to see through the bluff, that's all,' said Milo who watched as two sailors handed over some money and walked away from the stall, grumbling loudly. Milo looked up and down the street. As another group of sailors approached the stall, he jumped out and put a dollar on the table. The stallholder looked at him with surprise, and then saw the approaching sailors and set the pea rolling between the thimbles. The sailors stood behind Milo, watching carefully. The pea was passed rapidly from one thimble to the other, but still slowly enough for the onlookers to imagine they could follow it. The stallholder stopped moving the thimbles and looked at Milo, who picked up the dollar and paused before carefully placing it next to one of the thimbles. 'That one,' he said pointing. 'The pea's in that one.'

With an exaggerated sigh, the stallholder lifted the thimble and picked up the pea from underneath it. He peeled off some notes and pushed them across the table. 'Try again, boy?' he said. 'You sailors, you want to try?' Milo picked up the notes and walked back towards Arnie as the stallholder called him back. 'Hey boy, let me win it back.'

Milo ignored him. 'See how it's done?' he said to Arnie. 'He let me win when he saw the sailors coming. They'll think they can all do it and he'll win back far more from them than he lost to me.'

Arnie shook his head. 'Normally I'd call that clever, but he doesn't seem too happy.' He indicated the stallholder, who was approaching them, still shouting at Milo.

'He's just a poor loser,' said Milo, backing away.

'He seems to have some friends,' shouted Arnie as two uniformed men carrying rifles ran over. The stallholder gabbled quickly at the officers and shouted again, pointing to the boys.

'Let's get back to the boat, and fast.' Arnie didn't wait, but dodged behind the stall and ran back towards the docks. 'Come on,' he shouted over his shoulder.

Milo started forward but the policemen had separated and one of them was now blocking his route. He backed against the wall, looking around frantically for an escape. 'I haven't done anything wrong.' He kept his voice unnaturally calm; he knew they couldn't understand what he was saying, but didn't want to look guilty. 'I won the money fairly, but I'll give it back if he wants.' The men weren't interested. One held up the barrel of his rifle and cut Milo's shirt with the tip of his bayonet. The other took out some handcuffs and clipped them over Milo's wrists, pushing him up the street. Milo shouted out in every language he knew, but when he fell, they just dragged him over the rocks and potholes of the unmade road.

Milo was too scared to notice where they went until he was pulled through a gateway into a courtyard. Looking around him dumbly, all he could see was a wall of dark steel bars and arms waving through the gaps like snakes writhing in a pit. A door was unlocked ahead of him and he was thrown in amongst them.

It had all been too sudden. Milo couldn't work out what had happened. What was this place? Why had he been brought here? What had he done wrong? He crawled back through the heaving bodies and wedged himself against a corner of the walls. It was very dark and the fetid smell made him retch with nausea. He could barely see the daylight through the pressing mass of people. He could just make out a set of stocks in the centre of the cell, where an old man had fallen, held only by his thin wrists, his legs splayed out awkwardly against its base. Milo listened to the man's feverish, guttural moans and watched as his body started shuddering fiercely in regular spasms. Milo felt desolation overwhelm him like a black cloud. It seemed that his destiny was to be a victim and it was pointless to fight against it.

The day passed slowly. Milo could tell from the shouts of the prisoners when the guards approached and opened the gates, either to take someone away or add another poor wretch to the squalid mass. Each time his hopes grew that someone from the ship had come to explain that it had all been a mistake and to take him away. Each time his hopes faded as he was left, ignored by the other men. He unfixed his locket and rubbed it between his fingers. It was his only link with the outside world. In the darkness at the back of the cell, he couldn't tell when night fell and lost any sense of time, falling into a daze which was somewhere between sleep and despair.

Chapter Ten

A hand shook him and pulled him to his feet. He followed blindly into the harsh brightness of a new day. Someone thrust his arm into a steel bracelet and clamped it shut around his wrist. With a jerk, he was dragged along with a dozen other men chained together, while the policemen kicked and jabbed at them with their bayonets. Milo stumbled along with rising hope; surely someone must see him. Someone would help him. The chained men were taken towards the centre of the town, and led into another cell in the back of one of the few stone buildings near the main Plaza. The guards unlocked him and took him into a small courtroom where, facing him, he saw the two policemen who had arrested him. He tried to speak, but they ignored him and continued talking amongst themselves. He heard the judge rap his gavel and he just understood the words 'sixteen soles' before he was led back to the courtroom cells. Sixteen soles! Milo couldn't believe it. That's more than he'd earn for the entire passage.

As the guard locked the gate behind him, Milo saw that another sailor had been brought in, and lay snoring intermittently against the wall. Milo felt some hope. He approached the man and shook him gently, but he was out cold. Damned sailors, Milo swore softly: why can't you ever rely on them? He slapped the man's face, frightened that he might suddenly retaliate. 'Wake up, for Christ's sake, wake up!'

The sailor opened one eye and then the next. 'What, what is it? Where am I?' Consciousness spread over him and he looked around the cell slowly. 'I've been in worse,' he said after a while and looked at Milo. 'Where are you from, boy? You're not from hereabouts.'

'No, sir,' Milo judged it prudent to remain respectful. 'I'm from the Hanover, but the police grabbed me and put me in a cell. We weren't doing anything wrong, but they wouldn't listen.'

The sailor shook his head slowly, as if to check that it was still attached securely. ''Course they wouldn't, son. They don't need a reason to arrest you – mind you in my case, they usually have one. How much was the fine? – it's normally sixteen soles, but it could be less for a boy.'

'No, sixteen soles – that's the only thing I understood. That's nearly four pounds; where do they think I can find that sort of money?'

The sailor laughed. 'I see you don't understand the local customs. It's about the same rate as the crimpers would charge. They arrest the sailors and the Captain has to pay the fine to get them back. They don't need a reason. The policeman gets a cut, so does the jailer – even the judge. There're not many people who make an honest living in Callao.' The sailor looked at Milo and saw the tears starting to roll down his cheeks. 'Don't worry, lad, the Captains know how it works. Your skipper'll come and get you.'

'You don't know Captain Brockman,' said Milo. 'He couldn't care less about his crew. He'll just say I fell overboard.'

'Not Bully Brockman?' asked the sailor. 'I served with him when he was a second officer, and a right vicious piece of work he was then. But don't you worry – he'll come. He'll have to report to the owners when he gets back, and while they're not too bothered about losing the odd sailor, it doesn't look good if a Captain leaves one of the boys behind.'

'I hope you're right,' said Milo gloomily. 'But from what I've seen, passage times are the only thing the owners are interested in.'

The guards came for his cellmate during the afternoon and handed him over to his Captain. As he stumbled off he shouted to Milo, 'What did I tell you? They'll come for you soon enough, you'll see. You be sure and give my regards to Bully Brockman. Good luck, lad.'

Milo had taken hope from the sailor's cheerful presence, but now that he was alone, his depression returned. In the evening the guards chained up all the men who remained, and dragged them back to the stinking hole on the edge of the city. As they approached, the smell hit him again.

Just one more night, he thought; they've got to come for me in the morning. I can take just one more night.

The morning arrived slowly. Milo watched the new arrivals chained and dragged off to court, but no one came for him. Slowly his hopes faded and his loneliness grew. Even when the occasional sailor was tossed into the cell, they were too drunk to talk, while everyone else acted as though he didn't exist. He even found himself missing his ship – something he'd never thought possible. It seemed that whatever he found, it was only to lose it again soon afterwards. Even if he got out of here, who would take on a boy from prison? He thought of the ragged beggars he'd seen in the doorways on his short walk through Callao. He couldn't end up like that. Surreptitiously he took out his locket and looked down at it. A band glinted dully where he had been rubbing it with his thumb. Holding it inside his jacket, he opened it and stared at the portrait. Sipan seemed so far away.

As that day dragged into the next, he became convinced that he'd been forgotten and that his situation was hopeless. After two days with no sign of rescue, he started to think about escape – but where could he go? He had little idea where he was, couldn't speak the language and he knew no one. On the third morning, the guards arrived to assemble the men for the court. Almost as an afterthought, one of them grabbed Milo and, without a word, chained him to the others and dragged him away. After the overwhelming stench of the town jail, Milo felt some relief as he was thrown into the court cells. But it was the lack of comprehension he found so oppressive – he had no understanding of what these men intended for him and was wholly unable to influence it. He slumped down helplessly onto the hard stone floor and resumed his pointless wait, while increasing apathy emptied his mind. But after several hours, a change in the normal sounds of the courthouse jail roused him, and he looked towards the doorway beyond the steel bars. A slamming of doors echoed down into the cell and with the respectful clicking of heels from the warders, a tall, slightly stooping European swept in and approached the heavy steel bars. He looked around carefully, inspecting the inmates. Another man hurried in behind him skipping to keep up. For the first time in days, Milo heard some words he understood. They were finally going to release him. But the taller man turned and walked away. 'No, he's not here after all.'

Milo scrambled to his feet and forced his way through the press of the crowded men. 'Sir, sir – please help me.'

The second European stared at him. 'Who are you, boy? What are you here for? Where are you from?'

Milo tipped his forelock, hoping to impress. 'From the Hanover, sir. I've been here several days, sir. I don't, I don't know what for...' His voice trailed off as he fought back the tears. He had to appear in control of himself.

The man didn't seem to notice Milo's distress. 'Have you been in front of the judge? What did he say?'

'Yes, sir,' Milo tried to breathe normally, but stammered with the relief at finally being able to talk to someone. 'I think he fined me sixteen soles, but I don't have it.'

'Of course you don't,' said the man tersely. 'What's the man thinking of? So your Captain went without you, then?' he asked Milo.

'I don't know sir. I haven't spoken to anyone. I don't know what's happening.'

'The Hanover left a couple of days ago. Looks like you're here to stay. I'd better speak to that fool of a judge.' His tone changed from terseness to deference as he addressed the taller man, waiting by the door. 'I'm sorry about this, sir. The man we're looking for doesn't appear to be here, but I'd better see about this boy.'

'Of course you must. I'll wait here for you.'

'Oh, you can't do that, Mr Hurst. I'm sure they'll let you wait in the office.'

'No, leave me here. I'll talk to the boy.' The taller man spoke with authority and didn't wait for agreement as he turned towards Milo. 'Well now, so what have you been up to? You can start by telling me your name. My name's Martin Hurst, by the way.'

Milo looked at him. In spite of his obvious importance and the deference shown to him, his eyes were friendly and bright with curiosity. In contrast to his impatient and severe manner, there was a warmth and interest in the way the man spoke. Milo found himself pouring out his experiences as though to his own father. The words tumbled out while the man listened to him carefully, nodding occasionally in sympathy.

The shorter man returned before Milo could tell his story fully. 'Seems he was out thieving,' he said. 'Tried to steal from one of the stallholders.'

'That's not true!' Milo shouted and flushed with anger. 'I won the money fairly.'

'Now, now,' said the tall man soothingly. 'We understand how these things work – we can sort it all out later.' He turned to his colleague. 'When are they going to let him go?'

'I'm sorry, sir, but the judge says he's not letting him out until the fine is paid.'

'Oh, he does?' said Mr Hurst. 'I think I'll have a word with him myself.'

~~~~~

Milo sat looking out of the window at the lush green garden which surrounded the house. His rapid change in fortune had left him bewildered. Martin Hurst, with a quiet but unquestioned determination, had him released from the courtroom jail within the hour and had taken him the few miles up to the city of Lima, which almost seemed like a silent retreat after the fevered activity of Callao. Mr Hurst's colleague, Otto Luschke, clearly disapproved, but Mr Hurst just laughed at him. 'Don't mind him, Milo,' he said. 'He's the Consul for the port of

Callao, and after what he's seen over the years, he's grown quite indifferent to anything that goes on down there.' Otto Luschke had nodded with some feeling.

Milo was confused. What Europeans had the power to get him released so quickly from prison? He stared uncomprehendingly through the carriage window until they pulled up at an imposing building and an elaborately uniformed guard opened the door and pulled down the steps. 'Welcome to our Embassy,' said Mr Hurst. 'Mr Luschke has agreed to make you an honorary citizen until we can decide what to do with you. Though I suspect that if he had his way, you'd be thrown right back in jail.'

They walked up the steps into the biggest hall Milo had ever seen. A gilded coat of arms faced the doorway and gloomy, austere portraits darkened the walls and staircase. Martin Hurst asked a footman to bring some food and led Milo into a small reception room. Milo fell upon the food hungrily and ate without saying a word. Mr Hurst watched him carefully until he had finished. 'Tell me about your family at home,' he said finally.

Milo looked at him warily for a moment. Hesitantly he put his hand inside his tattered shirt and slipped the chain from around his neck, gripping it tightly in his palm. Slowly he started to explain how the Bossanos had dismissed his father, forcing his brother to sea before he was ready. As he told of the storm, his tears returned and Martin held his shoulder tightly and shook him gently, as though to force him into the present. Milo opened the locket and held it out to Martin, who took it and looked down at the portrait. 'It's my father,' said Milo. 'I never knew him: he died before I was born. It was all my mother had to give me. After what the Bossanos did to us, I've got to get back.'

Martin snapped the locket shut and handed it back to Milo. 'Don't worry about that now; first we've got to decide where you're to stay. This embassy is no place for a child and I've got the impression that Mr Luschke here doesn't exactly approve of children. So that just leaves my house, I suppose. Would you like to come home with me?'

Milo had agreed eagerly. The rank smell of prison still permeated his clothes and he would have agreed to anything that kept him away from Callao. They left Otto in his office and returned to the carriage outside. During the short drive Martin Hurst described the places they were passing, but Milo took in none of it. As they pulled through a large gateway, they turned down a driveway which passed through grass as green as any on Šipan. To Milo it looked like paradise. 'What do you think of my gardens?'

111

asked Mr Hurst. 'The soil in these valleys is excellent, but it doesn't rain here and it needs irrigation. This was almost a desert when I took it over.' He pointed ahead through the carriage window. 'Welcome to the Villa Miraflores,' he said. Milo looked at the immaculate villa ahead – it was almost a palace, set on a small rise amid the lawns. Milo thought of Šipan – this was how it was meant to be. The grounds were perfect; everything was in order and nothing out of place.

'Are you the Ambassador?' asked Milo.

Mr Hurst laughed. 'Goodness, no. I haven't got time to be a politician. It would take far too long to get involved in the politics of this country – not that anyone can understand them anyway. No, I'm a farmer. I've got several plantations in the north, but they've made me the Honorary Consul for Trade. That's why I was down in Callao this morning – there's some problem with a shipment. Some fellow's gone off with the letters of credit – although he can't get far with them.' He opened the door as another uniformed footman pulled down the steps and he jumped down them. 'Follow me, Milo, I'll introduce you to Mrs Hurst.'

Milo went up the steps and through the high double doors. He had felt too numb to understand what was happening. Mr Hurst led him into a drawing room, sat him down and walked through the French windows into the garden. Milo watched as Mr Hurst entered a large conservatory and emerged after a few moments, talking excitedly to a woman. He stood up as Mr Hurst ushered her into the room. 'Lisa, my dear, this is Milo Beran. He seems to have lost his ship and I thought he could stay for a few days.'

Milo just stared. He hadn't heard anyone use his family name in nearly a year and as he looked at Mrs Hurst, he fell back onto the settee. Fräulein Wolff, he thought: the resemblance was extraordinary. The same colour hair, the same figure. But of course it wasn't her. It was just his imagination.

Feeling even more confused, he stammered a few words. 'I'm sorry, Miss... Mrs Hurst. Your husband has been so kind, but my ship... you see, I was arrested. Fined. I didn't know anyone. No one could understand me.'

Mrs Hurst walked over to him and held out her arms, smiling. 'I'm sure you can tell me everything later. Don't worry about it: we'll look after you.' Milo was overcome. After his short life at sea, he had forgotten that such warmth and kindness existed. His carefully sustained independence collapsed, and he abandoned himself to the warmth of her soft embrace.

It had taken a dozen baths before Milo had felt clean again. At home, so much of his life had been spent swimming in the clear waters around the island that he found the dirt and grime of Callao and the guano fields difficult to eradicate. But now, as he looked over the garden, he finally felt that he'd left the prison behind him. Mrs Hurst had listened to him carefully as he told her again about his arrest in Callao. Hotly he denied any thieving and when he explained how he had managed to win, she had clapped her hands with delight. 'What happened to the money?' she asked. Milo pulled out some crumpled notes from the back of his trousers. Mrs Hurst laughed. 'At least you've got something to show for it.'

Milo found an easiness about the household. Everything seemed so natural. Mrs Hurst hadn't forced anything on him, but had been a constant and sympathetic presence. She was such a contrast to her husband. While he was impatient and full of energy, she seemed so calm and easy-going. He had become so accustomed to aggression at sea, even in the simplest things, that he basked in her relaxed and even-tempered attitude. He wanted to stay forever.

'Would you like to stay here with us?' asked Lisa Hurst one morning. Two months had already passed, and each day Milo had woken expecting to be sent back to jail. He could still barely understand the transformation. 'Martin and I have been talking about it, and you don't want to return to sea and – well, we have no children. We seem to get on well, don't we, so we could look after you.' There was a trace of anxiety in the way she looked at Milo. 'We could keep each other company when Mr Hurst is away at the plantations. We could find a teacher to continue your lessons. The city might be small, but it's growing and more people are arriving from Europe every day. What with the sugar and the cotton plantations, now there's the guano as well, so there's a good future here.'

Milo had finally recovered. He felt he was no longer simply being buffeted by events. He no longer felt a victim. He had choices, however limited. His reply was simple and heartfelt. 'Yes, Mrs Hurst: I'd like to stay.'

The relief he had felt after he had said it was overwhelming. No longer did he have looming over him the fear of spending the rest of his life at sea or, worse, scrabbling to make a living in places like Callao. This way he was secure and could plan his future – plan his return to Šipan.

'Milo, I'd like you to meet someone.' Milo was so far away in his thoughts that he hadn't heard Martin and Lisa come into the room. He turned away from the window and Lisa introduced him to the young man who had followed them in. 'This is Mr Miller;

he's just finished University back home in Europe and he has agreed to give you lessons. He was brought up in Chile and I knew his family slightly when I stayed in Valparaiso. I think we're very lucky to find him.'

Robert Miller held up his hands. 'No, Mrs Hurst, it's the other way around. I didn't imagine that I would land on my feet quite so soon after arriving – that is, if Milo wants me.'

'I'd like to start lessons again,' said Milo. 'I've missed my old teacher back in Dalmatia.'

Mr Hurst smiled broadly. 'Everything seems to be falling into place. In a few days I've got to get back to the estates in Napeña Valley, but you and Mrs Hurst can come and join me – and Robert too, if he'll come.'

'I've heard a lot about them, Mr Hurst. I'd look forward to seeing them for myself,' Robert said.

'Well, that's settled then,' said Lisa, beaming with satisfaction. 'Since Mr Miller has himself only just arrived, you can explore Peru together. We normally join Mr Hurst in July or August for the winter, to escape the *garúa* – the mist makes it quite cold here, and it's much more pleasant further north. During the winter months it's often hard to remember that we're still in the tropics.'

'We'll leave you two to get to know each other. Milo, show Mr Miller around the house and we'll talk about all the details later.' Martin Hurst was a man who liked to leave details to others.

Left to themselves, Milo and Robert were at first wary of one another. Both wondered what the other was looking for in this opulent house. Robert was suspicious that Milo might be taking advantage of the Hursts and questioned whether he really deserved his education, let alone whether he was capable of understanding anything. For Milo's part, he considered that Robert was not serious enough and was simply looking to spend an easy time under the Hursts' roof for as long as he could. When, a few days later, they started their first lesson, the atmosphere was heavy and the conversation stilted. Robert finally put down his book. 'Milo, what is the problem? You're clearly holding back; what's the matter?'

'Nothing,' said Milo

'You can't always be this difficult. I thought you said you wanted to learn.'

Milo thought about what he was going to say. Whatever Robert's motives, they affected him directly. 'Back home in Šipan I had a teacher, Fräulein Wolff – she was so different from you. She didn't have to teach us, she didn't get paid for it;

we knew she just wanted to help us. But I don't understand why you're doing this. With your qualifications you could do better than a job teaching me.'

Robert looked at him with surprise. 'Is that what it is? You think I'm up to something, and here I was worrying about you. Yes, I do want a better job than tutoring, but you don't understand how the system works. To get a job in one of the trading houses I have to be articled as a clerk, and for that I need some money. My parents don't do that badly, but they haven't enough to pay for one of the best houses. I could do a lot worse than teach for a year or so, until I've made a few contacts and saved up my wages.' Robert saw that Milo was watching him carefully. 'Look,' he said, 'Let's get this straight. We're both going to help each other. I want to be here, the Hursts want us both here, and you want to stay here. No one's taking advantage of anyone.'

Robert was proved right. As their lessons progressed, they both forgot their fears. Robert was still young enough to take pleasure in learning for its own sake, and found himself struggling to keep up with Milo's questioning attitude and confident ability. Milo was impressed that Robert's apparently facile manner hid a genuine grasp of his subjects and together they developed an easy routine, so that in spite of their age difference, they became almost inseparable. Robert realised how protected his own childhood had been and that his own education afforded him independence. He wanted Milo to gain the same independence and took care that his teaching would at least contribute to it. Milo, in turn, revelled in the obvious pleasure which Robert took from his progress, and was mortified by Robert's disappointment at his occasional mistakes. Life for Milo had finally regained its balance.

The steamer service was notoriously unreliable and it could take up to a week to travel the few hundred miles north to the sugar port of Samanco. But the ship was generally comfortable and it was a relief to get away from the cloying dampness of Lima. Martin Hurst was waiting for them at the quayside and greeted them with his usual irrepressible energy. Without allowing them to rest, he marched them off along the quay, beckoning impatiently at the porters to follow them. He rushed them towards a hut behind the docks where a pale young man, only slightly older than Robert, was waiting outside. 'This is James Young. He's the engineer for my new railroad. Come on, we'll show you.' He ushered them into the shack.

Milo squinted in the darkness. On the other side of the room, a man was looking through a small window across to the port. In spite of the temperature outside he was dressed in a dark frock coat. He turned and smiled broadly. 'You must be Milo,' he said, holding out his hand. 'So we meet finally. I'm Emilio Vasco. I'm Mr Hurst's banker.'

Milo studied him with interest. Everything about the man was dark – his clothes, his hair, his shiny dark complexion – but in spite of that he had a wide and easy smile and his eyes twinkled with good humour. Milo walked over and shook his hand. 'I've heard so much about you, Señor Vasco. You've been such a good friend to Mr and Mrs Hurst.'

'Over here,' Martin Hurst interrupted impatiently. 'You'll like this, Milo. We've built a model of the port showing how the ships are to be loaded. Look at that.' He pulled the sheet off a table with a flourish, revealing a scale model of the proposed port. All the contours, rocks and islands had been recreated in detail. The new railroad track was shown as a cutting through the hillside, working its way down to the new quay to be constructed to the south of the bay. Real model trains ran on the miniature rails. 'The railroad will lead from the sugar refinery to the dockside here at Samanco. The sugar will be discharged directly into the ships.'

Even the banker was impressed. 'How long have you been working on this, Martin?' he said after he had studied it for several minutes. 'Is it all surveyed yet?'

'That's nearly finished. James has been working on it for months and has pegged out the entire route, right from the loading bays of the refinery. It's feasible and it's costed down to the last peso. Your bank could do well from this.'

Emilio laughed. He'd always enjoyed Martin's enthusiasm, but knew that it could sometimes result in impulsiveness. 'I'm sure you've got all the figures worked out to the last peso, but do you think we could get to the estate before you ask me to look at them?'

The Hursts' hacienda at Huacatambo was at the head of the long, narrow Napeña valley. The drive was dusty, but Milo was enchanted by everything he saw. The sparkling sea beyond the fields reminded him so strongly of Šipan that he almost wept at the memories of what he had left behind.

Martin Hurst was a proud guide to his estate. Although the sugar plantations had been there for many years, they were virtually abandoned when he had first acquired them. He took them through the valleys, explaining how the Incas had cultivated the lands for hundreds of years before the Spanish conquests. He showed them the old ruins spread throughout the area. A ruined fortress, hundreds of feet in length, was still intact and they inspected the massive stone walls, built with joints so tight a paper would scarcely fit between them. James Young was intrigued by the engineering of the old stone reservoirs. He was amazed by the sophistication of the ancient societies which had managed to build such elaborate structures, fed from local springs. They compared the marvels of centuries-old engineering with the apathy of the indigent Indians who had simply allowed the land to return to desert. Individual Europeans had created pockets of cultivation over the years, and the remains of Jesuit communities were still evident in the small chapels that remained, but until Martin Hurst had taken over, no effort had been made to exploit the rich soil commercially. He had seized the opportunities and pursued them single-mindedly; Milo admired the spirit behind the enterprise and the way Martin seemed to bring out the best in each worker. Milo could not help comparing Martin's approach to what his father might have done with the estate on Šipan had he been allowed to.

Martin Hurst's unswerving dedication to his estate and its workers was a revelation to Milo. Engineers had been brought over from Europe to re-establish intricate irrigation systems. In time, he had built systems so sophisticated that the fields could be brought to harvest in rotation, allowing the workers to move from one field to the next throughout the autumn. Although many of the estate's workers were still Negro slaves, Martin Hurst treated them all the same and was as proud of the villages he had built for them as he was of the machinery they worked. He recognised the need to invest, and spent even more money on transport than on irrigation, saying there was no point in growing a crop if you couldn't deliver it to your customers. He was the first to build a railroad between his estates and the refinery, and the success of the project now led him to continue the line to the sea.

Emilio Vasco examined the booming estates carefully. For nearly a week the two men stayed up each evening, late into the night, examining the plans and checking the figures, while James Young explained the systems he had designed. When everything had been settled, Emilio agreed to stay, on condition that Martin didn't mention work. Lisa had laughed at this. 'Martin can't last five minutes without thinking about work. I doubt that he could last an hour without talking about it.'

'Even if he does talk about it I won't be listening,' said Emilio. 'I haven't had time to talk to Milo yet, and I'm impatient to hear all about his adventures at sea.'

When the winter mists faded over Lima, they returned to the Villa Miraflores and Robert and Milo once again resumed the routine of their lessons. Milo studied Spanish as a beginner, as well as working on the English he had picked up on his voyages.

Lisa often joined them, sitting quietly in the corner, noting the rapid progress Milo was making. She would arrange reading tests, for which Milo prepared carefully, noting with delight how proud Robert became of his pupil's achievements – so the summer passed quickly, quietly and contentedly. Milo treasured the calm and security after his turbulent life, even though he could never take it for granted – he still half expected to wake up one morning to find himself shanghaied and alone again at sea. But as the time approached for their next visit to Huacatambo, Milo started to notice that Robert's attitude began to change subtly. He seemed more tense – almost preoccupied – and Milo feared that his life was about to be rearranged again. Robert ended their last lesson early, shutting his book with a sudden snap. Milo jumped slightly with surprise.

'Milo, I don't know how to tell you this,' Robert started hesitantly. 'After we return from Huacatambo, it's going to be different.' Milo said nothing. Was this the change he had been dreading? He looked warily at Robert, waiting for him to confirm his fears. 'I'm not coming back,' Robert said finally. 'You know I didn't intend to be a tutor for ever, and with what I've earned here, I'll have just enough after the winter to buy a clerkship in one of the trading houses.'

'Has someone offered you a place yet?' asked Milo cautiously.

'Yes, the Banco de Commerçio. They're quite small, but they're growing fast and are looking for ambitious men to join them. It's agreed that I shall join them when I return.'

'But they act for the Garcias. You know they're Mr Hurst's main competitors.'

'Only in business,' answered Robert. 'You know that Señor Garcia and Mr Hurst are on good terms socially.'

'From what I've seen, social relations don't seem to count for much in business,' said Milo. 'Knowing Mr Hurst, do you really think if it came to a business matter he'd give Señor Garcia the time of day? It would be a fight to the death.'

'Well, it's not going to come to that,' said Robert. 'The sugar and guano markets are both growing; there's enough room for everyone, and with the new railroad Mr Hurst will be in a strong position for the future. There's nothing to worry about, Milo. Anyway, it's about time you went to the Institute school and met some people of your own age. You can let the adults worry about business.'

Chapter Eleven

1868 – Four years later

The steamer edged alongside the new quay at Samanco and Milo and Emilio looked across to the new marshalling yards. The railroad had been completed over a year earlier and had proved a stunning success, with repayments already well ahead of schedule. Martin waited impatiently for the gangplank to be lowered, anxious to show them the proposed extensions to his plantations at Matotambo. James Young went on deck to organise the unloading of their luggage. As they gathered at the foot of the gangplank, Milo noticed for the first time the two women standing back from the group.

It was clear they were mother and daughter. The obvious resemblance, the way they stood holding on to each other, was too striking to miss. The daughter seemed quite young, perhaps a year or so younger than Milo himself. She was looking at him with the same expression as her mother, a sort of tolerant smile that made Milo feel they were laughing at him for reasons he couldn't understand. It made him feel uncomfortable; he had never been comfortable with Lisa Hurst's female friends. But the daughter was undeniably attractive, dark hair and trim figure; she was swinging unselfconsciously on her mother's arm. As James came down the gangway, Milo looked at him questioningly.

James stepped forward quickly. 'I'm sorry. Can I introduce Mrs Hellman and Alicia, her daughter? Señor Emilio Vasco and Milo Beran.' Milo bowed formally, feeling his face redden.

Before Milo could say anything, James suddenly looked around in surprise. 'But where's Mrs Hurst?' he asked. 'You said she was coming with you.'

'She's been delayed with family matters,' replied Milo. 'She'll be up in a few weeks.'

'Oh, what a shame!' said Mrs Hellman. 'Alicia and I were looking forward to having some feminine company.'

James was also disappointed. He, too, had been looking forward to Lisa's visit, intending to show her his latest improvements. She always made a point of inspecting his progress and he enjoyed her simple compliments. Still, he thought, Milo would be impressed. 'So, what do you think?' he asked gesturing at the marshalling yards around him. 'We've just added these new loading ramps.'

Lines of wagons rattled backwards and forwards across the points. 'They can't have anything to rival this in Europe,' said Milo as he looked around intently, trying to understand the apparently random manoeuvres of the busy steam engines.

James laughed. 'You'd be more amazed if you saw some of the yards back home. This is tiny by comparison, but I'm still proud of it. Now it's nearly finished I suppose I'll soon have to find another job. Perhaps Señor Vasco can find me something in Lima, and then I can see you both more often.'

As they walked towards the waiting carriage, Alicia and her mother fell into step alongside Milo. 'It's such a pity Mrs Hurst isn't with you,' Mrs Hellman said. 'We were hoping she'd be able to show us around the estate. Mr Hurst seems so busy.'

'I'll be happy to show you,' Milo said quickly. 'I could take you in the trap.'

'On horseback,' Alicia said firmly. 'Horseback is the only way to see an estate properly.'

Milo looked at her in surprise. 'Do you ride much?' he asked.

'Whenever I can, but Mama doesn't approve of me riding by myself.'

They stopped to wait as the luggage was brought up. 'I understand you're studying at the Institute in Lima?' Alicia said. 'How do you like it? I know a lot of the students there.'

'I wouldn't call it studying. Not any more. I've learnt most of what they had to teach me some time back,' said Milo. 'I'm going to leave soon. Mr Hurst wants me to move up here.'

'It's certainly a lovely place,' Alicia said. 'So much nicer than Lima.'

Martin led Emilio and the Hellmans towards the carriage waiting to take them to Huacatambo. James turned to Milo. 'Pretty girl,' he said.

Milo nodded thoughtfully as he watched them go. 'And she likes horse riding.'

After a while he turned back to James. 'Tell me about Matotambo. What do you think of it?'

'To tell the truth, I haven't had much to do with it. Martin seems to want to keep it to himself.'

'It doesn't make sense to me,' Milo said. 'He's got enough land already. Why doesn't he diversify? Emilio and I both think there's much more money to be made elsewhere.'

James sighed. 'It's never going to be engineers who make the money – there'll never be much left after the banks and trading houses have taken their cut. The best decision I ever made was to leave Chile and move up here – look at the state they're in. The country's falling apart and they can't afford engineers. They won't be able to afford anyone until they sort themselves out.'

'There's talk of an invasion,' Milo said.

'What with?' James led Milo towards the trap and pulled himself up into the seat. 'What do I know about it, anyway? I've never understood politics.' He shrugged and held out his hand to Milo and pulled him up beside him. 'D'you ever see that teacher of yours?' he asked, changing the subject. 'Robert Miller, wasn't it? You seemed to get on so well together.'

'Sometimes,' Milo said guardedly, throwing his bags into the back. 'He still visits, but I think he finds it difficult to make the time. He seems to be doing well with the Garcias. They're lucky to have him.' Milo stopped for a moment and frowned. 'I just wish he hadn't joined the competition. I don't want him to become an enemy.'

Milo held the reins of his horse as he waited for Alicia. He looked at her away in the distance. She had stopped on the brow of a hill and was staring across the fields. Her slight outline was silhouetted against the clear blue sky. With the Andes pale in the distance, the black mare she was riding completed the picture. She seemed so at home here. In the past few days they had ridden across the entire Napeña estates and she had hardly faltered. On horseback she was at ease, a graceful and skilled rider. Even though Milo himself had been taught by Martin's best scouts, she had found no difficulty in keeping up with him: she was a natural horsewoman. He already felt so relaxed in her company that it was strange to remember they had been together just a few days. He watched her as she rode up to him. 'Martin's expecting us,' he said, getting back on his horse. 'We'd better go.'

Martin was waiting for them at the old winery. He and Emilio were sitting together in the shade on the rickety porch. 'So, what do you think of Matotambo?' Martin asked, getting up.

'Wonderful,' said Alicia. 'The air's so clear. It's magnificent riding.'

They looked back to the estate they had just toured. In the far distance the peak of Huascarán – the highest in Peru – was just visible, and in the fields stretching towards the foothills, teams of workmen were uprooting the old vines and replanting the new ones brought up from the dockside at Samanco. My father would approve, Milo thought, admiring the undulating rows of new vines, their leaves shimmering in the clear air. 'It reminds me of Šipan,' he said after a few moments. 'The other side of the world, but almost the same.' He suddenly noticed the huge wooden wine press, carved from the dark carob tree. 'I used to help my father with one just like that, though ours was made from oak. All the villagers joined in with the grape harvest; we didn't have any slaves – well, not until Rusa Bossano arrived on the island.' He wondered again what had happened to the vineyards on Šipan. Although he had continued to write home, he hadn't received any reply for several years.

The estate foreman rode up to them and Martin turned to Alicia. 'I'm sorry, my dear, do you mind? There're some things I want to talk to Milo about. Antonio can take you back to Huacatambo.'

'Men,' Alicia snorted. 'Always talking about work.' She pulled the reins of her horse and nodded at the foreman. 'I prefer to ride than listen to business talk. I'll see you later, Milo,' she called over her shoulder.

Martin turned and sat down heavily. He took a deep breath. 'So. What do you think? Would you like to take this on? Learn how things are run?' He turned to Emilio. 'Don't you think it's time Milo joined me?' Emilio said nothing and looked questioningly towards Milo.

'I'm not sure that I should,' Milo started cautiously. Seeing Martin's face darken, he hurried on. 'I mean… it's difficult to see how I could add to what you've already done, and – well, perhaps I should think about doing something else.'

'What d'you mean, "something else"?' Martin asked in surprise. 'What else is there?'

Milo hesitated. 'Perhaps you should think about diversifying.'

Martin waved his arm impatiently, indicating the rows of vines. 'What's this if it's not diversification? Isn't this exactly what you're talking about?' He looked to Emilio for support. 'This could be making good money in a few years.'

Emilio couldn't help himself. 'Perhaps, but there are other things you could try.' Immediately he regretted speaking. Martin was looking at him strangely.

'There are always other things,' said Martin. 'But you've always backed my choices in the past. We might not make a fortune from the vineyards, but it'll be a good grounding for Milo to understand the soil and the climate. Who knows?' he added. 'After a while we might even plant some sugar in the fields over there.'

'But that wouldn't be diversification,' protested Milo. 'It would be more of the same.'

'Since when have you been such an expert?' said Martin irritably. 'What do you know about it?'

'Nothing. And I want to learn. But there are other opportunities. What about the railroads, for example, or mining?'

'Mining! You want to go back to the Chinchas and make your fortune from all that misery?' Martin was starting to shout.

'No, of course not: I didn't say that. But I've heard they're starting to work the nitrate fields down south, and the guano can't last forever.'

'Down south?' Martin stood up angrily and started to pace up and down. 'What d'you mean? What's wrong with what's on offer here?'

'Nothing, nothing,' protested Milo. 'But there's just the one crop, and how could anyone improve on what you've already achieved? I just can't see what I could do. You've got everything under control, you know everyone – all their families, all their problems. How could I fit in?'

'But you *do* fit in. Ever since you came here you've fitted in.' Martin stopped pacing and stood in front of Milo. 'Who's going to look after my plantations?' He looked at Milo sadly, almost embarrassed. 'I thought – that is, Lisa and I thought – ' he paused and his anger ebbed, as he looked away from Milo to the fields beyond. 'What's going to happen to all this? I know we haven't talked about it, but we'd hoped you'd want to stay. That one day you'd want to take over.'

Milo had never seen Martin so unsure of himself and wanted desperately to reassure him. 'I do want to stay. You've given my life back to me. Of course I'll stay here, if that's what you want. But I want to be sure that I can contribute something that's real. I mean, well – what happens if it all goes wrong?'

'What can possibly go wrong?' demanded Martin, his anger resurfacing. But he sat down suddenly, his shoulders sagging as though no longer prepared to argue. 'I'm sorry, Milo. I should have spoken about this before. Perhaps it's too sudden.' For several minutes he stared at the vines stretching towards the airless, snow-covered mountains. 'You know this is your home?' He said it almost absently. 'Whatever happens, I want you to know this will always be your home.'

Milo stood up unsteadily. This was the man who had taken him from destitution; who'd rescued him and looked after him; who'd educated him and given him everything he could wish for. Milo just wanted to hug him, but he knew Martin would shrink from any display of affection. The tears welled up in his eyes and he looked questioningly at Emilio, frightened at what he had to say. Emilio frowned and shook his head.

After an embarrassed pause, Milo said gently: 'It's one of my homes, sir. One of my homes. One day I have to return to Šipan.'

Martin stiffened as the words hit him. Silently he turned and untied the horse's reins. Hoisting himself into his saddle, he rode off slowly towards the fields.

Milo watched him go. 'That couldn't have gone much worse, could it?'

'I'm sure he'll get over it.' Emilio didn't sound convinced.

'But what can I do, Emilio? I'll join him here in Matotambo if that's what he wants, and I'll help him as much as I can. But he's got to face it: I'll have to return home sometime. That's where my family is – he must understand that.'

'I'm sure he does,' answered Emilio. 'But it can't be easy. You must give him more time.'

'Anyway,' continued Milo, 'I'm right to be worried about the huge amounts he's investing on the estate. Good times can't go on forever.'

Emilio looked at him uneasily. 'Don't worry about it, Milo,' he told him, with more assurance than he felt. 'The bank wouldn't have lent the money if we weren't sure of the future.'

'But the bank has got other investments – the mines, the railroads, the trading houses. It doesn't just rely on the sugar harvest. If the sugar price drops, the bank has the security of the plantations. The bank is covered whatever happens. It's Martin who's carrying the risk. Look at the Garcias: they've got investments outside their estates, whereas Martin simply reinvests every penny he makes.'

Not for the first time Emilio didn't quite know what to say to this precocious and rather serious boy. He'd watched him grow and mature and, as he looked at the strong, fair-headed young man in front of him, he realised that here was someone who from now on was going to make his own future. Milo had a particular way of looking at things and in spite of Emilio's respect for Martin Hurst, he felt a tremor of uncertainty – perhaps Milo was right.

'Martin and I have been friends for a long time, Milo. I can say things to him no one else can. If you want me to, I'll speak to him. I could suggest that you join Delgado's –that's our trading house – for a year and see how you like it. It wouldn't commit you to anything in the future and afterwards, even if you did decide to join him on the estate, then the experience wouldn't be wasted.'

'I'm not having anything to do with the guano trade,' said Milo emphatically. 'Not after what I've seen. I may not be able to stop it, but I'm not joining it.'

'I suppose there are other commodities,' Emilio said doubtfully. Guano was Peru's biggest export – why look anywhere else? 'There's the copper inland, and cotton here on the coast, but the markets aren't as big.'

'What about nitrates? I've heard they could be an alternative to guano.'

'But that's in the desert down south.' Emilio shook his head. 'It's too isolated. There are only a handful of families working the nitrate fields and you wouldn't fit in. The life's too hard and the business is too small.'

'It could grow,' said Milo.

Emilio recognised the expression in Milo's face and sighed. 'Oh, all right then. We occasionally do some business with a small agent in Iquique. I can give you an introduction.'

Milo said nothing for several minutes. 'No,' he said finally, coming to a decision. 'No. I suppose Martin's right. I've got to stay here. I know he doesn't really need me, but that's not the point. I owe it to him. There's no point my carrying on with my studies: I might just as well get started as soon as possible. I'll come back with you to Lima. I'll tell Lisa what I've decided, and make arrangements to leave the Institute. Just as I was getting to know Alicia, too.' He looked back across the fields. 'I suppose this will be my new home from now on.' The image of Alicia against the mountains suddenly flashed across his mind. 'She can come back and visit me here.'

~~~~~

The butler coughed softly outside the door. Milo looked up from his unpacking. 'What is it, Julio? Is Mrs Hurst downstairs yet?'

Julio shook his head. 'There's a – ' he paused, looking confused. 'There's a – a gentleman at the door. He's asking for you, sir. I couldn't understand him very well. He seems to be some kind of sailor, Señor Milo. I think he was saying something about your brother.'

'My *brother*?' Milo looked at him in astonishment. 'He was talking about my brother? Where is he?'

'In the conservatory, Señor Milo. I thought it best to take him around through the garden.'

Milo left his trunk and rushed down into the dayroom. He stopped at the window and looked through the glass. A young man in a blue smock walked up and down nervously, occasionally stopping to inspect the plants. Milo crossed the room to get a better view; there was something very familiar about him. As the sailor started to turn, Milo suddenly recognised him. 'Jurica!'

Milo rushed up to his brother, who looked at him in surprise. He stopped in front of him and held out his arms. 'It *is* Jurica, isn't it?'

Jurica looked at him and grinned. He took Milo's arms and pulled him roughly towards him. 'It's taken a bit longer than I expected, but I've finally made it.'

Milo hugged his brother tightly; the familiar smell of ship's tar clinging to Jurica's clothes made the years fall away, taking him straight back to the day he first went to sea. Milo released his brother and looked him up and down critically. 'Who did you sail with? When did you get here? How long have you been away? How are…'

'Whoa,' Jurica interrupted him. 'One thing at a time. I'll tell you everything but first…' he stopped as Lisa approached from the doorway.

'Aren't you going to introduce me to your friend, Milo?' she smiled at Jurica, giving no sign of disapproval at his shabby appearance.

'I told you they'd get my letters,' Milo ran over and clutched her arm. 'I told you he'd come and find me. You're not going to believe it,' Milo said proudly, leading her across the room, 'but this is my brother, Jurica.'

'However did you find us?' Lisa was astonished. But she recovered quickly and held out her hand formally. 'You really are very welcome, Mr Beran. Milo has told us so much about his family and about Šipan that I feel I know you all.'

'Thank you, miss,' Jurica said shyly. 'But it's Jurica, miss. Jurica Rosich. Andro Beran is my stepfather.'

'Of course,' she said, trying to hide her embarrassment. 'This is such a surprise. I didn't think I'd ever meet you.' She turned back to Milo. 'But if he's just come from his ship, he'll be hungry. I'll ask Julio to bring some food.' Lisa could see that Milo was shaking with excitement and was hardly listening. 'I'll leave you alone to talk.'

She left the room quietly, but Milo didn't notice; he was holding Jurica's arm tightly and bombarding him with questions. 'When did you leave Šipan? Where have you sailed from?' he asked impatiently, but as they started to talk, Milo became aware that his brother's replies were subdued. Jurica appeared reserved, almost guarded, unable to share his own exhilaration at the reunion.

Julio brought in several plates of food and laid them out on a small table. Jurica started picking listlessly at the dishes, replying only occasionally to Milo's excited chatter. Eventually Milo realised his brother was barely listening. 'What is it, Jurica?' he asked finally. 'What's the matter?'

Jurica looked up, his eyes watering. 'It's Mam,' he said slowly. 'She's, she's…'

Milo felt a stab of fear as he stared at Jurica, waiting for him to finish. 'She's what?'

Jurica looked down at the floor. 'She thought it was her fault you'd had to leave. She was convinced she'd ruined your life. She wouldn't stop blaming herself. We tried to talk to her, but it made no difference. She couldn't accept it and just sat on the terrace, gazing out to sea. If she said anything it was only to ask where you were. She couldn't face up to the real situation: she kept saying that Frano Bossano had to do something, though it was obvious he wasn't interested. We hardly saw him after you'd left; he simply never went out – not even to the mainland.'

'But Mam? How is she now?' asked Milo.

Jurica shook his head. 'I had to find a proper job, one that paid proper money. I couldn't stay in the docks. We all needed to eat,' he said the last words angrily and looked back to Milo, his eyes red with tears. 'I found a berth on a coaster. It was well paid and I wouldn't be away for more than a month or so. But when I told her, she became hysterical. Nothing Dad or I could say would calm her.'

Jurica was struggling to hold back his tears. Milo kneeled in front of him and grabbed his hands. 'Tell me, Jurica, tell me. What happened?'

'Dad said she'd be all right. That he'd look after her.' Jurica's voice broke. 'I was only away for a few weeks, but I couldn't shake off the feeling that something terrible thing had happened. As soon as we docked in Gruz I took a boat straight back to Šipan. Going through the Passage I knew. I just knew something was wrong.' Milo gripped his arms, too frightened to say anything.

'It happened soon after I'd left. They didn't find her for several days. They think she must have drifted across the bay. They think – ' he stumbled on his words. 'They think she must have jumped from the Point. They found her in Caesar's Passage. Washed up on the rocks.' Jurica suddenly collapsed and his head fell forward onto Milo's shoulder.

Milo held him tightly and rocked him gently. 'No. No. No.' He kept repeating it. 'Not Mam. Not Mam. It wasn't her fault. She did everything she could. She tried so hard. So hard.'

For several minutes they held each other closely. Eventually Milo pulled away, wiping his eyes. 'And Dad? He lived for her. He was completely devoted. What can he do now?'

Jurica shook his head slowly. 'He was so brave. He said he couldn't remember a time when he hadn't loved her and that after my father died, he'd managed to steal fourteen years of happiness. He said that in this life no man could ask for more. He'll meet both of them in a better place.'

'Oh! The poor man. He must be devastated; he doesn't deserve it,' Milo said and his face darkened. 'What has Frano Bossano on his conscience now? I've got to get back.'

'No,' Jurica said. 'There's nothing you can do. Not now. It's too late.'

'But why didn't you write to me? You could have written.'

'And what would you have done?' asked Jurica. 'What would have been the point? Dad had your letters and wanted to write back, but I told him no, I had to tell you myself. I'm the eldest son now and I had to see you. When I transferred to deep-sea ships I knew I'd have to pass through Callao.'

'But you could still have written.'

Jurica hesitated. 'I didn't know how you'd react. I didn't even know if you'd remember us. You might not have wanted to know.'

Milo looked bewildered. 'But why should I have forgotten? Why shouldn't I want to know? You're my family.'

Jurica looked around him. 'Because of all this. You'd told us about the new life you'd found here. How were we to know what you'd think? You've had it so easy. When I saw the house, I almost didn't come in. You have all this, while we had nothing. It would have been best if you'd forgotten us.'

'But I wrote offering help.'

'Help?' Jurica laughed bitterly. 'To Dad it felt like charity. He was too proud even to consider it. He said we could manage without you.'

'He didn't tell me anything in his letters. He stopped writing after a while.'

'That was after Mam died. He didn't want you to know. He didn't think he'd ever see you again.'

Milo stared at his brother. 'But of course he'll see me again.'

For Lisa it was a difficult afternoon. She watched anxiously as they left the house and walked round and round the garden, deep in conversation. Over the years she had succeeded in gaining Milo's trust because she had kept herself apart. She had never tried to suggest that he should look on her as his mother, and she had never even hinted that Milo should choose between them. Indeed, she had encouraged Milo to talk freely about Šipan, knowing that it would be useless even to try to suppress his feelings for his homeland. Unlike her husband, she recognised that Milo might one day return there. She understood that now Milo's brother had finally come for him, she had to leave the two of them to talk together alone. Even though she was consumed with curiosity, she knew it was not her world.

She was writing letters in her room when Milo knocked and entered, several hours later. She pushed away her papers quickly and turned to look at him, impatient to hear his news. 'Milo, what is it?' she said in alarm as she saw the desperate look on his face. 'Where's Jurica?'

'He's gone back to his ship,' Milo said. 'We're going to meet later.'

Lisa looked at him anxiously. 'You'd better sit down and tell me what happened.'

Milo walked across to the window and looked out. 'Jurica had to leave home too. My father still can't make a proper living. Mrs Bossano won't let him work with any of their tenants. It's very difficult.' He stood silently for several minutes.

Lisa knew there was something very wrong. 'What is it, Milo? What about your mother?'

Milo's face crumpled. 'That's what Jurica came to tell me.'

'Tell you what?' Lisa prompted him gently.

Milo let out a shuddering wail and collapsed at her feet. 'She died. She – she threw herself off the Point. She convinced herself that it was all her fault. Why? Why? Why?' He looked around him. 'If only she could have seen this.' With a desolate cry, Milo buried his head in Lisa's lap, lost in a merciless grief.

Lisa stroked his head helplessly. There was nothing she could say to comfort him. He wouldn't let her close to him. 'Poor boy. Oh, you poor, poor boy,' she whispered quietly.

Milo's sobs eased eventually and he looked up at Lisa. 'I'm sorry. I shouldn't make you suffer for me.' With an effort he pulled himself away. 'I've been happy here. I don't want to worry you. You've been good to me. Why should you have to grieve for my family after all you've done for me? I already owe you a debt I can't repay.'

'You don't owe us anything,' Lisa said. 'We felt about your mother as though she was part of our family too. We will grieve with you. I won't ever meet her now. She sounded a remarkable woman.'

'She held us together. It wasn't her fault. If Rusa Bossano hadn't interfered – ' Milo stopped suddenly. 'What's the use?' he asked.

Lisa smiled at him nervously. 'Milo?' she hesitated, desperately afraid of his answer. 'Are you going to leave us? Do you want to go back?'

Milo took her hand tenderly and shook his head. 'No. No. Jurica's right. There's nothing I can do about it – not yet anyway. There's nothing for me to go back for. Not until…'

'Not until what?' Lisa asked.

Milo stood up suddenly, and looked down at her, his watery eyes glistening. 'I can't stay on the estates after this,' he said resolutely. 'I can't have everything handed to me. After what Jurica said, everything's changed.'

'Why not? Lisa asked, taken aback. '*Why* has it changed?'

'Because as he was talking to me, I realised that if I went to work at Napeña, how could I ever leave? I could never get back to Sipan. He was right about something else as well. I *have* had it too comfortable. How could I face them at home if I didn't try to make my own future? How can I tell Martin about all the opportunities in this country if I don't search them out myself? I've got to establish myself by my own efforts. Emilio said I could join his agency house and learn about business. But I've got to stand on my own. I can't keep relying on everyone else. After my family has sacrificed so much, it's up to me to deserve it.'

Lisa said nothing. She accepted that it was Milo's decision and there was nothing she could say. She knew how devastated her husband would be and how much he had counted on having Milo join him. But she knew Milo was right.

As the two brothers talked together over the following days, Milo felt increasingly sure that his decision to seek independence was the right one. Jurica was unconvinced, but after many hours Milo finally persuaded him to leave his ship and join him at the Villa Miraflores. Milo dreamed that, together, they could build something truly lasting. His ambition dominated his thoughts and he put to one side everything that had happened in Matotambo with Alicia.

He had now left the Institute and started his search with single-minded application. Trade in Peru was dominated by guano, which he was determined to avoid. The minerals inland were closed to him – he wasn't a geologist or an engineer. The sugar plantations – even the cotton fields – would mean competition with Martin. But he was aware that Jurica was becoming increasingly frustrated – his brother had never felt comfortable in the Hursts' home, and he was beginning to chafe at the enforced inactivity.

"It's so isolated down there." Milo remembered Emilio's description of the Tarapacá desert and made further enquiries. Inexorably his searches narrowed down to the nitrate fields in the south. Jurica trailed after him on a tour of the trading houses, libraries and newspapers, baffled by his brother's enquiries. The region represented an entirely unique combination of geographical circumstances. Southern Peru was one of the most arid places on earth. The warm, contrary currents which met off its shores had produced a coastal strip where, although often damp, it never rained. This unique climate had created not only the conditions which allowed the guano from countless millions of seabirds to build up along Peru's shores, but it also created the vast deserts further inland. Ribbons of lakes had once stretched across the borders of southern Peru, Bolivia and Chile, but as the climate changed they had slowly evaporated, and the salts dissolved in the water had dried out and solidified on the parched lake beds. Sodium nitrate was a powerful fertiliser, and there were hundreds of thousands of square miles of it left on the surface. Just lying there, ready to be dug up and sold to the growing European market. To Milo it seemed almost too good to be true. He also saw another advantage. He could take Jurica away from Lima. It would be hard down there, but what did that matter? After his time at sea, Jurica would take it in his stride. The two of them could work down south together as independent nitrate operators. Together they would join the *salitreros*.

Emilio Vasco did what he could to help, although he was doubtful of Milo's success and disappointed that he had chosen not to join Delgado's. Jurica was doubtful too, but in the face of Milo's determined optimism, he finally gave way. Milo had painted such an exciting picture of how their business might grow that Jurica simply couldn't find the words to argue. Together, they set off south on an exploratory tour, clutching Emilio's letter of introduction to a small trading house in Iquique – one of only two which carried out desultory trade with a few shipping lines. Lisa watched them as they sailed off southwards – Milo resolute and optimistic, his brother sceptical. She didn't say which of them she thought was right.

'You know, Milo, I never thought I'd see somewhere that made Callao look good.' Jurica looked around him at the dusty bay of Iquique. It was a dismal sight. An oppressive air of lassitude hung heavily over the settlement – it could hardly be called a town. The few shabby buildings were dominated by the cliffs which rose above them, grey and barren. The only movement ashore was a solitary cart which rumbled along the potholed street by the seafront. Groups of ragged men squatting at a street corner stared incuriously as it passed. Although further inland he could see some two-storey buildings, the constructions which fringed the shore were falling apart. Only the occasional chicken pecking at the dust around the doorways gave any clue that they were inhabited. The only activity was a few listing ships, loading from decrepit lighters.

Milo shrugged. This might be where he was going to live, but he was here to work. He wasn't concerned by how it looked now, but by how it could develop in the future. Like Martin, he was impatient to begin and had hardly established a base with Emilio's agents before he started inland. For two months he criss-crossed the region, talking to the *salitreros*, inspecting the rudimentary refineries where the salts were converted into saltpetre. As he saw the hand-to-mouth existence of the families operating the primitive equipment, he became increasingly convinced that here was a sleepy industry awaiting a technological awakening. There must be a better way of digging up the saltpetre. There must be better ways of refining it. He knew there were better ways of transporting it than with herds of llama and alpaca.

Milo was convinced that this was what he had been looking for. Each day he found more opportunities to explore and more questions needing answers. Jurica watched his brother's growing excitement with uneasy detachment. Although he continued to accompany him on his inland tours, he did so with increasing reluctance. He found the dusty desert landscape suffocating and missed the feel of salt spray stinging his face. He felt frustrated and isolated. But Milo was too obsessed with his plans to notice. By the time they had returned to Iquique after visiting their tenth *oficina*, Jurica had finally had enough.

'I want to get back to sea,' he said as they settled back into their waterfront lodgings.

Milo was packing his samples into a bag to send up to Lima for analysis. 'Sea?' He looked up absently. 'Why? What's the matter?'

'I've had enough. I don't belong here.'

Milo looked at him blankly. 'What do you mean? What about the future we've talked about?'

'*You've* talked about it. Not me,' said Jurica. 'This isn't what I want. I've tried to go along with it, but it's not going to work.'

'It'll be all right, Jurica,' Milo turned back to his samples. 'As soon as I find my mine, you'll have plenty to occupy you.'

Jurica stood up and grabbed the bag and threw it on the floor. 'You're not listening. I said this isn't going to work.'

Milo was taken aback by his brother's anger. 'But I've told you what I'm trying to do down here. I've explained what we can achieve together.'

'Countless times. But it's obvious there's never going to be a place here for me. You're never going to let anyone near you.'

Milo picked up the bag and sat down. 'I'm sorry, Jurica,' he said after several moments' thought. 'I should have realised. I've been too preoccupied.' Milo looked up at his brother. 'I've been so caught up with my own plans, I didn't think.'

'From what I can see, you need an engineer, not an uneducated sailor like me. That James Young you're always talking about. Why don't you get him to join you? The one who worked with Mr Hurst?'

Milo struggled uncertainly to understand him. 'Perhaps you're right,' he said. 'But I wanted to build this together. The two of us.'

'I'm sorry, Milo,' Jurica's anger had passed. 'I really hope you achieve your dreams. I'm sure you will. But they're not mine. I'll get a passage up to Callao and find a ship there.'

There was a long silence as they both accepted that they were shortly to separate and rejoin their separate lives.

'Do you really miss the sea?' asked Milo finally. 'I always found it too random, senseless and brutal.'

'The officers can be brutal, but I manage to stay away from them. I just do my job and try not to attract attention. On a good ship there can be strong companionship.'

'And on a bad ship?' asked Milo, but Jurica just shrugged.

'Tell me,' Milo asked thoughtfully. 'In any of your voyages, have you ever come across Arnie Asche? We were shipmates. He was a couple of years older than me.'

Jurica shook his head. 'No. But there have been so many.'

'Traub?' asked Milo. 'Joachim Traub? He was first mate when I knew him.'

Jurica nodded, slowly recognising the name. 'There was a Captain Traub on a sister ship. They were both fitted out in France – a yard near Brest, but she was commissioned by another company. German, I think. It was a new line and I heard he'd only just joined them. I'm sure it was Joachim Traub.'

'What's the name of it?'

Jurica hesitated as he tried to remember. 'Minerva,' he said finally. 'I think it was the Minerva Line.'

There was another long silence. 'Milo?' Milo looked up. Jurica could see a look of incomprehension in his eyes. 'I'm sorry it hasn't worked out. Tell Mrs Hurst goodbye. She's a nice person. You're very lucky.'

Milo escorted his brother back to join the steamer at Callao. 'Perhaps when we next meet, it'll be on Šipan,' he said, as he they reached the quayside. 'One day I'll have my own estate and build a mansion on the seafront, and you can stay there as long as you like.'

Jurica laughed. 'And the Bossanos? What's going to happen to them?'

'I haven't decided yet.'

Jurica looked quickly across at his brother, but Milo's face was stony. Jurica hesitated. 'Frano Bossano…' he started.

'Do we have to talk about him now?'

'The way Mam always talked about him. I never understood. Why did she think he would help?'

'He didn't,' said Milo. 'He couldn't have cared less.'

'I've always wondered.' Jurica shrugged. 'Have you still got Mam's locket?' he asked. 'You remember? The one she gave you when you left?'

Milo reached inside his shirt and unhooked the gold miniature. He passed it to Jurica. 'I've worn it every day since then. It was the only link I had.'

'It was all she had left,' said Jurica opening the lid. They stared at the portrait.

'Did Dad really look like that?' asked Milo after a while.

'I was too young,' Jurica said. 'But Andro's been a good father. It hasn't been easy.' He looked up at Milo. 'But you're lucky: you've got another father now.'

Milo looked at him in surprise. 'I hadn't thought of it like that,' he said after a moment. 'Martin Hurst's been very good to me. But he's not my father.'

Chapter Twelve

1869 – six months later

The offices of Hermanos Delgado y Cia were just a dozen blocks from the Villa Miraflores, on the road leading from the main Plaza towards Callao. Milo entered them with mixed feelings. The guano trade had come to dominate every trading house along the entire length of the West Coast of South America. Although it created the revenues which allowed the development of mines and agriculture further inland, the easy money was always to be made from the deposits themselves. This had been quickly recognised by politicians who, in the well-established tradition of governments everywhere, national-ised them. The temptation of such riches put excessive strain on Peru's already fragile and volatile political system. Coup followed counter-coup, revolution followed counter-revolu-tion. The changes were sometimes so rapid that new govern-ments came and went without people even noticing. The trading houses which collected the commission for the govern-ment were essential in maintaining the politicians' wealth, so it made little difference to them who else was skimming off the cream. At times revolutionaries even bypassed the government completely and simply took control of the Chinchas them-selves, imposing the levy directly on the ships while they lay at anchor at the islands without bothering about any political considerations on the mainland. Such anarchy was a feature of the commercial life of Lima and the trading houses learnt never to take any side other than their own, and always to give generously whenever a new President knocked at their doors seeking contributions. The guano, after all, was free. The only cost was the gangs of Chinese who worked the deposits – and few of them lived long enough to collect any pay.

The growing export business allowed the banks several bites at the ripening cherry. Not only did they advance loans against the security of export shipments, but their associated trading agencies then arranged the sale of those goods at the port of departure, charging yet more commission. The financial com-munity had just two objectives – loan interest and commission.

Wealthy from the profits of the guano trade, the trading houses started to look elsewhere, to the sugar and cotton plantations and to the minerals further inland. These needed railroads, and railroads in turn needed imports of steel, machinery and rolling stock – all of which needed financing. The banks financed the entrepreneurs who did the work, using outside money to make fortunes for themselves. Henry Meiggs, who absconded from San Francisco owing millions, became spectacularly wealthy from his railroad lines, even returning to America to pay off all his creditors. But the rapid economic growth soon exhausted the reserves of the local banks and forced them to look outside for investment. Gradually, all but the most powerful local families were squeezed out of their ownership of their industries. The economy throughout the West Coast became dominated by European – principally British – money.

Milo realised that the key to success throughout South America was Capital, but nowhere more so than in the nitrate fields. If the nitrate fields were to be developed properly, then it needed investment, massive investment. But Delgado's had never dealt with the nitrate industry before. Would Emilio be prepared to lend on such an untested plan?

Milo was shown into Emilio's large office and sat down confidently. He was sure there was nothing wrong with his forecasts. And the figures, although substantial, were not beyond Delgado's resources.

Emilio picked up Milo's proposal and tapped it on the desk. 'No one can say you're not ambitious,' he said finally. 'You certainly don't intend doing things by halves.'

'Why should I? The nitrates are there. You've got the analysis reports. The saltpetre has twice the nitrogen content of guano. It's got to sell.'

'Perhaps,' said Emilio. 'But you'd still be competing with guano, and that doesn't cost as much to produce.'

'That's why we need the investment: to keep the costs down.' Milo indicated the report in Emilio's hands. 'It's all down there. We can sell into the same markets.'

'But plans can go wrong. What about price fluctuations? The volatility of sugar prices has already taken years off my life. I don't think my nerves could stand dealing with yet more commodities. Something always happens that you're not expecting.'

'Since James agreed to join me, he's been working almost non-stop on these plans. He's convinced the equipment he's designed will work. It'll leapfrog us across the competition.'

'Are you sure? Guano prices are unsteady, and even Martin's having a hard time trying to cope with falling sugar prices in Napeña.'

'It's all in the report. We'll be able to make profits even if prices fall.'

'And service these loans?' asked Emilio. 'It's a great deal of money you're asking for.'

'And it's a great deal of interest you could earn,' Milo retorted.

'Yes,' Emilio hesitated. 'But it's a big risk. And we're not a big company.' Emilio was silent for several minutes. 'No,' he said finally. 'It's too big, too ambitious for such an untested industry. Scale it down and come back to me, and I'll look at it again.'

Milo realised he had probably heard the final word. 'Someone might get there ahead of us,' he gave it one last shot.

'Let them,' said Emilio. 'We don't have to worry about competition down there. Guano's the competition, not the other *salitreros*. Anyway, if someone does invest ahead of you, we can see how they manage.'

'But think of the advantages of being first. If I'm right, we'd get a couple of years' lead.'

'And if you're wrong?' Emilio shook his head. 'Have you tried asking Martin?'

'I couldn't ask Martin. You know what he thinks.' Milo stared at him. Did Emilio really not understand? 'Shall I take it you're refusing? Do you want me to go elsewhere?'

Emilio returned Milo's stare. He wasn't going to be pushed. 'You can take it as a definite "perhaps".'

After finishing his work at Napeña, James had welcomed Milo's invitation to take a tour around Tarapacá. Milo's description had made it sound like an engineer's dream and it hadn't taken him long to see that Milo hadn't exaggerated. It was an industry in its infancy, ripe for technological investment. James needed no further persuasion and had returned to Lima to start work immediately on plans for a new nitrate refinery. But, as Milo sat waiting for him in the European Club, he realised he would have wasted James' time if Emilio wasn't prepared to back them.

He felt a hand on his shoulder and jumped with a start. 'Milo! How's things?' a voice said.

Milo looked up expectantly, but took several moments to recognise the man in front of him.

'Peter Calder. I'm sorry, I was expecting someone else.'

Peter sat down next to him. 'Haven't seen you since the Institute. James asked me to stop by and tell you he'd be late. I'm supposed to be meeting a friend, so I was coming here anyway.'

Milo nodded. If James was caught up discussing engineering, he could be hours. 'So where've you been keeping yourself?' he asked

'I went inland. Everything seemed to be all wrapped up here on the coast, so I thought I'd try the copper mines.'

'And?'

'It's not bad. I'm thinking of studying to become a geologist.'

'That'll take some time,' said Milo, but stopped as he noticed Robert Miller entering through the heavy oak door and beckoned him over. Robert, quickly ordering himself a drink from a passing waiter, came over and shook Milo's hands stiffly. He nodded briefly at Peter Calder.

'James with you?' Robert asked, looking around him awkwardly.

'No. He'll be here later.'

Peter Calder turned to Robert. When they had last met he had still been Milo's teacher. 'Are you still with Señor Vasco?' Peter asked politely.

Robert looked at him with surprise. 'No, no. I'm employed by the Garcias. I'm sure you've heard of them.'

'I'm sorry,' said Peter. 'You used to be with the Hursts, so I thought...' He turned back to Milo. 'But Señor Vasco. His bank seems to be expanding rapidly.'

'I think he's finding it difficult at the moment. The sugar prices are weak and many of the plantation owners are struggling.'

'As long as the guano prices keep up,' said Robert. 'With the level of loans outstanding, there'll be a nasty shock if they start to drop.'

'Emilio thinks they're steadying,' said Milo, 'although the guano people are still making fortunes.' He hesitated, perhaps he should sound Robert out about his plans? He turned to Peter Calder. 'Look, do you mind if I take Robert away? I want to discuss something with him.'

Peter Calder stood up. 'I'll go and find my friend.'

'I'm staying at the Villa Miraflores: you must come and visit. Mrs Hurst would love to see you again.' Milo shook hands with Peter and took Robert to a private booth. 'Tell me, Robert – have the Garcias done much business with the nitrate fields in Tarapacá?'

'Tarapacá? Why are you asking?' Robert considered the question. 'From what I understand, most of the saltpetre fields down there are worked by family *salitreros*. They're pretty simple affairs. The nitrate's on the surface and they just dig it up and load it onto herds of alpaca who carry it across to the small port at Iquique. They don't have much need of investment.'

'They certainly haven't invested much, but that's not the same thing as not needing it. James and I have been down there to look around. I'm holding an option on several *estacas* of land. I wanted to ask what you thought about it.'

'Since when have Delgado's invested directly?' asked Robert, looking surprised. 'They normally find their commissions quite sufficient.'

'It's not Delgado's – it's me. Well, James and me. I've researched the business in detail and I think there's a future for us down there. I'm hoping Emilio will back me, but it's looking doubtful. I wanted to know what you think.' Milo looked at Robert anxiously.

'You're not wasting any time, are you? So you've learnt everything I had to teach you and now, in less than a year, you think you know it all.'

'No. No, that's not fair.' Milo was taken aback at the criticism. 'It's an opportunity I might not have again. You should see it for yourself – there's practically nothing there. It's just a desert, with a few dusty shacks. The refining is primitive. According to James, with proper investment in machinery, he could increase production tenfold. I think there's a lot of money to be made.'

Robert sat thoughtfully, and finally drained his drink at a gulp. 'Perhaps you've got a point. Should I suggest it to Señor Garcia – or is it meant to be a secret?'

'No, no. Like you said before, there's plenty of room for everyone. The desert goes on forever and demand for fertiliser in Europe just keeps rising. If more people are prepared to invest, it would help everyone. We could even build a proper port in Iquique and ship the nitrates out directly.'

Robert laughed. 'No one can say you lack ambition,' he said. 'From what I've heard Iquique's a dump. But with your unshakeable confidence, I suppose you're telling Emilio the nitrate exports will soon be bigger than the guano business.'

'Well, the guano can't last for ever, can it?' replied Milo. 'So what d'you think?'

'It's interesting. Let me talk to the Garcias about it. I'll call at the Villa Miraflores tomorrow. Christ! What's that?'

A splintering crash stopped all conversation. They both jumped up as the ornate chandelier fell into the centre of the room, showering them with shards of broken glass. They looked across the room where a massive oak panel, torn from its fixings, was flying towards a group of men huddled in conversation. One of them looked up quickly but his piercing scream was smashed from his lips as the panel clipped his jaw, crushing it like paper as it ploughed through the furniture. Another huge tremor shook the building, loosening more panels, which started to fall from the walls into the room. 'Earthquake! Quick, outside,' shouted Robert, as Milo rushed after him into the street.

The scene outside resembled a battleground. Dust from the collapsing walls swirled fiercely through the street, like smoke from a broadside. The force of the downdraught whipped the falling plaster against their skin, searing their faces. Hardly able to stand, they staggered along the street. Robert froze as an unearthly sound made him clasp his hands to his ears. Just ahead of him a trench appeared, a gigantic tear rending the paved roadway. It moved towards him rapidly as he jumped to one side and pressed himself tightly against a trembling building. Milo caught up with him. 'Make for the Plaza de Armas – we've got to get into the open.' He pulled Robert away from the building as a crack ran up the wall like a giant snake. 'Come on.' They ran on through the stricken city. Screams of pain and terror mingled with the crashes of the falling ruins. Towards the coast, the flickering of fires could be seen from the docks of Callao, where the guano ships tried desperately to haul themselves out to sea, battening down for the inevitable tidal wave which followed the terremoto.

Robert and Milo reached the square as the tremors faded. 'The Villa Miraflores,' shouted Milo. 'I must get back to Lisa.' Without waiting for an answer he ran off into the darkness. People crawled out from under collapsed walls and the flattened roofs of the crumbling buildings. As they skirted Chinatown, they could see groups of people standing helplessly, staring at the ruined buildings, stunned by the shock of the sudden assault. Milo dodged through the growing crowds and tried to shut his ears against the anguished wails of the families destroyed beneath the rubble.

As he rushed down the driveway towards the Villa, he saw with relief that the house seemed almost untouched. Parts of the cornice lay smashed in a dusty heap on the grass below, but miraculously there seemed little damage.

'Sir! Sir!' Milo looked as Julio ran up to him. 'Mrs Hurst – it's Mrs Hurst.'

'Where is she?' asked Milo.

'Behind the house, in the conservatory.' Milo ran after Julio and stopped with shock at the sight. Even in the gloom, he could see that the conservatory, Martin's showpiece, now lay flattened on the ground.

Milo bellowed at Julio. 'Get all the staff together. Let's get some torches lit. We need to see what we're doing.' The butler ran off and Milo approached the ruins, his shoes crunching the broken glass into the earth. 'Quiet, everyone. Can you hear anything?'

Slowly the excited chatter subsided. Milo looked along the serious faces caught in the flaring light of the lamps. 'Over here!' The young chambermaid pointed to the remains of the brick wall which had supported the back of the conservatory roof. 'There. Can you hear it?'

Milo approached and listened carefully. There was a faint but definite sound. 'Get the torches over here. We've got to get these roof supports up. Two of you get on each end and lift.'

After removing the first three roof trusses, Milo organised the staff to scrape away the glass shards carefully from the remains of the brickwork. They worked their way slowly towards the centre.

'There she is!' Milo pointed to the strands of hair smeared onto a sheet of broken glass. The pale skin of her scalp could be seen through the blood-smeared glass. He pushed the other men to one side and went onto his knees, picking at the debris piece by piece. 'Get that light over here, and someone run and fetch Doctor Muñez. Carry him here by force if necessary. Now get some blankets and something for her to lie on when we get her out. We can't go back inside the house.'

It was impossible to tell her condition. She was covered with cuts. As Milo freed her, a maid washed her down, talking quietly to her while she did so. But Lisa moaned gently and didn't respond. 'How bad is it?' Milo asked the doctor when he arrived. But the doctor simply shook his head. He opened his case and started to examine her.

Milo looked at them for several moments until he turned away impatiently. 'We'd better see if anyone else is missing.' Milo walked around the house and ushered the staff towards the back lawns, relieved to find them all accounted for. 'We'll all have to stay out here for the night. It's not safe inside until we've inspected the house when it's light.'

Doctor Muñez finished his examination and approached thoughtfully. Milo watched his face as the flames of the torches reflected off his dark skin, giving him an almost sepulchral appearance. Milo waited for the Doctor to speak, his heart thudding in his chest.

'I don't know,' the doctor started slowly. 'I've examined her as thoroughly as I can and I'm not sure. It's too early to make a proper diagnosis.'

Milo interrupted impatiently. 'Doctor, please just tell me how she is. Don't hide anything, I'm prepared for more bad news.'

The doctor shook his head. 'No, no. It's not like that at all. It's just that I can't quite believe it. It seems she's had the most remarkable escape. I think one of the roof beams must have protected her because she's only slightly concussed, although her leg is broken. It seems that she's been very lucky, but we can't do anything more until the morning.'

'Milo. Wake up, it's me, James.' Milo slowly regained consciousness. The morning was well advanced and James Young was shaking his shoulder. 'Are you all right?' James crouched down beside him anxiously. 'The doctor's been, but I didn't want to wake you. He wants Mrs Hurst taken inside as soon as it's safe. I've checked it out carefully and I'm sure the house is all right. The bricks were able to slide over one another during the shocks – a stone building probably wouldn't have stood up so well. A lot of the façade will need replacing, but it's safe.'

Milo stood up and stretched, massaging his shoulder. He ached from the hard night outdoors. 'If you're sure,' he said uncertainly. He called out to Julio, 'Get the men to carry Mrs Hurst to her room, but be careful.' He turned back to James. 'What about Martin? We must tell him, otherwise he might hear about it from someone else and imagine the worst.'

'I've got an Indian guide who could ride up there.' James was anxious to do something. 'He knows the trails: he helped mark them out for the railroad, and I used him as a messenger when we needed extra supplies. He could be in Napeña in three or four days. I'll go and fetch him. He lives just down the coast, so I should be back in a few hours.'

Milo went over to Lisa Hurst. She turned to face him. 'They told me you pulled me out,' she said.

Milo reached over and found her hand under the covers. 'Nonsense,' he said quietly. 'How are you feeling? James says it's safe to take you back inside. How's your leg?'

'Painful,' she gave Milo a lopsided smile. 'Doctor Muñez has set it. He says I've got to stay in bed for several weeks.' She looked around at her staff clearing up the scattered debris. 'You know, Milo, it's funny. I was just doing some pruning and the next thing I knew you were pulling me from the wreckage. You can't be sure of anything in this part of the world.'

James returned with the messenger later in the morning. Robert Miller was with him. 'We met in the docks; he was checking out the damage for the trading houses.'

Milo handed the messenger the note he had written for Martin. 'You can't see Mrs Hurst now, but tell Mr Hurst she's fine. Tell him the Doctor's put her leg into splints, but she's quite cheerful. Look around the house before you go, so you can tell Mr Hurst that everything's all right.'

As the messenger took his horse away, Milo looked questioningly at Robert. 'So?' he asked. 'How is it down there?'

Robert shook his head. 'It's not too bad up here in Lima, but Callao's devastated. The floating dock has destroyed half the quay walls. It's going to be months before they can get it all back together.'

'And the ships?' asked Milo. 'What about the ships? Where are the crews?'

'It's difficult to tell,' said Robert. 'There must have been several huge waves. Most had put out to sea after the first tremors, and they're slowly making their way back into the bay. One ship fouled its anchor and couldn't cut it free. It was crushed into splinters by the first wave. There's hardly a trace of it left. Half a dozen ships were caught on the crest as they tried to escape and were swept hundreds of yards inland. Now the water's receded, you can see a furrow through the houses where a ship was dragged straight through the centre of town. Everybody's lending a hand – even the boarding houses are sending men out to help. It'll be several days before anyone will know exactly who's missing – even then ...' Robert trailed off. He knew what Milo thought of the cheapness of life at sea and searched for something else to say. 'There is one thing though,' he said more cheerfully. 'Until they get Callao working there aren't going to be many ships leaving. The price of your nitrates is going to go through the roof.'

Milo stared at him for several moments and, without another word, he turned and went back upstairs to Mrs Hurst.

Martin Hurst arrived from Huacatambo nearly two weeks after the earthquake. He had never trusted the steamer service and was too impatient to wait for it. Antonio, his estate manager, had protested that the trail was too difficult, but Martin had brushed away his objections. As Milo watched him sitting by Lisa's bedside, it was difficult to tell who was the invalid. Martin looked tired and grey, while Lisa had regained her spirits and was cheerful and laughing. 'The staff are still talking about it,' she told Martin proudly. 'Milo dug into the glass with his bare hands and rescued me. He was a hero.' Milo had given up correcting her. Nothing he could say had persuaded her that he hadn't risked anything to pull her out from the wreckage. He would tell Martin the truth later.

143

There was no doubt about it, he thought, as he left them alone together. The strain of dealing with the falling sugar prices was taking its toll; there was a greyness about Martin's skin which Milo hadn't noticed before. His walk had changed as well – he didn't stride as he used to, it was more of an amble, almost a shuffle. He talked about it with Emilio when he called later that day. 'He should have waited for the steamer service – but what's the point of telling him? You know he's always done exactly as he pleases, but at his age that's a long trip down from Napeña by horseback.'

Emilio Vasco glanced towards the staircase to check that Martin was still with Lisa. 'He still hasn't adjusted to your – what did he call it?' The banker pulled a face. 'He said it was your experiment. He made it sound as though you were an alchemist.'

'He does realise I'm not joining him at Napeña? You did make it clear, didn't you?' Emilio didn't answer and Milo buried his head in his hands. 'Oh, Emilio, you must tell him we're committed to it.'

'You're committed,' said Emilio, 'I told you I wasn't convinced. Anyway,' he added. 'It's not easy to tell Martin anything. He tends to hear what he wants to hear, and he's still expecting you to return to Napeña. He thinks you'll eventually realise how much he needs you.'

Milo looked at Emilio thoughtfully. 'I think you might be wrong,' he said after a few moments. 'You say you know him better than anyone, and you do, but what does that mean? Who really knows him anyway? He didn't build up all those estates by sentiment. He looks after his workforce, yes, but only because he thinks that's the best way of doing it. I've watched him. Before he goes into one of the houses, he checks in his book. They think he knows who they are, but he doesn't – how can he? There are just too many of them. He does what he thinks he should and worries about appearances, but it's calculated, you know. Yes, he'd like me to join him, but it's not sentiment – he's worrying about his estates, not me.'

'But that's not true,' Emilio said in genuine surprise. 'You know he treats you like a son. He wants to do the best he can for you.'

'Yes, but he also wants the best for Napeña. I've been thinking about it a lot. I even tried to talk to Lisa, but she just avoided the question. She knows nothing's more important to him than Napeña.'

'It's easy for you to be cynical, but you weren't there.' The force of Emilio's objection took Milo aback. 'You didn't see him after you'd left Huacatambo. He was trying not to show it, but I knew that inside he was devastated.'

'Was he?' Milo looked at Emilio calmly. 'How do you know? You can't be sure. Just think about it for a moment. He's been working on those valleys for over twenty years. When he started people thought he was crazy, but he showed them it was possible. Your bank backed him and made a lot of money from it – but you backed him, not the land. The land had been there since the Incas abandoned it. They managed and so has he. You've seen the way he shows people the ruins, the old forts and reservoirs. He's recreated it. What he wants from me is to continue his work. He doesn't want it abandoned like the Inca remains.'

'It's the same thing,' Emilio protested. 'He's created something which he wants you to take over.'

'No,' said Milo. 'He wants it to last. That's why he wants me. But if I don't take it on, he'll just carry on himself. For all that time he had only himself to rely on. He was on his own and I just don't believe that he'll ever forget that. Yes, he'd be delighted if I took it over, and he'll do anything – you know I mean almost anything – to persuade me to do it. But that's for the estate, not for me. I'm sure that if after all the pressure he's put me under I still want to do something else, then he won't stop me. He'll grumble about it, and make my life difficult. But he won't stop me. At heart, Napeña will always be his first concern. And why not? He created it.'

Emilio stood up and straightened his jacket. 'We'll find out soon enough. James will be back tomorrow, but you can tell him that I'm still not convinced.'

James and Milo had gone over their scaled-down plan until they could find nothing more to change, but they were still nervous as they presented it again to Emilio. This time Martin was in Emilio's office when they arrived. Satisfied that Lisa was safe, he'd enjoyed several days' rest and was now lounging in one of Emilio's leather armchairs. He listened impassively as Milo started to outline their latest proposals. 'We've been looking into the nitrate business very carefully, and James and I are convinced that the Tarapacá desert offers an incredible opportunity. We're going to exercise our options on the land, and then show them how it should be done.'

'So how come you've suddenly become such experts?' Martin asked caustically, unable to sit on the sidelines for long.

'But don't you see? It's just the same as the valleys when you first saw them,' Milo tried to project his enthusiasm. 'Nothing has been worked properly and there's been no investment. Nobody wants to spend money developing the fields while you can simply get a shovel and dig up guano and load it directly onto a ship. But there are over four hundred ships out on the islands waiting to be loaded. It took nearly three months before the earthquake, but now the chutes are damaged it's taking almost twice as long. And the guano won't last forever, while the nitrate reserves are almost unlimited – the dry salt lakes go on for hundreds of miles. But the key to it is investment. James has designed a new machine using steam power to crush the caliche – it could be the same as your irrigation system in the plantations. Next we've got to build a railroad.'

'Railroad!' Martin snorted. 'Railroads are for proper businesses. You won't get anyone to put up money for a line which can only carry nitrates.'

'Isn't that what they said to you when you wanted to build a railroad for your plantations?' Milo asked quickly. 'They all said it would never justify itself. And they were wrong. Now everyone's had to build their own line to be able to compete with you. It's true, isn't it?' Milo looked at him searchingly.

Martin shifted uncomfortably in his chair. 'One thing's for sure,' he said after a while. 'You're not getting the money from me. I'm not going to risk everything I've worked for to back this crazy scheme. If you just wanted a simple nitrate mine, I might consider it, but you're being far too ambitious, talking about railroads.'

'I'm not asking for your money, sir. I want your agreement.' Milo turned to Emilio. 'We've scaled down the plans. There's nothing left to cut, but it'll still work. It's your decision.'

The three of them looked towards Emilio. He stood up and starting pacing around the office in silence. Finally he walked back to his desk and sat down. He picked up the report, then threw it down and looked at Martin. 'And it's a difficult one,' he said. 'It could happen as Milo says, or it could collapse. But I can't ignore the fact that guano prices have been rising steadily since the earthquake. Way above the nitrate prices allowed for in his plans. My directors have authorised me to make the decision,' he hesitated again. 'And I think we've got to take the risk.' He paused. 'Congratulations, Milo. You seem to be in the nitrate business.'

Martin stood up suddenly and glared down at Emilio. 'You can't!' He said in disbelief. 'You can't take him away from me.'

'What?' Emilio looked up in astonishment. 'This isn't about you! This is a commercial decision, just like the ones I've made for you in the past. Milo's project is a risk worth taking. Just like yours were.'

'You must be crazy,' Martin said finally. 'At his age?'

Emilio cleared his throat noisily. 'Martin, we think we know Milo well enough by now to know what he's capable of. And you would be the first to recommend James' engineering talents. They've been demonstrated well enough in the past.'

'But Milo is too young,' protested Martin. 'He's still got so much to learn.'

Emilio laughed. 'When it comes to nitrates, we've all got a lot to learn. It's an entirely new business we're getting into. We've seen the chemical reports, and we've studied Milo's forecasts. Now he's scaled it down, I think Delgado's should be in there first. If it works out, it could push the bank into the first league.'

'Haven't you forgotten something?' There was a note of smugness in Martin's voice. 'What about Chile? You know they're claiming all that land down there. Every time they have an economic slump – which seems to be most of the time, they threaten to invade. What would you do if they took over the mines?'

'They'd never win against Peru,' Emilio said. 'Our navy is too strong. Our first ironclad should be here in a year or so. None of their ships could stand up to that.'

Milo interrupted impatiently. 'That's all in the future. According to our calculations, if the price carries on rising the way it has since the earthquake, our investment will pay itself back within a couple of years. That just shows the potential.' He looked at Martin. 'If the bank is prepared to back it, can we have your approval?'

'It doesn't sound as though you need it,' answered Martin curtly.

'No,' said Milo. 'I don't need it. But I want it.'

'And my plantations? What about them?'

'You'll think of something,' Milo laughed. 'You always have and you always will. Anyway, think of it as diversification. One day you might need a nitrate mine to back you up.'

Chapter Thirteen

1874 – Five years later

'I suppose it could be worse.' Emilio looked along the Iquique dockside.

'You should have seen it when I first came here,' said Milo. 'You can't imagine how much it's improved.'

'It's still got a long way to go,' said Emilio Vasco gloomily, looking across the bay.

'The first time I was in Callao, I could smell it before I could see it.' Milo indicated the two oarsmen heaving on the oars of their boat. 'I was rowing then. Now here I am taking you to see my own railroad. Half of the ships over there are loading with my nitrates.'

'You said it would happen, Milo. The Chinchas are starting to get worked out. The last I heard, there weren't even a hundred ships waiting to load. And now everyone's moving down here. They've all heard how much money there is to be made.'

'It hasn't been easy,' said Milo. 'It's a technical business – we don't have gangs of coolies to load the ships and just send them off. I couldn't have managed without James. He's been incredible – nothing seems to stop him. You see that beach over there?' Milo pointed to the furthest part of the bay, protected by a narrow headland. 'He's been studying the flow of the sea around the headland and he's designed a mole where ships can load alongside. He reckons he'll be able to load over a thousand tons in less than a day.'

As the boat pulled alongside the narrow wall, Emilio followed Milo ashore. 'That's the first investment I made. Remember? It was one thing I wasn't prepared to give up. You told me I was crazy.' Milo looked up at the small wooden building, still fresh with new paintwork. 'It's the first mission in Peru. When people start to see the benefit to trade, they'll be a string of them down the entire West Coast.' Emilio shook his head doubtfully. 'You'll see,' said Milo. 'The old days are nearly gone. The shipping lines will have to start looking after their seamen.'

'Another lesson I've learnt from Callao,' Milo said as they climbed into the waiting carriage. 'I've built my house well inshore, away from any tidal waves.'

'I suppose even Lima was like this once,' said Emilio, as they passed through the desolate scene which surrounded him.

'Cheer up, for heaven's sakes. You will when you see my garden. The railroad doesn't just bring the nitrates, but water as well. When I first came down here it was like being back on a ship; everything had to be brought in by boat – the water came in barrels from up the coast. James sunk a well near the mines and laid a private pipeline alongside the railroad track. To use water for a garden is still considered lunatic extravagance.'

The carriage swayed along the brown, dusty streets. Further inland Emilio saw that palms had been planted beside the paved walkways. The buildings had become newer and more substantial; several, still under construction, were hidden behind bamboo scaffolding. In the main square, the tumbledown Spanish church was being renovated after a century's neglect. As they turned in through a wrought iron gateway, Milo smiled as he pointed out the sparse but carefully tended plants ahead. 'Irrigation – that's the secret, isn't it?'

Milo has the same impatience as Martin Hurst, thought Emilio the next day. He clung tightly to the donkey, straining to find its footing on the sandy track which scaled the high ridges surrounding the bay of Iquique. Milo had insisted they leave before daylight, saying that the only way to understand the *oficinas*, where the raw nitrates were refined, was to see the desert as it was – they could return on the new railroad. As the derelict track led into the wilderness of the valley beyond, Emilio looked around him at the barren landscape. The earth lay as dun-coloured and dusty as when it was first created. The only signs of life – if it could be called that – were the dried bones of the animals which had perished under the weight of the loads carried from the mines. They lay desiccated and blanched from the relentless sun. But the next valley was like a scene from a snow-covered dream. Everything was covered in a ghostly white. The sun had baked the caliche into rock-hard boulders which lay strewn around a landscape almost suspended in time, awaiting the rain which never came. As a boy, in the crystal nights in the foothills of the Andes, Emilio had spent countless evenings looking at the moon through his father's telescope. This was how it had looked.

It was late in the day when they finally rejoined the track of the railroad and approached the cluster of new buildings, already camouflaged by white dust. The thudding of the steam hammer echoed around the small hills as it pounded the caliche. Along the valley were piles of excavated salts, like giant mole-hills, through which wagons rumbled ceaselessly, carrying the saltpetre to the *oficina* for purifying. It was a relief when night finally fell, bringing a silence that seemed almost primordial after the unnatural activity of the day.

'This could hardly be more different from the valleys around Napeña,' said Emilio, as they looked at the ghostly white buildings gleaming in the moonlight, silhouetted against the black sky.

'Even if we irrigated it, nothing would grow,' said Milo. 'It's completely lifeless. I often get the feeling that we're not sup-posed to be here, that we're intruding onto another planet.' They went back inside and joined James, who poured them each an *aguardiente*. Milo let the fiery liquid scorch the dust from his throat. 'Even Iquique seems entirely artificial, though I don't suppose I'll recognise it in twenty years.'

'Possibly,' said Emilio cautiously, as he sipped his drink. 'But I'm worried that the nitrate prices might be starting to fall.'

'Well, you can't say you haven't done well out of it,' said Milo. 'The new Delgado office must have paid for itself dozens of times over.'

'It's not all good times,' Emilio frowned. 'I don't see how we can go ahead with any more investment here until we see whether the prices are going to stabilise.'

'That's why I'm not a banker,' Milo laughed. 'You lend an umbrella when it's dry and ask for it back when it starts raining. All your loans have been paid back several years ahead of time. We've got thousands of pounds on deposit. Don't you have any confidence in us?'

'But what can you do if the price starts to drop?' replied Emilio. 'Don't you remember what you said about Martin's plantations?'

'That's different,' Milo said impatiently. 'Martin can't do much to increase his capacity and he's already producing almost as efficiently as he can. Out here we're only just starting. James is working on more improvements to the refinery. If we can keep on cutting our costs, then we should still survive a falling price. We can produce it cheaper and sell more of it.'

'The more you sell, the more the price will drop,' said Emilio. 'You of all people should know that.'

'No, I don't think so. Not yet, anyway: the market's too young and too small. Overproduction might be a problem when all the other operators get their mines working, but that won't happen for a couple of years yet. Europe's demand keeps on growing. They need these nitrates – we've just got to keep our nerve.'

'It's not a question of nerve,' said Emilio. 'The figures speak for themselves. You've done well over the past few years, but if the prices start to fall, then it'll be time to get out.'

Milo slapped the arm of his chair angrily. 'You still don't understand it, do you? You think that just because the prices have temporarily peaked, we should simply take our money, pack our bags and leave at the first sign of problems. I'm not that sort of person.' Emilio was taken aback at Milo's anger. 'Good things take time, Emilio, whatever they are. How long did it take Martin to establish his estates? He did it properly, building it up slowly. He studied the land, put in irrigation. He looked after his staff to a degree that made everyone else question his sanity. I feel the same way about this place. Yes, it might look like the backside of the moon, but it's got a future that will outlast me. We've got to keep investing, though.' Milo leant back in his chair, his anger passing like a summer thunderstorm. 'It's the same everywhere. Back home in Šipan I saw the estate start to fail, because they didn't understand the need to nurture the trees before you can harvest the olives. But once it's grown, it will last for centuries. It's no different at sea – the best seamen start young, when they can learn and adapt. By the time they're made into skippers, they're tough men who've already seen most of what they're going to face.' Milo stopped suddenly and the silence echoed around the room. 'This is an entire industry we're starting. I'm not running away as soon as we hit our first problems.'

Emilio sat thinking. Milo was usually so self-contained, so calm. He had obviously exposed a raw nerve; he normally appeared so confident that people rarely questioned him. He had such self-belief, without a trace of doubt. Why was he so sensitive? 'Time will tell, I suppose,' he said neutrally.

'I'm sorry, Emilio,' Milo was aware that his outburst had startled them. 'Try and understand. It's not just money – there's another debt I've got to repay. If it hadn't been for this country, for the Hursts – for their sugar plantations even – I'd probably still be at sea, or washed up as a beachcomber. Perhaps drowned in a shipwreck without anyone knowing. But I'm not. I'm here and I've got to make it work. I've got to give something back.'

Emilio shrugged. It wasn't the way he looked at it. For him, things were there for the taking and you tried to grab them before the next man. He decided to change the subject. 'But we've got a more immediate problem than the falling prices. In Lima they're talking about *estanco*.'

'*Estanco*?' asked James. 'What's that?'

'Expropriation,' answered Emilio. 'You know politicians. They can sense money. They've been checking out the nitrate business over the past few months, and they like its smell.'

'You think they'll nationalise it, like the guano trade?' asked James.

'There are two things that governments like to nationalise,' said Milo. 'Businesses that make lots of money, and ones which don't make any. When they take over the first, they usually turn it into the second.'

'But we can't let them buy us out, not after the work we've put into it.' James looked alarmed.

Emilio laughed. 'It happens everywhere. Someone told me about the Emperor Napoleon at an Imperial ball. He spotted a woman covered head to foot in diamonds, and an aide told him that her husband owned a tobacco company. The next day a proclamation was issued expropriating the entire industry. It's the same everywhere.'

'So what can we do about it?' asked Milo. 'You know I'm hopeless with politics.'

'As I was leaving Lima, I was told that a number of the bigger *salitreros* are organising a meeting to fight it, so instead of going on down to Valparaiso, I'll have to go back.'

'Who's going to be there?' asked Milo

'I'm not sure exactly – but Gibbs, of course, although his main workings are in Antofagasta, and that's controlled by Bolivia. I suppose Folsch will be there, and probably J.D. Campbell. But it's the Garcias who are organising it.'

'I should have been able to work that out myself,' said Milo. 'The Garcias seem to be at the centre of everything.'

'That's because they're so close to President Pardo,' said Emilio. 'I sometimes wonder whether the Garcias' business is just an extension of the government, or whether it's the other way around. But now the guano revenues are falling, the government's having problems meeting its debt repayments. They're desperate to find money from somewhere else.'

'So they're looking south, towards Tarapacá?' said Milo.

'I suppose it's inevitable,' said Emilio philosophically. 'But if I'm going to hold my own in a meeting with the Garcias, I wanted to see an *oficina* for myself.

'Can't Milo go with you?' asked James. 'He knows as much as anyone else about the nitrate business.'

'Possibly,' replied Emilio. 'But he knows next to nothing about Peruvian politics.'

'I have a feeling,' said Milo, 'that I'm about to learn.'

'What's happening here?' Emilio had to shout to make himself heard over the thumping of the steam engine.

'This is my invention,' James said proudly. 'Although the nitrate's soluble in water, we've got to crush it first, to help it dissolve. Some of the caliche is as hard as rock. All this used to be done by hand. You can imagine the improvement the steam engine's made.'

'Is it true the Garcias are working on a big new mine?' asked Emilio

'It'll be much larger than ours,' James answered. 'It's away to the south. But the caliche isn't so pure, it'll cost them more to refine and... and... well, they don't have my engineering talent, do they?' He added with a smile.

'I've known Miguel Garcia nearly all my life,' said Emilio. 'He doesn't need his own engineers to come up with ideas; he'll just steal yours. You don't seem to have much security around here.'

'There's no point – they can find out what we're planning as soon as I order the equipment,' said James. 'All the orders are now shipped through Valparaiso in Chile, and the clerks down there sell copies of all our requisitions to the highest bidder. It's almost impossible to keep anything secret. We just have to keep working to stay ahead.'

'And can you?' asked Emilio. 'Stay ahead, I mean?'

'We've got no choice if we want to keep in the game. The Garcias have much greater funds behind them; even you can't compete with their backers. But as long as you stay with us, then we'll make up for it. We're smaller and can move faster.'

'And you were here first,' said Emilio, looking around. A burst of steam hissed from a cylinder underneath the conveyor track. 'So you've already paid back your original investment, while the Garcias have still got a long way to go. Why don't you just leave things as they are? This place looks as though it could run itself now.'

'Don't start that again,' said James. 'You heard Milo last night, and I'm sticking with him. I've never met anyone like him, and I've worked with some pretty single-minded people in the past. Martin Hurst knew exactly what he wanted to achieve, but Milo's looking much further ahead. They both leave the details to me, but Martin Hurst always dealt with one project at a time, while Milo has the entire plan worked out – and what we've done so far is just a small part of it. He's looking ten years ahead, even getting a full-time chemist over from Germany. He says we'll need to certify the purity of our nitrates so that our customers can see they're getting a better product. I asked him: since we don't know the purity of our product, how can we say it's better? He just said that as soon as we find out, we'll make it better.'

'Milo might take a long-term view, but with all the uncertainties about, I'm not sure that the bank can afford to.' Emilio sighed. 'The nitrate market has followed the copper market to Chile and it's moved down to Valparaiso. I was on my way down there to see if it's worth opening another office. I'm worried we're spreading ourselves too thinly. I think we've got some difficult times ahead.'

~~~~~

Milo looked around the crowded room. He recognised many of the men from the numerous receptions at the Villa Miraflores, but a lot were strangers. 'Most of the European producers are staying away,' said Emilio. 'Either that or they're here just as observers. They're trying to keep their distance. Most of the people here are the small *salitreros*. Some of them are probably your neighbours.'

'In Tarapacá, your next-door neighbour can be a day's ride away,' said Milo. 'Who's that over there?' He pointed towards a burly, pasty-faced man sitting on his own. 'He doesn't look very cheerful.' The man was looking around the room, scowling at the company as though they had murdered his son.

'That's George Smith. Gibbs foreclosed on his loan and took over his mine. They gave him a partnership, but then gradually eased him out. It all seemed very carefully planned. They deliberately lent him more money than he could afford to repay, waited for the first sign of a dip in the prices, and then called in the loan and forced him to sell. Since then, of course, the prices have gone up steadily. Gibbs are the only company with enough resources to finance their own development, and they use tricks like that to add to their reserves.'

'What happened to Smith?'

'He lost everything. His wife went back to England, and no one knows how he manages to survive. He still likes to think he's a *salitrero*. He was one of the first, so people still show him respect. I suppose he's here because he thinks it gives him status.'

'It's a cruel place, South America,' observed Milo. 'If you succeed you can go to the top, but if you fail, you end up with nothing.' He looked up as the talking suddenly faded away. On the other side of the room, a group of men came through a side entrance and made their way to the front. At their head was a short, trim man, whose dark face and high cheekbones displayed his Indian ancestry. I'll say one thing about Miguel Garcia, Milo thought:: he doesn't make any pretence of having pure Spanish blood, not like most of the leading families here.

He lets his wealth speak for him. Milo looked back as a late-comer entered the room, and hurried to catch up with the Garcias. Robert Miller. So he's finally joined the nitrate business. Now we really are competitors, thought Milo.

The discussion started, but although Milo listened carefully to the speakers, he kept his own opinions to himself. It's their country, he thought; it's not for me to interfere. If there are representations to be made, Emilio understood how things worked. The meeting, as is usually the case in such matters, ended inconclusively. People felt better having aired their views and they could satisfy themselves that they had at least done something, but most people knew that it was President Pardo who would eventually decide what to do. The best that could be hoped for was that the Garcias would use their influence to suggest a tax instead of outright expropriation.

'Milo Beran!' Milo looked around, startled. Miguel Garcia was approaching him, with his hand outstretched. 'I hope you remember me, and my brother Ramon. We have been honoured to enjoy hospitality at the Villa Miraflores several times. How are Mr and Mrs Hurst?'

'Of course I remember you, sir,' Milo said shaking the hand. 'Lisa and Martin are well enough, thank you.' Milo was not going to discuss Martin's health with his fiercest competitor. 'What did you think of the meeting, sir?'

'These things never accomplish anything, do they?' answered Miguel dismissively. 'But it's good for us all to meet occasionally, to share our problems. If we joined forces more often, the industry would grow even faster. We're all in this together, aren't we?'

Your idea of working together is to have everyone doing as you say, thought Milo. Aloud he asked, 'Do you think the President will go along with *estanco*, sir?'

'If we're working together, you shouldn't call me 'sir'. We're almost equals now.' Milo noted the word 'almost' with amusement. 'You've done a fine job down in Tarapacá,' Miguel continued. 'I look over one shoulder and see Martin Hurst chasing me, and I now look over the other and find you close behind. Still,' he said cheerfully – displaying a row of crooked but very white teeth, heavy with gold fillings – 'it's a competitive world.'

'And *estanco*, sir?' repeated Milo.

'Ah, well, that's another matter,' Miguel said mysteriously. 'The government's got to get some money somehow, otherwise they'll have a string of failures among the banks holding their bonds.'

'And is yours one?' asked Emilio, joining the conversation. 'I had always understood that you didn't do any work with the government.'

'Not directly, no,' Miguel Garcia shrugged slightly. 'But we have certain, what you might call, arrangements, and it doesn't help to have all this uncertainty. It has to be resolved one way or another.'

'And *estanco*, sir?' repeated Milo, for the third time.

'No,' said Miguel finally. 'I don't think we'll have that, but we've got to meet them halfway. A production tax, I think. We can all live with that, can't we?' He half turned as Robert Miller approached. 'Robert! Come and join us. You know Milo and Señor Vasco?'

'Of course I do, Don Miguel. You know perfectly well that I used to live with the Hursts. You've asked me enough about them in the past.' Milo couldn't decide whether Robert was serious in revealing such a confidence, or whether he was just teasing.

'My memory! It's getting full of holes,' said Miguel, smiling smugly. Everyone knew he never forgot anything.

Milo returned to the subject. If he was going to have the benefit of talking to Señor Garcia, he wanted to make the most of the man's opinions. 'If Peru introduces a production tax, that'll help the Gibbs' Antofagasta mine. Bolivia has signed a treaty which leaves their mines tax-exempt.'

'Have you ever known the Bolivians to keep their word?' asked Miguel. 'But even if they do, the Gibbs have higher costs out there. I think we can manage to live with a modest tax, don't you?' Señor Garcia was looking over Milo's shoulder; clearly there was someone more important he could see and his attention had already moved on.

Milo decided to keep the initiative and held out his hand decisively. 'I've got to go now, sir, but it's been good to see you and your brother again. I'll give your regards to Mr and Mrs Hurst.'

Señor Garcia was already moving away. 'Yes, please do that,' he said absently before he was gone. Milo and Robert watched as the Garcias approached another group of men huddled deep in conversation. They parted like corn before a scythe as the Garcias established themselves at their centre.

'I don't know how you can work with him,' Milo said finally turning to Robert. 'You don't trust him, do you?'

'Why not? His motives are pretty straightforward – he just wants to keep the money he's already made, and make more of it.'

'And doesn't care how he does it?'

'That's not fair. He follows the customs of the country.'

'Is that what it's called?' Milo laughed cynically. 'I thought the word was corruption.'

Robert flushed. 'I admit he's very close to President Pardo, but there's not much he can do – even in his own country – without European money. The foreign banks have more power than any President.'

'Is that why they employ you?'

'They employ me because I can deal with the trading houses. They don't need European banks; they have access to their own funds. Anyway, there's a limit to what they can handle, even for two brothers – it's almost an empire they're running. They've got interests in almost everything that happens here, and at least their money stays in this country – it isn't sent straight back to Europe as with most of the firms.'

'Martin doesn't take money out,' said Milo. 'Neither do I. We're both reinvesting it.'

'For the moment, yes. But what about all the commissions, all the interest? All that goes straight out of the country. And when you start paying dividends from the profits, where's that going?'

Milo turned and watched the Garcias leave discreetly through the side door. 'You make them sound like a patriotic charity, fending off the marauding foreigners.'

'Charity?' Robert laughed. 'I never said the Garcias were running a charity. They're out for what they can get, like everyone else here. But I think they're fair. They're very thorough, and check everything very carefully before they commit themselves. You've got to get up very early to see something they haven't thought of.'

'Well,' said Milo, 'it seems they've managed to put off this *estanco*. For the time being, at least. Now I can get back to Tarapacá, but first I'm spending a few days at Villa Miraflores. Are you joining us?'

'I haven't seen Mrs Hurst for some time,' Robert answered. 'I feel rather guilty about it. Can I join you for dinner?'

Milo knocked at the panelled front door. Why don't I just open it? he wondered – it's not locked. It's taken me only a few years to turn into a visitor. Julio opened the door, pulling a long face when he saw Milo. 'Señor Milo,' he said reproachfully. 'You don't have to knock on the door. You live here. This is your home.'

'Thank you, Julio, I'll try to remember. Is Mrs Hurst here?'

'In the drawing room, Señor Milo. She has visitors.'

Milo was disappointed. Although Lisa often had visitors for tea, he had hoped that this time they would be alone. He entered the room, preparing himself for the polite but empty social conversation that was usually on offer at such gatherings. Lisa held up her cheek to be kissed before introducing her visitors. 'Milo, dear, you remember Mrs Hellman?'

'Mrs Hellman?' he asked in surprise. 'Yes, of course. We met in Huacatambo.'

'With my daughter,' said Mrs Hellman, shaking his hand.

'Yes, with Alicia. How is she?'

'Why don't you ask me?' The voice came from the chair behind him. He turned, and the unexpected memories of those few, fleeting days washed over him.

'Aren't you going to say hello?' asked Alicia finally.

Milo tried to make some sense of his thoughts. 'I, er – yes, yes,' he started, suddenly aware that he had been staring at her. He shook her hand formally, trying to cover his embarrassment. 'It's good to meet you again.'

The girl laughed, a familiar, bright and cheery laugh. 'You haven't forgotten me?'

Milo was flustered. How could he tell her how often he'd thought about her? 'No, of course not. I – I've missed you,' he said awkwardly.

'You rushed off and left me. Just as we were getting to know one another.'

'Yes, I'm sorry.' How could he explain about Jurica? About the sacrifice his mother had made?

'When I got back to Lima, they told me you'd already left for the desert. You told me you were going to stay in Napeña. How could you miss such wonderful riding?'

'It's complicated,' Milo said. 'I'll explain later.' Milo sat down next to her and absently took the plate which Lisa handed him. 'I did try and find you, but they told me you'd gone away.'

'I went off to Europe to stay with my aunt. My mother wanted some of the old country's sophistication to rub off on me, rather than mix with the bad company to be found in Lima.'

'Now Alicia, stop teasing. You know it upsets me when you say things like that.' Mrs Hellman didn't seem in the least upset. She seemed every bit as light-hearted as her daughter. 'You'll embarrass Mr Hurst.'

'Beran, Mrs Hellman,' said Milo, looking across to Lisa anxiously to see if she was upset by the mistake. 'Please, just call me Milo,' he turned back to Alicia. 'Are you going to stay here long?'

'Well now, that depends. I must give it some thought,' she said putting on an expression of mock seriousness. 'I don't think I've yet decided what I shall do. Although I'll probably find out in due course,' she added brightly. 'After I've done it.'

'Depends?' asked Milo. 'What does it depend upon?'

'What a silly question,' said Alicia. If she didn't have such a pretty nose, thought Milo, I would have said she snorted. 'It depends upon who I make friends with, of course, and I won't decide that until I've met everyone in Lima. My mother told me that I had to start here. So here we are.'

'Now, dear,' warned Mrs Hellman.

'Well, it's true,' said Alicia without embarrassment. 'And now Milo and I want to get to know each other again, so he's going to show me the garden.'

Milo jumped to his feet. Now he really was embarrassed. Should he have offered to show her around before she asked him? Or was she flirting with him? He really didn't know. But he kept his normal serious expression and held out his hand to help her up. 'I'm not such a good guide as the Hursts – they created it. But I'll be delighted to tell you what I know.' Alicia took his hand and stood up. She moves so gracefully, thought Milo, as he followed her into the garden: almost athletically. Most of the girls he had met seemed to shuffle on tiptoe, taking small steps so they wouldn't disturb the lines of their skirts. Alicia didn't seem to care. She was almost striding, apparently unconcerned by her appearance. As he explained the planting, he found she responded easily, saying what she thought without a trace of embarrassment or self-consciousness. Milo found it immensely refreshing. In business, he was accustomed to keeping his thoughts to himself, saying only what needed to be said, but socially it was very different. He had difficulty in understanding many of the social nuances, even after they were explained to him, and tended to say what he thought, expecting everyone else to be thinking the same. When in Lima he found himself constantly berated by Lisa for his lack of tact. 'Try being diplomatic, for a change,' she had once counselled him before attending an elaborate dinner party. 'Try concealing your views until you've established what other people are thinking.' When he had protested at such a cynical approach, she had told him: 'You can only talk frankly to a friend, and how frankly you can talk decides how good a friend they are.'

Alicia had no time for such constraint, and Milo warmed to her spontaneity and independent outlook. They were still talking in the garden when Lisa called out to them that Mrs Hellman was leaving. 'Why did you call me back so soon?' he asked later, when they were alone. 'We were just beginning to get to know each other.'

Lisa shook her head, as though dealing with a backward child. 'You know, Milo, you were out there for an hour. You can see her again.' She muttered something almost under her breath. Milo wasn't sure if had heard her properly.

'What was that?' he asked.

'Nothing,' said Lisa. 'Nothing important.'

After dinner that evening, Robert followed Milo into the library. 'So what did you think of the meeting?' he asked as they settled into armchairs. They hadn't spoken privately for some time and Robert was looking forward to hearing all Milo's news.

'It wasn't a meeting,' replied Milo. 'They were here when I came back.'

'What?' said Robert.

'Yes. And Lisa set it up. She as good as said so. She said that she hadn't expected it to go so well – although she denied it afterwards.'

'Milo,' said Robert. 'What are you talking about? You've been acting strangely all evening. What's the matter?'

Milo handed him an *aguardiente*. 'Have you ever met her?' he asked.

'Who, for heaven's sake?'

'Alicia Hellman,' said Milo staring into the distance.

'Oh. I see,' said Robert, checking the level of his drink. 'You'd better tell me about it.'

'But I don't understand why you have to leave tomorrow. What difference does a few weeks make?'

Milo felt miserable. He didn't know what to say to her. He'd already extended his stay for a week and the time had passed so quickly. 'Alicia,' he took her hand, but it lay limp and unresponsive in his. 'It's my work. I can't just ignore it. You're the one who's always concerned with independence: you should understand. It's what I do. And I've still got such a long way to go.'

'I can understand all that,' said Alicia. She was clearly angry and she pulled her hand away. 'Of course you've got your work, just like my father had his. Lima's always been a working city – but why can't you take some more time off? My father worked hard, but he made time to spend a couple of months up-country each winter. Why can't you do the same?'

'Because I'm not established yet.' Milo was almost pleading. 'I've got so much planned and it's going to take all my time; besides, they need me. But I'll be back in a couple of months, I promise.'

'But Milo, I've enjoyed this past week so much,' Alicia's anger faded quickly and she smiled at him. 'Haven't you had a good time too?' She reached and took Milo's hand again.

'Of course I have.' Milo was reassured as he felt her fingers squeeze his. This was how Alicia was meant to be: happy and affectionate. 'And we'll have lots more good times together. You'll only have to wait a couple of months.'

'But what's so important down there? Why can't they manage without you? Everyone says you've already made money; surely you can take a little time off?'

'It's not that simple, Alicia. I've only just started. We've hardly scratched the surface. The money's just a drop in the ocean compared to the fortunes that are going to be made. I've got to be there. There's so much happening and it's going to get very competitive; only a few of us can survive. I can't take time off now.' He looked at the disappointment in her eyes. 'Later, I promise you. When I've got properly established, then I can relax a bit.'

Alicia looked down at the table and sighed. After a while she raised her head and looked at him sadly. 'Are you always so serious?' she asked. 'Is it all really so important to you?'

'Yes,' said Milo. 'Nothing has ever been this important.'

Alicia said nothing. She just stared at Milo, her eyes questioning. He returned her stare and read the question in her eyes, not knowing the answer.

'And me?' Alicia asked finally. 'Am I important too?'

Milo flushed deeply. 'Of course you're important. This past week has been… it's been so different. I won't be gone long. I'll be back soon. We can pick it up from here. I promise.'

Alicia took a deep breath and stood up. 'I can't be expected to wait longer.' She turned and Milo watched her go.

Chapter Fourteen

Down in Iquique the nitrate market continued to fall, while Milo and James swam doggedly against the stream. Producers were suffering throughout Tarapacá; without the resources of the large European banks behind them, the smaller operators – nearly all locally owned – failed and were swept away in the current. Capitalism penetrated the length of South America and, like the forces of evolution studied here by Charles Darwin forty years earlier, it ensured that only the fittest would survive.

Sugar prices fell even further. Robert Miller, whose principal job was to represent the Garcias' interests to the European agency houses, had started to question his future in the country. At this rate, he thought, there would be nothing left in a few years. Of all the plantation owners, only the Garcias and Martin Hurst seemed secure – the Garcias because they didn't carry the burden of large interest and debt repayments to foreign banks, and Martin Hurst because his investment had ensured the efficiency of his estates. In spite of this, there was something wrong. He had been summoned – Martin never invited people – to the Villa Miraflores, but Martin still had not told him why and still he wouldn't come to the point. Robert was getting uncomfortable. He had never seen Martin Hurst so indecisive. His mind seemed to wander. Robert remembered the forceful planter of just a few years ago, someone who had never showed the least trace of self-doubt and of whom, to tell the truth, he had always been slightly afraid.

'What is it exactly that you want me to do?' Robert asked finally.

'Haven't you worked that out yet?' said Martin testily. 'I thought I'd made it quite obvious.'

'I understand that you want to plant the land at Matotambo, but what I don't understand is why there should be a problem.'

'Problem? I didn't say there was a problem,' said Martin, returning to his earlier rambling. 'I just said that you might be able to help me.'

'Look, Mr Hurst... Martin,' Robert tried again. 'You've spent half a lifetime creating new plantations. The entire Napeña Valley is a monument to your skill; why is this one so different? Why is it so difficult?'

'It's not that it's difficult,' said Martin. 'That is, it's not easy. The foothills are so much higher, you see. If there isn't enough head in the spring we might have to pump the water up. The soil's not as good, of course, but we should be able to get it right after a couple of years or so. No, I think it's going to be a good investment.'

Robert was starting to get irritated. 'So where's the problem?' he repeated.

Martin was silent for a while, studying his boots. Finally, without looking up, he said quietly. 'I haven't got the money.'

Those few words took a little while to sink in. Robert just stared. Irrationally he noticed the hair thinning over Martin's tanned scalp. This was the great Martin Hurst – the Sugar King, one of the richest men on the West Coast. What did he mean, he didn't have the money? Robert decided to say nothing. Martin would have to explain.

'Don't misunderstand me,' Martin continued, looking up. 'I'm not broke, or anything like that. I've still got all the plantations. It's just that I'm short of cash. Prices have fallen. They'll go back up again, I'm sure of it – that's why I want to develop the new fields. I'm sure it's the right thing to do – haven't I always been proved right in the past? It'll be no different this time.'

Robert was about to observe that Martin had been considerably younger then, but changed tack at the last moment. 'But why do you want to? You don't need the money. Why don't you just take things easy – enjoy your success? Spend more time here in Villa Miraflores and see more of Lisa.'

'The best way to enjoy success is to have more success,' said Martin, almost bitterly. 'If I just gave up now, people would say I was past it.'

'What do you mean, "gave up"? You've still got one of the largest plantations in the country; continuing to manage them properly is hardly giving up.' Robert thought for a moment. 'Anyway, I still don't understand why you can't afford it.'

'It's my fault, I suppose,' said Martin. Robert was surprised. He had never heard Martin take the blame for anything. 'I didn't believe that prices would carry on falling. So instead of selling direct, I built some warehouses near Samanco and put the crop into store, waiting for the price to rise again. But it didn't. The money I lost seems to have had a knock-on effect and the price has just carried on falling. I've used my final reserves to subsidise this year's crop.'

'Can't Emilio Vasco help you?' asked Robert. 'The two of you almost started out together – won't he put up a loan?'

'For the existing plantations in Napeña, yes. But it's the new fields. He says he can't justify the investment while prices are so low.' Martin shook his head. 'D'you know, he's never turned me down before. Not once, in over thirty years. He always trusted my judgement and it always worked out. Now he's so deeply involved in Milo's nitrate business, he's turned his back on the business that made him.'

'But perhaps he's right,' Robert said nervously, fearing Martin's reaction. If Emilio was right, then Martin was wrong. 'Why don't you just wait a while, and see which way the price goes?'

'And end up following the market, just like everyone else?' Martin's voice was rising. 'To take advantage of a price rise in the future, I need to invest now. That's how Milo did it.'

'But Milo only modelled his operations on yours. All the infrastructure he put in, the railroads and machinery, the workers' settlements. He saw how it worked in Napeña and copied it.'

'And look at him now!' said Martin. 'For the past three years he's barely broken even, but still Emilio is putting up even more investment. Why should Emilio back him and not me?'

Robert wondered. Why, with all that Martin had achieved, should he feel so insecure? His record would stand up to anyone's. 'This isn't about Milo,' said Robert. 'The market's not the same. He's talking about cutting costs, you're talking about increasing production – the two are completely different. If Emilio isn't prepared to back you, then why don't you just accept it?'

'Because all my life I've never been prepared to accept the unacceptable. There's always another way: the problem is to find it. That's why I wanted to speak to you.'

'No other bank is likely to put up the money, so I don't see what I can do.'

'I wasn't talking about another bank,' Martin hesitated. 'I wanted you to talk to the Garcias. Ask if we can develop it together in some kind of partnership.'

'The Garcias?' Robert stared at him incredulously. 'No, you can't! It's not possible.'

'Of course it's possible; it's simply business.'

'For them perhaps.' Robert's reaction was immediate. 'Perhaps also for me too, but don't tell me that your sugar plantations are just business. They're your life.'

'Nonsense,' Martin said shortly. 'Don't be sentimental. Milo was always saying that I should diversify, and this could be the way to do it.'

'But not with the Garcias. You've spent the past thirty years competing with them at every step, neither of you giving an inch. You can't just suddenly turn around and say that's all in the past, and now you're going to join them.'

'Why not?'

'Because it would never work. Even if the figures were right, the personalities aren't. Both sides would want to run things. I can't see you letting them anywhere near your estates.'

'I wouldn't have to,' Martin said emphatically. 'That's the clever bit, you see. We'd only be partners in the new plantation. They wouldn't have anything to do with Napeña. Let's see what they say.'

'Martin, you won't be able to control the Garcias. no one can.' Robert looked at him earnestly. 'Please don't ask me. Even if they do agree, you'll never forgive me for what could happen.'

'Ask them, Robert. Just ask them. I've got it all planned: a new design of irrigation system – and this time I'm going to plant along the contour lines.' For the first time Martin sounded enthusiastic. 'It's going to be my finest achievement. You'll see. If the only way I can get it done is to share it with the Garcias, then I'll share it.'

Robert made one last attempt. 'Have you spoken about this with Milo? If he finds out you've gone to the Garcias, I can't think what he'll say.'

'Well, we're not going to tell him,' said Martin. 'He'll find out when it's all finished. He's not the only one who can build things up. Now, will you ask them?'

'If you tell me I must, then I'll have no choice. But it –'

Martin interrupted him. 'Just ask them,' he said curtly.

Robert delayed approaching Miguel Garcia for several days. Since leaving the Hursts' employment he had been able to keep the interests of the two families separate. He found it worked better that they were competitors – that way their business affairs didn't overlap and everyone knew where they stood. The rôles were clear and unambiguous. At work, he was on the side of the Garcias; socially, he was the Hursts' friend. The idea that Martin would enter a partnership with the Garcias horrified him, the more so because of Martin's irrational objectives. He should be scaling things down, not trying to establish another plantation while the sugar price was through the floor. He toyed with the idea of speaking to Lisa Hurst, but he knew that the basis of their marriage was that she kept apart from his business. She knew well enough that to interfere could be disastrous and she never questioned her husband's work.

The Garcias' boardroom was an imposing but sombre place. Panelled with dark oak, imported from Spain, it was gloomy even on the sunniest days. Around the room were oil paintings of the extended family members, the founding fathers of the enterprise, apparently showing uniform disapproval of what was now being done in their names. They added to the shadowy feeling of menace that Robert always experienced here. The meeting had ended, and just Miguel and Ramon remained. Robert took a deep breath and put before them Martin's suggestion. Miguel was a keen card player and proud of his poker face, but it was clear that he was completely astonished. 'You're quite sure?' he asked several times, and Robert repeated that there was no question about it. Martin wanted a loan to develop a new sugar plantation.

Miguel shook his head sadly. 'Why doesn't he take it easy? He's got nothing left to prove. I've always admired him; he was usually one step ahead of us. He always seemed to know what was going to happen next.'

'So what do we do?' asked his brother.

'You're quite sure he wants to do this?' Miguel asked Robert, yet again.

'That's what he told me. He said it was just for the new fields and an extension to the railroad. He said whatever happened he'd still have the Napeña valley estates.'

'I think he must be slipping,' said Miguel. 'Firstly, at his age and after all he's achieved, he wants to roll the dice again; and secondly, he wants a one-way bet. What does he think would be in it for us? We put up the money to develop his fields and share any profits. If there aren't any profits, he just walks away and we're left with a loss-making sugar plantation. We've got plenty of those already. He can't think we're that stupid.'

Robert looked embarrassed. 'I'm not sure he's thought it through at all. He seems to think it's like the old times, when everything happened as he said it would. I don't think he's really thought about failure.'

'Even with the sugar price dropping every year for the past four years?' said Miguel. 'Three years ago, the nitrate price started chasing it. That was when I managed to talk the President out of *estanco*. I often think that was a mistake; if they'd bought us out then, it would have been at the top of the market. I suppose if Milo Beran were doing better, then Martin would have approached him for a loan.'

'I don't think so,' said Robert. 'I don't think he would ever ask Milo for money. Anyway I doubt Milo has got any to spare and he's got major commitments to the bank. I'm surprised that Señor Vasco's bank is still backing him. He must have a strong nerve.'

Miguel turned to his brother. 'What do you think, Ramon? Banker to the great Martin Hurst – we'd be allowed into the European Club next.'

'It's an interesting opportunity,' Ramon answered carefully. Unlike his flamboyant brother, he was quiet and reserved. People always assumed that Miguel was the dominant partner, but Ramon contributed an analytical approach to the business which often reined in some of Miguel's more excessive enthusiasms. 'I don't think we really want to start developing any more plantations until the price steadies, but if we can somehow get involved in Napeña, well...'

Robert cut in. 'I told you he's only prepared to offer the new land.'

'Perhaps,' said Ramon. 'But you also said that he's desperate. He might be persuaded to go further.' He turned to Miguel, 'Perhaps if we offered him something extra?'

Miguel thought about it. 'We'd need more security than just the new land. Mr Hurst is only proposing that we go paddling in the water. But if we offer him an additional incentive, then he might go in as far as his waist: or even his chest.' He stopped, and his gold-capped teeth glinted as he smiled at Robert. 'Who knows? If he slips, he might even find himself swimming.'

'Or drowning,' said Robert. 'What are you suggesting?'

'I think you should put it to him step by step,' said Miguel. 'If Mr Hurst wants us to advance the money to develop his new plantations, then we must have additional security. Otherwise, if it doesn't work out, we would lose the entire investment while he would have lost nothing. He must be able to see that.'

Robert nodded. 'Go on.'

'If he offered Napeña as security, then the balance would tilt the other way. Those estates are worth too much.' Robert nodded again.

'So if we put in something extra by way of cross-collateral, something he thinks matches the value of Napeña, then each party would be covered. That seems fair, doesn't it?' Miguel gave Robert a big grin.

When you can see his teeth, thought Robert, that's the time to back away. 'What would you offer?' he asked guardedly.

Miguel looked at Ramon, who nodded slightly. He turned back to Robert. 'What about a nitrate refinery?' he asked. 'You said he was talking about diversifying. This way he could exchange his sugar interests for saltpetre.' He paused and turned back to Ramon. 'What *oficina* can we offer him? It would have to be a good one to match Napeña.'

'California,' Ramon said after a moment's thought. 'Compagñía Salitrera de California. It's the only one that's big enough – we could pledge the shares. We've got the figures.'

'But that's your biggest operation in Tarapacá,' Robert protested. 'You can't give him that.'

'We wouldn't be giving it to him,' said Miguel sharply. 'We're talking about offering the shares as security – that's completely different. You can tell him all about it: he'll trust you.'

'You want me to tell him that you'll put up the money, but only if he offers the Napeña valley estates as security? He'll never agree.'

'Even if we throw in the California?' asked Miguel. 'It doesn't matter anyway; we don't have to do this deal. With the price of sugar as it is, what do we want to develop another sugar plantation for? See what he says. He might agree if he's desperate enough.'

Robert left them, and Miguel got up to check the door was firmly shut. 'What do you think, Ramon?' he asked. 'He might have heard that the President is talking about expropriation again. If it goes ahead, the nitrate fields would be confiscated.'

'*Estanco* has been talked about for so long that people scarcely think about it any more, but it can only be a matter of time before Pardo actually goes through with it. It'll happen within a year. Eighteen months at most.'

'Yes, I think so.' Miguel chuckled. 'It's about time we started thinking about protecting our assets down in Tarapacá. Have we set up the operating company yet?'

'All the contracts are in place. The California is just a shell. It doesn't employ anyone.'

'So if Martin Hurst comes in with us and defaults, then if *estanco* goes through, he could end up with government guarantees instead of his sugar plantations.' Miguel smiled at his brother, his gold teeth flashing. 'And we both know how much they're worth.'

Robert reluctantly told Martin what the Garcias had proposed. 'I really don't think you should do it,' he added. 'Why risk everything?' He managed to stop himself from adding 'at your time of life'.

Martin was intrigued by the possibility of owning an *oficina* and was too impatient to consider all the consequences. 'Milo was always telling me I might need a nitrate mine, so why shouldn't I have one securing my plantations?' He asked Robert. 'Wouldn't it be strange if I ended up in the nitrate business too?'

Robert had tried one last time to dissuade him. 'You would only get the California Company if the Garcias foreclose on Napeña. Think about it. If it came to it, would you really want to lose what you've spent so much time and effort creating? You know that people who do business with the Garcias usually come off worse.'

Martin interrupted. 'You seem to be assuming that the sugar price won't go back up. I'm betting it will.'

And staking everything on it, thought Robert, who couldn't think of any more arguments to use. If Milo were here, he would be able to do something, but he was still in Tarapacá. Since the nitrate prices started falling three years ago, Milo had been spending all his time between Tarapacá and Valparaiso.

'So I tell the Garcias that you'll do it?'

'Yes, do that.' Martin rubbed his hands together. 'It'll show Emilio Vasco that there are still plenty of people who'll back me.'

~~~~~

'The Bordés shipping agent has just confirmed it.' Milo handed the telegram to Emilio. 'They'll only pay £12 per ton.'

'And there's no one else?' Emilio didn't sound hopeful.

'Even if there were, Bordés has the only ships that can carry enough to make it worthwhile.'

'So we've got no choice?' Emilio looked worried. 'Can you survive at that price?'

Milo shrugged. 'Possibly. But what happens after that? The profit's being drained out of us. If we do survive, we'll have to find an alternative to Bordés.'

They were in the new Delgado office in Valparaiso. The Pacific telegraph had just been completed and Milo had made full use of it. The nitrate prices had been falling since the meeting in Lima and were still highly volatile. By monitoring the prices from agents in London and Hamburg, they had been able to survive by wringing the last few shillings from each consignment. On the margins they were operating with, a few shillings made the difference between profit and loss.

'It's going to get tougher. I just hope our cash reserves last out.' Milo stood up and walked to the window. The Delgado building was towards the south, on the hills leading towards the city's centre. From the office there was a view clear across the wide bay, which swept away to the north, towards Iquique and the nitrate fields. Today the sea was calm, the sun reflecting off the ripples which covered the gently undulating waves. Along the coast, the red earth seemed to glow in the sunlight. Although most of the nitrates were now exported from the ports to the north, Valparaiso docks were still busy servicing the railroads and mineral trade, although that too had suffered drastic price falls.

'It's our first real test. Commodities prices have fluctuated in the past, but the only way we're going to survive now is by cutting our production costs.' Milo turned away from the window. 'We need that new plant, Emilio.'

Emilio sighed. 'We're under pressure from every direction. How can you justify more investment when your operations have been skirting the edge of bankruptcy for the past six months?'

'We need to be able to ride out these price swings. We *have* to do more.'

'But you're already one of the most efficient operations in Tarapacá, and the smaller operators are acting as a buffer. As they go bust the supply reduces, and hopefully the prices will stabilise.'

'We've got to do more than that,' said Milo. 'We can't just sit here and hope for the best. Prices will stabilise one day; that's when we'll make the real money. We've got to be ready for it.'

'I went through some difficult times with the sugar market when Martin was getting established, but I've never seen anything like this. And the investment is so much greater. I sometimes wonder who controls things – the bank or the borrower. We've lent you so much money that we can't afford to ask for it back. You haven't got it, but if we took over your refinery instead, what could we do with it that you hadn't already done? It would be better to let you get on with it – if anyone could get our money back it's going to be you. Not,' Emilio hastened to add, 'that we're thinking of calling in the loans.'

'It's called capitalism.' Milo pointed across the bay. 'All those ships out there are its lubrication. Delivering the products of capital invested around the world. None of it would have been possible without steam – we'd still be breaking the caliche by hand. But steam-powered machinery now costs so much that only the banks can provide the necessary money. They lend to entrepreneurs who make more money and then hand back the balance, keeping a little of the profit for themselves. But ultimately it's the banks with capital that control things. They can spread their risks: people like me can't. Capitalism and the steam age go hand in hand.'

'Ships aren't powered by steam – only the coasters and the tugs.'

'They will be. Even now they're starting to put steam donkeys on sailing ships. Some of the newer ships can operate with just a few dozen seamen. One day they'll probably be running steamers with a crew of six.' Milo stopped and stared at the ships swaying at their anchors. He turned back to Emilio. 'If we don't order the new machinery, we could lose everything.'

Emilio was silent for several minutes. Finally he stood up and joined Milo at the window. 'That's a hungry monster out there,' he gestured towards the ships. 'You fill one of them, but there'll always be another waiting behind it. You're right, of course. You usually are. Demand isn't going to stop suddenly. I don't think we have a choice; we've got to stick with it.'

Milo let out a sigh of relief. 'Thank you, Emilio. I'll get James to start planning right away. I know it's risky, but it's right.'

'But I don't like gambling everything on one throw of the dice.'

Milo laughed. 'You've got plenty of other irons in the fire, Emilio. And when the price picks up, you'll have to think about adding a shipping line to them. We need a reliable alternative to Bordés.'

Emilio groaned. 'Can we just try to get through this year first?' he asked plaintively. 'You're like Martin Hurst talking about when the prices go back up. You are always the first to ask him why they should.'

'That's because Martin has spent so long with his plantations that he's forgotten about the competition. But even with the sugar price so low, he should be able to hold on. He's built up enough reserves over the years. Do you remember that time we visited his new vineyard in Matotambo?'

'How could I forget? But a lot's happened since then.'

'You remember he was talking about planting it with sugar cane?'

'I know. He asked me to lend him the money.'

Milo looked at Emilio in astonishment. 'What! He's crazy. What did you say?'

'For the first time ever, I turned him down. He wasn't very happy about it.'

'It would have been too expensive. With the present level of competition, he should leave things as they are and concentrate on Napeña.'

'That's what I told him,' said Emilio. 'And I just hope he listened. I can't think of another bank that would lend him the money, although he's still the most efficient producer in Peru.'

'I'm not talking about Peru. Sugar can be grown in dozens of places. What about the competition from the Caribbean islands? The British are investing heavily there. With nitrates, it's completely different. If the world needs saltpetre, it has to come to us. If we can control the supply, then we can control the price, and until the producers understand that and stop trying to undercut each other, the price will go down.'

'Is that capitalism, too?' asked Emilio.

'No, that's common sense,' said Milo.

James watched the rocket pierce the dark night sky, exploding in a climax of sparkling light which rippled around the seafront. Along the bay, the fleet of anchored ships were celebrating their departure under the light of the coloured lanterns swinging in their rigging. 'Homeward-bounders,' he sighed. 'It'll be our turn one day.'

'Not yet,' Milo sounded almost irritable. 'There's still too much to do. How long will it take before we can get the plant delivered?'

'Probably the best part of a year. Then we've got to ship it. And you know what Bordés is like.'

Milo frowned. 'I hope we can hold out that long. I wonder,' he stopped as the noise of sailors dancing washed over the quiet shore. 'I was thinking. Have you ever heard of the Minerva Line?'

James shook his head. 'You know no one else apart from Bordés can handle the volume.'

'Could you make some enquiries?'

James nodded, thinking of something else. 'Er – Milo?'

'What is it?'

'When the steamer takes us up to Iquique, are you staying here or going on up to Callao?'

'You mean am I going to visit Alicia?' Milo sighed. 'I wish you'd stop nagging me. You know how bad the situation is here. If we're to survive, I've got to squeeze everything possible from the operation.'

'But we can spare you for a few weeks – it's more than a year since you were last there.'

'Don't remind me. I've written to her and explained the situation down here. I'm sure she understands how things are – everyone's suffering. And you'll be too busy with the new machines to have time to look after anything else.'

'It'll take several weeks to prepare the plans,' said James. 'There's nothing you can do before then and this is probably your last chance. If you don't go back now, you'll lose her.'

Milo looked up as another firework burst above their heads. 'Before I had to leave Šipan and go to sea, I remember life being so happy, but since then something always seems to get in the way. I'm just afraid that if I went back, then she'd…' He stopped.

James waited for him to finish, but Milo just stared out at the darkness and said nothing. 'Afraid that if you went back then she'd what?' James asked after a while.

'All right. I'll go up and see her. But she'll have to understand that I can't stay for long.'

~~~~~

Milo had taken many risks during his short career. It was the nature of business in South America that the potential rewards made the gambles worthwhile, and Milo accepted this as a fact of life. He saw investment not as a bet, but as a straightforward decision based upon a cool examination of the situation. He did it calmly and without emotion. For this reason, he couldn't understand why he should feel so nervous as he waited in Mrs Hellman's drawing room for Alicia to come down. How would she greet him? Perhaps she had changed; perhaps she had found someone else. Why had he left it so long?

At first he couldn't think of anything to say. He stared at her as she came into the room; he had forgotten how striking she was, her dark, wavy hair cut to her neck and her sharp features and pale skin accentuating the attraction of her attentive expression. She sat down on the settee with a studied elegance and smoothed her skirt down over her knees. There was a teasing smile in her eyes, and all Milo could think of was relief that she didn't seem angry with him. 'So you've finally found time to come and visit me?' she said. 'It must have been very difficult to get away with all your responsibilities.'

If Milo noticed the sarcasm, he ignored it. 'It has,' he said emphatically. 'This has been the worst year we've had in Tarapacá. I still don't know if we can survive.'

'You haven't come all this way to talk about boring old business, have you?' Alicia tossed her head in impatience.

'Of course not,' said Milo. 'But it is important.'

'Not to me it isn't. All business is boring. Now where are you going to take me?' she asked suddenly.

Milo was taken aback. 'I'm – I'm not sure,' he hesitated. She must realise that I've only just come up from Valparaiso, he thought. He'd only been able to stop in Iquique for one night. 'Do we have to go anywhere?' he asked in disappointment. 'Can't we just stay here and talk?'

'I know,' Alicia said brightly. 'You can take me for a walk in the Alameda – that's always the place to be seen in Lima. There's probably a band playing and we can dance a turn or two. Afterwards you can take me to the Gran Bolivar for dinner.'

Although Milo couldn't find any enthusiasm for dancing, it was clear that Alicia was set on it. Once she had made a decision, there was little that could change it. She had a very simple view of life and couldn't understand why people spent so much time considering alternatives. Her approach was straightforward: if it seemed a good idea, just do it. Milo took her out to his waiting carriage; they could talk on the way. And at dinner. At least they could catch up with each other over a long dinner.

Milo watched the brandy swirl around the glass. He held it towards Alicia and looked at her through the tawny liquid, watching the candlelight casting a mellow, flickering glow across her face. She was still as direct and uncomplicated as he remembered her. He held the cognac under his nose and sniffed it, dismissing the waiter with a nod. He put down the glass, leant forward to Alicia and put his hand over hers. 'I've missed you so much,' he said anxiously. 'I'm sorry I couldn't get back any sooner.'

'Well, it's been your loss,' said Alicia cheerfully. 'I'd forgotten what a busy social life people lead here. I've hardly had a moment on my own. Judging by this afternoon, you'd better put in some dancing practice now you're back.'

'Dancing? You saw how enthusiastic I am. I'll be quite happy never to dance again.' Milo stopped and pulled his hand away suddenly. 'What do you mean, "now you're back"?'

'You won't be able to avoid dancing, you know. You'll be getting a lot of invitations.'

'Come back?' said Milo in confusion. 'I don't understand. I told you how difficult business is.'

'Well, of course you'll still have your business to look after. But you've got that engineer – what's his name? James, isn't it? You told me he's still down there, so I assumed he's going to look after things for you. You can go down occasionally, though.' Alicia smiled across the table, unaware of the alarm her remarks had caused him.

'Alicia, I can't stay. You don't seem to understand that.'

'You've got to go back?' Alicia finished his sentence and looked at him thoughtfully. 'I wondered whether you'd ever be able to make the commitment. But you're right, I don't understand. I thought perhaps now you're established, you were finally going to stay. I thought – ' she stopped suddenly. 'What does it matter what I thought? If you say you're going back, then I won't be able to change your mind.'

'But Alicia, please at least try to understand. I've already explained to you that it's my business and it's going to be very difficult.'

'And I've told you that I'm not interested in business.'

'No, I know,' Milo said more gently. 'Look, I've thought about it a lot while I've been down in Iquique.' He picked up her hand and held it tightly between his. 'Why don't you come back with me?' Seeing the look of shock in her face, he added quickly. 'Not immediately of course, but you could join me down there, after... after,' he paused and looked at her seriously for several moments before continuing. 'Alicia, can we get married?'

'How was your evening?' Lisa asked the next morning over breakfast. Her eyes were bright with curiosity.

Milo looked up from the table. 'We went dancing.'

Lisa looked at him in surprise. 'I didn't think you liked dancing.'

'I don't. Then we went for dinner at the Gran Bolivar.'

'That's better. And how did that go?'

'Then I proposed to her.'

'That's nice,' Lisa said it before realising what he had said. She jumped up and clapped her hands in delight. 'Oh Milo, that's wonderful! Congratulations: I'm so happy for you.'

'She turned me down.'

Lisa looked at him in astonishment. 'But why? What did she say?'

'She didn't say anything at first,' Milo replied mournfully. 'She just laughed. As a matter of fact she laughed for quite a long time. Long enough for me to get quite annoyed. She even found *that* funny.'

'But why? You seemed to get on so well. You had a good time when you were here before. Why should she laugh at you now?'

'Apparently she might have agreed if I wanted to stay here in Lima. It seems it was the idea of living in Iquique that she found so amusing. I think her actual words were, "Do you really think someone like me could live in that parched hell-hole?" I suppose I can see her point. There wouldn't be much for her to do down there, although it's growing fast.'

Lisa sat down next to him. 'Oh, poor Milo,' she said sympathetically, pulling him towards her and hugging him fondly. 'It will be all right, I promise. You'll get over it.'

Milo rested his head on her shoulder. 'Perhaps,' he said and closed his eyes in resignation. 'Perhaps. But things are so difficult down there. If we don't get James' new equipment in time, then ...'

'Then what?' Lisa prompted gently – but Milo didn't reply.

~~~~~

Robert became a helpless spectator of events. Martin's deal went ahead and he became re-energised as the years appeared to fall off him. Robert, sent up to Matotambo by the Garcias, looked on and wondered whether he might have been wrong after all. This was the Martin Hurst of old, tirelessly driving the teams of engineers and workmen to create new sugar fields from the abandoned land.

But a year later, when the first sugar canes were finally planted, the sugar price fell to its lowest level for thirty years.

Chapter Fifteen

Milo walked down the long, cobbled main street leading to the docks, where James was supervising the unloading of equipment. 'Is it all here?' he asked anxiously.

'No.' James looked up from his clipboard. 'There's no central refinery unit.'

'But everything was delivered to Bordés. We've got the signed receipts,' said Milo. 'We've even paid for it all. Will the rest of it work?'

James looked down at his list. 'No. It's virtually useless without it.'

'Damn them. They don't get commission on machinery so they probably held it up for something more profitable.'

Milo watched the jib of the tall crane swing across the ship's deck, tracing a black arc against the deep blue sky. 'Did you find out about the shipping line I told you about?' he asked after a few moments.

James was still checking his lists and didn't reply for several moments. 'Sorry,' he said, looking up. 'Minerva Line? Yes, I found their office in Bremerhaven, but they're too small. They've only got a two or three ships.'

'We can't let Bordés hold us to ransom. We've got to get that plant here. I'm going to send a telegram.'

Milo sent several telegrams, although it was a couple of months before he received his final answers. By this time the guano revenues had dwindled to a trickle and President Pardo's Government was fast running out of money; only the export income from nitrates could pull the country back from bankruptcy. They finally announced *estanco*. Owners of nitrate operations, including Milo, were ordered to surrender their shares and take compensation certificates in return.

In Lima, the Garcia brothers grabbed their chance. Knowing that he couldn't comply, they issued Martin Hurst with a demand for immediate repayment of his loan secured against Matotambo and Napeña.

In the Villa Miraflores, Lisa Hurst bit her lip. It was the only way she could stop shouting 'How could you?' She knew recriminations wouldn't help – at least Martin had told her about it. If she reacted the wrong way, he'd simply retreat into his shell and she'd never hear the truth. 'So you went into partnership with the Garcias to develop a new plantation?'

'I wouldn't say it was a partnership – more a sort of loan,' said Martin indistinctly. He looked quite miserable.

'And you pledged the Napeña plantations as security for the loan? So if you default, you give them your lifetime's work on a plate?'

'That's not fair, Lisa.' Martin seemed to care more about what Lisa thought of him than his financial problems. 'I didn't give it to them on a plate. They put up their biggest nitrate fields as cross-collateral – the California Company.'

'So if I understand the meaning of cross-collateral properly,' Lisa said tersely, 'instead of owning the estates in Napeña, you would own a nitrate mine in Tarapacá? What do you know about nitrates?' She shut her eyes to help herself understand the problem facing them. 'Why did you ever put up Napeña? – there wasn't any need for it.'

'It was like – er, a sort of insurance,' Martin was groping for an explanation of something he could hardly believe he had done himself. 'It was like a policy to insure against them taking up the security. If they foreclosed on the loan, they'd have to hand over the California mine, so I really never thought they'd do it. I saw the figures; it was too valuable for them to lose. Even with the low nitrate prices it was still making money – it was then, anyway. More than Napeña.'

Lisa looked puzzled. 'So why have they done it now?' she asked. 'Why don't they want to keep it?'

Martin bent his head and rubbed the back of his neck. 'Because the government has finally announced *estanco*. The Garcias have timed it perfectly – they must have been warned. They called in the loan and surrendered the share certificates for the California two days before expropriation was confirmed. Since the announcement, ownership of all the nitrate fields has been transferred to the Government. The shares no longer entitle us to the mine; they simply allow us to claim government certificates in compensation.

'Someone must have told them.' Lisa controlled her frustration tightly. At all costs she must remain sympathetic. 'You know how close the Garcias are to President Pardo. They knew that one day the government would take the deeds to the land.' She said this slowly, working out the implications carefully. 'So they waited until *estanco* was about to be announced before they called in the loan. And now all you get are government certificates instead of the shares?'

Martin Hurst nodded glumly. 'They're more like bonds. But they pay at 8% until they redeem them.'

'And will they?'

'Why shouldn't they?' replied Martin, stalling.

Lisa could think of a number of reasons, but felt she should go easy on him. She'd established the facts and she didn't want her husband to think she enjoyed reproaching him. She had to support him. 'Well,' she said brightly, 'perhaps with the prices as they are, government certificates are better than a nitrate field.'

Neither of them said anything for several minutes. Each was lost in their own thoughts of the consequences of such a disaster. Finally Lisa spoke. 'We must get Milo back here. If it's anything to do with nitrates, he'll know what to do.'

'We can't tell him about this,' Martin's reaction was immediate. 'I don't want him to know. I'll think of something. You mustn't tell him.'

Lisa stood up and walked across to Martin and looked down at him. 'Do you know, Martin, 'Sugar King' Hurst, that over the many years of our marriage you have said and done some very insensitive things? You have treated me like a backward little girl with no understanding of even the simplest ideas of commerce. You have left me on my own for months at a time, while you went off to carry out plans you didn't even see the need to tell me about, as though I was some kind of housekeeper. And now you are continuing to insult my intelligence by telling me that you can get out of this on your own. You know you can't, and I'm not going to let you even try. I'm going to send a telegram to Milo in the morning and when he's here, we're all going to sit down and work out what to do. You might not think so, but as far as I am concerned, Milo is part of our family and it affects him too. You've never found it in you to give him any praise for what he's achieved, and the greatest compliment you can pay him now – which is only what he deserves – is to ask for his advice.'

Lisa was struggling to hold back her tears: she knew Martin would only see it as weakness. 'You can't even face your oldest friend, Emilio Vasco,' she continued. 'You've probably got it into your head that he's failed you, or some such nonsense. I'm going there right now, and I can't understand why you didn't do it a year ago.'

Lisa felt quite exhilarated as she made her way to Emilio's office. After all these years of marriage, she had finally discovered that she had some influence over her husband. She'd been so accustomed to hearing of Martin's business from other people that she'd always assumed he wasn't interested in her opinions. That he had come to her and told her of his problems was a revelation.

Emilio rushed out as soon as he heard that Lisa was asking for him. He couldn't remember the last time she had visited his office. He ushered her in and instead of going behind his desk, he sat in the chair next to her. 'What is it?' he asked immediately. 'What's happened?'

'It's Martin,' she started. Emilio's face dropped. He'd seen it before in people who'd spent most of their time outside, living a physical life. And Martin hadn't looked his old self for some time now.

Lisa read the expression on his face. 'No, it's not that,' she said. 'Martin's fine: well, that is...' Briefly she explained the situation to Emilio, whose face darkened to match his sombre suit.

'What did he do it for?' he asked when Lisa had finished. 'Why didn't he just leave things as they were and slow down a bit?'

'It's what men do when they get older,' Lisa answered ruefully. 'But they don't usually spend just two years losing all the money they've managed to make in the first fifty.'

'It isn't lost yet,' said Emilio quickly. 'We'll have to speak to Milo. We've got to get Milo up here. I'll speak to the Garcias and make sure they don't do anything without checking with me first. We've still got time. I'll send a telegram to Tarapacá immediately.'

~~~~~

When Milo had last been in Callao, he had saved his business and lost Alicia. But it wasn't a choice, thought Milo. I couldn't just abandon things in Tarapacá, I was fighting to survive. She could have joined me there. Iquique had grown since the early days; soon it would have its own established society and she could have enjoyed herself. Afterwards, he'd continued writing to her, but his letters were never answered. Finally, he realised he had lost her.

He looked around. It was more filthy and depressing than ever. There were more beachcombers hanging around the docks, and the incessant noise from the Fandango houses seemed more raucous. Most of the buildings hadn't been painted for years, and the tottering bamboo frames could be seen where the mud daub had fallen away. Some of the damage from the earthquake eight years ago was still waiting to be repaired. The country had no money left. Just as the Spanish had plundered the gold of the Incas, so the European traders of the nineteenth century had taken what little wealth remained. The guano had all but gone and traders had moved down south to the nitrate fields.

Milo went straight up to Emilio's office in Lima. The telegram had given little indication of the nature of the emergency; open correspondence had forced Emilio to be vague. At first Milo had started imagining the direst catastrophes, until he controlled himself. There was no point in guessing at the problem – he'd find out soon enough.

Emilio couldn't help showing his relief when Milo arrived. 'I'm sorry I made it sound so melodramatic. Everyone is well,' he reassured him apologetically. 'But I had to get you here as soon as possible.'

Milo looked at him anxiously. 'With *estanco*, I had to come anyway. How bad is it?'

Emilio shook his head. 'It's not just you, I'm afraid.' He explained Martin's problem.

'How could he get himself into such a mess?' asked Milo. 'The certificates are backed by a consortium calling themselves Los Bancos Asosiados. Do you know anything about them? Are they worth anything?'

'Put it this way: since the guano revenues have collapsed, the government's credit is so bad that Henry Meiggs has issued his own currency.'

'But they're paying the income on the certificates?'

'So far, yes.'

'Martin should have spoken to me.'

'That's what we've all said. I think he wanted to keep it a secret, so you could see the new Matotambo sugar fields when they were finished.'

'And now they are finished I won't be able to see them because they'll belong to someone else,' said Milo. 'Why doesn't Martin simply hand over Matotambo and walk away?'

'The Garcias won't accept it. They want their pound of flesh and served notice on the Napeña estates.'

Milo thought for a moment. 'That means they have to hand over the certificates for the California Company in return.'

'They've already surrendered them. Under the terms of the contract they have to place the shares, along with signed open transfer documents, in escrow. Once these have been lodged, then Martin is put on notice to decide what to with them. If he doesn't pay up, the Garcias get Napeña and the California shares automatically revert to Martin.' Emilio laughed bitterly.

'They worked out that the shares are still valid as security, even though they now have to be exchanged for Government expropriation certificates.'

'How much longer does the notice period last before that happens?'

'There's just over two weeks left,' said Emilio. 'While I've been waiting for you to arrive, I've tried everything. I've called in every favour owed to me by the directors, but even after twisting their arms, not one of them will agree to fund the Hurst estates. I've spoken – pleaded more like – with the Garcias. They were very polite about it all, they said they'd look at any suggestion, but that business was business. The trouble is I can't blame any of them. If Martin weren't one of my oldest friends, I wouldn't back him myself.'

'I don't think money is the answer to this problem,' said Milo. 'It's not a sound proposition. Even if I had the money, I'm not sure I'd want to invest it in sugar. It's going to take a few years before that market stabilises. If Martin had just stayed with the Napeña estates, he could have cut back on the workforce, made a few savings and just waited it out. That's what the Garcias will do if they take it over. They know Martin runs a more sophisticated operation than they do and it'll be the first plantation to return to profit. It will take only a tiny increase in the sugar price.'

'If money isn't the answer, then what is?' asked Emilio.

'I don't know yet. Can you get me the accounts for the California Company? Will the Garcias let you see them?'

'I don't see how they can refuse. Under the terms of the option there's a disclosure clause. Martin's entitled to confirm they haven't been siphoning assets out of the company.'

'They didn't need to,' said Milo ruefully. 'They've persuaded President Pardo to do it for them.'

'But what about you?' asked Emilio. 'How will it affect your operations?'

'I'm not sure yet.' Milo scratched his head. 'Everything's still up in the air. You'd never believe the government has been planning this for so long. Apart from the bald announcement of expropriation, they've done nothing to make it work. Each of the *oficinas* has to be valued, and it'll take years to do it properly.'

'The government's so desperate to get their hands on some income they can't wait that long,' said Emilio. 'They've established an emergency commission of surveyors to arrive at a retrospective valuation for each owner. Ultimately it's got to come down to negotiation.'

'I'd better speak to them anyway and see what they're planning. Can you try and get hold of the California accounts? I'd like to study them before going to the Villa Miraflores.'

'The Hursts will be upset if you don't go there first. How long is it since you last saw them?'

'This is more important. I'll see you later.'

Milo eventually found the Government Surveyor's office temporarily installed in a disused customs shed. He walked straight in; there was no reception area and no one to challenge him. Inside it was chaos. Trestle tables had been set up the length of the shed and maps lay everywhere, some pinned to the tables, others still tightly rolled in decaying cardboard tubes.

'It isn't as bad as it looks,' a voice behind him said. 'It's far worse.'

Milo turned. 'Peter,' he said, surprised. 'It is Peter Calder, isn't it?'

'Of course it is, Milo. I haven't changed that much since the Institute, have I?' Peter looked Milo up and down. 'You look fit,' he said. 'Leading an active life down south, are you?'

'How did you know I've been in the south?' asked Milo. 'What are you doing here anyway? I didn't know you had an interest in the nitrate business.'

'I didn't,' Peter said shortly. 'Not until a couple of months ago, anyway. You remember I came back to Lima just before the earthquake? Afterwards the country seemed to be in such chaos that I decided to go to Heidelberg to study geology. It seemed the only thing in Peru that had any future. I've spent the past few years inland as an inspector of mines. Someone had to do it.'

'I've often wondered what happened to you. I'd never have thought you'd become a geologist, let alone work for the Government. At school you always told us you were going to be a pirate.'

'So?' he said triumphantly. 'It's taken me a little while, I admit, but now I've finally made it.'

'What are you talking about?' said Milo. 'Why don't you tell me why you're here?'

'I just did. I'm a pirate – employed by the government. I take what doesn't belong to me and give nothing in return.'

'Wait a moment,' said Milo, thinking rapidly. 'You don't mean this is your office? You work here?'

'I was the only one they could find at short notice. You're talking to the Head of the Compensation Commission.' Peter affected a modest bow. 'It's my job to decide how much compensation is due for stealing – oops, excuse me – for nationalising the nitrate fields they couldn't afford to buy. Your name's somewhere near the top of one of those lists over there.' Peter waved in the direction of another table piled high with what seemed like title deeds.

Milo was recovering from his astonishment at seeing an old school friend in such an unlikely place. 'It's really good to see you again, Peter. But do you mind if I ask you some questions? It's urgent.'

'I can't see what's urgent about deciding about how much money not to give away.'

'It's not about the certificates, it's about production quotas,' said Milo. 'How do they propose to operate the fields? They're so desperate for income, they've got to keep everything going.'

'Ah, that's different.' Peter Calder abandoned his facetious manner and looked serious for the first time. 'They haven't decided yet, but in the meantime immediate production cuts have been imposed on each *oficina* and temporary operation contracts given to most of the previous owners. That should keep the industry going for the moment and I think it'll stabilise prices. After that they'll be asking for formal tenders, offering fixed production contracts in return for operation agreements. That way they can concentrate on the more efficient producers – the others won't be able to compete.'

'Who decides on the tenders?'

'I'm afraid, Milo, that I do. So there's no point hoping you can bribe someone.'

Milo shook his head with mock sadness. 'How could you think that of me? I'm the one who did things by the book – remember?'

'You always said you did, but since you were the only one who had read it, we couldn't check whether you were telling the truth. Now, is there anything else you want?'

Milo had learnt all he wanted to know. He arranged to meet Peter the next evening, and returned to Emilio's office. Emilio sat at his desk behind a large pile of documents. 'Have you heard the news?' he asked as Milo walked in.

'It can wait,' Milo said impatiently. 'I've been speaking to Peter Calder – he's now the head of the Compensation Commission. The government's imposed new production quotas. Prices will have to start rising. I think we're through it; I think we've survived.'

Emilio stood up and, in an uncharacteristic gesture, he reached out and hugged Milo. 'Thank God,' he said. 'Thank God.'

Milo pulled himself away in embarrassment. 'We finally have a breathing space; it'll give us time to install the new equipment.'

'You've got to get it delivered first.'

'We will,' Milo said. 'Don't worry, we will.' He started skimming through the papers. 'I shouldn't think the Garcias were very happy about letting you have these. It seems to give details of all their operating costs.'

'Robert gave them to me.' said Emilio. 'I showed him the option agreement and he agreed they had no choice. I don't think he'll be too popular, though – the Garcias would have stalled for time. You can look at them in the office next door. 'But I still haven't told you the news,' Emilio continued, looking up from his desk. But Milo was gone.

It was over two hours later before he finally returned. Emilio looked up eagerly. 'Have you found anything?'

'There's a lot there.' Milo replied, sitting at his desk. 'But even more that isn't.'

'What do you mean?' asked Emilio in alarm. 'Robert said the production figures were complete.'

'They are. But only up to the time the Garcias did the deal with Martin. After that, although they left ownership of all the nitrate fields and the equipment with the California, they transferred the operation of it to a separate company.'

'But that would have broken their agreement with Martin,' Emilio protested. 'He could claim that they've defrauded him.'

'No, he can't. All the fixed assets remain in the name of the company, so technically its value remains the same. But everyone who runs the place – all the management, even the labourers – was transferred to a separate operating company. The California company pays them to manage the *oficina*, and in return it's contracted to buy all the refined nitrate they produce.' Milo stared across the room thinking deeply. 'They must have known – even back then.'

'Known what?' Emilio looked blank. 'I don't understand.'

'They must have known about *estanco*, or at least had a pretty good idea that it was likely to happen.'

'People have been talking about it for years.'

'Yes, but each time it was the Garcias who persuaded the President not to go ahead with it. They must have known they wouldn't be able to prevent it forever, so they made contingency plans.'

'So you reckon the President told them that he was finally about to announce *estanco*?' Milo nodded. 'But how does it help the Garcias to have a separate operating company?'

'They knew how bad the country's finances are. Each time there's been a coup, each departing President has cleared out the country's coffers before leaving. President Pardo seems to have been relatively honest, though. It wasn't his fault that there was nothing left when he came to power.'

'But I still don't understand how a separate company helps them.'

'Think about it,' Milo said impatiently. 'The Government has nationalised the assets – the nitrate fields, the refineries, all the equipment, but they haven't nationalised the people. So after nationalisation, who's going to run it for them?'

There was a long silence. 'I see,' Emilio said at length. 'In effect, the California can't operate without a separate production contract, so the Garcias are counting on continuing to run the *oficina*, even though they don't own it.'

'I think they realised that Martin couldn't possibly run a refinery and they knew the certificates wouldn't be redeemed for years – if ever.' Milo hesitated. 'You know, Emilio, I think Martin might be better off letting the Garcias run it. He can sit back and collect the 8% income.'

'But that's what I've been trying to tell you,' Emilio said. 'The Bancos Asociados have just gone bust. There won't be any income, not any more. The certificates are worthless.'

'Christ!' Milo slumped into a chair with his head buried in his hands. 'I thought if he lost Napeña, at least he'd have the California. But this means he could lose both.'

'You know how far Martin and I go back together? We've been through some difficult times, but I thought all that was in the past.' Emilio shook his head sadly. 'I suppose it's about time we went and told him.'

Milo looked up suddenly. 'You say we've got two weeks? Can I use your telegraph? We might just pull it off.'

Chapter Sixteen

As they waited for Martin and Lisa in the hall, Milo searched for the right approach. Should he be sympathetic and understanding, or practical and matter-of-fact? Sympathy might seem patronising, but merely to be practical might seem callous and he was desperate to show them how much he cared. He remembered several years ago, when he'd told Alicia that nothing was as important as his work. He wondered now whether he had been wrong; what could be more important than the Hursts? Perhaps he'd been wrong about Alicia, too. But as he looked around him, he felt reassured by the warmth of the memories which surrounded him. He'd forgotten the simple pleasure of familiar things and familiar company. He'd forgotten how much he'd missed the calm comforting presence of Lisa. In his isolation in Iquique he felt that some of the harshness of the Tarapacá dust must have deadened his senses. Now, in spite of the desperate circumstances, once again he felt immediately at home. He decided he would just try to be himself.

Martin came slowly down the stairs, Lisa a few steps behind. The sight was so formal and Martin's manner so cold that Milo felt his awkwardness return. Martin asked after Milo's operations in Tarapacá, but his tone was distant, almost hostile. Milo realised how difficult he must find it to seek help, and tried to ignore his apparent resentment. Lisa manoeuvred them into the drawing room. 'Well?' she asked. 'Emilio has told you everything?'

Milo nodded warily. 'I've been going through the figures for the California Company.' He looked towards Martin and tried to lighten the heavy atmosphere. 'But when I said you might need a nitrate mine, I didn't expect you to take me seriously.'

Martin smiled grimly. 'Even if I don't get the mine, I'll still get the income from the certificates.'

Milo glanced quickly at Emilio. 'I'm afraid you won't.'

'You think I don't understand? They're backed by the government.'

'I'm sorry, Martin,' Emilio didn't know how to break the news gently. 'The banks defaulted this morning. The country's bankrupt.'

Lisa gasped. 'But the certificates? What about the certificates?' She stared in disbelief at her husband, slowly realising what was happening to them. 'They planned it this way, didn't they? They knew that any certificates issued by the Government would soon become valueless. They managed to pass them on just before the banks defaulted. They've taken over Napeña and left us with nothing.'

Martin squirmed uncomfortably under Lisa's gaze. 'The certificates might be worth something one day.' There was an unfamiliar tremor in his voice. 'What about the accounts? Did you find anything?'

'They seem to be getting the best out of some quite old equipment,' Milo answered. 'On balance, if things were arranged normally, I'd choose to take the company rather than fight for Napeña.'

'But that's ridiculous,' protested Emilio. 'If the government's defaulted on the certificates and the company no longer owns the land, how can the shares be worth anything?'

'What difference does it make how much they're worth?' Milo looked at Emilio impassively. 'No one is about to buy or sell anything. We're just talking about the Hursts and the Garcias. Which does each prefer? The Napeña estates, or the California Nitrate Company?'

'Well, that's obvious, isn't it?' Martin looked disgusted. 'A bit of a waste of time you coming here, if that's the best you can think of.'

'I was coming anyway.' Milo saw Martin was fidgeting impatiently and he hurried to finish. '*Estanco* affects everyone in Tarapacá. We all need to know what's going to happen. Nitrate production is a big industry now, bigger than the guano trade ever was. Bigger than sugar. It won't just stop overnight and we haven't just packed our bags and left. We're all still hard at it down there. At the moment it doesn't make any difference to us who owns the nitrate fields; we're too busy trying to keep our production going. It's a bit like the sugar plantations.'

Martin spluttered. 'You're always saying how different they are,' he said sarcastically.

'I said that the markets are different,' said Milo. 'The production is much the same. Once the sugar fields have been planted, the main expense is the cultivation and refining. With nitrates, the cost of digging them out of the ground is small. The money goes on taking it to the *oficinas* and turning them into saleable saltpetre. So the government now owns the raw caliche – what are they going to do with it? They can't sell it – it's not pure enough, so there's no market for it. It's the refineries that are important. That's where nearly all the investment has gone – into the transport and the refining. Perhaps, in a few years time, as we go deeper, we'll have to invest in extraction. But there are still hundreds of thousands of square miles of nitrates just sitting on the surface. If the government shut us down, what are they going to do with it? They need us. They didn't understand that it's not the same as guano – they can't just load it onto ships and carry it away.'

During his explanation Milo had noticed Martin's truculent manner was softening as he started to realise the possibilities. 'So the same companies could continue to operate the refineries, even though they don't own the nitrate fields?'

'Exactly,' said Milo. 'Instead of selling our own saltpetre, we'll be charging the government for producing it. It won't make a lot of difference to us. If the government want to sell their expropriated nitrates, then they're going to have to pay us to refine them.'

'But can't they do it themselves?'

'Who with?' asked Milo. 'This is a technical business. If the owners leave, then the refineries will collapse. How are they going to replace an engineer like James Young?'

Milo turned to Lisa. 'Do you remember Peter Calder at the Academy? The rather studious one, who was always losing his glasses? I met him again this afternoon. He works for the government, in charge of the compensation procedures – since there's no money to pay it, it's a waste of time. But he's also allotting the production contracts, and that's vital. He told me that at least the government have done something right by cutting production – I've been telling everyone it's the only way to stop prices falling. I don't like this nationalisation, but at least we can now control the supply. When we've got the contracts we should be able to carry on almost as before.'

Martin shook his head. 'Wait a minute. I don't understand. How can you be so sure that you're going to get a production contract? If you don't, your refinery will be useless.'

'Precisely!' Milo looked at Martin, earnestly trying to help him understand. 'That's just the point. The refineries and mines will be useless unless the government allow us to keep running them. They're desperate for the income. It's simple, don't you see? Emilio once told me that we owed the bank so much money that they couldn't afford to foreclose. He said that, in practice, the real control had been transferred from them to us. It's the same with nationalisation. Who else knows how to refine the caliche? We've spent all these years developing our processes – there isn't anyone else with enough knowledge. As long as we charge a realistic price, they've got to involve us.'

Emilio was frowning. 'Don't the Garcias know all this? If what you say is true, why are they prepared to lose the company?'

'Of course they know it. They worked it out before they gave you the Napeña deal.' Milo pointed to the pages of accounts. 'The California Company owns everything – all the nitrate fields, all the refineries. But as I told Emilio, it doesn't own the operation. According to their accounts, all their managers are employed by a separate company which has a contract to run the refinery for the next five years. It's like owning a hotel – the building isn't worth much without the staff to run it.

'Your option,' continued Milo, 'is over the shares in the California which owns the mine and refinery, the land and all the assets. If you exercise it, you have to hand over Napeña, but rather than getting the shares in return, you'd be left with government certificates instead. The Garcias are betting that whatever happens to the Company or to the certificates, they'll still be able to operate the refinery. And it's a pretty safe bet that you won't suddenly put in a team to run it, even if the contracts allowed it. They might lose title to the Company, but they'd probably written it off anyway. They'll get title to Napeña instead. That's why they lent you the money.'

Lisa frowned. 'I'm not sure I've got this right. You're saying that because we've defaulted on a loan to develop a relatively small sugar plantation, the Garcias can exchange the shares of a worthless nitrate company for the deeds of the most efficient sugar producer in Peru.' She held up her hand against interruptions. 'Having done that, they can still keep the income from both the sugar and the nitrate production?'

'You've forgotten one thing,' said Milo. 'Because of a cut in production, the nitrate price has finally stabilised – which will allow them to get a proper price for refining.'

'Tell me something, Milo.' Lisa was the first to break the silence. 'Does this mean that your own company can now survive?'

Milo felt his eyes watering as he looked at her. She had done so much for him and now, when she was facing the loss of everything, she was still thinking of him. 'Yes,' he said softly. 'We'll survive. The certificates will have to be redeemed at some time. The local Peruvian banks aren't so important now, but the European banks have too much at stake just to walk away from them. So the longer term doesn't worry me – one day we'll get ownership back. But in the meantime, the revenues are the only thing that counts.' He turned to Emilio Vasco. 'I'll start doing the figures as soon as I can, but no one else can operate our refineries. James and I have lived with them for over eight years. When the production contract is confirmed, I'll reschedule the loan repayments.'

'Whatever difficulties you've had over the last few years, I never once doubted that you'd find a way to honour your debts, just like your father always has.' Emilio stopped, suddenly realising what he had said. 'I'm sorry,' he said. 'But sometimes you two are so much alike that I tend to forget you're, well …'

Martin interrupted brusquely. 'I'll take it as a compliment. But as far as I can see, the Garcias are still going to get away with it, and steal my plantations.'

'Well, I can talk to them about that,' Milo said. 'After all, the production contract hasn't been agreed yet and – well, perhaps there is an alternative.'

'But you said the government office would have no choice.' Martin, who thought he had understood the situation, now looked puzzled again. 'You said that the existing operations on site were the only way they could refine the saltpetre.'

'No. I said that the existing refinery was the only way to refine my nitrates. The California Company is different.'

Martin frowned. 'You're playing with us,' he said. 'Why don't you just explain what you mean?'

'Normally we couldn't possibly bid for a refining contract for the California fields – they're too far away: but expropriation has changed everything.' Milo looked across to Emilio. 'You remember I told you about the Pampa Blanca?' Emilio nodded slightly.

Martin was becoming increasingly impatient. 'Where's all this leading?' he asked.

Milo turned to him. 'Some of the *salitreros* have already given up. When they heard about the expropriation, they guessed that government promises might be worthless and tried to sell for whatever they could get. They just wanted to get out. We bought some certificates for a mine called Pampa Blanca. It's near the California – in fact their railroad runs right past it. The certificates hardly cost anything – even before *estanco* it was struggling. We weren't intending to work it. I just wanted to hold it in reserve, just in case. But now, with the California, perhaps we could think about operating it.'

'I don't see how,' said Emilio. 'You'd never get an operating contract, and their equipment is too old to make a profit. That's one of the reasons they sold the certificates – they knew it would have to be shut down.'

'If we used the existing equipment, yes,' said Milo. 'But what about our new plant? Instead of installing it in our existing fields, it's just possible that we could install it in the Pampa Blanca.' He looked across to Martin. 'It's what you call diversification.' He saw Martin smile faintly.

191

Emilio cried out in disbelief. 'You can't! You haven't got it — it still hasn't been delivered!'

'The Garcias don't know that,' Milo said calmly.

'Anyway, you need that equipment yourself.' Emilio shook his head. 'No, it's a crazy idea. It would never work.'

'It might — just,' said Milo. 'The plant operates with an entirely new process, so it's virtually self-contained. We just need some steam hammers, but we can pick those up cheaply enough now. But that's not the point anyway. It's not what we think that counts: it's what the Garcias think. At the moment they're assuming they're safe, because no one else can operate the California. But if they thought we could install a refinery, then they might think twice about letting it go.'

'They wouldn't if they found out the refinery doesn't exist.'

'But it does exist,' Milo looked at him steadily.

'Perhaps,' said Emilio, looking away. 'But not in Valparaiso. They can easily check.'

Milo shrugged. 'I'm hoping they don't, but even if they do — '

'Hoping?' Martin interrupted. 'Is that it? You're going to tell them you're going to operate a refinery you don't even have.'

Milo sighed. 'Isn't it about time you had some faith in me? Why don't you just trust me?'

Martin looked around the room for support, but no one replied.

'What have we got to lose?' Milo continued. 'We can bid for the operation contract whatever happens, and worry about the plant afterwards. We've taken bigger gambles. But if we could get the refinery operating, it would be the most efficient in the territory. To be honest, I don't know if we can do it, but the important thing is to act as though we can.'

Emilio turned to Martin. 'Milo thinks that the earlier figures in the California accounts probably still give a fairly accurate idea of what their production costs are. Nothing much has changed in their processes.'

'We can pitch a tender so they'd be losing money if they tried to match it.' Milo explained. 'We could probably put in a bid low enough to persuade Peter Calder to give us the production contract, and after that we'd have to see what we could do.'

'Would you have enough capacity?' asked Martin.

Milo rubbed his chin. 'Probably not, but again, no one else knows that — all that counts is what the Garcias think, and they must be assuming they're going to keep the production contract. If I can persuade them they might lose it — they know they can't make the same income from Napeña for several years yet. From what I've seen of them, they always value a bird in the hand at least four times more than one in the bush.'

Once again Lisa summarised. 'So you're going to tell your friend Peter that you can refine the California nitrates at a lower cost than the Garcias?' She hesitated. 'Even though you don't actually have a refinery?'

Milo ignored her irony. 'If necessary, but I don't need to tell him yet; the only people I need to speak to are the Garcias,' Milo said. 'It comes down to a simple poker game. I have to convince Miguel Garcia that he doesn't hold all the cards; that he should fold. At the moment he thinks he can take over Napeña as well as getting a production contract for the California. If I tell him that Peter Calder has offered me the contract, then even if he suspects I'm bluffing, it would be one hell of a risk for him to bet that I'm wrong. It could cost him a fortune. Is he going to risk losing a secure nitrate production contract which brings in steady income, for the chance of owning the Napeña estates?' Milo looked across to Martin. 'He's not as sentimental as you are, and I'm betting he doesn't overplay his hand. I just hope I'm right. I'll find out tomorrow.'

~~~~~

Milo rubbed the locket. Absently he pulled it from inside his shirt and inspected the dull band of gold, newly polished by the constant chafing of his thumb. He thought he'd lost the habit years ago. He looked up as he heard footsteps approaching along the corridor, and frowned as he saw Robert approaching.

'I'm truly sorry about this mess,' Robert said. 'I did everything I could to stop Martin from getting involved with the Garcias. I warned him what they were like, but you know Martin; he doesn't even listen to advice, let alone consider taking it.'

'You were in it as well?' Milo asked harshly.

'Milo, believe me. I was helpless. I can't influence the Garcias any more than I can Martin. They all knew what they were doing. Martin should have checked things more carefully, but he didn't have Emilio to help him.'

'So you're saying it's all Martin's fault? I suppose you'll be saying next that he deserves everything that's coming to him?'

'That's not fair,' Robert was starting to get angry. 'I've never had anything but kindness from the Hursts, and I'm the last person to want anything to happen to them.'

'No,' said Milo. 'I am.'

Without another word, Robert escorted Milo along the corridor and left him in the gloomy boardroom. Milo sat warily under the reproachful eyes of generations of Garcias. As Miguel

Garcia entered, with Ramon close behind, he stood up and greeted them both with elaborate courtesy. 'Four years, isn't it?' he asked. 'Four years ago we discussed expropriation, and you said it wouldn't happen.'

'Did I?' said Miguel vaguely. 'I don't think I ever said it would never happen; only that it wouldn't happen just then. Afterwards, it's always been possible – Mr Hurst should have known. We didn't force him into it.'

'Perhaps not, but you planned it, didn't you? You knew they'd do it one day. You cut the heart out of the company before you pledged it to Martin Hurst.'

'It was unfortunate that Robert decided to let you see the accounts without – how shall I put it? Without letting me explain them to you.'

'There was nothing to explain,' Milo said sharply. 'It's quite clear what you were trying to do.'

Miguel spread his arms wide. 'We are running a business. We take the opportunities we find. Personally I feel very sorry for Mr and Mrs Hurst, but what can I do? This is about economics, not personalities.'

'Why should you feel sorry for them?' asked Milo.

Miguel looked puzzled. 'The expropriation, of course. The default on the certificates.'

'Why should that affect them?'

'Affect them?' Miguel started to look flustered. 'Haven't you heard? Didn't Mr Hurst explain everything? I thought that's what you wanted to talk about – to see how you can get Mr Hurst's plantations back.'

'I don't know why you should think that,' said Milo, looking puzzled himself. 'With the state of the sugar market, I think Mr Hurst is well out of it. I understand that the British Sugar Company has decided against investing in Peru and is concentrating on the Caribbean. It's going to be difficult to compete.'

'Where did you hear that?' Miguel Garcia frowned and turned to his brother. 'Do you know anything about this?' he asked. Ramon shook his head, but said nothing. He was watching Milo closely.

'No,' continued Milo, 'I wanted to discuss the refining operations after I've taken over the California.'

'You?' Miguel resumed his puzzled look. 'But you know that the California now belongs to the Peruvian Government? You have to wait for the valuation of the Compensation Commission.'

'Of course I know,' said Milo. 'You forget that they've taken my fields as well. But they still need me to operate them. I'm talking about who's going to operate the California.'

Miguel relaxed, and smiled broadly. 'Ah, the operation contract,' he said. 'That has yet to be decided, but like you, I can't see the government has much choice in the matter – who else can do it? It wouldn't change anything; the California has been run by a separate management company since, well, since ...'

'That is the way we do things.' Ramon Garcia saw where his brother was leading and interrupted quickly. 'The land, the nitrate deposits, we keep separate. We invoice the operating company for the caliche they use. It would have been the same if Mr Hurst had become the owner. As it is, well ...' He shrugged.

'You don't really think the government will lease you back the refinery and give you an operating contract?'

'Give? Did I say they will give it to me?' Miguel winked conspiratorially. 'But I'm sure I can persuade them one way or another.'

'With Peter Calder in charge of allocating the contracts?' Milo asked. 'You know he can't be bribed.'

Miguel shrugged. 'Ah well, that's the way it goes. But what other choice does he have? Who else can do it?'

'Mr Hurst didn't tell me that you still intended to operate the refinery. This might change things.'

Miguel smiled again. 'Mr Hurst probably didn't realise that the government would have to allocate operating contracts. Of course, this business is quite new to him.' He thought for a moment. 'You said you wanted to discuss the refining operations. What exactly did you want to talk about?'

'The railroad,' said Milo. 'I naturally assumed that once you'd finished with the California, I could lease part of your railroad – I didn't think you'd need it.'

'Of course we'll need it. How else can we transport the saltpetre?'

'But I assumed you were giving up the California. That's why you wanted to take over Napeña instead.'

'We can do both,' said Miguel defensively. He was starting to seem less confident.

'Señor Garcia,' Milo replied as pompously as he could, 'you're not seriously proposing to take over Mr Hurst's sugar plantations and still try to run the nitrate fields you've handed over in return?'

'Why not?' asked Miguel. 'It's not illegal.'

'Perhaps not,' said Milo. 'But you're known to be friendly with President Pardo, and people might think that he arranged it all. After all, the timing is a little bit too good to be true, don't you think?'

'People can think what they like,' said Ramon.

'Including Peter Calder? If he offers you a contract immediately after you've taken over the Hursts' estates, then people might think he's in on it. I don't think he'd like that.'

Ramon shifted uneasily. 'But he isn't. It's got nothing to do with him.'

'And another thing,' Milo said. 'Since the Banks have defaulted, I understand President Pardo is going to London to look for new backers. I don't think they will be too impressed if they think the President just uses the country's money to hand out to his friends – that's what it'll look like, you know. It certainly will after I've told everyone.'

'You can say what you like,' said Ramon. 'We've done nothing illegal. We've got the right to refine the California nitrates. It's President Pardo's problem, not ours.'

'I don't think you understand,' said Milo. 'You have a choice. Either the sugar plantations or the refining contract. Not both. If you want to take over the sugar estates, then I won't let you win the operating contract for the California. Personally I hope you opt for the sugar. Mr Hurst has decided to take things easy at last, and I really don't want him still going backwards and forwards to Napeña.'

'You're right, Señor Milo: I do not understand,' Miguel bared his teeth in a forced smile. 'You talk about giving us a choice. How can you prevent us from getting the operating contract?'

'Because if you decide to keep Napeña, I will bid for it myself,' Milo said.

Miguel breathed in sharply and looked at his brother questioningly.

'Señor Beran,' said Ramon, taking over the conversation. 'Your nitrate fields are almost at the other side of the desert. How do you propose to refine the California caliche from there?'

It was Milo's turn to smile. 'I see you aren't aware of everything. That's the trouble being up here in Lima – you're too far away from things. That's why I prefer to base myself in Iquique.'

'Señor Beran, please,' said Ramon. 'Could you perhaps answer the question?'

'Of course,' said Milo. 'Some people have found the government certificates the final straw. If they have no refinery, then they have no stake left. A neighbour of yours – he owned the Pampa Blanca: you probably know it – decided it was time to get out. He didn't want much for the certificates. He said they were worthless anyway.'

'So you hold the certificates,' Miguel leered at him. 'What does that matter? The certificates don't entitle you to the nitrates.'

'No, but the government will still prefer them to be worked. You're aware, of course, that we've ordered new refining equipment?' Milo's mouth suddenly felt very dry. 'It's sitting in Valparaiso docks – I'm sure your spies must have told you.'

Miguel looked questioningly at his brother, who shook his head. 'You can check if you like,' Milo continued. 'There aren't many secrets in Valparaiso. It was intended for my own fields further south, but I'm going to send it to Pampa Blanca instead. I've discussed it with Peter Calder and shown him my estimated prices. He's going to recommend that we're given the contract. After all, with the new plant, who can touch us?'

'What capacity does it have?' asked Ramon quickly.

Milo smiled. 'I see you're starting to understand. Of course it won't be able to handle the entire output of the California at first, but with the temporary production cut-backs ordered by President Pardo, we'll manage.'

'We'll undercut you,' said Miguel, looking distinctly unhappy.

'You can't,' said Milo. 'At the refining price I've offered the government, you'd lose your shirts. Don't forget I've seen your figures. They might be a couple of years out of date, but they can't have changed much.'

'I wouldn't be so sure about that,' Miguel sat back in his chair, attempting to look relaxed, but he wasn't smiling. 'Anyway, we can afford to subsidise the prices for a while. That should keep you out.'

'Señor Garcia,' Milo said levelly. 'Exactly what do you think I've been doing for the past eight years in Tarapacá? Do you realise how much money we've invested in our operations down there? You, on the other hand, have handed it over to managers and kept them starved of money. As the price has dropped, you've simply cut corners. They run it well enough, but the refinery is old and if you attempt to match our prices, then your losses will be colossal. Think of it – every day thousands more soles wasted, and the next day, another few thousand. Day in, day out. And what for? I thought you said sentiment has no place in business?'

'Even if you did undercut us,' Ramon said. 'How would you transport it? You haven't got a railroad.' Miguel had been doodling on a pad; now he looked up.

'That's what I told you when I came in. Use yours, of course. The railroad wouldn't be much good to you with nothing to carry, would it? I'd pay you a fair market price, taking into account the fact that you will have no use for it.'

'We wouldn't sell,' Miguel snapped.

'What? And throw away yet more money? You're not the kind of man who cuts off his nose to spite his face. Once we've got the contract, you'll have no choice but to sell. Anyway, if

197

we're offering the government such an attractive price, what's to stop my friend Mr Calder from printing a certificate and just taking the line? You think he wouldn't?'

Miguel looked nervously across to his brother. Ramon's impassive face betrayed nothing. He looked back to Milo questioningly. 'Señor Beran. Do you know what we think? We think you're bluffing. You'll never carry it off, and you know it.'

Milo looked slowly from Ramon to Miguel. 'Try me.' The challenge was unmistakable. 'If you want to discover whether I'm bluffing or not, then go right ahead and take Napeña. Just try me. After what you've tried to do to Martin Hurst, I'd enjoy seeing you cut to pieces.'

Neither brother said anything. They both looked down at the table. The silence grew.

Milo stood up suddenly. 'It's been a pleasure talking to you both, but I've got things to do. Perhaps you can let me know your decision? I will need time to finalise my bids. Personally I hope you will choose to take the plantations. The California will go well with the Pampa Blanca. I'll wait for you tomorrow morning at the Villa Miraflores. Shall we say nine o'clock?'

Milo walked towards the door and turned. 'Napeña or the California. Not both.'

Chapter Seventeen

If Lisa was nervous she managed to hide it well. The following morning she seemed as bright as ever, although Martin was sombre and said little as they sat at the breakfast table waiting for the Garcias. Martin stood up as he heard Julio open the front door but Milo shook his head. 'It's too early. I think it's for me.'

Martin sat down again abruptly and watched Milo leave the room. As they sat waiting, Lisa and Martin felt that time was being stretched to breaking point. Martin got up and started pacing up and down the room. 'Where is he?' He suddenly stopped and slapped the table with the palm of his hand. 'Why isn't he here with us?'

He looked up as Julio knocked on the door and entered. 'Señor Emilio Vasco,' he announced stiffly, sensing the tension in the house.

Emilio followed him into the room. 'Where's Milo?' he asked.

Martin scowled. 'He went to meet someone. He seems to find his own business more important.'

Emilio looked at Lisa who shook her head. 'I'm sure he has his reasons.' He sat down next to her and they waited.

After nearly half an hour, Julio finally returned with Milo. 'The Señors Garcia have arrived. I've shown them into the dining room as you instructed.'

Lisa turned to Milo, sensing his suppressed excitement. 'Are you ready?' she asked quietly. Milo nodded. She stood up and headed towards the dining room.

'Where are you going?' Martin asked her in surprise. 'This doesn't concern you.'

'Not concern me?' Lisa hissed at him. 'Of course it does. Everything you do concerns me.'

'But you're a woman,' protested Martin. 'The Garcias won't do business with a woman in the room.'

'Then let them leave,' said Lisa. 'If the Garcias have decided to let us keep Napeña, then they'd tell us even if there was a snake in the room. If they haven't, they'll leave anyway.'

Milo pushed Martin gently from behind. 'She's right, you know. Now let's go.'

Martin shook his head in disbelief. 'What's going to happen next?' he muttered under his breath.

Without thinking, Milo automatically sat at the head of the table. 'I hope you don't mind meeting in the dining room. I thought it would be easier to talk.' He gestured towards Lisa. 'Also Mrs Hurst wanted to be present. I'm sure you have no objection.' It was not a question.

Miguel Garcia bowed towards Lisa. 'It's always a pleasure to see you, Señora Hurst, under any circumstances.' As he smiled, the dull glint of gold was unmistakeable.

That's a bad sign, thought Milo 'Have you thought about what I said last night?' he asked quickly.

'Oh yes, Señor Beran. My brother Ramon and I have thought a lot about the situation.'

'And?' asked Milo. He reached inside his shirt and unconsciously started rubbing his locket.

'It was clever of you to suggest we check with Bordés. You seemed so confident that we almost didn't bother.'

Milo nodded slightly, but said nothing.

'We asked them about this new refining equipment you told us so much about,' Miguel continued. 'They told us they hadn't completed the delivery yet.'

'Not all of it,' said Milo. 'But most of it.'

'They also told us that the balance of the consignment was still in London.'

'I see,' said Milo.

'It was a good try,' Miguel wagged his finger. 'But not good enough. If you're going to try a bluff like that, you should cover your tracks better.' He glanced down the room as he heard Martin breathe in sharply. 'Did you know he was bluffing, Señor Hurst? Did he tell you? He did it quite well, though: I nearly believed him.'

Lisa reached out and took Martin's hand. Emilio Vasco watched them across the table and smiled weakly.

'Only a detail,' said Milo. 'I admit it isn't in Valparaiso. Actually it's down in Callao. The central refinery unit is, anyway.'

'Señor Beran, this is never going to work. Why don't you admit you're not holding a strong enough hand?' In spite of his apparent confidence, Miguel Garcia was playing nervously with his gold tie pin. 'You haven't got a refinery to install in Pampa Blanca.'

Milo looked at him impassively. 'Have you ever heard of the Minerva Line?' he asked finally.

Miguel glanced at his brother. 'Minerva? Should I?'

'Bordés isn't the only shipping line in the world.' Milo turned to Lisa. 'Can you ring the bell for Julio?' There was an awkward silence as they waited for the butler.

'Julio, can you ask my visitor to come in?' Milo turned back to Miguel Garcia. 'You're right, of course. You should never overplay your hand. Word about that sort of thing spreads quickly.' Milo stood up and walked towards the door as it opened. 'May I introduce Captain Traub?'

Joachim Traub had hardly changed. The curly black hair spreading over his collar was now streaked with grey, and his face was more weather-beaten, but he still exuded a raw strength. His huge chest strained against his jacket and his stomach was still flat. He looked around the room, saw Lisa and went up to her. 'Mrs Hurst? Milo has written so much about you. It's an honour to meet you.' He turned to Martin and clicked his heels formally. 'And you also, Señor Hurst.'

'Captain Traub arrived yesterday.' Milo followed him to the table and introduced Emilio and the Garcias. 'He's with the Minerva Line. A small line but, unlike Bordés, a reliable one.' Milo beckoned Joachim to sit opposite him. 'Captain Traub tells me all the equipment is safe, and he can unload it in Iquique in a couple of days.'

Joachim nodded. 'I'll be pleased to see the back of it and get out of the Pacific. The wind's too fickle and it's difficult to make good passage times.'

Milo turned back to Ramon. 'You should have waited until you saw my hand. What d'you think of it now?'

Miguel Garcia stared at Joachim for several minutes. 'How do we know this isn't another bluff?' he asked finally.

'Show him the bills of lading, Captain. You can see the Bordés stamp on them and the description. They're the missing parts.'

Joachim pulled a bundle of documents from inside his jacket. 'And if you still don't believe it, you can even go and look at them in Callao. It's nearer than Valparaiso.'

Miguel skimmed through the documents and handed them to his brother. Ramon read them more slowly, before finally looking up and nodding almost imperceptibly. Miguel sighed deeply. 'It seems you weren't bluffing after all.' He stared at Milo who looked back impassively, saying nothing. 'I've always coveted the Napeña estates, but I suppose Matotambo will have to do instead. If we keep the production contract, then I suppose we haven't done so badly.' The two brothers collected their papers and started to leave. At the door, they turned. 'Señora Hurst. Gentlemen.' They both bowed curtly.

'It wasn't the hand I was dealt – it was the hand I made,' said Milo, standing up. 'Yesterday you thought you'd get Napeña, as well as keeping the California contract. It all looks a bit different now – but that's South America for you. Things can change so fast here, don't you agree?' Milo stood up. 'Let me see you out.'

Emilio challenged him as soon as he returned. 'Do you mind telling us what's going on?'

Milo laughed. 'Captain Traub was bringing the equipment anyway. Three months ago, when I discovered Bordés hadn't delivered everything, I decided we couldn't risk waiting for them, so I cabled Minerva Lines. James had found out where they were based. I wanted them as an alternative shipping line for the nitrates, but they didn't want the business. They thought the saltpetre market was too big and too volatile for them, but they did agree to send Captain Traub for the equipment in London and we shared the cost of bringing it here with a consignment for Ecuador. Captain Traub had already arrived in South America – he'd cabled me to say he was unloading in Guayaquil – so I knew he could be down here in a week. But it was close.' He turned to Joachim. 'You cut it fine, didn't you?'

'I'm sorry, Milo. We set sail from Guayaquil as soon as you told us to come down. But the wind only picked up towards the end of the passage. We should have been here several days ago.'

'You would have saved us from a sleepless night if you had,' said Milo.

'Sleepless night? I didn't think you let little things like that worry you.' Lisa stood up and hugged him tightly. 'Thank you,' she said, pulling away. 'We shouldn't have doubted you.'

Martin coughed nervously. 'I suppose I should thank you, too.' he said grudgingly. 'But let's just wait until the papers are signed.'

'What can I do with him?' asked Lisa. 'They've managed to keep Napeña for you, and you can't even say thank you properly.'

'But you've had to give up Matotambo,' said Emilio.

Martin smiled wanly. 'I only wanted it for Milo, and I don't think he needs it any more.'

~~~~~

A ship's master is also her servant. As soon as Joachim Traub had completed the delivery of equipment to Iquique, he had little time to stay before seeking new cargoes. A ship is on a never-ending treadmill – having discharged one consignment, the search begins immediately for the next. After sharing their precious few days together, Joachim set sail for Valparaiso and Milo threw himself back into his work.

As he predicted, the Peruvian Government's expropriation of the *oficinas* had little practical effect on operators with production contracts. If he was nervous about the eventual outcome, he didn't show it. As he foresaw, the centralisation of the nitrate sales finally brought some order to the market and the price steadied. For the next two and a half years, along with some of the other owners who had kept their nerve, he surreptitiously bought up production contracts of *salitreros* who were unable to borrow against their certificates. Control of the nitrate industry narrowed even further and profits finally started to rise.

The great entrepreneurs in South America during the second half of the nineteenth century had few political ideals; they dealt with things as they found them. Even the extraordinary conditions in the Chinchas shocked few of them and if they meddled in politics, it was to make money. If people like Martin Hurst invested in improving the conditions of their workforce, was that idealism, or simply the realisation that people who were well fed and well housed work better than people who weren't? What did they care about politics? Just as long as they were given a reasonable opportunity to get on with things, they were content to leave the politics to others. There were no great Quaker dynasties here to run their businesses as models for social reform.

But politics and commerce are rarely far apart. For the past ten years, Chile had been looking at the growth of the nitrate fields to the north with envy and frustration. Milo had been right about their intentions – their economy was in chaos, despite the mineral reserves inland – but their invasion, when it came, was not unprovoked.

Further inland, the Bolivian Government, contrary to treaty and without any discussion, imposed a tax on the Gibbs' operation in Antofagasta. Chile decided to resolve the disputed ownership of the borders once and for all and finally declared war. In turn Peru, citing a secret treaty with Bolivia, declared war on Chile. The three countries had previously been content to leave their boundaries undefined, but by 1879 the wealth of the nitrate fields no longer allowed it. The War of the Pacific came down to money. Whatever each country gave as its reason for going to war, they all knew that whoever won would control the world's entire reserves of nitrates.

The odds were heavily in Peru's favour. Its naval fleet included South America's first ironclad, the Huascar, whose power dominated the coast. Chile attempted a blockade of Iquique, but the Peruvian Navy managed to break through. But, on October 8th 1879, the Huascar was captured, and Peru's maritime power collapsed. By the end of the year, the entire Tarapacá province was taken by Chile, and the following year, to most people's surprise, they were even in occupation of the sugar plantations in Napeña, several hundred miles north of Lima. But Chile's argument was with Bolivia and Peru, not with the Europeans, whom they carefully left alone. They were well aware that it was Europe that ultimately controlled most of the nitrate fields of Tarapacá and provided the capital for continuing investment.

The California Company, however, was still being operated by the Garcia family, and they were Peruvian. Following Chile's occupation, their production contract was terminated and they had no choice but to abandon their investments in Tarapacá, which had now become Chile's most northern province. Indeed, few South American-owned operations survived. If they were Chilean, most had gone bankrupt before the war. If they were Peruvian, they were forced to retire to the north, having no future in a region that was now part of Chile. In the six years following the war, the number of companies dropped from 123 to 30, operating just 42 *oficinas* and producing ninety-seven percent of Tarapacá's output. Of these, more than three-quarters were European-owned.

Milo considered the operation of markets carefully. He calculated that there was no such thing as intrinsic value. The Incas had valued gold as enduring ornaments, while the Europeans melted them down into bars and hoarded them in bank vaults. Who was right? The value of something was simply what you could persuade someone to pay for it. It really didn't matter what you thought of it – merely what you were prepared to sell it for.

Milo now owned Peruvian Government certificates for several *oficinas*. The government was even less able to honour them following its defeat and anyway, Tarapacá was now occupied by Chile. What would happen to the certificates? More importantly, how much were they worth?

Once Chile had taken the nitrate fields from Peru, the country's economic prospects were transformed. The money to be made was as great as the income from their entire exports of minerals. But like Peru after *estanco*, they needed the Europeans to run things for them and above all they needed European capital. Milo finally decided that Chile ultimately would have no choice but to honour the Peruvian certificates. If they wanted to encourage investment in the industry, then ownership had to be established. Chile didn't want the *oficinas*: they just wanted their slice of the sale proceeds. Emilio Vasco's bank was more enthusiastic, and decided to finance Milo's purchases of more certificates. Some desperate *salitreros* were selling for as little as a shilling in the pound, and at that price Milo decided they were cheap.

On the 11th June 1881, Milo's decision was finally vindicated. Chile agreed to transfer ownership of the nitrate fields back to holders of valid certificates. Their value soared. Milo, James Young and Emilio Vasco, along with a number of others – mainly Europeans – who had speculated correctly and purchased certificates for a fraction of their face value, made fortunes overnight.

It was a massive breakthrough. By agreeing to honour the Peruvian certificates, Chile removed all uncertainty and the scope for further borrowing became immense, far exceeding the limited resources of Chile itself. Milo was drawn irresistibly towards the vast accumulations of money controlled by the wealthiest and most dynamic commercial Empire the world had ever seen. Britain's position was unassailable. True, there were some German and French banks financing some of the nitrate industry, but the liquidity of the London Stock Exchange meant that British money dominated it. To hold his own with the competition, Milo needed to match their resources, and London was the only place where such sums could be found. Although it remained a technically based business, capital and investment were now the keys to success, and Milo's understanding of money was unchallenged. He had known the nitrate industry from its cottage beginnings, with dusty old machines in shacks clinging precariously to the Tarapacá desert. Now it had grown into a business of worldwide importance.

But as he prepared to leave for Europe, Milo still had mixed feelings. It wasn't that he was finally abandoning his supporter of so many years; Emilio Vasco had given his blessing and they both agreed that it was time that someone else shared the huge risks. But in spite of this, when Milo finally embarked on one of the Bordés Line's fastest clippers, the feeling of satisfaction, that should have been his due, was absent. He shipped on board on the morning of departure, missing the traditional celebrations. He wasn't homeward bound – Šipan, not London, was his home and however close the two might appear rom such a distance as the West Coast of South America, the reality was that while he was in London, the Adriatic would effectively remain as distant and unattainable as it did in Iquique. He had promised himself that when his job was done, he would return home. But in spite of his growing wealth and influence, he knew that South America still offered great challenges. This first trip back to Europe was to be purely business. However strong the attraction, his home would have to wait. He hadn't finished yet.

Milo saw the London Stock Exchange of the early 1880s at first hand. Šipan had once been part of the stable and enduring

Dubrovnik republic that had controlled the trade routes of the Southern Adriatic for many hundreds of years. But as their northern neighbours found alternative sources for their goods and alternative markets, the power of the Venetian and Dalmatian republics had withered. It was now the British Empire which dominated trade across the world. The massive reserves of capital provided by the City of London were the powerhouse for colonial development or – depending upon your point of view – exploitation.

Throughout the next decade, rising affluence in Victorian Britain no longer restricted investors to established families with old money. The growing middle classes – even skilled workers – were acquiring surplus funds which attracted a range of hungry stock market jobbers offering seductive schemes for their enrichment. The market-makers promoted new industries, especially those based overseas, which promised dazzling returns without the opportunity to examine the extravagant claims at first hand. The nitrate industry was ideal. After the war, production was booming and dividends mushroomed. Agricultural production could hardly keep pace with the world's rapidly growing population, and investors were assured that Chile's huge reserves could supply the world's need for fertilisers for decades to come. Best of all, it was a monopoly. Chile saltpetre – as it became known – could be found nowhere else in the world.

In the London Stock Exchange in Chapel Court, Milo had tapped into an almost inexhaustible supply of capital. Led by the colourful 'Colonel' John Thomas North, successive nitrate companies were formed and floated on the Exchange to an increasingly enthusiastic reception. By the end of the decade the shares of North's quoted nitrate companies would soar up to eight times their original price.

Milo had always considered that Valparaiso represented a major and cosmopolitan trading centre, but London made it look almost as unimportant as Dubrovnik. He could scarcely believe the scale of the capital available and the hunger of the banks to discover new industries in which to invest. While they knew nothing about the nitrate industry, they seemed to think this was a positive advantage and saw, in the proposition that Milo outlined to them, an industry they could make money from. But their enthusiasm made him cautious.

Free of the constraints of expropriation and working under the relative stability and encouragement of Chile, Milo could see that circumstances were finally right for the expansion of the industry in the way he had always foreseen. He was convinced that its future would dwarf its past. He decided to keep something back and simply whet the appetite of his British investors, by issuing just enough shares for his capital requirements. He knew that if all went well, if he could keep up the dividends, the investors would keep coming back for more. He kept to himself that he still held certificates for a number of other nitrate fields – and he certainly wasn't going to tell them how cheaply they had been bought. If interest in nitrate shares grew as he anticipated, and it was discovered that he had more to sell, it would only depress the price. He returned to South America, confident the best was yet to come.

Chile had entered the Nitrate Age. During the following decade, world consumption would surge more than six-fold. In the seven years following Chilean occupation, capital investment nearly doubled. The sudden impact on a small economy was huge. Managers, technicians and skilled workers were imported from Europe and the improvements largely bypassed Chilean society. It became a European – principally British – business, which just happened to operate in South America. But there were considerable advantages to Chile and they were grateful for everything they could get. The almost feudal system of estates was virtually destroyed by the money on offer to workers in the desert of Tarapacá. Slowly a middle class was to evolve, and political ideas filtered down throughout society. Ownership of the capital was consolidated into European hands, leaving Chile with the leftovers. But even the leftovers were substantial, and the country rapidly became the most sophisticated in South America.

~~~~~

'It's finally finished.' Milo led Emilio Vasco past the ships alongside Iquique's new breakwater. He stopped and watched them load. 'When James first designed it, people said there would never be enough business to make it pay.'

'The problems I had trying to syndicate the loan,' Emilio smiled at the memory. 'But the dock was full as soon as they finished it, and now we're planning a second one.'

Milo turned as they reached the end of the quay and looked around the bay. A wide, tree-lined avenue skirted the coast, disappearing around the headland. Milo looked back at the ships. 'Iquique's changing so fast. It's getting almost sophisticated; I wonder what Alicia would have thought of it. Everything's so new.'

'Not everything,' Emilio said, pointing across the street to a small wooden building set back from the newly paved roadway. 'That's my first office – d'you remember it? Somehow it survived the last earthquake. But we've moved uptown now: we're safer there.'

'Safer from earthquakes or the crimpers?' They walked on along the quay and stopped in front of a substantial brick building. 'This is the new mission,' said Milo. 'We've established one in Valparaiso as well and we're slowly starting to ease out the crimpers. Joachim Traub gets his replacement crew from them when he's down here. They don't give kickbacks, so only the honest skippers use them. But they're hard places to keep in order and Valparaiso's much worse than here. It's run by an American, John Hardy, who used to be a professional wrestler; I don't think anyone else could keep it under control. The missions are alcohol-free – it wouldn't work otherwise – but it means they're always short of money. I've been supporting them ever since they opened.' Milo looked back across the bay at the deceptively calm sea. 'Sailors need all the help they can get. The skippers still pay the mission the normal three months' advance, but they only take what we're owed for the lodging and hand the rest back to the sailors when they leave. The waterfront crimpers despise them.'

'You'll never get rid of them completely,' Emilio said.

'We've got to. The world's trade can't depend on a handful of cut-throats. The shipping lines will have to change. They can't go on treating the seamen as expendable and let them go through what I went through – they'll have to start looking after them. The number of ships is growing too fast; how are they going to attract new sailors and train new officers? They can't.' Milo stopped and looked back at the ships heaving slowly in the swell. 'I should start a shipping line. Get someone to run it who doesn't treat the men as animals. Someone who doesn't rely on the sort of crimpers you find in San Francisco and Callao.'

'Fortunately Iquique's not quite as bad,' Emilio said.

Milo looked around. 'No. It's turning into a real city. Every new street is having water pipes installed under it. I'm still using the pipeline James put in for me. I used to be the only one with water, but now everyone's got it.'

'Not everyone, but enough of them.' Emilio gestured towards the large main square ahead. 'They couldn't have built all that without a water supply. It's been a big investment – not big enough for London perhaps, but we managed to float the water company on the Valparaiso Stock Exchange.'

'At least in Chile they care whether something has value, like a water company,' said Milo. 'In London they're only interested in how high they can push the share price. They don't really care about the business. If a jobber declines a stock he doesn't like and then sees other people paying huge sums for it, he doesn't say "what an idiot" and walk away. Instead he thinks he must have missed something, and goes back and starts buying even faster to make up for his late start. If someone else is buying, then he thinks it must be worth something. People don't seem to understand that a stock has a value simply because it's bought.'

'I don't know that's it's any different in Valparaiso,' said Emilio. 'We have some pretty sharp operators there as well.'

'The London operators only think they're sharp. In fact all they're doing is following everyone else. The jobbers turn stocks into a fashion. They float the shares, but restrict them to influential friends so the public can see people buying, but can't get any themselves. Demand increases and the price goes up; then, when it's high enough, they finally sell at a huge profit. The market-makers are like patent-medicine sellers who've placed someone in the crowd. Punters see someone starting a queue to buy and they join it, afraid they're missing out – even though they don't know what they're queuing for. They keep pumping in hot air, until the bubble bursts.'

Emilio shrugged. 'If people want to gamble with their own money, I don't see why you should want to protect them. But the nitrate industry isn't a gamble; it's a good investment. You're paying healthy dividends, and with production increasing so fast, the shares can only go up.'

'That's the problem. Production could be rising too fast. If we don't do something about it, we'll see unsold nitrates on the quayside and falling prices for the first time in ten years.'

'I can't see why it should worry you,' Emilio said. 'You've invested all the money you've raised. You can ride out any fluctuations in price far better than any of your competitors.'

'Yes, and it's not the future that worries me. I've still got old Peruvian certificates for new fields. Most *salitreros* are just concentrating on their existing operations, producing all they can. But in a few more years they'll all be worked out and they'll need to find new ones. That'll be the time to sell – they'll be worth far more then.' Milo paused. 'But in the short term they've got to cut back on production, otherwise the price will start to drop. We've seen it before – before *estanco*.'

Emilio laughed. 'I don't think the government in Chile has even thought of nationalisation. They're too busy dreaming up ways of spending the tax that's still flooding in. You know it's the first time their government has ever balanced the books? They're as anxious to keep the prices up as we are.'

They stopped in front of a large, granite-clad building and Milo looked up at the shining stone façade. 'Impressive – it's certainly a change from the shack on the coast.'

Emilio led Milo between the carved columns of the ornate entrance and crossed the marbled hall to his office. 'So, what do you think?' he asked as he sat behind his desk.

'Magnificent. Has Martin seen it?'

'No.' Emilio frowned. 'It wasn't finished when he was here and I don't think it's likely that he'll be down again. When did you see them last?'

Milo thought for a while. 'I suppose it must have been over a year ago. I haven't had time to go to Lima since then.'

'I was with them last month. Martin said he'd written telling you he'd finally sold out.' Emilio frowned. 'He accepted the offer from the British Sugar Company. But I'm worried about him. Now he hasn't got the estates to occupy him, he seems to have aged even more. I don't think he's got the strength to come down here again. I'd never realised before how much older he is than Lisa. After he's gone, I can't see what's left to keep her here.'

'It's about time I visited them,' said Milo. 'I've got to visit Arica shortly, so I'll go on up from there.'

He travelled up two months later. As he pushed open the gates he was reassured by the familiar driveway stretching towards the Hursts' villa, the garden as perfect as it had ever been. As the imposing front door opened, Milo rushed forward and grabbed the servant by the arm. 'Julio. It's good to see you again.'

The butler bowed stiffly. 'We read about you in the papers, Señor Milo, and are all very proud.' Although he was trying to keep his expression impassive, his delight was clear.

For the first time Milo thought of what his arrival, as a small boy, must have meant to this rather formal house. 'How is everyone?'

'Señora Hurst is very well – ' Julio hesitated before adding, '– but Señor Hurst is not what he used to be. He's resting upstairs, but Mrs Hurst is in the conservatory.'

'No need to announce me, Julio. We'll go straight through.' Milo started towards the back of the house.

'But Señor Milo,' Julio protested, hurrying after them. 'Señora Hurst isn't alone, there's someone with her. Senor...'

Milo interrupted him. 'It doesn't matter; she'll be pleased to see me, whoever she's with.' He strode off through the day-room into the conservatory.

When Martin had rebuilt the conservatory after the earthquake, he had doubled its size. Lisa Hurst was hardly visible behind the huge plants at the far end, sitting in a bamboo chair facing him. She looked up as he approached and her face dissolved into smiles as she rushed over to greet him. 'Milo! What a surprise,' she said, holding Milo tightly. 'Why didn't you tell us when you were coming?'

'I decided on impulse. I suddenly realised how long it was since I last saw you. I've come straight from the docks.' Milo broke away impatiently. 'How are you? How is Martin?'

Lisa had recovered from her surprise, but Milo sensed she was ill at ease. 'What is it?' he asked. 'Is Martin all right? Tell me.'

Lisa laughed nervously. 'No, no, it's not that. Martin's fine, that is, he's not too bad. It's just that, well...' She stopped speaking and Milo followed her look across the conservatory. A figure rose slowly from the chair opposite Lisa's.

'Robert Miller,' Milo said abruptly. 'What's he doing here?' he turned back to Lisa. 'You'd think he'd stay away after what he's done.'

Lisa started to protest, but Robert cut across her angrily. 'And exactly what have I done? You're not still blaming me for what happened with the Garcias? I told you I had nothing to do with it.'

'Please, both of you.' Lisa gestured to Robert to keep quiet. 'This is my house,' – she uttered the words firmly – 'and I will not allow you to quarrel. Whatever you think he's done, Milo, Robert remains our friend. He still visits us regularly and we're always pleased to see him. I can't understand why you continue to think he's our enemy. He's always tried to help us. If the two of you would only talk about it...'

Milo looked at Robert coldly. 'We don't have anything to talk about.'

Robert flushed. 'Perhaps not, but you seem to have forgotten that the Hursts are my friends too. They don't share your low opinion of me.'

'That's only because Lisa is soft-hearted,' said Milo. 'She always thinks the best of everyone. Martin understands what kind of person you are, but he knows how upset Lisa would be if he told her.'

Lisa cried out. 'That's not true. You're just like Martin: you both think you know what's best for me. Robert has never done anything wrong.'

Robert shook his head sadly. 'Martin doesn't blame me for what happened. He knows I tried to stop him. Why do you still hold me responsible for something I couldn't control?'

'Control?' Milo said angrily. 'It was you who organised everything. You were the go-between. I've always suspected it was your idea in the first place. You encouraged Martin to develop the second plantation and then, when Emilio wouldn't lend him the money, you suggested he approached the Garcias. You knew how much they wanted Napeña, and thought it would promote your career if you got it for them.'

Robert sighed. 'That wasn't how it happened.' He looked at Milo earnestly. 'You're determined not to believe me. I know it's your way of repaying Martin and Lisa, but they've helped me too, and I'm not going to compete with you to establish who's most in their debt. You like to pretend that you've protected them against me. Of course you helped them, but it was from the Garcias – not from me.'

'Do you expect me to believe that Martin would have risked his entire estates without your encouragement?' Milo asked fiercely. 'He always trusted you – otherwise he would never have dealt with the Garcias. He was far too clever to get caught out by them. It was only because you persuaded him that it was safe.'

'There's no point talking about it, is there?' Robert said. 'There's nothing I can say to convince you that I did everything I could to prevent it.'

'Only because it's not true,' said Milo, but before he could continue, a noise made him turn.

Martin Hurst stood stiffly at the doorway. 'I'm afraid it is true,' he said quietly. 'Julio told me you were here.' His voice had a slight tremor, but his eyes were clear. 'I heard the shouting and guessed what it was about. Even though you won't accept it, you've got to know what happened.'

Martin walked slowly into the room; his lean frame was now wasted and frail. He eased himself into a chair. 'Robert's right. He did all he could to stop me, but I wouldn't listen. You don't want to believe that I could be so stupid, but I was. I think I just wanted to show everyone that I hadn't lost my touch.' Martin laughed bitterly. 'I'd already enjoyed every success there was, but it didn't seem to be enough. It seemed as though all my achievements had been forgotten. When Emilio refused to make any more loans to me, I just couldn't believe it – he was only interested in nitrates. He didn't have time any more for my sugar estates. He seemed to have forgotten about all the business we'd done together.'

'But that can't be true,' Milo protested. 'You didn't need to prove anything to anyone. The evidence was all around us. You can't have forgotten that I spent every summer in Napeña? You created that out of nothing. I was so proud of you, I wanted to copy you – I did copy you.'

'But I wanted you to join me, not copy me.' Martin said sadly. 'But you decided you didn't want to be involved and went off to the desert instead. If you'd stayed, we could have developed the plantations together.'

'But I wouldn't have created them,' said Milo. 'I wanted to do something myself. I felt that if I didn't, I might just as well have stayed in Dalmatia and starved.' Milo's eyes started watering. 'I owed it to my mother, and to Vigo. I had to make it on my own to make it all worthwhile. If they hadn't tried to get a better life for me, they'd both still be alive now. I didn't want their deaths to be meaningless, when I was responsible for them.'

Lisa took Milo's hand. 'Isn't it about time you stopped blaming yourself? They would both be proud of what you've achieved. We all are.'

'It's your achievement, too.' Milo smiled at her weakly. 'You made it possible by everything you've done for me, and I wanted to show you that it hadn't been wasted.' Milo looked back to Martin. 'But what I couldn't understand is why you went to the Garcias. There were plenty of other people you could have gone to.'

'Because I thought Robert could make it easier for me,' Martin replied. 'I thought he'd be able to persuade them. After all, the sugar market was very weak and I needed help to convince them, but he was against it from the start. When Miguel Garcia suggested I put up Napeña, Robert begged me not to do it. But I thought I knew better. I was just a silly old fool.'

Milo looked at him. Underneath his almost permanent tan, his lined face was grey and wasted. Suddenly Milo realised that Martin was now an old man, and had been for some years. Perhaps he had fooled himself into thinking that Martin was still the vibrant and determined businessman who had first cowed the magistrate into releasing him from jail.

'But why didn't you ask me? I could have helped.'

Martin looked across to Robert. 'He still doesn't understand, does he?' Turning back to Milo, his voice was resigned. 'I couldn't ask you. I wanted to show you that I was still more powerful than you. Everyone was starting to talk about what you were doing in Tarapacá. Every time we got a newspaper it was full of how you were creating a new industry down there – it was as though it was the first time it had happened. I wanted to remind you that I'd done it first, that I was still Martin Hurst, the Sugar King.'

'To remind me?' Milo let out a long, slow breath. He let go of Lisa's hand and approached Martin's chair. 'I could never forget that without you, I'd probably be just another nameless, forgotten victim of a shipwreck – at the bottom of the sea, or eaten by sharks. I owe you and Lisa everything.' Milo paused. 'But it isn't just gratitude. You were the only one who had any principles, the only one who cared about the workers and their families. I looked up to you. I'm one of the few people who can really understand what you've achieved. I admired you.' He appealed to Robert. 'Why didn't you tell them? – you know what I thought. I told you often enough.'

'I tried,' said Robert. 'I even told him that you were blaming me because you didn't want to believe it was Martin's idea. But he wouldn't listen to me. Neither of you would.'

Lisa stepped forward and took Milo's arm. 'For all your cleverness, there's still a lot you don't understand. Other people make mistakes – you can't seem to accept that. You shouldn't think the less of them for it. It's what people do, but they try and work around them. But it was Martin's mistake, not Robert's. You can't accept that Martin could do anything wrong.'

Milo looked slowly from Robert to Martin. 'I suppose I've made mistakes, too,' he said finally.

Lisa looked at Milo earnestly. 'We can dismiss other people's experience as their mistakes, but we think of our own mistakes as wisdom. But one way or another we've all managed to get on with things and we've all survived. Isn't that what's important?'

'My mother didn't survive, neither did Vigo.' Milo said it without thinking and his face cracked with grief. 'I'm sorry, I didn't …' He put his head in his hands. 'They're the ones who've paid for it all.' His cry echoed around the still room.

Lisa put her arms around him, but his body remained stiff and unyielding. No one said anything for several minutes. Each of them had their own memories. With an effort Milo tried to recover himself. 'I've done what I could for them. I've tried to make the best of everything. I didn't do so badly, did I?'

Only Lisa could see the pain etched deep in his eyes.

Chapter Eighteen

Over the previous two decades the Chilean city of Valparaiso had established an unassailable position as the capital of the nitrate industry, and inevitably it came to supplant Iquique as Milo's new base. The industry was changing rapidly and, with almost unrestrained growth, the development of new fields used up capital in a way that couldn't have been imagined when he started. The scale of the industry was vast. Gradually he started to withdraw from the operations and concentrate on the commercial side. For the first time in over ten years, he started to think about things outside his work. There was no longer the sense of being a pioneer, of establishing an industry. It was already established.

Milo walked through the doorway into his home. Is this really my home? he thought, looking around him. Rather than the trouble of maintaining another house, he kept a suite of private rooms for his personal use – they were linked to an office on the ground floor that was occupied by his trading staff. But the proximity to his work was becoming irksome. There must be other things beside work – companionship, for example. Had he sacrificed that for his single-mindedness?

At least there was still James – when he wasn't out inspecting the refineries. He joined Milo after work, passing through the connecting door into the spacious living room. He usually had several engineering problems he wanted to discuss, but tonight he could sense that Milo was restless. The weather was appropriately overcast and although it wasn't yet evening, it was almost dark. Clouds had been building up throughout the day and they hung heavily over the bay. Shrieks of wind occasionally whistled through the window frames. The dreaded norther was on its way.

James waited while Milo poured them both a drink, and as the approaching storm rattled against the shutters, Milo asked suddenly, 'Where do you think of as home?'

James looked up in surprise. 'Home?' he asked. 'Why do you ask?'

'You know I want to go back to Šipan one day. But what about you?'

'There's nothing like that for me.' James sighed. 'I told you that both my parents died when I was young and I hardly remember them. I was brought up by some sort of cousin. I never did understand the relationship properly. She paid for all my studies, but only out of duty – she never liked me.'

'How can you be so sure? Isn't it worth trying to contact her again?'

'No. You can tell these things. I left as soon as I could and I haven't heard from her in years. I suppose she thinks I was ungrateful, and perhaps she's right. I suppose she did what she could, but somehow it never felt like home. In my earliest memories I couldn't wait to get back to boarding school.'

'You know, James, my first recollections are of such happiness. I realise that memories can play tricks on you. But in my mind, it still seems that my early childhood in Šipan was so … so easy – easy and contented.' Milo pulled himself away from his recollections. 'I suppose it's just a dream, just my imagination.'

'So why don't you go back? You've done everything there is to do here. Isn't it about time you started to enjoy yourself instead of working so hard?'

Milo hesitated. 'It doesn't feel as though I'm ready yet; I haven't quite finished. But what about you? Why don't you go back?'

'I don't know. It's difficult to explain. Knowing that I could go back home has always been a sort of touchstone for me. It's as though I could compare myself against something that doesn't change. But if I went back it would crystallise everything I've achieved here, and I don't think I'm ready for that. The point about home is that it's always there, and in one's memory it never changes. You only discover how you've changed when you go back to it.'

'I wonder,' said Milo thoughtfully. To him Šipan could never change. 'It's so long since I've heard from my family,' he hesitated. 'I had a couple of letters from my brother after he left, and my father even wrote a few times, but the letters soon stopped. Perhaps they found it all too painful. I thought it best not to write – what could I say to them? I'll go back, but only when I've finished here. When I've made up for everything that's happened to them.'

'But you could have sent them money. Wouldn't that have helped them?' suggested James cautiously, anxious not to appear critical.

'You don't know my father. He's far too independent to accept it.' To James' surprise, the suggestion seemed to cheer Milo up. 'Where would you go if you went back?'

'Near London. I'd want to keep in touch with South America, but in the country – Kent, perhaps. I suppose I could afford to live anywhere now. It's funny: I don't feel any richer. I've always done well in South America, but I've been so caught up with work there's never really been anything I wanted to buy. All my satisfaction has been from creating things. Perhaps I should get an estate here. The valleys behind Valparaiso are so green and beautiful, but I don't think I'd ever be able to relax with the business on my doorstep. I'd have to make a clean break.' He hesitated. 'I'd like to … perhaps, to find a wife. I don't seem to have had any time for it yet, but I'm still not too old, you know.'

As he said it, a gust of wind hit the window with a dull thump and they both laughed.

'Do you think someone out there is trying to tell us something?' Milo got up and shut the curtains against the storm. 'I lost my chance with Alicia, and hardly a week goes past without me thinking about it. I still can't be sure that I did the right thing. It didn't seem like a choice then, but as the time's gone on, I wonder whether it was.' James had rarely heard Milo so introspective; he was always such a private person.

'You know,' Milo continued, 'I heard someone call me "The Nitrate King" the other day. It's funny the way things seem to balance themselves out. I've had all this success – but what have I got to show for it? I'm still alone.' Milo watched a gust of wind ruffle the curtains. 'It's suitable weather for feeling sorry for ourselves, I suppose.'

'I'm not feeling sorry for myself,' James said. 'I wouldn't change a thing that's happened to me here. It's been a fantastic adventure, and I'm really proud of the things I've done. When I first came out I never dreamed of what would happen. Suddenly, after I started working with Martin, anything seemed possible. I just worked out what had to be done and the money was always there. I just had to go ahead and do it. No engineer could have asked for more.

'But at times it's been harsh,' James continued. 'I think I've earned the right to enjoy other things. Out in Tarapacá the nights are so clear, I've started studying the stars. Perhaps I could build a proper telescope and study astronomy. I don't want to stay out here working on nitrate refineries for another twenty years and then return home a dry and spent old man, spending all my time looking back and saying how much better things were here. There's still a future for me here outside nitrates.'

'Perhaps, after Alicia, I should find myself a Dalmatian wife,' Milo said. 'Life there is much too hard for women to ask their husbands to choose between them and work. Anyone who tried to would remain a spinster. Trouble is, there aren't many suitable Dalmatian women in Valparaiso. But I'm still only just thirty,' Milo mused. 'Thirty-four,' he added after a while.

The crash of thunder shook the building. James walked across the room and pulled the curtains aside. 'It's going to be a bad one,' he said. 'I hope the ships are secure. Valparaiso isn't the place to be when there's a storm from the north.' He turned from the window. 'How long is it?' He saw that Milo didn't understand. 'Since Matotambo, I mean. I always think of our partnership as starting then. You asked me to join you down in Tarapacá just after Martin bought that vineyard.'

'Vineyard? If only he'd kept it as one.' Milo clearly wasn't happy at the memory. 'I suppose it must be over sixteen years ago. Of course the Garcias have got it now, though I doubt that they're able to make much from it. It was perfect land for wine, but a bit too high for sugar. I suppose that's why Martin planted it – he didn't want to do anything too easy. He liked a challenge.'

James smiled at the memory. 'When we started, did you ever think the nitrate industry would be so much bigger than the sugar business? Did you ever think we'd outgrow Emilio? You know our combined operations are capitalised at more than his entire bank?'

'But he's achieved his ambition. He always said he wanted to make his bank one of the biggest, and he's certainly done that.'

'He deserves it,' said James. 'No one could have been more loyal. It's because he learnt it from Martin, back when I first joined him. I hear he's looking for new investments now.'

'It's extraordinary that under Chile, the industry looks more secure than it has for years.' Milo mused. 'Now the London stock market is so deeply involved it seems we can't do anything wrong. I still find it amazing the way people are attracted by a new business they don't quite understand. I even heard people were queuing up to buy shares in a South African nitrate company. It took months before anyone realised there aren't any nitrates in Africa.'

The noise of running feet outside made him stop. 'What's that?' he asked. A long low wail started from by the docks. Slowly it rose in pitch, undulating and wavering. 'It's the siren. Someone must be in trouble.' Milo went to the door. As he opened it, a gust of wind almost ripped it from his hands. In the street, people were running down towards the docks. Milo braced himself against the force of the wind as James joined him. 'There, look!' It was getting very dark, and from the harbour a maroon flew high into the dark sky. 'It's from the bay. Let's go.'

They ran down the street, hunched against the full force of the gale which funnelled between the buildings, buffeting them as they ran past the alleyways. As they reached the docks they could see a ship anchored dangerously close to the beach. The crew was hauling desperately on the capstan, trying to pull on the anchor cable to heave themselves out of danger. The sea cascaded past them, the waves building in the shoaling water and crashing against the shore. The ship seemed almost close enough to touch, but there was nothing they could do. The sailors strained at the spokes of the anchor capstan, but the sea was too strong for them. A fierce gust caught the bows of the ship, throwing her sideways. She veered wildly against the chain until it snagged at the end of its scope. The ship turned and chased back again and as it did so, they could see the second anchor chain hanging uselessly from the leeward side. 'It must have broken,' shouted Milo. 'They've only got one anchor holding them.'

The ship ran to the end of the scope of its single chain, juddering to a halt as the anchor was dragged along the seabed. The ship slowed and headed up into the wind; as it did so the force on the chain subsided and the anchor rebedded itself. A shred of foresail was torn loose, catching a gust which forced the bows around. The ship scudded off in the opposite direction. 'It's not going to hold,' shouted Milo. They watched helplessly. A rescue team was assembling below them on the beach, bracing themselves against the fury of the wind screaming across the bay. The crests of the crashing waves were whipped high across the shore, drenching the onlookers in a cold, salty spray. The ship was now gaining speed, as though charging at an unseen target. From onshore the anchor chain could be clearly heard through the wail of the storm, clanking as the men strove to pull it in. But each link they gathered in weakened the anchor's hold. Their task was becoming hopeless.

As if realising it, the men stopped heaving. The onlookers could see one of them pointing out to sea. Milo and James followed the direction of his arm. Out in the darkness, a clear line of white foam could be seen bearing down on the shore. The random sea had combined into one huge wave which towered over the rest. They looked back to the ship. The crew rushed towards the masts and scrambled up the ratlines. The ship reached the end of its scope and barely seemed to pause in its headlong attack as the anchor was ripped from the sea bed. Unrestrained, the bows of the ship were forced away from the wind and the ship turned broadside on to the sea. The massive wave appeared to dip slightly like a bull before a charge, and then it roared forward, burying its base deep under the hull, while its white crest scoured the decks clear.

James and Milo thought the land shook as the keel was flung against the base of the rocks, but it could only have been their imagination. All that was visible of the ship was its masts heaving uncontrollably in the white cauldron. They watched the foremast, where three sailors had taken refuge. The sea forced it back against its stays. It buckled like a straw, pitching the men into the water even as their hands held their grip. Their bodies were lost among the stricken flotsam thrown ashore.

As though regrouping for one final effort, the wind appeared to ebb and for a moment the scene before them appeared almost static as the light faded. In the unfamiliar silence, a man's scream was heard clearly from across the water, but it was silenced suddenly in a rush of water. With a final blast, the wind hurled itself against the stricken ship and lifted it clear across the rocks and smashed it down a hundred yards from the shore where it struck with the crash of splintering timber. The decks were now awash, while half a dozen men still held their grip on the mizzen mast above. The mast couldn't hold up much longer.

A flare from the rescue team ashore was fired into the sky. Its eerie white light lit up the driving spray like the crystals of snowflakes. As the flare reached its height, they saw the rescuers levelling a tube towards the ship, and with a dull 'whoosh' a cable was fired towards the mast. Buffeted by the wind, it veered away and was lost in the darkness. A second flare was fired, and a second line aimed. This time, they heard a faint shout as the rope fell across the rigging. They could just make out an officer clambering down to secure it. Milo watched as a sailor joined him and together they struggled to attach the shore line to the mast. Another yell, and Milo looked out to sea. A row of three breakers was bearing down on the ship. No one could survive this. He watched, trembling. The first wave reared up onto the stricken ship and scoured the decks clean. After it had passed, he saw a man run up from below, desperately timing his moment to escape, only to be caught by the second wave as it buried the decks in foam. As the water cascaded off the decks, the man was gone. The final wave smashed itself against the ship, which keeled over until its remaining mast was level with the water. But still the remaining men clung on, their feet buried in the sea. As the wave receded, the water was sucked from underneath the hull and the mast straightened and started to heel into the wind. The shoreline tautened.

How it held was a mystery. The ship turned and shifted against the rocks, wedging its broken back against the rocky outcrops. Taking the opportunity of a brief calm, a bosun's chair was winched along the line. The officer pulled it in and helped the first seaman climb into it. The rescue team heaved on the line and ferried him back along the rope. As he dropped onto the beach and waded ashore, a loud cheer echoed around the bay. The rescue team ran the chair out again without pausing.

The team on shore worked rapidly. With four of the five men ashore, the chair was sent out for the remaining officer. Even before it reached the mast, he leapt across to it. The onlookers could hear the slight shift in the wind. It was a chilling sound: a deep rumble, like an earthquake. The rescuers starting heaving at the line, in a desperate race against the sea. The storm was not to be deprived of its final prey. The angry wind hit again like an explosion. The ship quivered, as its back was snapped in two like a twig. It toppled into two halves, and buried its mast finally beneath the sea. The rescue line had parted: the final crewman was lost.

A cry came from the crowd. One of the rescue team was yelling, pointing into the spray. As the waves ebbed back out to sea, in a clear stretch of water between the rocks and the shore, they saw a figure struggling at the end of the line. The rescuers heaved again with new hope. One of them hurried towards the breaking waves, tying a rope around his waist as he ran. Two others followed him. Another flare shot up into the sky. The onlookers were now silent. No one said a word as they watched the final survivor fight for his life.

The rescue team hauled in the line, but the body at its end was overwhelmed by the foam. The rescuer from the beach staggered into the sea, the waves swirling around his chest. As he waded in deeper, the team on the beach paid out his rope. Gradually he approached the victim. Another wave crashed against the shore and for a moment both men were lost from sight.

'He's got him,' shouted a voice. The two figures merged for a moment. The rescuer grabbed at the body and secured a second rope under its arms. The men on the beach heaved as fast as they could, intent only on getting the two men ashore. Finally they pulled them onto the beach. The wind howled, as though deprived of its due. The rescue team carried the two survivors beyond the reach of the frustrated sea.

Still the crowd was silent. They peered into the darkness at the two figures laid out on the beach. Yet another flare lit up the sky. Slowly, the rescuer's body moved. He pushed himself to his knees and looked across to the sailor lying on his back. The onlookers waited. Finally, they saw the officer move. He turned, wriggling onto his front and vomiting seawater. He pushed himself up slowly until he, too, swayed unsteadily on his knees. The two men kneeled together as though at prayer. The crowd erupted into wild cheering.

Milo and James followed the excited crowd back up the hill towards their office. They were too shaken by the drama to talk. A man was pressing against the crowd ahead of them, making his way back towards the beach. He was huge, even by European standards, and towered over the excited spectators who parted to let him through. Milo shouted at him as he passed. 'Mr Hardy, Mr Hardy. Over here.'

The man paused and looked around him until he eventually located Milo and pushed his way towards him. 'What happened?' he asked. 'Did they get the last one off? I've taken the other survivors back to the mission.'

'Thank God,' answered Milo. 'It was a near miracle that he's alive. I don't know how badly he's hurt. They ought to take him to the hospital.'

'No,' answered the man. 'The mission's nearer and they've sent some nurses over.'

'You must go. I'll call in tomorrow morning.' Milo watched the man make his way down towards the sea. James looked at him questioningly.

'That's John Hardy,' explained Milo. 'From the seaman's mission. The sailors love him, or they're terrified of him – either way they're lucky to have him.'

Milo went back early the next morning to see the survivors. He looked across the bay. The wind had dropped and the sky was pale as though washed out, exhausted by the storm. Wisps of grey cloud scudded across the weak sun. John Hardy met him at the entrance. He seemed cheerful. 'How are they?' Milo asked.

'Remarkably well, except for the last one. I haven't got their names yet – do you want to see them? They're all in the first floor dormitory.'

'I don't want to disturb them.' Milo suddenly felt embarrassed. 'I just want to let them know they we'll look after them.'

John Hardy knew Milo's history and understood his feelings. 'We're doing everything we can. When they've recovered, then you can probably do more. In the meantime it might help the officer to have a visitor. He seems to be a bit depressed.'

Milo followed him upstairs. The sailors were sitting by the window, talking quietly amongst themselves. They were all wearing a varied selection of seaman's jerseys that Mr Hardy had managed to find for them. Milo greeted them shyly, not wanting to intrude. 'You did well last night,' he said. 'It must have been terrifying.'

The men were bound together by the closeness of their experiences. One of them touched his forelock. 'Thank you, your honour,' he said before turning back to his shipmates. Milo stared at them. "Your honour?" Is that what he was to them? He realised with shock how far he had come from the life of an ordinary sailor. He followed Mr Hardy across to the bed set apart at the far end of the room. The nurse looked across to them and stood up. As they approached the bed, the officer turned his head to face him, staring with unfocused eyes.

Milo stopped. 'My God,' he said.

John Hardy looked up at him in alarm. 'What is it?' he asked. Milo's face was white.

Milo approached the bed slowly. 'It can't be,' he whispered under his breath. 'Not after all this time.' He leant over the sailor in the bed. The man raised his arm weakly and Milo reached out and held his hand. John Hardy looked across to Milo, bewildered at the sight of the tears streaming down his face. He started to speak, but there was nothing to say.

Milo was muttering something to himself. He strained to hear. 'What is it?' he asked. 'What's wrong? Can I do anything?'

Milo shook his head and clung to the sailor's hand. 'How many lives?' he started. 'How many lives have you got left, Arnie?'

Arnie opened his eyes and blinked slowly in recognition. Finally, he squeezed Milo's hand and smiled weakly.

Chapter Nineteen

'We were shipmates,' Milo told James excitedly. 'For nearly a year we were almost inseparable. I can't believe it – Arnie's part of my past.' He grabbed James' arm. 'He knew me before … before –' Milo groped for the words in frustration. 'Before all this,' he said finally, waving his arm to indicate the office. 'It's unbelievable. It's as though he's come back from the dead. They say he'll be fine after a few days' rest. We've got so much to talk about.'

James looked on, not knowing quite what to say. Milo had returned from the Mission chattering like a child. It had taken James almost a quarter of an hour to discover the reason for the excitement. 'An old shipmate.' Milo kept repeating it, unable to accept that he'd found a part of his past that he thought was lost forever.

Arnie recovered rapidly, barely remembering his rescue. The last thing he could recall was running up the rigging as a wave crashed onto the deck. Milo forgot his work in the excitement of showing Arnie around. James noticed the pride with which he told people that Arnie was 'an old shipmate', surprised at how few people realised that Milo had ever been to sea.

Milo made Arnie tell him everything that had happened to him since sailing away from Callao, nearly twenty years earlier. He had always wondered about Captain Brockman. Did he make any effort to find him?

'Bully Brockman? You're joking. He said you weren't worth it.' Arnie laughed at the memory. 'You were so small then. I begged him to let me look for you, but he said that no one would worry about one boy, but that if I went missing as well, he'd have to come and find me and he'd make sure I'd never forget it. I had no choice. We sailed the next day, and it was a voyage I'll never forget. He never let up; he drove us like cattle. He and that first mate, Streicher. There wasn't a day when the ship wasn't over-canvassed. How we didn't lose a mast I'll never know. We made a record time to the Western approaches, but after that the wind backed, and it took a week to beat up the Channel. The owners liked him, but if a man had sailed with him once then if he had any choice in the matter, he'd never go with him again.'

'And you, Arnie?' asked Milo. 'What happened to you?'

'I managed to save up a bit of money. I took six months off and put myself through college. I got all my navigation papers and finally got my master's ticket, although I was only second mate on the ship that brought me here. I was master of one ship, but it was only a coaster, not deep-sea. To get a captain's berth, you need contacts, and they're difficult to find.'

'What about your family? Couldn't they help?'

'We've sort of drifted apart. That's what the sea does to you. You spend so much time worrying about what might happen next that you sort of forget the past. I really feel that if I don't get a ship soon, it'll be too late.'

'We'll find you one, don't you worry.'

To James it seemed that Milo was occupying another world, all thoughts of business had suddenly disappeared. Milo acted like a fourteen-year-old – the age at which he and Arnie had last been together. Arnie himself was quite bewildered at the attention he was getting. He had no means of gauging the extent of Milo's fortune, and at first he worried that Milo was spending too much money on his care. A full-time nurse was always in attendance, and Milo insisted that a doctor visit four times a day. Milo arranged for tailors to produce complete wardrobes to replace Arnie's lost possessions. Arnie wondered where all the money was coming from.

When Arnie was well enough, Milo took him on a trip inland to see the valleys. Milo thought the sight of the green, lush valleys would help Arnie's convalescence and raise his spirits. Arnie had never seen anything so carefully organised. Behind their own carriage, three others followed carrying an elaborate picnic, and he lost count of the number of staff there were to serve it. Finally, Arnie took James to one side. 'Can Milo afford all this? He's spending so much money on me and it's not necessary. I don't need it.'

James laughed. 'I wouldn't worry about it, Arnie. It would take him a hundred years to spend everything he's got. Didn't he tell you about our business?'

'He told me that you were partners in a nitrate operation. But that's all.'

'It's one of the biggest in Chile,' said James. 'Don't worry about him.'

'But he doesn't seem to have a proper home. Why does he stay in those rooms?'

'Oh, I see,' said James. 'I suppose you'd expect him to have a lavish mansion. All I can say is: wait until you see his place in

Iquique. When he's down here, he doesn't like the bother of running another house. He finds it easier just to have rooms next to the office.'

'Has he really made so much money?' Arnie pondered. 'I always knew he was special. Did I tell you he saved my life? I was washed overboard – I thought it was the end. But Milo didn't give up on me. He got the crew to launch a boat and row out, even though they could all have drowned. I don't know how he persuaded them, but there was something about him even then – in spite of his size, he always seemed so grown up and mature. He always had an answer for things. I didn't think he'd stay at sea; in a funny way it didn't seem big enough for him. He seemed destined to make a name for himself and I always thought I'd hear of him again. I didn't expect it to be as a result of a shipwreck.'

James nodded. 'I know what you mean. He seemed middle-aged when I first knew him. He'd only been living with the Hursts a short time, so it couldn't have been long after you last saw him. He was always so serious, but it was extraordinary. If I showed him anything we were building I only had to explain it once, and he never forgot. He was always so keen to impress me. I think he felt it was the only way he could pay back the Hursts for taking him in and looking after him. Once he'd decided to operate a nitrate field, he put everything into it.' James hesitated. 'It was as though he was worried he wouldn't live up to his potential. He's always taken things so seriously and is desperate to avoid making mistakes. I think he's always cared more about his own expectations than anyone else's. I suppose in many ways he's had a difficult life, but it's good to see him enjoying so much time with you.'

Arnie frowned. 'But I'm worried about taking up *too* much of his time. His work must be suffering. In any case, I can't stay here for ever. I'll soon have to find a ship.'

'But he told you not to worry about that, didn't he?'

'Well, yes,' said Arnie. 'But I assumed he was joking.'

'Milo never jokes about work. If he said he'll find you something, then he will. He's always talking about establishing a competitor to the Bordés line, but he's never had the time. Or the opportunity,' he added, looking at Arnie thoughtfully. 'And as for worrying about the delay, it's done him so much good. I've never seen him so animated. Tell me –' James lowered his voice, even though they were alone – 'when you were with him at sea, did he ever talk to you about his brother?'

Arnie thought back to the days they had spent together, talking about their families and what they were going to do when they were older. 'Vigo,' he said. 'He was drowned. Milo talked about him a lot: seemed to worship him. I don't think he'd got over it.'

'He still hasn't,' said James. 'I think that having you here reminds him of Vigo.'

Arnie thought for a moment. 'His father died at sea, too. He used to have a locket. Did he ever show it to you? With a little picture of his father? It was a fine piece.'

'He still has it. He wears it all the time. I don't think he's ever taken it off. Sometimes at night in Tarapacá he'd show it to me, and tell me about his family, and that island he came from. Šipan.'

'Yes, Šipan. He always used to say that he'd got to get back there one day. There was something he had to do.'

Arnie had been in Chile for several months, and James could tell that Milo was becoming increasingly restless and unsettled. Problems with the refineries were brushed off in a way unthinkable just a few months previously. It was clear that his thoughts were elsewhere. The fundamentals of commerce were changing, too. It was now the time of corporations, not individuals. Martin Hurst had already discovered that the capital required had now become too great – a single man might start a business and develop it into a major enterprise, but no single man could continue to provide the huge capital that a growing company now needed. Corporations needed outside investors, and the easiest way to find them was to float their shares on the London Stock Exchange. But it wasn't straightforward. As Milo had discovered earlier, the problem was to decide how much the shares were worth.

After several years of difficulties, nitrate prices had finally rallied and the industry was once again flourishing. There were now more than seventeen quoted companies, accounting for nearly 3% of the Exchange's total capital. This was a colossal sum to be concentrated in just one industry, located in an uninhabited desert on the remote West Coast of South America. As the *Financial News* reported at the time: "The company promoter has only to whisper the magic word 'nitrates' and the market rises at him, whether he hails from Antofagasta, Talfal or Tarapacá. Gold can no longer conjure up premiums in Chapel Court like nitrate. It is the spell which draws the biggest crowd and causes the greatest flurry among premium hunters."

The South American nitrate bubble of the late 1880s had the classic ingredients of unsustainable speculation. It was a little-understood industry, based far away, which furnished investors with the hope that normal rules of finance might not apply. It offered a glorious future, based upon no solid past, and no one could say with certainty that this glorious future would never arrive. But above all, it involved greed. 'Colonel' John Thomas North, who counted Randolph Churchill and Nathan Rothschild among his friends, was still leading the boom. He sold his *oficina* Ramírez, which had cost him just £5,000, to the Liverpool Nitrate Company, a company he also controlled, for £50,000. Another paper wrote of the creation of: "a new aristocracy of finance, a new sort of parasite in the shape of promoters, speculators and merely nominal directors; a whole system of swindling and cheating by means of corporate juggling, stock jobbing and stock speculation." Unlike today's speculators, investors then looked for dividends, and during the late 1880s the nitrate companies were offering dramatic returns. But the fevered speculation meant that prices now soared beyond the ability even of a company to repay the investment. Money raised from new share issues was immediately paid out again as dividends – there was no other way to maintain the rapidly growing prices.

Milo knew it couldn't last and was happy not to become involved. He left the brokers to arrange the sale of his certificates. But what was left for him? What was there to keep him? He started thinking again of a different future, a future away from nitrates. Perhaps his work was finally complete, and it was now the time for him to move on.

'You remember what we were talking about – before the storm?' Milo asked James one evening. 'Since Arnie's been here I've been thinking about it more and more. I don't see what's left for me, and – well, what would you say if I sold up?'

James looked at Milo in astonishment. Although Milo had always talked about finishing the job, James had always thought that when it came down to it, Milo would never be able to leave the industry he'd helped create. 'But you'd come back?' he asked. 'You couldn't just abandon everything?'

'What's to keep me in Chile now? Suddenly I don't feel –' he shrugged. 'I don't know. I don't feel *hungry* any more. The time I've spent with Arnie has been, well, almost peaceful. I've spent so much time alone, and I can't ignore what's happening in London. I've still got most of the Peruvian certificates and the Stock Market would grab them. I'll keep my shares in the refineries – I don't think I could bear to sever all my connections: this is still my industry. But it's the time to sell the nitrate fields. I'll hand over the running of them to someone else who can develop them. It's not my future any more.'

James saw the faraway look in Milo's eyes. 'Where will you go?' he asked.

'I'll go home. It's time I met the Bossanos again. I think I'm ready for them now. I'll tell Arnie that I'll go back to Lima to say goodbye to Martin and Lisa. Then I'm taking him home.'

~~~~~

How many times had Milo listened to the celebrations of the homeward bounders? Since he'd first heard them in the Chinchas all those years ago, he'd wondered when it would be his turn. Last night, the rousing cheers echoing around the bay had been for *his* ship. Now it was *his* turn; he was finally homeward bound. The ships at anchor sounded their sirens to wish the departing ship safe passage home. The boys jumped around the rigging, the lanterns swinging brightly high up in the cross-braces, while James had provided the fireworks which lit up the evening sky. At last the celebrations were for him.

Milo now watched the last faint edges of the South American coast disappear into the haze. What did he feel? It was difficult to tell. There was a deep sadness at leaving the Hursts and Emilio Vasco. He recalled his final visit to Lima. Emilio and Lisa were as active as ever, but Martin had become even more frail, and the frustrations of his inactivity were evident. He felt worried at leaving James alone with the business, as well as anxiety at the dangerous passage around the Horn to Europe. But above all he felt excitement. Excitement, and unreasonable optimism, at finally going home.

He was also proud, not of the fortune he had created, but that he had helped to create an industry that would long outlast him. He was proud that the Tarapacá nitrates provided the world with an alternative to the cruel desperation and inhuman misery of the guano deposits. He had contributed to the development of Iquique from a dusty, derelict and isolated settlement into a modern, self-sufficient city.

Milo looked up at the masts. Did I really climb to the top of them, he wondered? Now the ships had steam winches and donkey engines to turn the anchor capstan and hoist the sails. Where had all the good chanteymen gone? But the Captain at least was of the old school. A tough old seafarer nearing the end of his time at sea, Milo had liked him at first sight. He was the sort of man who didn't need brutality to run a good ship. Outwardly he seemed good natured – almost affable, if such a thing were possible in the Captain of a nitrate clipper, where passage times counted more than anything else. But all his crew knew that underneath he possessed a steely and determined authority.

Captain Gross had come highly recommended. Milo had interviewed him in their office; he didn't intend to spend the next two or three months with an arrogant bully. The Captain explained that he had once owned two ships of his own, but they had both foundered, within three months of each other. Even though it had forced him back to sea at a time when most men of his age were looking towards the land, his sailing career had been full of setbacks and he appeared to take the calamity remarkable calmly. Captain Gross explained that his setback was made more bearable by his wife and daughter, who had ignored his protests and insisted upon returning to sea with him, as they used to in the past.

The shipping line had considered themselves lucky to find him, and offered him one of their newest clippers; and even to Milo's unpractised eye, Captain Gross had kept the ship like the day it left its slipway in Greenock. Having spent half a lifetime working under the threat of a possibly catastrophic fire, he noted approvingly the regularly spaced barrels of nitrate water lashed down to the deck. Only water saturated with saltpetre stood a chance against a nitrate fire, a fear which was never far from the crew's mind.

The passenger cabins were comfortable, although Arnie chafed at having no part in the running of the ship. He knew of the Captain's reputation as a tough, but fair seaman and regretted that there was no vacant mate's position. He had almost refused to come with them, insisting at first that he would wait until a paid berth became free. But Milo asked him to think about what kind of ship was likely to have a free mate's berth on the West Coast of South America. Arnie took his point and reluctantly shipped with them as passengers.

Although Milo had travelled countless times up and down the West Coast, he had always used the steamer service as the only way to make good time against the prevailing winds. He hardly remembered his last voyage to London, when there had been so much to occupy him in preparing for his meetings with the London brokers. Now he had time to feel the unfamiliar cant of the deck, heeling against the southerly winds, and he staggered as the ship was suddenly backed as her bows buried themselves in a long rolling wave. He clung on to keep his balance and watched as the Captain's daughter emerged from the cabin and walked steadily towards her seat at the rail without missing a step. She moved across the deck with an unconscious grace, swaying easily to counteract the rolling of the ship. She sat and pulled from her basket a small embroidery frame and started to prepare her threads. Milo approached her. He had seen her only briefly when they were loading, and never close to. She looked up as he came. She had light, almost mischievous, grey eyes which looked at him confidently with a level gaze. Her skin was unfashionably bronzed from the sun. Unlike the ladies' social circle of Valparaiso, she seemed unconcerned about social conventions. She was perhaps twenty-six, and had the self-contained and confident manner of someone who knew her own mind.

She looked at him enquiringly, putting her needlework to one side in her basket. 'Mr Beran?' she asked. 'We are honoured to have you with us. I've heard a lot about you.' She seemed amused when Milo stumbled against the rail as the ship lurched into a wave, giving him the feeling she might be making fun of him.

'Miss Gross?' he asked, regaining his balance. 'I heard that you and Mrs Gross were on board. I hope for your sakes that we have a comfortable passage.'

'For our sakes?' she said sharply. 'There isn't much that the sea can offer that my mother and I haven't already experienced, and I'm sure my father will take good care of us all.'

As if to move the conversation onto safer ground, Milo indicated the embroidery. 'May I see?' he asked. He inspected it carefully, admiring the skill and effort which had already gone into the half-finished pattern.

'I've had a lot of practice,' she said, as though reading his thoughts. 'This is the Sugar Loaf mountain in Rio,' she explained. 'We had to put in for repairs on our way across. It's been some years since we were last there. My father always tried to avoid the place because of the yellow fever.'

Milo noted that she seemed entirely unconcerned by the dangers she had faced, as though the extent of her travels was entirely natural for a woman. 'How old were you when you first went to sea, Miss Gross?'

'Herta – please call me Herta,' she smiled at him. 'For almost as long as I can remember. After his first trip as captain, my father said he had never imagined it could be so lonely, and he decided to take us with him after that.'

'Lonely?' repeated Milo, thinking of the captains he had known. 'I'd always thought that you could have anything if you were a ship's captain. It's the nearest you could get to being an Emperor.'

'Being an Emperor must be very lonely at times, too. To have absolute power is a difficult responsibility to carry. A ship's captain has to keep his distance from the crew, even the officers.'

'And you?' asked Milo. 'Do you have to keep your distance?'

Herta laughed. 'It's the crew who tend to avoid me. My father is always hoping that he'll take on board a bright young mate, a future captain, who'll fall madly in love with me, marry me and make me happy ever after. But most of the young officers are far too afraid of their captain to make advances to his daughter.'

'Well, at least that doesn't apply to me,' said Milo, but he reddened as soon as he realised what he had said. 'I mean being afraid of your father,' he added hastily. 'He's a fine seaman.'

'I think it unlikely that there's anyone you're afraid of,' Herta said, before picking up her embroidery. Was it Milo's imagination or did he detect a slight flush in her cheeks. Probably just the wind, he decided.

The ship made its slow way further south, beating far out into the Pacific before tacking towards the Horn. Milo returned many times to join Herta at her embroidery stool. She had been to so many places that her interests were wide and her observations perceptive. At first Milo remained slightly nervous of her, wary of her sharp tongue. Although many of the women he had met in South America had a streak of independence, they usually kept their opinions to themselves. Herta felt no such constraint, she was lively and funny, and Milo started each day looking forward to their talks together. As the weather got colder, Herta moved her seat next to the donkey engine's boiler where she and Milo could talk together, warm and snug even in the frequent gales.

Cape Horn, when they finally reached the South Atlantic, displayed none of the temperament which had earned it such a fearsome reputation. The gales had died away and the sea was smooth as Milo and Herta stood at the rail and stared out to Horn Island itself. The small chapel was the only reminder of the innumerable lives lost in these dangerous waters, lives sacrificed in the name of Trade.

They turned northwards and were finally heading towards Europe. The weather eventually started to get warmer, and a steady following wind drove them quickly into the tropics and the equator.

'Are there to be any initiations?' Milo asked Herta on the day they were due to cross the line. 'My own is still vivid to me; I crossed it the first time with Arnie. Although when I was reminding him about it just now, he pretended to have forgotten all about it.'

'You crossed together?' Herta asked with surprise. 'I knew you'd been shipmates, but I hadn't realised that you had started together.'

'Yes, and if you'd seen us then, you would have said that Arnie would be the one to jump ship, while I stayed at sea. So much depends upon the crew and its officers. We had a fine first mate – Joachim Traub. If he'd stayed on board, then perhaps I would have turned out to be a sailor.' Milo looked out at the blue sea, his memories brimming over. 'That was a good ship.'

'They can be so different,' Herta said, as though continuing his thoughts. 'I remember when we were crossing the line once, one old sailor asked the second mate how it was that he'd been over the line so many times but he'd never seen it. The mate said to him that perhaps this time they would be lucky. He got out his sextant and stuck a hair across the lens. I've never seen anyone so excited as that old sailor was when he looked through it. "There it is," he shouted across the decks. "I've seen it. I've seen the line." '

Milo laughed, but Herta hadn't finished. 'The funniest bit was when he suddenly stopped and started shouting "We're going to hit it: we've got to turn back." He came rushing back to my father begging him to change course. The only way my father could calm him down was to show him the hair. You should have seen his face. I thought he was going to murder the mate there and then. He saw the funny side eventually, and he was chuckling about it for the rest of the voyage. He's probably bored everyone he's met with that story ever since.' She was silent for a while until she added, 'That one event, shared by everyone, bound the crew to-gether more tightly than any bullying threats. People can get very close on a ship.'

With Herta's cheerful company, Milo found himself enjoying the voyage in a way he had never experienced before. As the routine of the passage became established, even Arnie finally relaxed, and he and Herta swapped endless stories about the places they had been. But as they made their way further north, Arnie started to become anxious. Unable to contribute to the running of the ship, he was pacing up and down the decks when Milo passed by, hurrying to join Herta by their usual place by the rail. Arnie stepped out and stopped him. 'Milo, I'm sorry, but I've got to ask you.'

Milo had been thinking about other things and he looked at him in alarm. 'Ask me what? What is it? What's the matter?'

'It's just that ...' Arnie didn't know quite how to start. 'Well, you remember telling me that you were going to try and help me find a ship?'

'Yes, of course,' said Milo. 'What about it?'

'Well,' Arnie hesitated. 'I don't want you to go to any trouble, but we're going to arrive soon and – well, afterwards we might not see one another.'

'Might not see one another? What on earth are you talking about?'

'When we get to England you'll have so much work to do, you won't have time to worry about my ship.'

Milo looked at Arnie in consternation. 'I've been so stupid,' he grabbed Arnie's arm. 'You must have been worrying about this ever since we left. I've been so selfish, spending all my time with Herta. We'll go and find Captain Gross and tell him about our plans right now.' Milo turned and rushed off down the companionway.

'Plans?' said Arnie watching Milo's retreating back. '*Our* plans?' For the first, although not the last time, Arnie discovered that the only plans Milo ever had were his own.

'I'm not talking about a huge fleet,' said Milo a short time later. They were sitting around the Captain's table. 'Perhaps eventually between six and a dozen ships. From the figures Captain Gross has given me, I calculate that once you've got the shipping contract, it should take only a year to eighteen months to recoup the cost of each ship. And if we start building in Maine, he says we can get good ships for even less. We've got three skippers, so we'll start with three ships.'

'Three?' asked Captain Gross.

Milo smiled. 'You, Arnie and Joachim Traub. We'll send him a telegram when we get to Hamburg. Meanwhile, is there anything else we need to decide?'

Captain Gross and Arnie looked at one another, scarcely able to believe what they had heard. Arnie was the first to speak, 'But how can you confirm a shipping contract when we haven't even got a ship?'

Milo laughed. 'Once I give you the contract, you'll have to make sure you find the ship pretty fast.'

Arnie looked puzzled. 'It's not that simple,' he said.

Milo stopped and looked at him anxiously. 'Why shouldn't it be?' he asked. 'Have I forgotten something? You're the experts – you must tell me.'

'No, it's not that,' said Captain Gross slowly. 'Between us we should be able to manage. Once the contract is confirmed, we can buy a couple of old ships to get us started, until we can get more modern ones built. It's just that …' The Captain looked unusually uncomfortable.

'You must tell me everything,' said Milo. 'If you can see a problem, then you must tell me.'

'Frankly,' Captain Gross said after a while. 'I don't think that either of us can afford to subscribe for any of the capital. We can't accept a partnership unless it's allocated fairly. If you put up all the capital, then it wouldn't be right for us to hold any of the shares.'

Milo looked slowly from Captain Gross across to Arnie, who was looking down at the floor. 'I suppose you're right,' he said finally. 'The shares should be allocated according to the capital invested.' He paused. 'But who said I was putting up any money?' he asked brightly.

Arnie looked up. 'So how are we supposed to pay for all these ships?' he asked with a trace of bitterness. His new dream didn't seem to have lasted very long.

'I'm sorry,' said Milo. 'I thought I had explained. 'Once my certificates are floated in London, they'll be backed by some of the biggest banks in England. If you hold a shipping contract from us, then it will be as good as money. The banks in Hamburg will fight to advance the funds to buy ships, even without the security of the ships themselves.'

'But I don't understand. What will you be getting out of it?' asked Captain Gross.

'I'll be getting my prayers finally answered,' said Milo. 'All I've ever wanted is to have my cargoes shipped at a reasonable price, but I couldn't run a shipping line: I didn't know enough about it. Even though I'm handing over control, I'll still have a substantial stake and my successors couldn't possibly do it without you.'

'You're now making it sound as though we're doing you the favour,' said Arnie.

'But you are,' replied Milo. 'And Joachim, when he joins you. I get you all to do the work, I finally get the nitrates shipped at a lower cost, *and*,' Milo looked around the table dramatically, 'I get a share in what I have no doubt will be a very profitable shipping line. All that without putting up a single silver shilling.'

The day before their arrival at Liverpool, Herta and Milo spent their last evening looking across the grey colours of the Irish Channel. 'You seem to have made my father very happy,' she said. 'I've haven't seem him this excited for years. I must thank you for your help.'

'Your father is helping me, too. That's one of the advantages of commerce; when you get to a certain size, things become simpler. If my meetings with the bankers in London go well, then I should be able to confirm everything within a couple of months. I can then go to our agents in Hamburg before leaving for Dalmatia.'

'A couple of months? Are we to stay in Liverpool for that long?'

'No, but your father needs to finalise the delivery of this cargo. After that he's planning to take you on ahead with Arnie to Hamburg. They can start looking around for suitable ships before I meet you there.'

Herta looked crestfallen. 'I hadn't realised that you would be leaving us. Somehow I thought we would stay together.'

'We'll be back together shortly, I promise.'

Milo thought of the last time he had made the same promise.

Chapter Twenty

Having made his decision to sell, Milo no longer felt the attraction of London. He was aware during his conversations with the City bankers that something was missing. He felt an emptiness in conducting his business, and found the endless demands of the merchant banks frustrating. In the strange city, where no one knew him, he chafed at the long, aimless evenings spent alone in his hotel. He made enquiries about the Dalmatian hostel in Limehouse, but no trace of it remained. Ma Babich was another character who had disappeared from his life. He was used to being alone, but he had never before felt so lonely.

So much had happened that he'd rarely had time to consider things outside his work, but as the frustrating days slowly passed, he found himself able to look at things in new ways and discover new possibilities. Surrounded by the almost palpable greed of the City of London, he started to realise how much he was missing Herta. She had taken his mind off the things that usually preoccupied him. He had laughed with her at things which previously would have simply puzzled him. It was as though she had discovered a different person inside him. He even wondered whether the circumstances of his life had stunted his personality. Perhaps Herta had found the child in him. Whatever had happened, he knew he had to go back to her as soon as he could. She had made him happy.

As he thought about it, he understood the irony. The worst times of his life had been spent at sea – but so had the happiest. With Arnie's friendship and Herta's unfailing liveliness, love and humour, the past few months had been like no others. He understood that his life could be different.

He had few doubts about his decision to leave the nitrate industry and return home, but he suddenly realised that he had little idea about what to do next. It had seemed sufficient to wait until he arrived on Dalmatian soil for everything to be resolved, but now, as his home finally seemed attainable, he knew it wasn't as simple as that. He had always wanted to build his own home by the Adriatic, and the idea was taking hold of him and its grip growing stronger. But apart from that, his plans were entirely vague. He had given no thought to how his dream was to be turned into reality. Desperately he cabled his agents in Hamburg who traded regularly with the Adriatic, and arranged for them to send someone to make enquiries. To Šipan.

But as he waited to hear back from them, he felt apprehensive. He feared that his homeland might prove to be a mirage created by his memory. Over the years, the ideal of his tranquil island of Šipan had become so fixed in his mind that he was now afraid that it might be simply his imagination. James had said that the memory of home never changes, but perhaps the reality does. His father and brother – would either of them still be there? What would he find when he returned?

He had felt that Arnie's rescue had liberated him, but in Herta he had found something more. It seemed so long since he had felt able to enjoy happiness. He was not going to lose it again.

*****

Herta had also found the past few months unsettling. After all her time spent at sea, she considered that she had become entirely self-contained – she prided herself she had the seaman's ability to accept whatever life threw at her. She knew that at sea anything could happen – and it usually did. When her father's ships were lost, she realised that she had little choice but to accompany him for as long as was necessary. She had no regrets about it. That was how things were and although she had, on occasion, enjoyed flirting with the officers she had come across, she didn't allow herself to miss them when they moved on. She had wasted no time feeling sorry for herself, always finding her own company sufficient. But since arriving back in Hamburg, instead of her habitual cheerfulness, she had felt unusually troubled. Whenever she started to do something, a picture of Milo would enter her mind and distract her. She thought fondly of the serious, slightly worried expression, melting instantly into spontaneous laughter as she told him her stories. She knew that she had attracted him and, in turn, she had found his combination of seriousness and an almost childish lightheartedness challenged her desire to remain independent.

At first she considered that they might even have a future together, but she quickly dismissed the idea. Her mother watched her moods change until, after several weeks, she finally dared to raise the subject with her independent daughter. 'You mustn't lose faith. He'll come back. The two of you were inseparable,' she said. 'He wouldn't have spent so long with you unless he cared.'

Herta greeted her advice with insincere laughter. 'You should know better than that, especially after the time you've spent at sea,' she replied attempting to dismiss the idea. 'You've seen how easy it is to form attachments at sea, which dissolve the moment the ship docks. Relationships always feel more vivid at sea.'

'But this was different,' said Mrs Gross. 'You always seemed so natural together. You both responded equally to one another; there seemed to be a gravitational force pulling you together. But above all he seemed a different man when he was with you – happy and relaxed. You can't just ignore the effect you had on him. Nor that you got on so well.'

'I'm not ignoring it,' Herta protested. 'I could never forget it. He had insights which had never occurred to me. He looked at situations in a completely different way. He made his achievements sound so easy, when I know they weren't. And I think he enjoyed my company too. I think he was genuinely interested in the things I told him. But what's the point? There's too much to separate us. He's wealthy and I've got nothing.'

'But he's going into partnership with your father,' Mrs Gross protested. 'They'll be working together.'

'You know that's not true,' said Herta. 'He might say they're partners, but Milo is in charge. The ships might be shared, but the shipping contracts will always be his. You know I couldn't hold myself back if I thought Father's interests were at risk. It wouldn't work.'

But in spite of her outward certainty, inwardly she remained troubled and undecided, unable to accept the situation with her normal equanimity and strength of mind.

'We'll see,' said Mrs Gross. 'He'll be back.'

'Oh yes, he'll be back,' said Herta. 'But only as our paymaster.'

But Herta was proved wrong even earlier than Mrs Gross had anticipated. Milo suddenly cut short his business in London, having achieved all that was important to him. He rushed across to Hamburg.

Herta was sitting with her mother in the parlour, forcing herself to concentrate on her embroidery, when a loud banging on the door started to shake the house. Herta glanced up at her mother in alarm. Mrs Gross looked back impassively. 'I'll go,' she said.

Herta put her embroidery to one side and stared anxiously along the dark hallway.

Milo rushed down the corridor, knocking the pictures with his shoulders as he passed. As he faced her, he suddenly seemed embarrassed at the noise he had been making and stopped uncertainly. 'I'm sorry,' he said. 'I thought you were out. I've come straight from the port. I, er…' Milo hesitated.

Herta flushed with excitement. She didn't dare believe that he had come to see her. 'I'm afraid my father isn't here, he's…'

'I don't want to see your father,' Milo stopped in confusion. 'I mean, I want to see…' he stammered, before saying finally, 'I want you.'

Mrs Gross followed softly along the corridor and entered the parlour behind him. 'What did I tell you? I said he'd come back for you.' But Herta didn't notice. Her mother backed out of the room. 'I'll leave you two alone,' she said quietly. But they didn't hear.

'She makes me happy.' Milo said to Captain Gross a few days later. 'She once told me that you had always wanted to take on board a young officer to make her happy. I'll try, but I know that she makes me happy.' Milo was speaking very formally and Captain Gross was amused by his nervousness. Milo was normally so self-contained, but he had sensed immediately that Milo had arrived in Hamburg in a state of confusion. There was a change, too, in his daughter. He noticed that they seemed to share an intimacy which he hadn't noticed before. Herta seemed more focused now Milo had returned. More alive. He noticed that she looked at Milo constantly, as though to reassure herself that he was still there.

Herta's parents were taken aback by the speed of their daughter's decision to marry. Although Mrs Gross had confidently prophesied the outcome, privately she had always found it difficult to decide upon Milo's true feelings. He had always appeared so reserved. Now he was to be their son-in-law, they found him almost embarrassed. He was so used to taking control that he appeared unsure how to behave with them. He had transformed not just their daughter's life, but theirs as well. He had come like a sudden squall, bringing Arnie to work as their new partner, and shipping contracts which would establish them for the rest of their lives. Things didn't happen this way, they thought. They would wait and see.

But they both had to admit that Herta's and Milo's happiness together was genuine. Whatever reserve Milo showed to them, he had no inhibitions with their daughter. With her, he always seemed unfailingly cheerful and talkative, speaking unceasingly of their future together.

'The agents have finally confirmed it.' Milo rushed into the small front room where the Grosses were sitting talking with

Arnie. Milo was too excited by his plans for their wedding the next day to notice the dull atmosphere in the room. 'They've found us somewhere near Dubrovnik to rent for our honeymoon,' he continued. 'They've found some estates on the market that we can look at. We'll be happy there,' he said turning to Herta. 'We'll have our own villa by the waterside. We can grow fields of fruit trees and vines and olive trees. I'll make it just like the Napeña valley.'

Milo looked across to Captain Gross. Although he was straining to look pleased at Milo's news, he was finding it a struggle.

Milo couldn't understand why the two of them appeared so listless. 'What is it?' he asked. 'What's the matter? Is there a problem?'

Captain Gross merely shrugged slightly. 'Nothing for you to worry about – not the day before your wedding.'

Milo changed before their eyes. His excitement had evaporated and he sat down and looked across the table with a steady, serious expression. 'Tell me what's happened.'

Arnie interrupted. 'The bank won't confirm the loan. And if you're going away, well…' he trailed off.

Captain Gross filled the short silence. 'I'm sure he misunderstood,' he started.

Milo held up his hand. 'Please. Just tell me what happened.' Captain Gross looked across to him. Milo was looking at him calmly and expectantly, his calculating eyes showing no emotion.

Captain Gross sighed faintly. 'It seems the bank doesn't believe the contract is real. They say you've been dealing with the Bordés line for so many years. They haven't come out with it directly, but they suspect that we're making it up. That's why they spun it out for so long. They were afraid to reject us, just in case it was true.'

'Why didn't you tell me before?' cried Milo. 'I could have spoken to them.'

Captain Gross looked towards the window as though this had nothing to do with him. 'I didn't want to trouble you,' he said, wondering whether he had ever really believed in the good fortune Milo had brought to them.

His wife interrupted him. 'The truth is that he felt embarrassed at approaching his future son-in-law. He's been brought up to be self-reliant, and the old seadog felt it a sign of weakness to ask for your help.' She looked across at her husband. 'I told him not to be so silly, but he wouldn't listen.' She shook her head. 'He never does,' she added.

Milo turned to Arnie. 'You should have told me.'

'I've only just found out. I knew you wanted to leave tomorrow and I was worried that nothing had been confirmed, so I pushed them for a decision.' Arnie looked a little embarrassed as he continued. 'I thought of what you would do, so I told them that if I didn't hear from them by the end of the day, I'd go somewhere else.'

Milo laughed. 'Good for you,' he said.

'Well, my bluff hasn't done us much good. They seem to have called it – I haven't heard from them. Now what do we do?'

'You do exactly what you threatened,' said Milo. 'Never bluff if you're likely to be caught out – remember I taught you that on the Hanover? We'll go to another bank. Now I'm here, I can provide all the confirmation needed. We'll go to my agents first thing,' Milo stood up. 'I'd go there now, if I could.'

'But the wedding,' protested the Captain. 'You can't go there on your wedding day.'

Milo looked across at him, but his words were addressed to Herta. 'My work has always taken priority over everything else. That's why I've decided to leave most of it behind in South America. But this isn't work: this is family now. Mrs Gross is right – you didn't think I could just leave you here without doing anything, did you? It will only take a few hours in the morning – it won't delay the wedding.'

Captain Gross, himself accustomed to respect as a ship's Captain, had never seen anything like it. His reservations about Milo's ability and importance were swept away as he saw the treatment which Milo received. Even though they had hardly sat down in the agent's office, an attendant who, judging from his uniform, ranked alongside a Field-Marshal, ushered them into the large office of Herr Weiss, the company's Director. Captain Gross watched closely, fascinated by Milo's single-minded approach. Scarcely allowing time for introductions, Milo was direct to the point of rudeness. He cut across Herr Weiss' summary, as though not listening to a word of it. But he took in everything he needed to know and began to outline his requirements. This was a side of Milo that the Captain hadn't seen in those carefree days of passage: determined and relentless.

Herr Weiss made the occasional note on a pad in front of him as he listened to the proposition. 'I think we can try the Holstein Bank,' he said finally. 'We can help you draw up the written shipping contracts, and then perhaps we can get together at the bank tomorrow or the day after?' He looked towards Milo, seeking his confirmation.

'Now,' said Milo shortly. 'I can't wait. I have a wedding to go to and tomorrow I'll be on a train to the Adriatic. You can make the arrangements with the bank on the basis of a normal letter of credit. We can establish the shipping contract and the terms of the loan when I return. For the moment I will give you written authority for consignment of ten thousand tons of Chile saltpetre, free-on-board in Hamburg. That will allow you to issue an immediate letter of credit to be drawn on any bank.'

Captain Gross gasped. Milo had just sold nearly fifteen thousand pounds' worth of saltpetre with the sale proceeds to be paid over directly to him and Arnie. He was simply giving it to them.

Milo looked from Captain Gross across to Arnie. 'It's not a gift. We'll treat it as a loan for the time being. We can arrange the partnership papers when I return.' He turned back to Herr Weiss. 'Now, is there anything else?'

This was the first time that Milo had been to his agent's Hamburg offices, but Herr Weiss was fully aware of Milo's business methods and was accustomed to conforming to his rapid decisions. The agent had made a small fortune from Milo's decisive dealing when the nitrate prices were at their most volatile. If he was surprised, he didn't show it. Instead he just made a few notes on his pad and nodded his assent. 'There is one more thing,' he said. 'Our enquiries in Dubrovnik have had some more results.' He picked up some papers.

'Our agent reports that the Bossitos...'

'Bossanos,' Milo interrupted. 'Their name is Bossano.'

The banker acknowledged the correction. 'Mrs Bossano appears to have quite a high level of expenditure. Apparently she has quite expensive tastes and insists that most of her purchases, clothes and household items, are brought in from Vienna. In addition it seems that she's sending money across to her family on the mainland – they seem to have tastes as lavish as hers. However,' he flipped through the report, searching for a particular paragraph. 'Yes, here it is,' he continued. 'However, it appears that the income from the estate has been dropping steadily for many years and has all but dried up. According to our information, Mr Bossano is now heavily in debt and the banks are starting to get concerned.'

Herr Weiss shuffled the papers together. 'Perhaps the agent can tell you more when you arrive.' He handed them to Milo, who took them without a word. He saw Milo's distant expression as though, in his mind, he was already there.

Their wedding was simple. Joachim Traub had left his ship in Bremerhaven and he rode along the coast for the ceremony.

Arnie was best man and seemed bewildered by the speed of events. In response to his brief speech, Milo got up to reply, as though reporting to a meeting of shareholders. He announced that the banks had confirmed the loan facility and that Captain Gross had secured two ships which needed only a few weeks' work in the dry docks. A third would be delivered in a few months. Herta led the enthusiastic applause, and Milo sat down quite oblivious of her amusement. She wondered how long it would take before he could accept his new life.

James was quite delighted at Milo's sudden announcement and although he couldn't be there, he arranged for their Hamburg agents to lay on a fireworks display, a suitable reminder of alterative uses of saltpetre. A telegram was received from Martin and Lisa Hurst and another from Emilio Vasco. Milo picked up another telegraph, but quickly saw that it had come from Robert Miller. He had never mentioned Robert to Herta and he wondered fleetingly whether he had been wrong about him. He put the paper to one side – all that could wait.

A private railway carriage took them away on their honeymoon. The train pulled them steadily southwards through Bavaria, Austria and into the Italian peninsula of Istria. From Rijeka they transferred to a ferry and finally the gaunt islands off Velebit gave way to the green pine forests of Southern Dalmatia. The ferry threaded its way along the rugged coast towards Dubrovnik and the Elaphit Islands. Herta became enchanted by the gentle, silky mist which wrapped the southern islands in a beguiling warmth. Milo counted them off, one by one. His enthusiasm was so infectious that Herta became as excited. 'Is that it? Is that Šipan?' she would cry as they approached another island. Finally the wooded shores of Jakljan come into view, separated from Šipan by that narrow channel where Milo had spent so much of his childhood. 'You've talked so often of Caesar's Passage,' she said. 'How did it get its name?'

Milo laughed. 'It's probably untrue,' he said. 'But it's a good story. Šipan was said to be the ancient island of Tauris, where the fleets of Caesar and Pompey fought for domination of the southern Adriatic. Caesar chased Pompey's navy back towards the island, into the bay of Šipanska Luka, but he waited until daylight before attacking. He was in no hurry: Pompey's fleet was trapped – there was nowhere for them to escape. But in the morning, when Caesar sailed in, they were gone. Caesar didn't know of this narrow passage – you can't see it unless you know it's there. Pompey's fleet escaped.'

'Then it should be called Pompey's passage,' Herta said with spirit.

'Some people do,' said Milo. 'But Caesar beat him in the end, so I prefer to name it after the winner, not the one who ran away.'

The villa by the Rijeka Dubrovocka was elegant and spacious. Neither Herta nor Milo was accustomed to inactivity, but they slowly relaxed as they gained confidence in each other. The carefully planted grounds led through a series of canals down to a small stone quay at the water's edge. They sat under the shade of the palms, talking and planning. As the days passed, Herta was aware of an increasing number of visitors, but Milo kept them mysteriously secret and refused even to explain the reason for their visits. Although she knew that she would find out in due course, she was intrigued by Milo's increasing excitement. It was almost bubbling over one morning when he took her down to the water's edge and pointed out a steam launch approaching from Dubrovnik. The boat pulled in at the dry-stone quay at the foot of the gardens, and two men stepped ashore as the boatmen held them off. One, a dark-suited man, carried a leather briefcase and a serious expression. The other, in complete contrast, had long flowing hair and a ruby-coloured jacket with a silk cravat. Milo took Herta down to the quay to greet them.

'Herta, this is Mr Popovich,' he said, indicating the dark-suited man. 'He represents the Hamburg agents. And this,' Milo turned to the other man, 'is Doctor Bonnetti. They are coming with us to Šipan.'

Herta's heart fell. She had spent weeks imagining her first visit to Milo's home; it was something she wanted to savour with Milo, not share with strangers. 'But can't we go alone?' she said plaintively. 'For our first visit, couldn't it be just the two of us?' She turned to Mr Popovich. 'I'm sorry, I don't mean to be rude, but you will understand this is our honeymoon, and my husband hasn't been home for nearly thirty years.'

The man bowed stiffly. 'Of course I understand, but Mr Beran…' he turned to Milo seeking support.

Milo cut in. 'If we were just going there as a visit, then of course we would go alone, but I need Mr Popovich to help me with some business, and Doctor Bonnetti has prepared a surprise for you.'

The gleaming private steam launch ferried them across the Kolocepski Canal towards Šipan. Herta tugged at Milo's arm as they reached Caesar's Passage, aware of the distant expression on his face. The light wind cooled their faces. The water rose and fell, washing around the rock which breached the surface of the water to his left. Milo stared at it. In his memory it had been more like a small mountain. As the boat passed through the narrow passage and turned back towards Šipanska Luka, he compared the shoreline with his fading memories. Fewer fishing boats were moored against the quayside; many were neglected – their formerly bright paintwork peeling away, leaving ugly scars on their hulls. Milo remembered, almost with shame, the pride his brother Vigo had always taken in his boat. Several hulks were hauled up the slipway, but their damaged hulls had been abandoned. He looked across to the boatshed where his father had occasionally worked, but it was firmly shut. Finally, he turned to look up towards his house. He could see the wall of the terrace and the vine trellis shading it. But nothing moved. The house gave no sign of its occupants.

Taking Herta by the arm, Milo escorted her up the steep pathway where he had run as a boy. He stopped at the doorway built into the wall. He pushed the door open and walked through. He looked across the low wall to the shimmering Adriatic stretching along the skyline. In front of the wall, on the terrace, a thin, grey-haired man sat at the table. He looked up slowly, and something stirred deep in his watery eyes.

'Father!' Milo kneeled in front of him. 'It's me. Milo. I've come back.'

Slowly, very slowly, Andro Beran reached out to Milo's shoulder and stared at him wordlessly. He pulled his son towards him and hugged him tightly.

'I knew you'd come,' he whispered eventually. 'I told your mother, you'd come back, but she... she,' he pulled himself away and stared at Milo with eyes etched with sadness. 'Have you heard? Did Jurica tell you?'

Milo nodded and took his father's hands. 'Yes, I know. You must miss her so much. But you never failed her. It wasn't your fault.' Both men stood silently for a moment, lost in their thoughts. Eventually Milo stood up. 'This is my wife, Herta,' he said. 'We're here on our honeymoon.'

Andro pulled himself to his feet, his tall figure was wasted and his back stooped, but deep in his listless eyes there was a glimmer of renewed hope. He put his arms around Herta and embraced her. 'Welcome to Šipan,' he said simply.

They made their way back down to the port. Doctor Bonnetti was sitting in the open space in front of the bay, drawing on a pad. Herta looked over his shoulder at the emerging sketch of a porticoed mansion. She watched for a few moments as the building took shape in front of her. 'You are an artist, Doctor Bonnetti?' she asked.

'An architect, Madam,' he replied.

'This is the surprise I had for you.' Milo left his father and joined Herta. 'I've commissioned the Doctor to prepare designs for our home. I've bought all this land, from in front of the open space here, across to the end of the quay.' Milo indicated with a sweep of his arm. 'We're going to build our own villa overlooking the bay, and we'll surround it by gardens. I have given Doctor Bonnetti instructions that nothing is to be spared. It will be a home fit for a Nitrate King.' Milo put his arm around her waist and pulled her closely towards him. 'And his Queen.'

They watched as the architect shaded in the columns and added the final details to the drawing. Milo pulled himself away. 'Mr Popovich and I have some other business to attend to, but I'll leave you with Doctor Bonnetti. He can show you the ideas he's been working on.'

Milo left Herta and followed Mr Popovich along the stony path up the hillside. The agent's formal clothes looked ridiculously out of place in the soft, green landscape. His father kept pace alongside him, keeping stiffly erect as though to defy all the years that had passed. As they reached the top, the blanket of dark trees covered the valley ahead of them, freshened with the random burst of bright spring growth. Along the pathway, the gates of the Villa Bossano were rusted and screamed on their hinges as they were forced open. The driveway was now overgrown, the vineyard scarcely recognisable, its vines concealed by the uncontrolled weeds which had taken over.

The noise of the gate brought someone from the house. Milo saw a short, stocky man in a frayed straw hat approach them. Frano Bossano had not aged well. His cheeks were blotched and bloated, his eyes dull and suspicious.

'What is it? Who are these people?' The voice came from the house behind. Milo looked over Frano's shoulder. Rusa Bossano was hurrying along the driveway, her screeching voice grating amid the gentle rustle of the leaves. She looked towards Milo's father. 'Is that Andro Beran?' she continued. 'Tell him we have nothing to say to him. Tell him to get off our land.'

Andro sighed and started to turn, but Milo caught his arm. He looked up questioningly.

'Stay,' said Milo. 'I want you to stay.'

Rusa Bossano was now standing just in front of her husband. 'I told you,' she shrieked. 'Order him to leave.' Frano Bossano said nothing. He was looking from Milo to the agent as though knowing what was about to happen.

Rusa faced Milo angrily. 'And who are you, sir? What do you want here and why have you brought that man with you?' She indicated Andro, who looked down at the ground uncomfortably.

'My name is also Beran. You might remember me.' Milo paused. 'Milo Beran. "That man", as you call him, is my father.'

Rusa hesitated only briefly. 'All the family's the same to me. Each of them worthless. Now get off our land.'

'Rusa, please.' Frano spoke without conviction, gesturing her to keep quiet.

Rusa turned back to him in anger. 'I know you've always been spineless,' she said fiercely. 'But can't you even keep people away from private property?'

'I think I know,' his voice lowered to an inaudible mumble.

'What was that?' Rusa hissed with impatience. 'Speak up, will you?'

'I said,' Frano spoke more firmly, 'I think I know why they're here.'

'What are you talking about?' Rusa asked in a shrill voice. 'Why do we have to allow Berans on our land? Send them away.' She turned and started back to the house.

'Your land?' Milo called after her. He turned to Frano. 'Don't you think you ought to tell her?'

'Rusa!' Frano Bossano's voice was sharp with unfamiliar authority. His wife turned slowly and faced him.

Milo stepped forward. 'It appears that your husband hasn't told you,' he started, 'but he's built up some quite substantial loans – all of them secured against this property. Perhaps he has used the money to support your, your – lifestyle.' Milo almost spat the word out. 'However, that is none of my business. Give me the papers.' He addressed these last words to Mr Popovich, who reached into his inside pocket and pulled out a bundle of documents.

'These are the loan notes.' Milo waved them at Rusa Bossano, who looked at him uncomprehendingly. 'The bank was only too happy to accept the offer I made for them,' he continued. 'That means, Mrs Bossano, I now hold the first charge over this property and this gentleman is a bailiff.' He turned to Mr Popovich. 'I think you should show them the other documents,' he said without emotion.

The agent pulled another paper from inside his jacket and held it out towards Frano Bossano.

'That,' said Milo, 'is formal notice of repossession.'

Frano took the paper dumbly. He stood without reading it; instead he looked past Milo, along the valley. He looked up at the hills above them and turned to look back at the house. His eyes were moist and his breathing was laboured. He walked back to Rusa, and held out his arms to her.

Rusa took a step backwards, and then launched herself at her husband in an uncontrolled frenzy. 'You've betrayed me,' she screamed, beating her fists furiously against his chest. 'You've destroyed everything.' Her strength ebbed suddenly, her body buckled and she fell to the ground, wailing hysterically. 'I always knew you were worthless.' Her anguished voice reverberated in the calm air.

Milo walked over to where Rusa Bossano lay sobbing. 'You see, Mrs Bossano, you were wrong.' She forced herself to look up at him. 'This isn't your land any more. It belongs to me. This is the Beran estate now.' Milo looked at her contemptuously and strode off.

'Stop! Come back!'

At first Milo didn't realise his father's words were addressed to him and he continued up the driveway.

'Milo! Stop!'

He turned. His father was holding out his arm towards him as if to beckon him back. 'You can't do this. Come back.'

Milo walked back slowly, looking at his father with blank incomprehension, bewildered by Andro's look of utter misery. Warm tears were coursing down his face and he seemed barely able to stand. He was on the verge of losing control completely, but Milo was totally unable to understand his distress.

'Dad? What is it? What's the matter?' He stopped in front of Andro and took his hand and held it in his. 'Why can't I do this?'

'Because,' started Andro, but he stopped and looked at Milo in profound despair. He gestured towards Frano Bossano. 'Because he's your father,' he said finally.

Chapter Twenty-One

Milo was stunned. He stared aghast at Andro, struggling to assimilate what he had said. Frano Bossano staggered back as though punched in the stomach, stumbling against his wife, lying prostrate on the gravel path. She looked up at him in disbelief. 'What did he say?' She couldn't understand what was happening. She was hanging to her world only by the thinnest thread.

'Don't listen. Don't listen.' Frano kept repeating the words, more to himself than to anyone else.

Rusa Bossano slowly climbed to her feet. 'You? His father?' she looked at him in disbelief. 'You couldn't be, we, we... What is he talking about?'

Milo ignored them and remained staring desperately at his father. 'How? How can it be true? It can't be. I mean – how could he be?'

'I'm sorry, Milo. You had to know.' Andro was distraught. 'If you're going to take over the estate and evict the Bossanos, you had to know. I can't keep it a secret any more. Before, it was different. We – that is, I mean ... your mother and me, we didn't see how it would help if we told you. She worried about it so much at first, after you were born. But after we decided to get married, we always thought we could explain it to you when you were older, but it never seemed the right time. The years passed, and Vigo and Jurica were so pleased to have a little brother to play with, and after a while we didn't think it mattered any more.'

Milo was about to answer, but stopped. Instead, he reached inside his shirt and pulled out the locket. 'And this?' he asked. He unfastened the chain from his neck and held it out to Andro. 'I've always known you as my father, but since I was twelve years old I've carried this portrait everywhere, thinking it was the natural father I never met.'

'But it is your father,' Andro said sadly. 'We can't choose our natural fathers any more than they can choose their sons.' He took the locket and studied it. 'Olga told me about it. She thought it was the right thing to do, to give it to you.'

'But every time I looked at it, I felt hatred. Of what the Bossanos did to us all.'

'It was all she had,' said Andro. 'She desperately wanted to give you something to remember her by. I think she knew then that she was never going to see you again.'

'But it's of him.' Milo looked fiercely at Frano Bossano. 'He's done everything he could to forget about me; why should I want to remember him?'

'If Olga never blamed him, why should you? She wanted you to think of your family, of us here in Šipan, not just of your father. Yes, he took advantage of her, but it wasn't without affection. She was alone with two small boys. He promised to marry her and the only thing she did wrong was to believe him.' Andro looked across to Frano. 'Of course he was different back then. He really wasn't a bad man, just weak. That was before she got her claws into him.'

Milo watched Rusa Bossano for several moments. 'How could Mam bear to live on the same island as that woman?' he asked. 'I would have found it impossible.'

'She had no choice,' Andro said simply. 'You boys were the most important thing she had. She had to do whatever was best for all of you. Though she always worried most about you.'

'That explains why.' Milo appeared to be speaking to no one in particular. 'Is that why?'

Andro heard, but didn't know how to respond. After all this time, how could he explain to Milo how it really was? 'You have to understand our situation. Olga, that is your mother and I, we thought ... until you were old enough to know – why tell you? We couldn't see how it would help. We...' his voice trailed away and he looked at Milo in desperation.

'Is that why?' Milo looked vacantly into the distance.

'I don't understand,' said Andro, 'Is that why what?'

'Is that why I've always felt so different?' Milo turned fiercely upon Andro. 'Is that why?'

'I can't say,' said his father helplessly. 'I only know that you were different.'

Milo shook his head angrily. 'After everything I've done, after all I've been through – put other people through. I finally come back home to this? To find the home I've always dreamt about never really existed?'

'It did exist, Milo. We were happy together, weren't we?' Andro pleaded. 'Until Vigo, that is, after Vigo...'

'But if he was my real father, why didn't he help us?' Milo interrupted. 'We went there together. You, Mam and me. We needed help. We stood in that room up there and begged him for it. If he was my real father, how could he refuse?'

'You must ask him that,' Andro looked towards Rusa Bossano. 'Perhaps his wife wouldn't let him?'

251

'At least you could have told me then,' said Milo. 'I had a right to know,'

'Yes, you had a right. But after Vigo died, how could it help you to know? How could we explain to you that your own natural father had rejected you? It would have achieved nothing, so we decided to stay silent. It was the most difficult decision we ever made together, but we couldn't see how the truth would ever make you happy.'

'Happy?' Milo repeated in astonishment. 'When I find that my entire life has been built on an illusion?'

'No,' said Andro desperately. 'No, it wasn't an illusion. We were happy. But nothing was ever the same after Vigo died. I just found it too painful. After you'd left, so many times I sat down to write and tell you, but I just couldn't do it. That's one of the reasons I stopped writing. I thought that if you were building a new life out there, we might just, well … just fade away. But now you've come back, and you want to take over the estate, I didn't have any alternative. This time I had to tell you. You had to know.' Andro gestured towards Frano. 'Now, if you want him, there he is.'

They both stared at the Bossanos. Rusa was sitting gazing into space, totally unable to take in the changes forced upon her. Frano appeared to be mumbling to himself quietly. Milo looked at them in disbelief. Was this man really his father?

He turned back to Andro. 'But why did he dismiss you? How could anyone be so completely heartless?'

'That was her.' Andro didn't even bother to look in Rusa's direction. 'She made him. She'd been after me for years. Although she told everyone else how common I was, it seemed that's what attracted her. She made my life hell. When I finally left, part of me was glad to get out of there.' Andro noticed that Frano was looking at him in disbelief. 'You should have realised that she made it up. It was her, not me,' he told him. 'Your wife couldn't take rejection; all she wanted was to get her revenge. She lied to make you get rid of me.'

Frano's shoulders sagged. This final revelation about his wife was ultimately devastating. He looked at Rusa in anger. She stepped backwards and for the first time in her life, she was afraid of him.

Rusa saw her husband through a misty haze of confusion. Where had she gone wrong? She clung to the tatters of her destroyed pride. 'It's not true,' she cried. 'It was him. He always wanted me. They all wanted me. I was, I was –' she stopped as she saw the cold faces surrounding her. She looked back to her husband, but Frano turned away. With a terrifying howl of desolation, she fell to her knees.

Andro looked away, his sympathy spent. 'That they should dismiss me, on top of everything else, almost destroyed me. What could I say to your mother? I'd always been so much in love with her and she'd made me so happy. I didn't know how I could bear her misery. She knew it meant you'd have to go away, and she just couldn't take it. I tried to talk to her, to get her interested in the future, tell her you'd come back – but she just started to fade away. Every day it seemed there was less of her.

'I didn't know what to do. I could have exposed him, but Olga wouldn't let me. She was afraid of how that might affect you. She didn't think you'd understand. How could you be expected to comprehend what it was like back then?' Andro looked at him helplessly. 'We were no more than peasants. We had no land, no rights to anything. If any of the Bossanos took against us, there was absolutely nothing we could do. I was doing my best to look after her, after her husband died.' Andro suddenly went white with suppressed rage. 'And if he, Frano Bossano, decided to take up with any of the islanders, what could be done to stop him?' His face crumpled. 'My Olga. She was helpless. He told her she'd have to leave the island. Instead of standing by her, instead of looking after her, he tried to send her away.' Andro stopped, as if to collect himself. There was complete silence, interrupted only by Rusa's intermittent sobs. It was as though the entire island was listening intently, waiting for what he would say next. Nothing stirred. Even the constant foaming of the surf through the rocks seemed to recede into stillness.

'She told me only when she realised it was over. I don't know why she waited so long. I would have done anything.' Andro started again, gazing vacantly into the past. 'Right until the end, she still thought he would help, she couldn't believe he could just abandon her like that. Not after … not after everything that had happened. She was convinced he cared, and perhaps in his own way he had, but afterwards he wouldn't listen. He thought that normal rules didn't apply to him and told Olga that it was finished, and there was nothing she could do about it. And he was right, she was on her own. At first she even tried to hide it from me.' To Andro the memory was still vivid. He felt his old emotions return, undiminished by the passage of time. 'I did my best. I remember her expression as she told me. I can never forget it. She was overwhelmed with fear and shame – there was remorse and so much guilt. How could I not forgive her? How could I not feel her despair? My heart melted with her distress. I loved her, I'd always loved her. And I hoped that one day she would love me. Perhaps she had been foolish, but what of it? I knew we could be happy together and I couldn't let Frano destroy her. I had to stop him.

'I went to talk to his father, old Mr Bossano,' Andro continued. 'In spite of his faults he cared about Šipan. I think he cared about the islanders as well, but who can say now? At first he was angry; he smashed his fist down on his desk so hard I thought it would break. Then he seemed to take control of himself, but I could see the effort it took. I could see exactly what he was thinking. Shock, disgust – yes. But also resolution. He knew that whatever his own views, he had to stand by his family and his only son. I think he finally decided that, in the end, it was his fault for having let Frano run so wild, but he understood what he had to do. Unlike Frano, he recognised his responsibilities towards us. It was almost feudal, but it was the only kind of honour he knew. He offered me the job of estate manager. Don't misunderstand me,' Andro said hurriedly. 'I didn't ask for it and I didn't want it, but just try and imagine our situation. What else could we have done? We couldn't change anything. Olga would soon grow big with her baby and her husband missing nearly a year. Even though I knew she had little choice, I still felt that it was me who was taking advantage of her. I was so relieved when she finally agreed to marry me. Relieved and proud – she had always been the prettiest girl on the island. We decided for the baby's sake, for your sake, that we had to continue as though you were our son.' Andro looked at Milo. 'Did we do wrong?' he asked. 'We didn't want to deceive you, but what else could we do? We were trying to protect you.'

As he told his story, Andro appeared to grow. His back was straight and some of his old strength seemed to return to him. Milo looked at him and felt his body starting to tingle with pride, recognising him finally as the hardy, fearless man whom he had always thought of as his father. 'As for him,' Andro gestured contemptuously towards Frano. 'I told old Mr Bossano that if he ever strayed again, I'd kill him. The old man knew I was serious. He called him in and stopped his allowance there and then; he told Frano that he was restricted to the island and must never tell anyone about it. I caught up with Frano after I left his father. Then, just the two of us opposite each other, just as man to man, suddenly he seemed so weak. I could hardly believe it; it was as though there was nothing there. I told him what I would do to him if he ever went near a girl from the island. No one had ever spoken to him like that before, and he just crumbled. Since then he's acted as though it never happened. He simply hasn't had the courage to recognise his responsibilities. Look at him!' Andro indicated Frano, who was cringing with self-pity. 'Please believe me, Milo, if only for your mother's sake. We did what we could for you, even if it wasn't enough.'

Milo was quiet for several minutes. Slowly a big tear welled up and ran down his cheek, and soon he was weeping uncontrollably. 'My poor mother,' he finally managed to cry out between sobs. 'What must she have gone through? And I never knew, I never had the chance to talk to her, to thank her.' Milo reached towards Andro and fell blindly into his arms. The two men hugged each other, lost together in their grief.

Finally Milo pulled away and looked at Frano with profound incomprehension. 'Haven't you got anything to say to me?'

Frano shuffled nervously. 'You wouldn't understand,' he said. 'It's all right for you; you've finally landed on your feet. Your future's secure.'

'Is that it?' Milo asked, scarcely able to believe Frano's reaction. 'Don't you care about everything that's happened in the past? Yes, my future's secure, and I intend to keep it that way. We've had enough misery as a family to last several generations.'

'Misery? What about me? How can you ever know how I feel?'

Milo smiled faintly. 'When I first arrived in South America, I was arrested and thrown in jail. After three days I had given up all hope; there was no one within thousands of miles who could help me, no one who knew that I was even there – no one who cared. I had never imagined that such despair was possible. My mind was empty. I had been reduced to just a body; I was no better than an animal. Yes, I know how you feel.

'But I was lucky,' Milo continued. 'I was rescued by a kind man and his wife. There are kind men in this world, you know. He took me in and gave me a home. He helped me grow up and I adored and admired him. It was like having a second father. But I never mistook him for my real father and he never wanted me to. We both knew which was which. If he was here now, we'd both recognise you as an impostor.' Milo turned back to Andro. 'Whatever happened in the past, you're my real father.'

~~~~~

Milo threw the stone high into the air and watched it fall into the foaming sea at the entrance to the Passage. A wave slapped against the rocks below him and a gust of wind blew the spray across his face. Wiping the salt water from his cheek, he gave a last look out to sea and then turned and walked back along across the headland towards the stone quay. At the boathouse he went inland and climbed up the short hillside. Along the valley leading up to the estate house, he passed his workmen planting new rows of vines, and he stopped and bent down next to one of the new plants. A fresh, green shoot had spurted up and wrapped itself around the training wire. He pulled it through his fingers, and looked around him. Beyond the vine-yards rows of olives, fresh and green, marched up the hillsides. From beyond the hills he could hear the constant rumbling of the surf on the rocks.

He heard Herta calling him and stood up and walked to-wards the house. As he approached he could see she had left Pasko on the grass and was running up to him. She stopped as she saw him and held out a telegram. Seeing the sadness in her face, he reached for it slowly, fearing what it must say. He read it, and then read it again. Finally, he pulled Herta towards him and, holding her tightly, he looked down at the baby playing on the grass. Their son, Pasko, was already nearly a year old.

Milo looked past him, towards the gardens beyond, their lush greenness contrasting with the barren, brown hills which had encircled him in Iquique. He thought back at the events which had taken him to such an unlikely place and which had finally enabled him to come back here. The man who had taken him in, sheltered him, given him hope and allowed him to succeed, was now dead.

Milo handed the telegram back to Herta. 'He was an extraor-dinary man,' he said. 'There'll never be anyone like Martin Hurst. The world is too complicated now. He created his business quite literally with his bare hands. The directness of his approach will always be a model for others, but no one will be able to copy him. Soon they'll lose sight of what the fundamen-tals of business really are. The stock markets will take over and the people involved will be forgotten. Martin had his faults, but he made money for his investors and didn't need to do it at the expense of his workers. He recognised that each of them contributed something. There are many people grateful to him.'

'What do you think Lisa will do?' asked Herta.

'Come back to Europe, I think. There's no reason for her to stay now. James Young has already come back – he finally found that estate in Kent.' From the table Milo picked up a newspaper which had been sent a few days earlier from Chile. 'The nitrate age is finished. It's the industrial age now,' he said, passing the paper to Herta. 'You see, it's finally happened. I said it would. They're striking at the docks. With the wages most of them get paid, who can blame them? The workers in the nitrate fields will be next, and when the news reaches London, share prices will crash.'

Herta said nothing as Milo gazed along the green valley. 'Who could ever have imagined strikes? When I started I had barely a dozen people. We all lived together. We depended upon each other. But things move on. There're nearly twenty thousand people working out there now. No single operator can look after them. It's time they looked after themselves.'

Milo looked back towards his son. 'Our future is here; my part is over. The nitrate industry will continue, but for someone else it will be a new start.' For a moment he almost lost control as he remembered the weight of responsibility that had been lifted from him. He reached out and took Herta into his arms. 'If Martin Hurst could turn a great desert into countless miles of fertile plantations, just imagine what we have left to do on an island like this. No one living here will want for anything. Šipan is my home.

'We can give Pasko the childhood I missed.'

Epilogue – 2001

The signs of what Milo achieved are everywhere on Šipan. Locals will tell you the island once had so many olive trees that it featured in the Guinness Book of Records, but most are gone now – dead or dying. There aren't many fishermen left either, although many of the islanders are still seamen. It's not as dangerous as in Milo's time, when one ship out of three ended its days at the bottom of the sea.

Milo wasn't the only Dalmatian to make his fortune from Chile saltpetre. From the island of Koloèep, just a few miles from Šipan, Pasko Barburizza also established his business in Valparaiso. He went there long after Milo, and made his money from shipping. "My only mistake," he was to say later in life, "was to send an empty ship back to Chile. I did it just once." He, too, returned home – most Dalmatians try to, although there's still not much work for them. He built the small quay, where I often moor *Calypso*, and donated it to the island. Although he never married, his business still thrives in Valparaiso.

Few people outside the West Coast of South America are aware of the importance of the nitrate industry, not just for the countries involved, but for the world at large. It was the First World War that finally brought it to an end. Cut off from supplies, Germany developed a synthetic process for manufacturing nitrates, and that was it. A few operations still exist even now in the Tarapacá desert, but the rest are abandoned. You can visit one, just outside Antofagusta. Humberstone, it's called, after the engineer J.T. Humberstone who developed the refining process named after him, and who himself joined the ranks of the *salitreros*.

But what of Šipan? As I look across the small bay of Šipanska Luka, it is now only in my imagination that I can picture what Milo achieved after his return. The huge mansion is still there – just – as his grandson struggles to keep it standing, but the olive oil press has been thrown out to make way for the hotel bedrooms, and the remains of the machinery now lie rusting in a field that was once an orange grove. This afternoon I wandered through the valley where the crumbling terraces have been washed away by the torrents of the winter rains. The vines have long since outgrown their training wires and their gnarled, desiccated branches wave barrenly in the breeze, abandoned and forgotten. It is just an echo of what Milo had once created after he'd returned.

Few people who visit Šipan can ever forget it. Go and see for yourselves. You'll ask how such a hauntingly beautiful place could have suffered such neglect for a second time. Yet it happened.

How it happened would fill another book.

Andrew Smyth
sv *Calypso*
Šipan, September 2001